WHEN BEAUTY TAMED
THE BEAST

WHEN BEAUTY TAMED THE BEAST

Eloisa James

WINDSOR
PARAGON

First published 2011
by Piatkus
This Large Print edition published 2012
by AudioGO Ltd
by arrangement with
Little, Brown Book Group

Hardcover   ISBN: 978 1 4713 0294 7
Softcover   ISBN: 978 1 4713 0295 4

British Library Cataloguing in Publication Data available

Printed and bound in Great Britain by
MPG Books Group Limited

This book is dedicated to my fabulous editor, Carrie Feron. She always pushes me to my very best writing, but with this book, her editing brought the novel to a whole new level. This one's for you, sweetie.

ACKNOWLEDGMENTS

My books are like small children; they take a whole village to get them to a literate state. I want to offer my heartfelt thanks to my personal village: my agent, Kim Witherspoon; my website designers, Wax Creative; and last but not least, my personal team — Kim Castillo, Franzeca Drouin, and Anne Connell. I am so grateful to each of you!

ONE

Once upon a time, not so very long ago . . .

Beautiful girls in fairy stories are as common as pebbles on the beach. Magnolia-skinned milkmaids rub shoulders with starry-eyed princesses and, in fact, counting two eyes in each bright-eyed damsel would result in a whole galaxy of twinkling stars.

That sparkle makes it all the more sad that real women rarely live up to their fictional counterparts. They have yellowing teeth, or spotty skin. They have the shadow of a mustache, or a nose so big that a mouse could ski down it.

Of course there are pretty ones. But even they are prone to all the ills that flesh is heir to, as Hamlet had it in a long-ago complaint.

In short, it's a rare woman who actually outshines the sun. Let alone all that business about pearly teeth, the voice of a lark, and a face so beautifully shaped that angels would weep with envy.

Linnet Berry Thrynne had all of the above, except perhaps the claim to lark-like melody. Still, her voice was perfectly agreeable, and she had been told that her laughter was like the chiming of golden bells and (though not larks) linnet songs were often mentioned.

Without even glancing at the glass, she knew that her hair was shining, her eyes were shining, and her teeth — well, perhaps they weren't shining, but they were quite white.

She was just the sort who could drive a stable boy to heroic feats, or a prince to less intrepid acts such as whacking through a bramble patch merely to give her a kiss. None of which changed a basic fact:

As of yesterday, she was unmarriageable.

The calamity had to do with the nature of kisses, and what kisses are purported to lead to. Though perhaps it's more accurate to point to the nature of princes. The prince in question was Prince Augustus Frederick, Duke of Sussex.

He had kissed Linnet more than once; in fact, he had kissed her a great many times. And he had vehemently declared his love for her, not to mention thrown strawberries at her bedchamber window late one night (which had made an awful mess and had driven the gardener into a fury).

The only thing he hadn't done was offer his hand in marriage.

"It's a shame I can't marry you," he had said apologetically, when the scandal broke the evening before. "We royal dukes, you know . . . can't do everything we'd like. My father is slightly deranged on the subject. Really, it's most unfortunate. You must have heard about my first marriage; that one was annulled because Windsor decided Augusta wasn't good enough, and she's the daughter of an earl."

Linnet was not the daughter of an earl; her father was a viscount, and not a very well-connected one at that. Not that she'd heard of the prince's first marriage. Everyone who had watched her flirting with him in the last few months had unaccountably forgotten to tell her that he was apparently prone to courting those he couldn't — or shouldn't — marry.

The prince had bowed sharply, turned, and abruptly left the ballroom, withdrawing to Windsor Castle — or wherever it was that rats went when the ship sank.

This had left Linnet alone but for her dour chaperone and a ballroom of gentlepersons, a circumstance that led her to quickly re-

11

alize that a great many maidens and matrons in London were eagerly — if not gleefully — certain that she was a hussy of the first degree.

Within moments of the prince's retreat, not a soul would meet her eyes; she was faced with a sea of turned backs. The sound of upper-class tittering spread all around her like the hissing of a gaggle of geese preparing to fly north. Though, of course, it was she who had to fly — north, south, it didn't matter as long as she fled the scene of her disgrace.

The unfair thing was that she wasn't a hussy. Well, not more than any girl bowled over by a prince.

She had enjoyed snaring the greatest prize of them all, the blond and winsome prince. But she hadn't had any real hope that he would marry her. And she certainly would not have given her virginity to a prince without having a ring on her finger and the approval of the king.

Still, she had considered Augustus a friend, which made it all the more painful when he didn't pay her a call the morning following her humiliation.

Augustus wasn't the only one. In fact, Linnet found herself staring out of a front window of her townhouse, the better to convince herself that no one was coming to call. No one. Not a soul.

Ever since she'd debuted a few months earlier, her front door had been the portal to the Golden Fleece — i.e., her dowered, delectable self. Young men pranced and trotted and strolled up that path, leaving cards and flowers and gifts of all kinds. Even the prince had lowered himself to make four morning calls, an unheard-of compliment.

But now . . . that path was nothing more than a row of flagstones shining in the sunlight.

"I simply don't believe this has come out of nothing!" her father said now, from somewhere behind her.

"I *was* kissed by a prince," Linnet said dryly. "Which might have counted as nothing, if we hadn't been seen by Baroness Buggin."

"Kissing — pah! Kisses are nothing. What I want to know is why it is being reliably reported that you are carrying a child. *His* child!" Viscount Sundon came, stood at her shoulder, and looked with her at the empty street.

"Two reasons. Neither of which involves a baby, you'll be happy to learn."

"Well?"

"I ate a bad prawn at Lady Brimmer's

morning musicale last Thursday."

"So?" her father asked.

"It made me ill," Linnet told him. "I couldn't even make it to the ladies' retiring chamber. I threw up in a potted orange tree." She shuddered a little at the mere memory.

"Uncontrolled of you," the viscount commented. He hated bodily processes. "I gather that was taken as a sign of childbirth?"

"Not childbirth, Papa, the condition that precedes it."

"Of course. But you do remember when Mrs. Underfoot spewed in the throne room, narrowly missing His Majesty, the King of Norway? That was no prawn, nor a baby either. Everyone knew the lady had drunk herself into a standstill. We could put it about that you're an inebriate."

"Would that solve my problem? I doubt many gentlemen wish to marry a drunk. At any rate, it wasn't just the prawn. It was my gown."

"What about your gown?"

"I wore a new ball dress last night, and apparently my profile gave people cause to think that I was carrying a child."

Her father swung her around and peered at her middle. "You don't look any different

14

to me. A bit chilly around the shoulders, perhaps. Need you show quite so much bosom?"

"Unless I want to look like a fussocking matron," Linnet said with some asperity, "then yes, I do need to show this much bosom."

"Well, that's the problem," Lord Sundon said. "You look like Bartholomew ware. Damn it, I specifically told your chaperone that you had to look more prudish than anyone else in the room. Do I have to do everything myself? Can no one follow simple instructions?"

"My ball gown was not revealing," Linnet protested, but her father wasn't listening.

"I have tried, God knows how I've tried! I postponed your debut, in the hopes that maturity would give you poise in the face of the *ton*'s undoubted scrutiny, given your mother's reputation. But what's the good of poise if your neckline signals you're a wanton?"

Linnet took a deep breath. "The affair had nothing to do with necklines. The gown I wore last night has —"

"*Affaire!*" her father said, his voice rising. "I raised you with the strictest of principles —"

"Not *affaire* in the French sense," Linnet

interrupted. "I meant that the disaster was provoked by my gown. It has two petticoats, you see, and —"

"I want to see it," Lord Sundon announced, interrupting in his turn. "Go and put it on."

"I can't put on a ball gown at this hour in the morning!"

"Now. And get that chaperone of yours down here as well. I want to hear what Mrs. Hutchins has to say for herself. I hired her specifically to prevent this sort of thing. She put on such a priggish, puritanical air that I trusted her!"

So Linnet put on the ball gown.

It was designed to fit tightly over her breasts. Just below, the skirts pulled back to reveal an under-dress of charming Belgium lace. Then that skirt pulled back, showing a third layer, made from white silk. The design looked exquisite in the sketchbook at Madame Desmartins's shop. And when Linnet had put it on last night, she had thought the effect lovely.

But now, as her maid adjusted all those skirts while Mrs. Hutchins looked on, Linnet's eyes went straight to where her waist ought to be — but wasn't. "My word," she said, a bit faintly. "I really do look as if I'm with child." She turned to the side.

16

"Just look how it billows out. It's all the pleating, right here at the top, under my breasts. I could hide two babies under all that cloth."

Her maid, Eliza, didn't venture an opinion, but her chaperone showed no such reticence. "In my opinion, it's not the petticoats so much as your bosom," Mrs. Hutchins stated. Her voice was faintly accusing, as if Linnet were responsible for her cleavage.

Her chaperone had the face of a gargoyle, to Linnet's mind. She made one think of the medieval church in all its stony religious fervor. Which was why the viscount had hired her, of course.

Linnet turned back to the mirror. The gown did have a low neckline, which frankly she had considered to be a good thing, given how many young men seemed unable to drag their eyes above her chin. It kept them occupied and gave Linnet license to daydream about being somewhere other than a ballroom.

"You're overly endowed," Mrs. Hutchins went on. "Too much on top. Put that together with the way the dress billows out, and you look as if you're expecting a happy event."

"It wouldn't have been *happy*," Linnet

pointed out.

"Not in your circumstances." Mrs. Hutchins cleared her throat. She had the most irritating way of clearing her throat that Linnet had ever heard. It meant, Linnet had learned over the last few months, that she was about to say something unpleasant.

"Why on earth didn't we see it?" Linnet cried with frustration, cutting her off before she could launch her criticism. "It seems so unfair, to lose my reputation and perhaps even my chance at marriage, just because this gown has too many pleats and petticoats."

"Your manners are at fault," Mrs. Hutchins said. "You should have learned from your mother's example that if you act like a hussy, people will take you for a jade. I tried to give you tips about propriety as best I could over the last months, but you paid me no mind. Now you must reap what you have sown."

"My manners have nothing to do with this dress and its effect on my figure," Linnet stated. She rarely bothered to examine herself closely in the glass. If she had just looked carefully, if she had turned to the side . . .

"It's the neckline," Mrs. Hutchins said stubbornly. "You look like a milking cow, if

18

you'll excuse the comparison."

Linnet didn't care to excuse it, so she ignored her. People should warn one of the danger. A lady should always look at herself from the side while dressing, or she might discover that all of London suddenly believed her to be carrying a child.

"I know that you're not *enceinte*," Mrs. Hutchins continued, sounding as if she were reluctant to admit it. "But I'd never believe it, looking at you now." She cleared her throat again. "If you'll take a word of advice, I'd cover that chest of yours a bit more. It's not seemly. I did try to tell you that several times over the last two months and twenty-three days that I've been living in this household."

Linnet counted to five and then said, stonily, "It's the only chest I have, Mrs. Hutchins, and everyone's gowns are designed like this. There's nothing special about my neckline."

"It makes you look like a light frigate," she observed.

"What?"

"A light frigate. A light woman!"

"Isn't a frigate a boat?"

"Exactly, the type that docks in many harbors."

"I do believe that it is the first jest you've

ever told me," Linnet said. "And to think I was worried that you might not have a sense of humor."

After that, the corners of Mrs. Hutchins's mouth turned down and she refused to say anything more. And she refused to accompany Linnet back to the drawing room. "I've naught to do with what's come upon you," she said. "It's the will of heaven, and you can tell your father I said so. I did my best to instill principles in you, but it was too late."

"That seems rather unfair," Linnet said. "Even a very young light frigate should have the chance to dock at *one* harbor before she's scuppered."

Mrs. Hutchins gasped. "You dare to jest. You have no idea of propriety — none! I think we all know where to put the blame for that."

"Actually, I think I have more understanding of propriety and its opposite than most. After all, Mrs. Hutchins, I, not you, grew up around my mother."

"And there's the root of your problem," she said, with a grim smile. "It's not as if her ladyship were a felt-maker's daughter who ran away with a tinker. No one cares about that sort. Your mother danced like a thief in the mist while everyone was watching her. She was no private strumpet; she let the world see her iniquity!"

"A thief in the mist," Linnet repeated. "Is that biblical, Mrs. Hutchins?"

But Mrs. Hutchins pressed her lips together and left the room.

Two

Castle Owfestry
Pendine, Wales
Ancestral Seat of the Dukes of Windebank

Piers Yelverton, Earl of Marchant, and heir to the Duke of Windebank, was in a considerable amount of pain. He had learned long ago that to think about discomfort — a blasted, silly word for this sort of agony — was to give it a power that he didn't care to acknowledge. So he pretended not to notice, and leaned a bit more heavily on his cane, relieving the pressure on his right leg.

The pain made him irritable. But maybe it wasn't the pain. Maybe it was the fact that he had to stand around wasting his time with a roaring idiot.

"My son is suffering from acute diarrhea and abdominal pain," Lord Sandys said, pulling him closer to the bed.

Sandys's son was lying in bed looking gaunt and yellow, like tea-stained linen. He

22

looked to be in his thirties, with a long face and an unbearably pious air. Though that might have been due to the prayer book he was clutching.

"We're desperate," Sandys said, looking indeed quite desperate. "I've paraded five London physicians past his bed, and bringing him here to Wales is our last resort. So far he's been bled, treated with leeches, given tinctures of nettles. He drinks nothing but asses' milk, never cows' milk. Oh, and we've given him several doses of sulfur, but to no effect."

That was mildly interesting. "One of those fools you saw must have been Sydenham," Piers said. "He's obsessed with sulfur *auratum antimonii*. Gives it out for stubbed toes. Along with opium, of course."

Sandys nodded. "Dr. Sydenham was hopeful that the sulfur would relieve my son's symptoms, but it didn't help."

"It wouldn't. The man was enough of a fool to be admitted to the Royal College of Physicians, and that should have told you something."

"But you're —"

"I joined purely as a kindness to them." He peered down at Sandys's son. He was certainly looking the worse for wear. "It likely didn't make you feel any better to

23

trudge all the way to Wales to see me."

The man blinked at him. Then he said, slowly, "We were in a carriage."

"Inflamed eyes," Piers said. "Signs of a recent nosebleed."

"What do you gather from that? What does he need?" Sandys asked.

"Better bathing. Is he always that color?"

"His skin is a bit yellow," Sandys acknowledged. "It doesn't come from my side of the family." That was an understatement, given that Sandys's nose was the color of a cherry.

"Did you eat a surfeit of lampreys?" Piers asked the patient.

The man looked up at him as if he had sprouted horns. "Larkspy? What's a larkspy? I haven't eaten any of it."

Piers straightened up. "He doesn't know the history of England. He's better off dead."

"Did you ask if he'd eaten any lampreys?" Sandys said. "He hates seafood. Can't abide eels."

"More to the point, he's deaf as a post. The first King Henry ate lampreys, one of the many mad kings we've had in this country, though not as cracked as the current one. Still, Henry was thickheaded enough to have eaten a surfeit of eels and

24

died of it."

"I am not deaf!" the patient said. "I can hear as well as the next, if people would just stop mumbling at me. My joints hurt. They're the problem."

"You're dying, that's the problem," Piers pointed out.

Sandys grabbed him by the arm and pulled him away. "Don't say such a thing in front of my son. He's no more than thirty-two."

"He's got the body of an eighty-year-old. Has he spent much time consorting with actresses?"

Sandys snorted. "Certainly not! Our family goes back to —"

"Nightwalkers? Hussies? Mollishers, mopsies, or mackerels? Though mackerels brings fish back into this conversation and you already told me that the man can't abide seafood. But what about fish of the female variety?"

"My son is a member of the Church!" Sandys blustered.

"That settles it," Piers said. "Everyone lies, but churchmen make an art of it. He's got syphilis. Churchmen are riddled with it, and the more pious they are, the more symptoms they have. I should have known the moment I saw that prayer book."

"Not my son," Sandys said, sounding as if he actually believed it. "He's a man of God. Always has been."

"As I was saying —"

"Seriously."

"Hmm. Well, if not a mopsy —"

"No one," Sandys said, shaking his head. "He's never — he's not interested. He's like a saint, that boy is. When he was sixteen, I took him to Venus's Rose, in the Whitefriars, but he didn't take the slightest interest in any of the girls. Just started praying, and asked them to join him, which they didn't care for. He's a candidate for sainthood."

"His sainthood is about to become a question for a higher authority. There's nothing I can do."

Sandys grabbed his arm. "You must!"

"I can't."

"But the other doctors, all of them, they gave him medicines, they said —"

"They were fools, who didn't tell you the truth."

Sandys swallowed. "He was fine until he was twenty. Just a fine, healthy boy, and then —"

"Take your son home and let him die in peace. Because die he will, whether I give you a solution of sulfur or not."

26

"Why?" Sandys whispered.

"He has syphilis. He's deaf, he's diarrhetic, he's jaundiced, he's got eye and joint inflammation and nosebleeds. He likely gets headaches."

"He's never been with a woman. Ever. I swear it. He hasn't any sores on his private parts or he would have mentioned it."

"He didn't have to be with a woman," Piers said, nipping his coat out of Sandys's hand and shaking his sleeve straight again.

"How can he have syphilis without —"

"It could have been a man."

Sandys looked so shocked that Piers relented. "Or it could have been you, which is far more likely. The rosy ladies you visited as a youth infected the boy before he was even born."

"I was treated with mercury," Sandys protested.

"To no avail. You still have it. Now, if you'll excuse me, I have important things to do. Like treat a patient who might live for another year."

Piers strolled out, finding his butler Prufrock in the hallway. "I wonder how you ever get anything done," he said to him. "It must be hard to run a household when you have to conduct all your business in the corridors so you can hear every golden word that falls from my lips."

"I do not find it a particular problem," Prufrock said, falling in beside him. "But then I have lots of practice. You don't think that you were a trifle hard on Lord Sandys?"

"Hard? Was I hard? Surely not. I told him exactly what was wrong with his son, and what to do next — in short, go home and wait for choirs of angels, because there are no miracles on this side of the divide."

"It's his *son* that's dying. And if I got you right, he gave the poor lad the illness. That's a blow, that is."

"My father wouldn't have minded a bit," Piers assured him. "If he had another heir, that is. But Sandys has a whole passel of children. An heir and more to spare."

"How do you know that?"

"The Church, you fool. He put this boy into the Church and seems to have trained him up to it from an early age, too. The heir must be rousting about in brothels just like good old Pa. Sandys would never have allowed the spare near a Bible if he were, in fact, the heir. This one is expendable, which is a bloody good thing, under the circumstances."

"Your father the duke would be greatly disturbed at the very idea that he'd passed on a disease of this nature," Prufrock said.

"Perhaps," Piers said, pretending to consider it. "And perhaps not. I'm amazed my father hasn't married a fresh young thing of twenty. Or sixteen. Time's a-wasting, and at this rate he'll never have the spare he needs."

"His Grace was devoted to Her Grace and wounded by the terrible events of the past," Prufrock said with a palpable lack of attention to the truth.

Piers didn't bother answering that. His leg hurt as if someone had stuck a hot poker into his thigh. "I need a drink, so why don't you rush ahead like a good butler and meet me at the door of the library with a strong brandy?"

"I'll keep walking next to you in case you keel over," Prufrock said.

"I suppose you have visions of breaking my fall," Piers said, giving his scrawny butler a sidelong glance.

"Actually, no. But I would call for a footman, who could drag you along the corridor. It's marble, so you might get a concussion, and that might make you a bit kinder to your patients, not to mention your staff. You had Betsy in tears again this morning. You seem to think scullery maids grow on trees."

Thank God, they were getting close to the library. Piers paused for a moment, the idea of amputation flitting through his mind, and not for the first time. He could get one of those Egyptian bed-things that Cleopatra had herself carried about on. Walking would be a damned sight more difficult, but at least he'd be free of this infernal pain.

"Your father has written," Prufrock told him. "I took the liberty of putting the letter on your desk."

"Took the liberty of steaming it open, more like," Piers said. "What does he have to say?"

"He expresses some interest in your marital future," Prufrock said cheerfully. "It seems that last missive you sent him, the one listing all your demands for a spouse, did not dissuade him. Rather surprising, I must say."

"The one that called him an idiot?" Piers asked. "Did you read that one too, you pestilent polecat?"

"You're quite poetical today," Prufrock observed. "All that alliteration in the service of mopsies and mollishers, and now for your lowly butler. I'm honored, I assure you."

"What's the duke writing about now?" Piers said. He could see the library door. He could almost feel the brandy going down his throat. "I told him that I wouldn't accept a wife unless she was as beautiful as the sun and the moon. Which is a quote from literature, in case you don't know. And I added quite a lot of other provisions as well, ones guaranteed to send him into a frothing fit of despair."

"He's looking for a wife," Prufrock said.

"For himself, I would hope. Although he's waited a bit long," Piers said, failing to summon any particular interest in this news. "Men of his age don't have the balls they once had, if you'll excuse the vulgar truth of it, Prufrock. Lord knows you have more delicate sensibilities than I do."

"I used to, before I began working for you," Prufrock said, pushing open the library door with a flourish.

Piers had one thing in mind. It was golden, tasted like fire, and would cut the pain in his leg.

"So he's looking for a wife," he repeated without paying any attention to the words, but heading straight for the brandy decanter. He poured out a hefty dose. "It's been a rotten day. Not that it matters to me, or you, for that matter, but there's nothing I can do for that young woman who showed up at the back door this morning."

"The one who's all swollen in the belly?"

"It's not the usual swelling, and if I cut her open, I'll kill her. If I don't cut her open,

31

the disease will kill her. So I took the easier of the two options." He threw back the brandy.

"You sent her away?"

"She had nowhere to go. I turned her over to Nurse Matilda, with instructions to bed her down in the west wing with enough opium to keep her mind off what's happening next. Thank God this castle is big enough to house half the dying people in England."

"Your father," Prufrock said, "and the question of marriage."

He was trying to distract him. Piers poured another glass, smaller this time. He had no wish to stick his head in a bottle of brandy and never come out again, if only because he'd learned from his patients that overindulgence meant that brandy wouldn't blunt the pain anymore. "Ah, marriage," he said obediently. "About time. My mother's been gone these twenty years. Well, *gone* isn't quite the word, is it? At any rate, darling *Maman* is over on the Continent living the good life, so His Grace might as well remarry. It wasn't easy to get that divorce, you know. Probably cost him as much as a small estate. He should make hay while the sun shines, or in short, while he's still able to get a rise every other day."

32

"Your father's not getting married," Prufrock said. Something in his tone made Piers glance up.

"You weren't joking."

The butler nodded. "It is my impression that His Grace sees you — or your marriage — as a challenge. It could be that you shouldn't have listed quite so many requirements. One might say that it fired up the duke's resolve. Got him interested in the project, so to speak."

"The devil you say. He'll never manage to find anyone. I have a reputation, you know."

"Your title is weightier than your reputation," Prufrock said. "Additionally, there is the small matter of your father's estate."

"You're probably right, damn you." Piers decided he could manage another small glass. "But what about my injury, hmm? You think a woman would agree to marry a man — what am I saying? Of course a woman would agree to that."

"I doubt many young ladies would see that as an insurmountable problem," Prufrock said. "Now, your personality . . ."

"Damn you," Piers said, but without heat.

THREE

The moment Linnet returned to the drawing room, her father groaned aloud. "I turned down three marriage proposals for you last month, and I can tell you right now that I'll never receive another one. Hell, I wouldn't believe you a maiden myself. You look four or five months along."

Linnet sat down rather heavily, her skirts floating up like a white cloud and then settling around her. "I'm not," she said. "I am not pregnant." She was starting to feel almost as if she truly were carrying a child.

"Ladies don't use that word," Lord Sundon said. "Didn't you learn anything from that governess of yours?" He waved his quizzing glass in the air the better to illustrate his point. "One might refer to a delicate condition, or perhaps to being *enceinte*. Never to pregnancy, a harsh word with harsh connotations. The pleasure, the joy of being of our rank, is that we may

34

overlook the earthy, the fertile, the . . ."

Linnet stopped listening. Her father was a vision in pale blue, his waistcoat fastened with silver buttons inset with ivory poppies, his Prussian collar a miracle of elegance. *He* was very good at overlooking anything earthy, but she'd never been as successful.

At that moment a long banging sounded at the door. Despite herself, Linnet looked up hopefully when their butler entered to announce the visitor. Surely Prince Augustus had rethought. How could he sit in his castle, knowing that she was being rejected by the *ton?* He must have heard about the disastrous events of the ball, the way no one had spoken to her after he left.

Of course, the prince had taken himself away while the news was still spreading through the ballroom. He had walked out the door with his cronies without a backward glance at her . . . and after that every face in the ballroom turned away from her. Apparently they were only waiting to see what his reaction was to being told she was carrying a child.

Yet he, if anyone, knew it to be a taradiddle. At least, he knew the child wasn't *his.* Maybe that was why he threw her over so abruptly. Perhaps he too believed the stories and thought she was pregnant by another man.

The cut direct from an entire ballroom. It had to be a first.

The caller wasn't Prince Augustus, but Linnet's aunt, Lady Etheridge, known to her intimates as Zenobia. She had chosen that name for herself, realizing as a young girl that Hortense didn't suit her personality.

"I knew this would come to grief," she announced, stopping just inside the door and dropping her gloves to the floor rather than handing them to the footman to her right.

Zenobia relished a good drama, and when inebriated was prone to informing a whole dinner table that she could have played Lady Macbeth better than Sarah Siddons. "I told you once, if I told you a hundred times, Cornelius, that girl is too pretty for her own good. And I was right. Here she is, *enceinte,* and all of London party to the news except for me."

"I'm not —" Linnet said.

But she was drowned out by her father, who chose to avoid the question at hand and go on the attack. "It's not my daughter's fault that she takes after her mother."

"My sister was as pure as the driven snow," Zenobia bellowed back.

The battle was properly engaged now, and there would be no stopping it.

"My wife may have been snowy — and God knows I'm the one to speak to that — but she was certainly warm enough when she cared to be. We all know how fast the Ice Maiden could warm up, particularly when she was around royalty, now I think of it!"

"Rosalyn deserved a king," Zenobia screamed. She strode into the room and planted herself as if she were about to shoot an arrow. Linnet recognized the stance: it was just what Mrs. Siddons had done the week before on the Covent Garden stage, when her Desdemona repudiated Othello's cruel accusations of unfaithfulness.

Poor Papa was hardly a warrior like Othello, though. The fact was that her dearest mama had been rampantly unfaithful to him, and he knew it. And so did Aunt Zenobia, though she was choosing to play ignorant.

"I really don't see that the question is relevant," Linnet put in. "Mama died some years ago now, and her fondness for royalty is neither here nor there."

Her aunt threw her a swooning look. "I will always defend your mother, though she lies in the cold, cold grave."

37

Linnet slumped back in her corner. True, her mother was in the grave. And frankly, she thought she missed her mother more than Zenobia did, given that the sisters had fought bitterly every time they met. Mostly over men, it had to be admitted. Though to her credit, her aunt wasn't nearly as trollopy as her mama had been.

"It's the beauty," her father was saying. "It's gone to Linnet's head, just as it went to Rosalyn's. My wife thought beauty gave her license to do whatever she liked —"

"Rosalyn never did anything untoward!" Zenobia interrupted.

"She skirted respectability for years," Lord Sundon continued, raising his voice. "And now her daughter has followed in her footsteps, and Linnet is ruined. Ruined!"

Zenobia opened her mouth — and then snapped it shut. There was a pause. "Rosalyn is hardly the question here," she said finally, patting her hair. "We must concentrate on dear Linnet now. Stand up, dear."

Linnet stood up.

"Five months, I'd say," Zenobia stated. "How on earth you managed to hide that from me, I don't know. Why, I was as shocked as anyone last night. The Countess of Derby was quite sharp with me, thinking I'd been concealing it. I had to admit that I knew nothing of it, and I'm not entirely sure she believed me."

"I am not carrying a child," Linnet said, enunciating the words slowly.

"She said the same last night," her father confirmed. "And earlier this morning, she didn't look it." But he peered at her waist. "Now she does."

Linnet pushed down the cloth that billowed out just under her breasts. "See, I'm not *enceinte*. There's nothing there but cloth."

"My dear, you'll have to tell us sometime," Zenobia said, taking out a tiny mirror and peering at herself. "It's not as if it's going anywhere. At this rate, you'll be bigger than a house in a matter of a few months. I myself retired to the country as soon as my waistline expanded even a trifle."

"What are we going to do with her?" her father moaned, collapsing into a chair as suddenly as a puppet with cut strings.

"Nothing you can do," Zenobia said, powdering her nose. "No one wants a cuckoo in the nest. You'll have to send her abroad and see if she can catch someone there, after all this unpleasantness is over, of course. You'd better double her dowry. Thankfully, she's an heiress. Someone will take her on."

She put down her powder puff and shook her finger at Linnet. "Your mother would be very disappointed, my dear. Didn't she teach you anything?"

"I suppose you mean that Rosalyn should have trained her in the arts of being as dissipated as she herself was," her father retorted. But he was still drooping in his seat, and had obviously lost his fire.

"I did not sleep with the prince," Linnet said, as clearly and as loudly as she could. "I might have done so, obviously. Perhaps if I had, he would have felt constrained to marry me now. But I chose not to."

Her father groaned and dropped his head onto the back of his chair.

"I didn't hear that," Zenobia said, narrowing her eyes. "At least royalty is some sort of excuse. If this child is the result of anything less than ducal blood, I don't want to hear a word about it."

"I didn't —" Linnet tried.

Her aunt cut her off with a sharp gesture. "I just realized, Cornelius, that this might be the saving of you." She turned to Linnet. "Tell us who fathered that child, and your father will demand marriage. No one below a prince would *dare* to refuse him."

Without pausing for breath, she swung back to her brother-in-law. "You might have

40

to fight a duel, Cornelius. I suppose you have pistols somewhere in this house, don't you? Didn't you threaten to fight one with Lord Billetsford years ago?"

"After finding him in bed with Rosalyn," Linnet's father said. He didn't even sound mournful, just matter-of-fact. "New bed; we'd had it only a week or two."

"My sister had many passions," Zenobia said fondly.

"I thought you just said she was white as snow!" the viscount snapped back.

"None of them touched her soul! She died in a state of grace."

No one was inclined to argue with this, so Zenobia continued. "At any rate, you'd better pull out those pistols, Cornelius, and see if they still work. You might have to threaten to kill the man. Though in my experience if you double the dowry, it'll all come around quickly enough."

"There's no man to shoot," Linnet said.

Zenobia snorted. "Don't tell me you're going to try for virgin birth, my love. I can't imagine that it worked very well back in Jerusalem. Every time the bishop talks about it at Christmastime, I can't help thinking that the poor girl must have had a miserable time trying to get people to believe her."

"I can't imagine why you're bringing scripture into this conversation," Linnet's father said. "We're talking about princes, not gods."

Linnet groaned. "This dress just makes me look plump."

Zenobia sank into a chair. "Do you mean to tell me that you *aren't* carrying a child?"

"I've been saying that. I didn't sleep with the prince, or anyone else either."

There was a mournful pause while the truth at last sunk in. "God Almighty, you're ruined, and you didn't even eat the gingerbread," her aunt said, finally. "What's more, just displaying your waistline to its best advantage would be no help at this point. People would simply assume that you had, as one might say, taken care of the problem."

"After the prince refused to marry her," the viscount said heavily. "I'd assume it myself, under the circumstances."

"It's unfair," Linnet said fiercely. "With Mama's — ah — reputation, people naturally expected that I might be rather flirtatious —"

"That's an understatement," her father said. "They thought you'd be a baggage, and now they know you're one. Except you're not."

"It's the beauty," her aunt said, preening a little. "The women in my family are simply cursed by our beauty. Look at dear Rosalyn, dying so young."

"I don't see that it's cursed *you*," the viscount said, rather rudely.

"Oh, but it has," Zenobia said. "It has, it has, it has. It taught me what could have been, had I not had the chains of birth holding me back. I could have graced the world's stages, you know. Rosalyn too. I expect that's why she was so —"

"So what?" the viscount said, leaping on it.

"Irresistible," Zenobia said.

Linnet's father snorted. "Impure, more like."

"She knew that she could have married the finest in the land," Zenobia said. "And you see, that same dream caught our darling Linnet in its coils and now she's ruined."

"Rosalyn could not have married the finest in the land," the viscount said. "There's a reason for the Royal Marriage Laws, you know." He pointed a finger at Linnet. "Didn't you even think of that before you created such a scandal with young Augustus? For Christ's sake, everyone knows that he up and married a German woman a few years ago. In Rome, I believe. The king himself had to get involved and annul the marriage."

"I didn't know until yesterday," Linnet said. "When the prince told me so."

"No one tells girls that sort of thing," her aunt said dismissively. "If you were so worried about her, Cornelius, why didn't you trot around to those parties and watch over her yourself?"

"Because I was busy! And I found a woman to chaperone her, since you were too lazy to do it yourself. Mrs. Hutchins. Perfectly respectable in every way, and seemed to grasp the problem, too. Where is that woman? She assured me that she would keep your name as white as the driven snow."

"She refused to come downstairs."

"Afraid to face the music," he muttered. "And where's your governess? She's another one. I told her *and* told her that you had to be twice as chaste to make up for your mother's reputation."

"Mrs. Flaccide took insult last night when you said she was a limb of Satan and accused her of turning me into a doxy."

"I'd had a spot or two of drink," her father said, looking utterly unrepentant. "I drowned my sorrows after I was told to my face — to my face! — that my only daughter

44

had been debauched."

"She left about an hour later," Linnet continued. "And I doubt she's coming back, because Tinkle says that she took a great deal of silver with her."

"The silver is irrelevant," Zenobia said. "You should never make the best servants angry, because they invariably know where all the valuables are kept. Far more important, I expect your governess knew all about any billets-doux that royal twig might have sent you?"

"He didn't write me any love letters, if that's what you mean. But early one morning about a month ago he did throw strawberries at my bedchamber window. She and Mrs. Hutchins said at the time that we mustn't let anyone know."

"And now Flaccide is out telling the world about it," her aunt announced. "You really are a fool, Cornelius. You should have paid her five hundred pounds on the spot and shipped her off to Suffolk. Now Flaccide is out there turning one strawberry into a whole field. She'll have Linnet carrying twins."

Linnet thought her governess would likely leap at the chance. They'd never really liked each other. In truth, women rarely liked her. From the moment she debuted four months

45

ago, the other girls had clustered into groups and giggled behind their hands. But no one ever let Linnet in on the joke.

Zenobia reached out and rang the bell. "I can't think why you haven't offered me any tea, Cornelius. Linnet's life may have taken a new corner, but we still have to eat."

"I'm ruined, and you want tea?" her father moaned.

Tinkle opened the door so quickly that Linnet knew he'd been listening in, not that she was surprised.

"We'll have tea and something to eat along with it," Zenobia told him. "You'd better bring along something for reducing as well."

The butler frowned.

"Cucumbers, vinegar, something of that nature," she said impatiently. When he closed the door, she waved at Linnet's bosom. "We must do something about *that*. No one would describe you as plump, my dear, but you're not exactly a wraith either, are you?"

Linnet counted to five again. "My figure is exactly like my mother's. And yours."

"Satan's temptation," her father said morosely. "It isn't seemly so uncovered."

"No such luck," Linnet said. "I got a prince, but the king of darkness never made an appearance."

46

"Augustus couldn't be even a minor devil," her aunt said consideringly. "I'm not surprised he didn't manage to seduce you, now I think on it. He's a bit of a nincompoop."

"There shouldn't be styles that make a young girl look like a matron with a babe on the way," Lord Sundon stated. "If there is, I don't want a part of it. That is, I wouldn't want a part of it if I were the type to wear dresses. That is, if I were a woman."

"You're getting more foolish every year," Zenobia observed. "Why my sister ever agreed to marry you, I'll never know."

"Mama loved Papa," Linnet said as firmly as she could. She'd fastened on to that fact years ago, in the aftermath of a confusing evening when she'd encountered her mother with another gentleman in an intimate setting, engaged in a very intimate activity.

"I love your father," her mother had told her at the time. "But darling, love is just not enough for women such as myself. I must have adoration, verses, poetry, flowers, jewels . . . not to mention the fact that François is built like a god and hung like a horse."

Linnet had blinked at her, and her mother had said, "Never mind, darling, I'll explain it all later, when you're a bit older."

She never got around to it, but Linnet had somehow managed to garner enough information to interpret what had caught her mother's attention with regards to François.

Now her father's eyes flickered toward her. "Rosalyn loved me the way Augustus loves you. In short: not enough."

"For goodness' sake," Zenobia cried. "This is enough to send *me* into the Slough of Despond! Let poor Rosalyn rest in her grave, would you? You make me rue the day she decided to accept your hand."

"It's brought it all back to mind," the viscount said heavily. "Linnet takes after her mother; anyone can see that."

"That's quite unfair," Linnet said, scowling at him. "I have been a model of chastity this season. In fact, through my entire life!"

He frowned. "It's just that there's something about you —"

"You look naughty," her aunt said, not unkindly. "God help Rosalyn, but this is all her fault. She gave it to you. That dimple, and something in your eyes and about your mouth. You look like a wanton."

"A wanton would have had a great deal more fun this season than I had," Linnet protested. "I've been as demure as any young lady in the *ton* — you can ask Mrs. Hutchins."

"It does seem unfair," Zenobia agreed. A golden drop of honey suspended itself from her crumpet and swung gently before falling onto the pale violet silk of her morning dress.

"I hope that you told the countess that I was never alone with Augustus at any point," Linnet said.

"How could I do that?" Zenobia inquired. "I'm not privy to your social calendar, my dear. I was as shocked as the dear countess, I can tell you that."

Linnet groaned. "I could strip naked in Almack's, and still no one would believe that I wasn't carrying a child, no matter how slim my waist. You practically confirmed it, Aunt Zenobia. And Papa dismissed Miss Flaccide, and I'm quite sure that she's saying wretched things about me all over London. I truly will have to live abroad, or in the country somewhere."

"French men are *very* easy to please, though there is that inconvenient war going on," Zenobia said encouragingly. "But I've got another idea."

Linnet couldn't bring herself to ask, but her father asked wearily, "What is it?"

"Not it — *him.*"

"Who?"

"Yelverton, Windebank's heir."

"Windebank? Who the devil's that? Do you mean Yonnington — Walter Yonnington? Because if his son is anything like his father, I wouldn't let Linnet near him, even if she *were* carrying a child."

"Very kind of you, Papa," Linnet murmured. Since her aunt had not offered her a crumpet, she helped herself.

"Reducing, my dear. Think about *reducing*," Zenobia said in a kindly yet firm tone.

Linnet tightened her mouth and put extra butter on her crumpet.

Her aunt sighed. "Yelverton's title is Duke of Windebank, Cornelius. Really, I wonder how you manage to make your way around the House of Lords, with your spotty knowledge of the aristocracy."

"I know what I need to know," the viscount said. "And I don't bother with that I don't need. If you meant Windebank, why didn't you just say so?"

"I was thinking of his son," Zenobia explained. "The man's got the second title, of course. Now let me think . . . I do believe that his given name is something odd. Peregrine, Penrose — *Piers,* that's it."

"He sounds like a dock," Lord Sundon put in.

"Mrs. Hutchins called me a light frigate this morning," Linnet said. "A dock might be just the thing for me."

Zenobia shook her head. "That's just the kind of remark that got you in this situation, Linnet. I've told you time and again, all that cleverness does you no good. People would like a lady to be beautiful, but they *expect* her to be ladylike, in short: sweet, compliant, and refined."

"And yet you are universally taken for a lady," Linnet retorted.

"I am married," Zenobia says. "Or I was, until Etheridge passed on. I don't need to show sweetness and light. You do. You'd better polish up some ladylike chatter before you get to Wales to meet Yelverton. His title would be Earl of Marchant. Or would it be Mossford? I can't quite remember. I've never met him, of course."

"Neither have I," Lord Sundon said. "Are you trying to match Linnet off with a stripling, Zenobia? It'll never work."

"He's no stripling. He must be over thirty. Thirty-five at least. Surely you remember the story, Cornelius?"

"I pay no attention to stories," the viscount said testily. "It was the only way to survive under the same roof with your sister."

"*You* need to do a treatment to clean out your spleen," Zenobia said, putting down

51

her crumpet. "You are letting bile ferment in your system, Cornelius, and it's a very powerful emotion. Rosalyn is dead. Let her be *dead,* if you please!"

Linnet decided it was time to speak. "Aunt Zenobia, why would you think that the duke would be interested in matching me with his son? If indeed that's what you were thinking?"

"He's desperate," her aunt said. "Heard it from Mrs. Nemble, and she's bosom friends with Lady Grymes, and you know that her husband is Windebank's half brother."

"No, I don't know," the viscount said. "And I don't care either. Why is Windebank desperate? Is his son simpleminded? I can't recall seeing any sons around Lords or in Boodle's."

"Not simpleminded," Zenobia said triumphantly. "Even better!"

There was a moment of silence as both Linnet and her father thought about what that could mean.

"He hasn't got what it takes," her aunt clarified.

"He hasn't?" Sundon asked blankly.

"Minus a digit," Zenobia added.

"A finger?" Linnet ventured.

"For goodness' sake," Zenobia said, licking a bit of honey off one finger. "I always

52

have to spell everything out in this house. The man suffered an accident as a young man. He walks with a cane. And that accident left him impotent, to call a stone a stone. No heir now, and none in the future either."

"In fact, in this particular case," her father said with distinct satisfaction, "a stone isn't a stone."

"Impotent?" Linnet asked. "What does that mean?"

There was a moment's silence while her two closest relatives examined her closely, as if she were a rare species of beetle they'd found under the carpet.

"That's for you to explain," her father said, turning to Zenobia.

"Not in front of *you*," Zenobia said.

Linnet waited.

"All you need to know at the moment is that he can't father a child," her aunt added. "That's the crucial point."

Linnet put that fact together with various comments her mother had made over the years, and found she had absolutely no inclination to inquire further. "How is that better than simpleminded?" she asked. "In a husband, I mean."

"Simpleminded could mean drool at the dinner table and Lord knows what," her

53

aunt explained.

"You're talking about the *Beast!*" her father suddenly exclaimed. "I've heard all about him. Just didn't put it together at first."

"Marchant is no beast," Zenobia scoffed. "That's rank gossip, Cornelius, and I would think it beneath you."

"Everyone calls him that," the viscount pointed out. "The man's got a terrible temper. Brilliant doctor — or so everyone says — but the temper of a fiend."

"A tantrum here or there is part of marriage," Zenobia said, shrugging. "Wait until he sees how beautiful Linnet is. He'll be shocked and delighted that fate blessed him with such a lovely bride."

"Must I really choose between simpleminded and beastly?" Linnet inquired.

"No, between simpleminded and incapable," her aunt said impatiently. "Your new husband will be grateful for that child you're supposedly carrying, and I can tell you that your new father-in-law will be ecstatic."

"He will?" Lord Sundon asked.

"Don't you understand yet?" Zenobia said, jumping to her feet. She walked a few steps, and then twirled around in a fine gesture. "On the one side, we have a lonely duke, with one son. Just one. And that duke is obsessed with royalty, mind. He considers himself a bosom friend of the king, or at least he did before the king turned batty as a . . . as a bat."

"Got that," the viscount said.

"Hush," Zenobia said impatiently. She hated being interrupted. "On the one side, the lonely, desperate duke. On the other, the wounded, incapable son. In the balance . . . a kingdom."

"A kingdom?" the viscount repeated, his eyes bulging.

"She means it metaphorically," Linnet said, taking another crumpet. She had seen rather more of her aunt than her father had, and she was familiar with her love of rhetorical flourishes.

"A kingdom without a future, because there is no child to carry on the family name," Zenobia said, opening her eyes wide.

"Is the duke —" Lord Sundon began.

"Hush," she snapped. "I ask you, what does this desperately unhappy family need?"

Neither Linnet nor her father dared to answer.

Which was fine, because she had only paused for effect. "I ask you again, what does this desperately unhappy family need? They need . . . an *heir!*"

"Don't we all," the viscount said, sighing.

Linnet reached out and patted her father's hand. It was one of the rather unkind facts of life that her mama had been extremely free with her favors, and yet she had given her husband only one child, a daughter, who could not inherit the major part of her father's estate.

"They need," Zenobia said, raising her voice so as to regain her audience, "they need a *prince!*"

After a minute or so, Linnet ventured to say, "A prince, Aunt Zenobia?"

That gained her the beatific smile of an actress receiving accolades, if not armfuls of roses, from her audience. "A prince, my dear. And you, lucky girl, have exactly what he needs. He's looking for a heir, and you have that heir, and what's more, you're offering royal bloodlines."

"I see what you mean," the viscount said slowly. "It's not a terrible idea, Zenobia."

She got a little pink in the face. "None of my ideas are terrible. Ever."

"But I don't have a prince," Linnet said. "If I understand you correctly, the Duke of Windebank is looking for a pregnant woman—"

Her father growled and she amended her statement. "That is, the duke would perhaps acquiesce to a woman in my unfortunate situation because that way his son would have a son —"

"Not just a son," Zenobia said, her voice still triumphant. "A prince. Windebank isn't going to take just any lightskirt into his family. He's frightfully haughty, you know. He'd rather die. But a prince's son? He'll fall for that."

"But —"

"You're right about that, Zenobia. Be gad, you're a canny old woman!" her father roared.

Zenobia's back snapped straight. "What did you say to me, Cornelius?"

He waved his hand. "Didn't mean it that way, didn't mean it that way. Pure admiration. Pure unmitigated admiration. Pure —"

"I agree," she said in a conciliatory tone, patting her hair. "It's a perfect plan. You'd better go to him this afternoon, though. You have to get her all the way to Wales for the marriage. Marchant lives up there."

"Marriage," Linnet said. "Aren't you forgetting something?"

They both looked at her and said simultaneously, "What?"

"I'm not carrying a prince!" she shouted. "I never slept with Augustus. Inside my belly I have nothing but a chewed-up crumpet."

"That is a disgusting comment," her aunt said with a shudder.

"I agree," her father chimed in. "Quite distasteful. You sound like a city wife, talking of food in that manner."

"Distasteful is the fact that you are planning to sell off my unborn child to a duke with a penchant for royalty — when I don't even have an unborn child!"

"I said this would all have to happen quite quickly," her aunt said.

"What do you mean?"

"Well, let's say that your father goes to Windebank's house this very afternoon, and let's say that Windebank takes the bait, because he will. As I said, the man is desperate, and besides, he would love to meld his line with royal blood."

"That doesn't solve the problem," Linnet said.

"Well, of course not," Zenobia said, giving her a kindly smile. "We can't do everything for you. The next part is up to you."

"What do you mean?"

Her father got up, obviously not listening. "I'll put on my Jean de Bry coat and Hessians," he said to himself.

"*Not* the de Bry," Zenobia called after him.

58

He paused at the door. "Why not?"

"The shoulders are a trifle anxious. You mustn't seem anxious. You're offering to save the man's line, after all."

"Sage-green court coat with a scalloped edge," her father said, nodding, and disappeared through the door.

"Aunt Zenobia," Linnet said, showing infinite patience, to her mind. "Just how am I supposed to get a child of royal blood to offer to the husband I've never met?"

Zenobia smiled. "My dear, you aren't a woman of my family if you have to ask *that*."

Linnet's mouth fell open. "You don't mean —"

"Of course, darling. As soon as your father signs those papers, you have . . . oh . . . twelve hours before you really should leave for Wales."

"Twelve hours," Linnet echoed, hoping she was mistaken in what she was thinking. "You can't possibly mean —"

"Augustus has been following you about like a child with a string toy," her aunt said. "Shouldn't take more than a come-hither glance and a cheerful smile. Goodness' sake, dear, didn't you learn anything from your mother?"

"No," Linnet said flatly.

"Actually, with your bosom you don't

even need to smile," Zenobia said.

"So you really mean —" Linnet stopped. "I — I —"

"You. Augustus. Seduction. Bed," her aunt said helpfully. "Twelve hours and only one prince . . . should be quite easy."

"I —"

"You *are* Rosalyn's daughter," her aunt said. "And my niece. Seduction, especially when it comes to royalty, is bred in your bones. In your very bloodline."

"I don't know how," Linnet said flatly. "I may look naughty, but I'm not."

"Yes, you are," her aunt said brightly. She rose. "Just get yourself a child, Linnet. Think how many young women manage to do it and they haven't nearly your advantages, to wit, your body, your face, your smile."

"My entire education has been directed at chastity," Linnet pointed out. "I had a governess a good five years longer than other girls, just so I wouldn't learn such things."

"Your father's fault. He was frightened by Rosalyn's indiscretions."

There must have been something about Linnet's face, because Zenobia sighed with the air of a woman supporting the weight of the world. "I suppose I could find you a willing man if you really can't bring yourself to approach the prince. It's most unconventional, but of course one knows, one cannot help but know, of establishments that might help."

"What sort of establishments?"

"Brothels catering to women, of course," Zenobia said. "I do believe there's one near Covent Garden that I was just told about . . . men of substance, that's what I heard. They come for the sport of it, I suppose."

"Aunt, you can't possibly mean —"

"If you can't seduce the prince, we'll have to approach the problem from another angle," she said, coming over and patting Linnet's arm. "I'll take you to the brothel. As I understand it, a lady can stand behind a curtain and pick out the man she wants. We'd better choose one with a resemblance to Augustus. I wonder if we could just send a message to that effect and have the man delivered in a carriage?"

Linnet groaned.

"I don't want you to think that I would ever desert you in your hour of need," her aunt said. "I feel all the burden of a mother's love, now that darling Rosalyn is gone."

It was amazing how her aunt had managed to ignore that burden during the season and indeed for years before that, but

61

Linnet couldn't bring herself to point it out. "I am not going to a brothel," she stated.

"In that case," Zenobia said cheerily, "I suggest you sit down and write that naughty prince a little note. You're wise to choose him over the brothel, truly. One hates to start marriage with a fib involving babies. Marriage leads one into fibs by the very nature of it: all those temptations. One always orders too many gowns, and over-spends one's allowance. Not to mention men." She kissed the tips of her fingers.

"But I wanted —"

"I am so pleased not to be married at the moment," Zenobia said. "Not that I'm happy Etheridge died, of course. Ah well . . ."

Zenobia was gone.

And what Linnet wanted from marriage was clearly no longer a question worth discussion.

FOUR

"You must be joking," Piers said to Prufrock. "I sent my father a list of requirements for a wife that was a page long."

"It made fascinating reading," Prufrock said. "I especially appreciated the part where you admitted your incapability in bed. And the tear stain just there on the page —"

"It wasn't a tear," Piers said irritably. "It was brandy, you fool."

"Oh good," Prufrock said. "Because I hate to think that you were weeping all over the letter. Not when you could be wailing in your lonely bed."

"Why wouldn't I wail?" Piers said, wondering whether to have another glass. Better not. "You show me the man with an injury like mine who isn't broken-hearted over the dark future that lies before him."

"Dark and *dire* future," Prufrock amended. "Don't lose your alliterative touch now, right at the climactic moment."

"The despair of never having a good woman at his side, the bitterness of knowing a sticky little hand will never curl around his thumb, the —"

"Or to get to what really matters, years without shagging," Prufrock said.

"Is that an attempt to make me feel better?"

"It's not all it's cracked up to be," he said, with an unmistakable lack of conviction.

"Where did you go to school?" Piers inquired. "You're altogether too literate for a butler. Most butlers I know say things like *As you wish, my lord,* and leave it at that. Our conversation should be along these lines: *Prufrock, bring me a wench.* And then you would say, *As you wish.*"

"What would be the good of that?" Prufrock inquired. "Under the circumstances?"

"Good point," Piers muttered. "Well, I think I'll go for a swim. Tide's in."

He left the castle by the west door, still puzzling over his butler. As he'd thought since he hired Prufrock a year ago, the man must be in service to his father, to wit: a spy. That went without saying.

But where on earth had the old man managed to find a butler like that, a Prufrock-like butler, with a sense of humor and a

64

sharper tongue than Piers himself? In short, probably the only butler in the world whom Piers would keep in the castle even knowing that he was a bloody spy?

The only possibility was that his father actually knew or understood something about him, and since that was impossible, he dismissed the thought.

The bathing pool was carved straight out of rock on the edge of the sea, and was filled by the high tide but protected from the worst of the waves. It was a magnificent sight, a rock basin gleaming sapphire blue as the light began to fade. The sea had calmed the way it often did just at twilight, and he stood for a moment looking past the pool at the way the sea rippled on and on, following a dim gold trail of light.

Then he shook himself and pulled off his clothes. If he'd learned anything about his leg in the past years, it was that if he didn't exercise every day it hurt like the devil. He'd skipped the swim yesterday, and he was suffering the consequences today. Not that it didn't ache as a matter of course, but without swimming, he found himself in the kind of pain that he couldn't bear without thinking about opiates.

Not good, those moments, nor opiates either.

He dove off a rock, deep into the water, feeling his hair pull free — damn, forgot to take out the ribbon again — and his body rejoice as his leg kicked free without carrying the weight of his body. Without thinking, he began to propel himself forward, shooting through the water in the way he couldn't on land.

Hand over hand he went, ten lengths, twenty . . . at fifty he was tired, but he forced himself through another ten, and then pulled himself onto the rocks in one smooth gesture, water sluicing off his shoulders and arms. Before the injury, he never paid much attention to his body. Now he found himself pleased with the strength in his shoulders and chest. Though the doctor in him knew that was nothing but rubbishing vanity.

"My lord," a young footman said, stepping forward and handing him a large piece of toweling.

Piers looked up at him. "You're new. What's your name?"

"Neythen, my lord."

"Sounds like a terrible illness. No, more like a bowel problem. *I'm sorry, Lord Sandys, your son has contracted neythen and won't live a month. No, no, there's nothing I can do.* Sandys would have preferred hearing that

66

to syphilis."

Neythen looked perplexed. "My mum always said I'm named after a saint, not an illness."

"Which one?"

"Well, he had his head chopped off, see? And then he picked it up and carried it down the road a time. All the way back home, I think."

"Messy," Piers said. "Not to mention unlikely, though one has to think of chickens and their post-mortal abilities. Did she think that you would inherit the same gift?"

Neythen blinked. "No, my lord."

"Perhaps she was just hopeful. It behooves mothers to look ahead to this sort of possibility, after all. I'm tempted to behead you just to see if she was right. Sometimes the most unlikely superstitions turn out to have a basis in fact."

The footman stepped back.

"God, you are young, aren't you? Now why did Prufrock send you down here? Not that I don't appreciate the towel."

"Mr. Prufrock told me to tell you, my lord, that there's a patient waiting."

"There's always a patient or two around the place," Piers said, drying his hair. "I need to have a bath first. I'm covered with salt."

"The sign isn't up, so Mr. Prufrock said to inform you."

"No, bath before patient. My life is enough of a shambles without my butler telling me what to do."

"This one's come all the way from London," Neythen said. "And he's a big lord."

"Big, is he? Probably too fat for his heart. Pick up my cane and give it to me, if you would."

Neythen did so. "He's not fat," he said. "I saw him coming in. I mean that he's important-looking. He's dressed all in velvet and thin as a rail. And he's wearing a wig."

"Another dying man," Piers said, starting up the path. "Just what we need around here. Pretty soon we're going to have to put in our own cemetery out back."

Neythen didn't seem to have anything to say to this.

" 'Course you won't be there," Piers assured him, "since you can carry your head back home and be buried in your own village churchyard. But I'm starting to feel like a dark version of the Pied Piper. They come to Wales to find me, they die. The next day, more of the same arrive."

"You cure some of them, don't you?" Neythen asked.

"A few," Piers said. "Mostly not. For one

thing, I'm an anatomical pathologist, which means that I'm really better with dead bodies. They don't twitch, and they don't get infections. As for the live ones, all I can do is observe them. Sometimes I don't know anything until after they're dead, and then it's too late. Sometimes I cut the cadavers open and I still don't have the faintest idea what went wrong."

Neythen shuddered.

"You're doing the right thing to become a footman and not a physician," Piers told him, making his way up the rocky path to the castle. "We surgeons are always cutting up people, dead or alive. It's the only way to learn what's inside, you know."

"That's revolting!"

"Don't worry," Piers said. "If you manage to walk your decapitated body home, then I can't cut it open and find out what happened to you, can I?"

Neythen kept quiet.

"Don't even think of quitting," Piers added, pushing himself over the last rock and onto the flat path. "Prufrock will have *my* head if more of his staff leaves because of my ill-considered remarks."

Neythen's silence seemed to indicate that he wasn't quitting yet.

Piers reached the house. "I suppose I'll

have a look at that patient before I bathe."

"Like that, my lord?" Neythen asked.

Piers looked down at himself. He'd wrapped the towel around his waist. "You said there's a patient waiting, didn't you?"

"Yes, but —"

"There's nothing I like more than meeting velvet-clad peers while wrapped in a towel," he said. "They're going to lie to me anyway, but it keeps them alert."

"Lie?" Neythen asked, sounding shocked.

"It comes with the peerage. Really. It's only the poor who bother with honesty, these days."

FIVE

Linnet left the drawing room and walked straight to her mother's chamber, the one place where she was sure not to be disturbed.

Not much had changed since her mother died. It was still the same flowery boudoir that it had been when Rosalyn was alive, minus the most important thing: the sparkling, charming person who had made it her own.

Who had made her husband love her, no matter how unfaithful she was. Who had made all those other men love her too.

Who had loved Linnet for more than her beauty.

Linnet sat down at the dressing table just as she had when she was a mere fourteen, devastated by her mother's sudden death. There was dust on the silver brushes; she had to remind Tinkle to make sure the maids cleaned the rooms properly.

She touched each one, remembering how her mother used to sit on the stool, brushing her hair and roaring with laughter at whatever Linnet told her. No one ever laughed at her jokes the way her mother had. Rosalyn had the gift of making you feel like the wittiest person in the world.

Linnet sighed. Her mother would have loved the joke about the light frigate docking at the pier.

And then she would have dabbed on scent and rushed away to meet some darling, delicious man, her eyes still twinkling.

Finally Linnet took her finger off the silver brush and raised her head. Rosalyn's portrait dimpled from the wall. Linnet smiled, and without even glancing at the mirror before her, knew that precisely the same dimple had appeared in her cheek. Precisely the same curls, like pale primroses. The same wide blue eyes, the same naughty cherry mouth, the same . . .

Not the same.

Oh, she had her mother's charm. She knew that. She could twinkle at a man just the way her mother used to, and it was an odd man who didn't get a faintly glazed expression in his eyes. Zenobia called it the "family smile," and said it was their greatest inheritance. But what Linnet didn't do was . . .

Follow through.

She didn't even like being kissed, if the truth be told.

Kisses were messy, and *saliva* — well, saliva was disgusting.

She'd always thought that one day a man would stroll into the ballroom and she would realize that he was the one whom she could tolerate kissing. But no one appeared who sparked that realization, not once during the season. That was why she flirted so wildly with the prince.

A girl who is flirting with a prince is generally excused from flirting with other men, who understand exactly why, so it isn't as if she is being rude. Besides, in her spare moments, Linnet generally twinkled at them, to keep a whole crowd about her. It made her feel as if she were on stage, à la Zenobia.

Who would have thought that the biggest thing of all — that quality of her mother's that had practically defined her — would be so definitively missing in Rosalyn's only daughter?

And yet, so it was.

Not only did she not desire men, she didn't even like them very much.

They were big, and hairy, and tended to

73

smell. Even her father, whom she loved, acted like a little boy. He complained and whined and carried on in the most tiresome fashion. They were all like little boys, she thought. And who could desire a little boy?

Her mother's voice sounded in her head and she answered it irritably: hung like a horse or not, men were still pitiful creatures.

But it made her think of something. If the earl was incapable, then . . .

Then he was incapable.

They wouldn't have to kiss. She wouldn't have to put up with all that was implied by a man hung like a horse, which (thank you, Mama!) had revolted and horrified her for years.

All she had to do was appear to be carrying a child long enough to marry him, and then pretend to have lost the babe.

She'd never met a man yet whom she couldn't charm into a good temper. She'd learned at the feet of a master, after all. Her mother had kept her father sweet-tempered — even after he had to throw Linnet's French tutor out of the house, and roust another lover out of his new bed.

In fact, she could make a rational argument for marriage to Piers. She would never cuckold him, for one thing. (A man with his problem had to be afraid of that possibility.)

74

She was the best he could have hoped for: both beautiful and chaste. Practically saint-hood material, really.

She stood up and took a last look around her mother's room. "I miss you," she told the laughing portrait on the wall. "I do miss you." But the words pulled at her heart, so she hurried from the room.

Six

That night at supper, Linnet's father reported that the Duke of Windebank had
leaped on his proposal with undignified
speed. "He apparently knew all about you.
And Zenobia, it was clear you were right.
He was unshaken — if not privately delighted — at the sound of Linnet's little
scandal."

"Linnet was the talk of the *ton*," Zenobia
said, "long before last evening's unfortunate
events."

"He wasn't nearly as interested in her
beauty as in her education, if you can
believe it. I told him Linnet had about as
much education as any girl should, and that
she was the cleverest woman *I* knew, and
that shut him up. I can't think why he didn't
ever marry again. His wife took off for
France years ago, didn't she? Took the lad
with her as well."

"She was French, of course. He got a

divorce," Zenobia said. "The rumors were that it cost him two thousand pounds sterling to buy his freedom. And then he never did a thing with it." She shook her head. "He could have had any number of possible heirs by this time."

"What I don't like is all this royalty-mongering," Lord Sundon said. "Absolutely cracked on the subject of monarchy, if you ask me. He told me that a great-great-great aunt on his father's side was intimate with Henry VIII."

"Wasn't he the king who had six wives?" Linnet asked.

"Had 'em and murdered 'em," Zenobia said with relish, waving her fork. "Just like the story of Bluebeard, except it was all true."

"At any rate, Windebank is happy because he's got the blood of the Tudors in his veins, and now he's getting the blood of the Hanovarians as well, through our Linnet."

The viscount was looking a good deal happier than he had that morning. "All's well that ends well," he said, finishing his glass of wine. "Someday we'll look back on this whole episode and laugh."

Linnet couldn't quite imagine that.

"I suppose you sent the prince a note," Zenobia said to Linnet.

She nodded, though she had done nothing of the sort. "I'm meeting him in Vauxhall tonight." In reality, she planned to have a nice nap in the carriage while it tooled around London.

"Vauxhall?" Zenobia asked dubiously. "Luckily it's a warm night, but it seems an odd place for an assignation. One would think that he could whisk you away to some sort of royal lodge."

"He probably will," her father said. "Just be sure you're back here in the morning. Windebank wants to meet you. I told him we wanted to send you off to Wales as soon as possible. No point in hanging around London."

In their household, her mother had drawn all the fire for her improprieties. But sometimes Linnet thought her father was just as improper, in a different way. A shabbier way, if the truth be told.

"I think this will all work out better than it might have otherwise," her father went on. "After all, Augustus could never have married you. And there isn't a single duke on the market this year. Someday Marchant will be a duke."

"She could have done better than a limp lily," Zenobia pointed out. "I assume the duke is obtaining a special license?"

The viscount nodded. "Of course. He's bringing it with him tomorrow. And he sent a messenger to Wales this very afternoon, so his son will have some warning. It isn't in the normal course of things to acquire a wife and a child without notice, you know."

"You'll have to make sure the marriage takes place quickly," Zenobia said, "just in case Linnet's visit to Vauxhall tonight doesn't have the desired effect."

"Well, as to that . . ." her father said.

At the note in her father's voice, Linnet stiffened. She knew it, had heard it a million times. "Papa, you can't simply send me to Wales without a chaperone!" she said fiercely.

"Hate to bring up a painful truth, but you've got no further use for a chaperone," he said evasively. "Though we might we able to persuade Mrs. Hutchins to accompany you if you insist."

Zenobia narrowed her eyes. "Do you mean to tell me, Cornelius, that you are thinking of sending your only daughter into the wilds of Wales without your escort?"

"It's not a good time for me to leave London," Lord Sundon said, starting to bluster.

"I do not feel comfortable taking a journey of that length by myself, especially when I am going to meet a *Beast*," Linnet said. She kept her voice light but firm, precisely as her mother would have done. And just to make absolutely sure that he understood her, she fixed him with a glare that she'd learned from her aunt.

"The Earl of Marchant has been unfairly maligned," the viscount said. "Heard all about it from his father. He's a brilliant physician, don't you know. You remember his mother stole him away to France; well, he got a university degree over there. Then he returned here and did the same at Oxford and then he was admitted to the Royal College of Physicans at the age of twenty-three, which is practically unheard of, and then he went off to Edinburgh and did something or other there, or maybe he did that before the Royal —"

"Cornelius," Zenobia said, cutting through his bluster, "you are a precious coward."

"I'm not a coward!" the viscount said. "I have important things to do here in the city. The House of Lords is meeting, I'll have you know, and I'm very important — very important indeed. My voice is required, essential."

"You're a cringing coward," Zenobia said. "You don't want to go up there and face

80

the Beast yourself, even though you are sending your daughter — your pregnant daughter — into the countryside to marry him."

Now that Zenobia had got hold of the story, Linnet began to feel like one of those maidens who hung around King Arthur's court and invariably found herself in the coils of a great serpent. Her aunt instinctively turned any event into a melodrama, though one had to admit that this was worthy of a little drama. "You are throwing your daughter onto the mercies of a *wild man*," Zenobia said, her voice rising.

Rather surprisingly, the viscount did not back down. "I've already made up my mind. I shall not go to Wales."

Linnet knew that sulky tone of voice; he wouldn't go. "Why not?" she asked, before Zenobia could jump in.

"I am no pander for my daughter," her father thundered. "I may have been a cuckold to my wife, but I will not double my shame by pandering my only child."

"You already have," Linnet snapped back. "You bartered me off this very afternoon, by lying about the child that we all know I'm not carrying."

Lord Sundon's jaw was rigid. "Your mother never would have spoken to me in such a fashion."

That was true. Linnet could not remember a single occasion on which Rosalyn's voice lost its sweet, musical tone. Whereas Linnet's voice grated with the anger she couldn't keep inside. "I'm sorry to disappoint you, but the tone of my voice doesn't change the truth."

"The truth is that every girl is bartered off in some fashion or other," Zenobia said. "But I really think that you should accompany poor Linnet, Cornelius. What if Marchant takes one look at the girl and refuses to marry her?"

"He won't," Lord Sundon said flatly. "We all know that —"

At that moment the door opened and Tinkle entered. "His Grace the Duke of Windebank begs your indulgence."

"At this hour?" the viscount asked.

"Is he outside?" Zenobia demanded.

It appeared that the duke was indeed in his coach, waiting to see if Lord Sundon could spare him a moment.

"Bring him in," the viscount said. Then, turning to Linnet. "I suppose he couldn't wait until tomorrow to meet you."

"He can't see me," Linnet said, alarmed. She looked down at her slim profile. "In this dress, I don't have any evidence of royal

82

progeny."

"I told him you were barely showing," her father said. "Just sit down quickly. We'd better see him in the rose drawing room."

The Duke of Windebank had to be sixty, but he looked younger and very handsome. He had a regal profile, worthy of a coin, which seemed fitting for his rank. A Roman coin, Linnet decided.

"Miss Thrynne," he said, bowing. "You are as beautiful as the world has described."

Linnet dropped a curtsy, judging it to the precise inch to indicate respect for a duke. "I am honored to meet you, Your Grace."

"Now," he said, turning back to Linnet's father and aunt. "I took it upon myself to interrupt you at this hour because I decided that I should personally escort Miss Thrynne to Wales. My son is a brilliant man, absolutely brilliant."

He paused.

"But he does have a reputation for irascibility," Zenobia said, giving him her version of the family smile. "Please do be seated, Your Grace."

Despite his youthful aspect, the duke creaked when he sat down, like a chair left out in the rain. His eyes were suddenly wary. "My son has been much maligned."

"I suggest we dispense with the pleasantries," Zenobia said, rearranging the drape of her garments. "After all, we are soon to be family. Lord Marchant may be rather surprised, if not shocked, at the arrival of his bride, and it's only natural that you wish to accompany dear Linnet, Your Grace."

"Well, that's settled," Linnet's father said, dispensing with any pretense of reluctance.

The duke looked from the viscount to Zenobia. "Will Miss Thrynne travel with a chaperone? Yourself, perhaps, Lady Etheridge?"

"No need for that," Zenobia replied cheerfully. "She's ruined. No point in guarding an empty stable, so to speak. Would you like to bring Mrs. Hutchins with you, my dear?" she asked Linnet.

Linnet looked from her father to her aunt and something familiar panged in the general region of her heart. But it was an old pain, a familiar pain, and easily shrugged off. "I think not," she said. "If you don't mind, Your Grace, I shall just come by myself, with my maid, of course. As my aunt says, the circumstances certainly suggest that a chaperone is not necessary."

The duke nodded.

"If you'll excuse me," Linnet said, rising, "I have an appointment at Vauxhall."

The gentlemen scrambled to their feet,

and Zenobia followed, after accepting (in a most theatrical fashion) the duke's help in rising.

After which Linnet climbed into a carriage, instructing the family coachman, Stubbins, to drive around London wherever he wished, and leaving her relatives with the happy, if quite mistaken, impression that Prince Augustus was vigorously debauching her.

It could be that she would never return to London, she realized, staring out the window. The city passed before the carriage in a long, dreary string of gray houses, made even dingier by a thick layer of coal dust.

That would mean she might not see her father again, as he never left the city. Or Aunt Zenobia, who left only for the most raucous of house parties.

At the moment, that idea was entirely untroubling.

SEVEN

In a caravan made up of three carriages and eight groomsmen, Linnet and the Duke of Windebank finally arrived in Wales two weeks later. Since the duke had only one subject of conversation at every meal — his son — by then she knew enough about her future husband to introduce him to the Royal College of Physicians herself. That is, if he hadn't already joined their ranks.

After the first few days of incessant talking about Piers, Linnet had banished the duke from her carriage, with the excuse that her condition, combined with the jouncing of the coach, made her nauseated.

She had then discovered that lying flat on the ducal cushions was remarkably comfortable. And since she had an iron-clad stomach, she had read happily through their journey, lying on her back and munching apples.

What she'd seen of Wales through the carriage windows was green: a dark, alive green that seemed drenched with water and wind. She'd never smelled the sea before, but she knew what it was immediately, deep in her bones. It was wild and fishy and free, and made her dream about long sea voyages to islands she'd never heard of.

When she wasn't contemplating the sea, she thought about the physician she was about to marry. According to his father, he had been unfairly labeled as a "beast" because of his impatience with the hoary medical establishment.

"Doctors," Windebank had told her, "are old fools. Take fevers, for example. Piers discovered that, by their combination of blood-letting and heating the internal temperature, doctors were actually killing their patients. Members of the Royal College fought him tooth and nail until he finally put his patient record against that of an eminent practitioner, Ketelaer. Ketelaer lost all but three of his patients, and from about the same number, Piers lost only one."

So she was marrying a genius. It did sound as if he had a tendency to lose his temper when crossed, but she was confident that she could manage him.

The morning of their arrival at the castle,

she wound some linen cloth around her waist to give her a slightly thicker profile, and regarded herself in the mirror. Apart from her waistline, she looked precisely like a princess in any one of a hundred fairy tales: clear blue eyes, reddish-gold hair, beautiful skin. Plus the family smile.

She would give herself two weeks to ensure that her fiancé (perhaps husband, by then) was desperately in love with her, and then she meant to confess that she wasn't carrying a child.

The castle was set on the cliffs, and as the carriages started up the road, the sun was rising hot and yellow to their left. "Enjoy this sunshine," the duke said. She'd allowed him to join her carriage for the final leg of their journey. "I'm afraid that Wales is infamous for its wet weather. I do wish that you could talk my son into moving to London, my dear. I know he could do so much good there. Not that I'm suggesting that he have a regular *practice,* of course. He will be a peer of the realm. But he could consult on the most interesting cases."

There was something about the duke's descriptions of his son that was a little . . . odd. As if he didn't know him very well, although that couldn't be the case.

Linnet leaned forward in anticipation as

they neared the castle. It was massive, built of light gray stone, and had four or five turrets that she could see. "Is it very old?" she asked.

"Ancient," the duke said, looking out as well. "Been in the family for generations. One of my ancestors won it in a game of piquet. Piers had to make extensive repairs, since no one had lived in it for ages."

The carriages drew up in an enclosed area outside a great arched door.

"Ah, there you are, Prufrock," the duke said, leaping out.

The butler seemed quite young for his position, probably only in his thirties, and so thin as to be stork-like, with skin the color of milky tea. "Your Grace," he said, bowing.

His eyes moved to Linnet, who had just stepped from the carriage with the help of a groom. He didn't have that butler's knack of keeping an impervious face; his eyes widened and one eyebrow flew up in an unexpectedly charming manner.

"This is Prufrock," the duke said. "Miss Thrynne, my son's fiancée. I'm sure Piers informed you of our impending arrival."

Prufrock ushered them through the huge doors straight into a great, open room with a huge staircase going up either side. The door was as thick as Linnet's hand was wide, and clearly built to withstand sieges.

"Where shall we find my son?" the duke asked. There was something in his voice, some sort of barely suppressed joy, that made Linnet wonder.

She took off her bonnet and pelisse, and handed them to a footman.

"Lord Marchant is in the west wing, and he has been informed, of course, of your arrival," Prufrock said. "I sent a footman there as soon as we caught sight of your carriages. I expect he will join you any moment. If Miss Thrynne wishes to refresh herself, I can escort her and her maid to her chamber. Perhaps Your Grace as well?"

"Nonsense," the duke said. "We left our inn only a matter of an hour or two ago. Patients are housed on the third floor, aren't they, Prufrock?"

"Yes, but —"

The duke strode off. Then he hesitated, turned around, and grabbed Linnet by the wrist. "I'll take you with me," he said, as if to himself. Before she even opened her mouth to reply, they were halfway up the left hand flight of stairs.

"Your Grace," she gasped, catching up her skirts.

"Come along, come along," he said over

his shoulder. Now that they were finally at the castle, he seemed to be possessed by a ferocious compulsion. He towed her down a corridor.

Linnet concentrated on keeping up, though she could feel her heart beating faster and faster. At any moment she would meet the paragon she was to marry. She'd formed a picture of him in her mind: tall and willowy, with a limp that gave him a slight tilt to the side, a face lined by pain but imbued with the quite remarkable beauty that his father still possessed.

They rounded a corner. She could hear voices now. The duke walked even faster, pulling her along behind him. A door at the end of the corridor stood open and the duke dove through.

They were in a room with six beds, most of them occupied. A group of young men was clustered around a bed to the left. The duke let go of her arm at last and stepped forward. "Piers," he said, his voice suddenly hoarse.

None of the men looked around at the interruption. Most of them were younger, probably students, and all were intently focused on the patient.

"A teaching session," the duke breathed.

Linnet's eyes darted over the men, immediately locating her fiancé. In fact, he was speaking. "Miliary fever. Presents with rash, febrile state." His voice had the ring of utter authority. "The eruption appeared on the third day, which is conclusive evidence." Marchant had a longer chin than she would have imagined, but the rest of him was perfect: sleekly blond hair, wildly intelligent, lean, with an arrogant look.

That was what got him the nickname of *Beast* — that arrogant look, as if he were more intelligent than anyone in the room. Still, she could see a kindness in him that belied the label.

His costume was exquisite. Frankly, she would never have thought to see a morning coat of that magnificence in Wales, or indeed anywhere outside London. Her father would have envied it, which was saying a great deal.

A young man to the right of the bed spoke up, rather hesitatingly. "Huxham says the rash might appear on the seventh, ninth, or eleventh day."

"In my experience, eruption occurs on the third day," her fiancé replied. His voice was just the sort to soothe a fretful patient, Linnet thought, wondering why he had a French accent, before remembering that he'd spent most of his life in that country, with his mother.

"Your experience is worthless," some graceless student snarled from the other side of the bed. She could not see him since he was obscured by the other men. "And so is Huxham's. The man was flailing in the dark. Seventh, eleventh; he might as well say that the eruption comes with the new moon. It's all magic to him."

"This eruption was accompanied by oppression and sinking spirits," her fiancé responded, his voice a quiet reproach. "Lobb explicitly mentions those symptoms in connection with miliary eruptions."

"Wouldn't you have sinking spirits if you found yourself covered with a disgusting, crusty eruption?" the harsh voice said.

Beside her, the duke shifted to the side to see the speaker, and then smiled. Linnet's heart sank as she grasped the meaning behind that smile.

"Here, you in the bed, aren't you finding your condition sinking, if not oppressive? That eruption means someone might as well start carving your gravestone, so why not be depressed?"

"Yweth," came from the bed.

"Now this is fun," the man said. "Someone ask him what color the sky is, why don't you?"

No one said anything.

"Bwuu," the patient offered.

There was a crack of laughter.

"You're an ass," the blond doctor stated. Linnet agreed. How could that lout make fun of a dying man?

Just then the group of young doctors parted, and she could see who was spouting all this incivility. "The ass in this room is the person who diagnosed a patient without asking him a single question. Now this man has a thick tongue, leading to that amusing lisp. Could be dry, could be swollen. Either way, not a good sign. If it's dry, it could mean miliary fever. But if swollen, what would that indicate?"

Her first impression of the rude man was that he was big — huge, in fact. The blond doctor was tall and lean, but this man was even taller, and much bigger. His shoulders seemed twice as wide as those of the other men. He was all muscle, with a kind of predatory force that looked out of place next to a sickbed. In fact, he looked as if he should be out leading hordes of Vikings . . . berserking, or whatever it was those men did for a living.

He'd been pointing out something on the patient's chest, but he looked up and their eyes met. Instantly his face went stony.

What was beautiful in his father was harsh in him; his blue eyes were frosty, like bitter winter. He didn't look civilized. No one would put that face on a coin, Roman or otherwise. He looked too tough . . . too . . . too *beast-like,* she suddenly realized.

Her heart skipped a beat, but his eyes moved over her face and then down her body, as if she too were a patient he was diagnosing. Quite carelessly, without looking away from her, he said, "It's petechial fever, numbskull. He should have been put in the east wing, not the west, though he's likely no longer infectious. You should stick to sawing off legs; you're an ass when it comes to diagnostics."

And then, "Look who's here! My father actually managed to find a woman more beautiful than the sun and the moon." There was a faint ring of contempt in his voice that made Linnet's backbone stiffen.

"Piers," the duke said.

His son's implacable eyes moved from Linnet to the duke, standing next to her. "And accompanied by Dear Old Dad, no less. Well, this will be a jolly party. Guess what, fellows?"

The other doctors were frankly gaping. Unlike the earl, they each had a quite normal reaction to Linnet; she saw that in one lightning glance.

"I'm getting married," he said. "To a woman who apparently has a remarkable wish to be a duchess. Aren't I the lucky one?" He walked forward, around the end of the bed.

Linnet just stopped herself from stepping backward. She realized with a jolt of nerves that she could either stand up to him, starting now, or she'd spend the rest of her life being bullied.

Because he was a bully, no question about it. He walked over until he was standing too close to her, using the fact he was so much bigger to intimidate her.

"My father did inform you that I'm planning to live a normal life span, didn't he?" Marchant said, his voice liquid with distaste.

"He didn't mention it," she managed, grateful to hear her voice unshaken. The contempt in his eyes was so thinly veiled that her back went rigid. "Sometimes plans change," she added. "One can only hope."

"My plans rarely do. I wouldn't want you to have scampered all the way to Wales just because you thought I was lining up pall-bearers."

"The duke told me everything essential about you, and your reputation provided the rest," she said.

His eyes drifted slowly down her body again. "Interesting. There are a few things he seems to have forgotten to tell *me*."

Linnet turned to the duke. Surely he'd mentioned the baby in his letter — that is, the baby she was supposed to have? Marchant's eyes had definitely paused at her thickened waist.

But the duke was staring at his son like a greedy man in front of a French custard. There was a great deal more going on here than she had realized.

"And you must be my father," Marchant continued. His voice was not in the least welcoming.

"I am," the duke said, his voice halting. "I am he."

There was a painful silence. It was clear that Marchant wasn't going to say anything else, and the duke didn't seem to have the nerve.

"Now we all know who each other is," Linnet said brightly, "perhaps we should go downstairs and leave this poor patient to himself."

The man in bed had propped himself up on his elbows and was staring in fascination. "Not on my account," he said, his swollen tongue making a mangle of the sentence.

Marchant looked from the patient to her. "Beautiful *and* cheerful. My, my, this really is my lucky day, isn't it?"

"A delightful family reunion of this nature brings out the best in everyone, don't you think?" She turned and walked to the doorway, where she paused and turned around. Just as she expected, the men were staring after her, including — she noticed with a pulse of pleasure — her own fiancé, not to mention the patient. "Doctor?"

"I believe that's my cue," Marchant said. For the first time she realized that he was leaning on a cane clutched in his right hand. She watched as he made his way toward her. Oddly enough, his huge body gave the opposite effect to the gentle list to the side that she had expected.

He lurched as he walked, moving like a wounded but still ferocious lion, all the more dangerous for his injury.

"Don't tell me that His Grace forgot to inform you that your future husband is a cripple," he said, reaching the door. He had walked straight past his father without seeming to notice the way the duke's hand started toward him and then fell to his side.

Linnet decided to hold the family smile back for a better moment. "He mentioned it," she said. "Perhaps I shouldn't take your

98

arm, in case I topple you?" She ignored the fact that he hadn't offered his arm.

He narrowed his eyes. They both knew that he was built like a brick house, and her hand on his arm wouldn't shake him.

"You're playing a deep game," he said.

"So, are the three younger men your students?" she asked. They walked down the corridor. Behind them, she could hear the duke introducing himself to the remaining doctors.

"You can count to three," he said approvingly. "That bodes well for our offspring."

"And here I thought *we* weren't having offspring," Linnet said.

"It is true that the responsibility for the business rests on your shoulders," he said, walking with a sort of rolling gait that sent him stalking just before her. "Though I must say that my father's letter seemed to imply you were more precipitate in that regard than you appear to be."

The worst thing she could do was to skip to catch up with him. He was obviously far too accustomed to young doctors tagging along at his heels.

He turned his head. "Didn't you hear what I said?"

"Unluckily for me," she said sweetly, "I don't know what the word *precipitate* means, so I missed the compliment you were giving me."

"I was talking about that scrap of royal blood you're supposedly carrying in your womb," he growled.

Linnet glanced over her shoulder. There was still no sign of the duke or the medical students. "What of it?"

He stopped again. "There's no baby in that belly, Miss Thrynne. The fact that you have tied a cushion around your waist may be sufficient to confuse my father, but not me." He started walking again.

Linnet looked at his shoulders and realized that she would have to curb this habit of his, or she would spend the rest of her life scrambling after him. "Is it your limp that makes you walk like this?" she asked, raising her voice.

"What do you think?" he said, halting again. "Do you suppose that I stagger like a drunken sailor for the pure pleasure of it?"

"I don't mean the stagger," she said. "I mean the way you're scurrying along the corridor like a kitchen maid afraid of the cook."

He froze for a moment and then, rather to her surprise, gave a bark of laughter. It sounded rusty, as if from disuse. "I'm bored by corridors," he said.

100

"I'm bored by people's shoulders."

His eyes were remarkably lustrous in the dim light of the corridor. He didn't have his father's beauty, but Linnet began to see that he had his own. It was a more brutal, stronger kind, a sort of beauty that burned from his eyes.

"Bloody hell. You're not what I expected."

"I must not be quite as famous as you are," she said, catching up to him. He didn't offer, but she put her fingertips on his right arm, thinking that would at least keep him at her side.

"With that face, I would imagine that polite society knows all about you."

"And what do you know of polite society?"

"Not a thing," he said, starting to walk. He didn't mention her touch, but he did slow down to keep beside her.

"At the moment, I'm more notorious than famous," she said, taking the bull by the horns.

"Because of that baby you don't actually have," he said. "Odd, that. I thought the gentry were more outraged by babies, than the lack thereof. Did you start wearing the cushion as some sort of joke?"

"I put it on this morning just for you," she said.

"How did you figure out that my father

would be unable to resist you, under the circumstances? It was a remarkably clever ploy, given his obsession with the family name." For the first time there was a germ of admiration in his voice.

"Thank you," she said.

"Not that it's going to work."

Linnet was thinking precisely along those lines, though she saw no reason to let him know. "Oh, but I think we're perfectly suited," she said, just to needle him.

"A barking-mad doctor — that's me — and a wickedly conniving beauty — that's you — limping along together in a lifetime of happiness? I hardly think so. You've been reading too many fairy stories."

"Who says I can read? I can barely count, remember?"

He glanced at her and she decided, once again, to withhold the family smile. "I'm starting to think I may have been wrong about your abilities. You can probably count all the way to ten and back."

"That just warms my heart," she cooed. "Since it comes from the great doctor and all."

The corner of his mouth curled up. "So just when did you think you'd inform your husband about the royal baby that doesn't exist?"

"I could have lost the babe."

"I'm a physician, remember?"

"I thought you were a surgeon."

"I do it all," he said, starting to speed up again.

She tightened her fingers on his arm, feeling muscles flex as his arm took the weight of his body, leaning on his cane.

He looked sideways, slowed down, but didn't say anything.

"So you're a surgeon," she prompted, and asked once more, "Are those men all your students?"

"I don't have students," he said in a disgusted tone. "I leave that for the fools in London. What you saw are hopeless idiots who found their way here to make my life hell. You may have noticed the driveling idiot in the front, the blond one. He's the worst."

"He looks old to be a student," Linnet said.

"Sébastien. My cousin. He's actually not a bad surgeon. Claims to be writing a book on the subject, but actually he's just got the wind up, so he's hiding here."

"Hiding from what?"

"He seems to be convinced that Napoleon is losing his mind. It wouldn't surprise me. He's Marquis Latour de l'Affitte, by the way, so it's a miracle he made it through the last ten years with his pretty head intact."

They reached the stairs leading down to the main floor. "If you want to keep holding onto me, you'll have to move to my left side," Marchant said. "Though, of course, there's always the possibility that you could descend the stairs all by yourself."

Linnet moved to his left side, just to irritate him. She curled her fingers under his arm this time. She rather liked all that muscle under her hand. It felt as if she were taming a wild beast.

"I suppose you think I'll fall in love with you," he said.

"Quite likely."

"How long do you give yourself?" He sounded genuinely curious.

"Two weeks at the outside." And then she did give him the smile — dimples, charm, sensuality and all.

He didn't even blink. "Was that the best you've got?"

Despite herself, a giggle escaped, and then another. "Generally, that's more than enough."

"I suppose I should say something reassuring at this point." He pitched his voice to a groveling apology. *"It's not me, it's you."*

Then: "Oops! Got that backwards. *It's not you, it's me.*"

"I suppose your injury gives you immunity," she said, having already figured that out. She'd miscalculated when she counted his incapability as a plus. It made him uninterested in her charms, which meant their marriage would never work.

The duke was simply going to have to reconcile himself to the lack of an heir.

Marchant's frosty blue eyes flickered over to her and then away. "Something like that."

"I didn't mean to mention it, if it's a sore subject," she said, making up her mind to irritate him all she could. "I'm sure it must be difficult to feel that you're . . . what is the phrase? A pussycat. A powder puff."

"Pussycat?" To her disappointment, he didn't sound irritated, just wryly amused. "I think of myself more as a . . ."

"Yes?"

"I'll have to think about it. To find the perfect phrase, you understand."

"Don't fret," she counseled him. "I'm sure I can solve our little problem once we're married. Wales is likely full of strapping lads, ready to do their lord a favor."

"*We* don't have a problem," he snapped.

She bit back a smile. "Oh, but we do," she said. "Your father has promised your hand

105

in marriage to me, and the announcement has already been sent to the *Morning Post*."

"Do I look as if I give a damn about that?"

"Your father will."

"The father I just met five minutes ago, for the first time in twenty-six years?"

"Yes, well," she said. "Here I am. Your fiancée. Probably the only one you'll ever be offered, too."

There must have been something in her tone that gave her away, because he gave another one of those rusty barks of laughter. "I'm *not* marrying you, and I can tell that you're in agreement — but damned if I wouldn't consider it, if things were different."

"Now, now," she cooed, curling her hand more tightly around his arm and giving him another smile.

"Oh, give it up," he said. "You're not marrying me, any more than I'm marrying you. What's your name, by the way?"

"Miss Thrynne," she said. "My father is Cornelius Thrynne, Viscount Sundon."

"I'm an earl," he said. "But I suppose you know that, since you apparently made a dead set at my poor father, bewitching him with stories of princely issue. How did you find out his weakness for royal blood?"

"My aunt was aware that he claims Henry

106

VIII as an ancestor," she said, eyeing his big frame. "I don't see much resemblance, though; he was certainly shorter and fatter than you are."

The butler was waiting in the entry as they reached the bottom step. "This is Prufrock," the earl said. "He knows everything that happens in this castle and farther abroad. Though really, Prufrock, you should have warned me that my father planned to breach the fortress. I would have left."

"My conclusion precisely, my lord," the butler said. He bowed to Linnet. "Your maid is in your bedchamber, Miss Thrynne, if you would like to join her."

From the top of the steps came a clamor of voices as the doctors walked down, led by the duke.

"Hell and damnation," Marchant said. He turned toward the archway. "You — open the door," he snarled at a footman, who sprang into action.

Linnet was looking after him with some amusement when he suddenly turned around. "And you," he said to her. "Come with me."

She laughed. *"You,"* she said mockingly, "run away and hide now, why don't you? I think the big, bad wolf is coming."

For a moment his face darkened and his

eyes narrowed in an almost frightening fashion. But then he held out his hand. "Please."

She might as well. "All right," she said. But she didn't take his hand. They went out the massive door into the sunshine.

"The sun's still out," Marchant said, squinting up. "All morning, which is practically a record. It rains most of the time in Wales."

"Will you take me in the direction of the sea?" She could smell a saucy, salty freshness and faintly hear the sound of waves. She didn't have her bonnet, which meant she might get freckles, but at the moment she couldn't bring herself to care. Mrs. Hutchins said that freckles were vastly unattractive, but Mrs. Hutchins was far away, in London.

"This way," the earl said. "You may hold my arm if you wish." He would never wait for her to retrieve her bonnet, so she'd have to go without it.

"Very courteous of you. You'll be ready for Almack's any moment," she said, curling her fingers around his arm again.

"Almack's? What's that?"

"A place where all the best sort go to dance on Wednesday nights," she said.

"Sounds appalling."

"It can be tedious," she said, considering.

He looked sideways at her. "You don't like dancing?"

"It's fine," she said, without much enthusiasm.

"But what do ladies do if they don't dance? My mother lives for it. She's furious at me about the lack of dancing in her life at the moment."

"Why?"

"It's Seb's fault. He sent his mother and mine off to Andalusia to make sure nothing happens to them in Paris if Napoleon gets an itch to invade England. And, of course, nothing *has* happened, so instead the ladies are longing to be back in the ballroom."

Linnet said nothing. She would love to travel, to see places like Andalusia, or Greece, or even further afield. In fact, she would willingly give up dancing forever for the chance to see the Parthenon.

"So what's your name?"

"I told you," she said, frowning. "Miss —"

"Your given name."

"Linnet," she said. "But it's quite inappropriate for you to use it, now that you've informed me that you're not my fiancé."

"But I haven't informed the *Morning Post* yet," he said. "So I suppose we're still technically betrothed. Mine is Piers, by the way. Don't call me Marchant; I loathe the name."

The path curved and ran alongside a tiny house. "What's this?" Linnet inquired.

"The guardhouse. It seems that at some point in the castle's less-than-illustrious past a man was stationed here, the better to manage a smuggling operation," Piers said.

Linnet opened her mouth to ask more, but they rounded the bend and suddenly, there below them, was the sea. It shone like a great sapphire in the sunlight.

"It's so beautiful!" Linnet breathed, dropping his arm. "I had no idea."

"You've never seen the sea?"

She shook her head. "My father prefers London all year round. Is that a pool?"

"Yes. It's carved from the rock. Drains and then fills again with the tide."

"Do you raise fish in it?"

"I swim in it, of course. If I can tolerate my father's presence long enough, you can give it a try." He started down the path. "Not that you'll have the nerve."

She narrowed her eyes, staring at his back.

A moment later he turned around. She had folded her arms and was waiting. "You're a pain in the arse," he said impatiently.

She waited.

He leaned hard on his cane and let out a ragged groan. "My leg. The pain is excruciating."

But he walked back to her. The wind coming off the sea whipped his dark hair out of its queue, and it swirled around his head. Linnet laughed, because there was something about him that made her feel . . .

Weak.

Ridiculous. She curled her fingers across his arm. "Ladies don't swim," she informed him.

"Yes, they do. I've sent quite a few of my patients off to the coast. I generally do with women whose problems stem from their love of pastries. Send them there for female complaints too. As I understand it, they roll out to sea in a carriage, and then their maids tip them into the water."

She digested that. "I would think one's clothes would make one sink."

His eyes were wicked, full of laughter. "Stripped, you fool. The maid takes her mistress's clothes off and she slips, fish-like, into the water."

"Oh."

"I swim naked as well," he said, "but without a bathing machine."

"What about privacy?"

They were making their way down the

111

rocky path that led to the pool. He negoti-
ated it with ease, seeming to know precisely
where to place his cane.

"I can't say I really give a damn, but Prufrock kept sending patients down here, so I
finally decided to keep my pump-handle to
myself. See that sign?" He nodded toward a
piece of wood hammered into the ground,
with a red crossbar. "If I swing the crossbar
vertical, like that" — he pulled it up — "no
one in the household dares to continue."

She nodded.

He pushed it horizontal again. "If you
decide to go swimming, be sure to put up
the crossbar."

Linnet opened her mouth to say *Oh, I
couldn't,* and then shut it again. Why
couldn't she? She wasn't a debutante who
had to watch herself every moment to make
sure she wasn't labeled improper.

She was a ruined woman. If nothing else,
ruined women were presumably allowed to
swim.

The very thought made her grin.

"What's so funny?" Piers asked, irritably.

"The thought of you wiggling around in
the water," she said. Adding, "Lord Marchant," just to annoy him a little more.

"I don't wiggle," he retorted. "I'll show
you, if you like." They had reached the edge

of the pool, so he dropped her arm. "I generally dive in here." He pointed to a flat rock overlooking the basin of water.

Linnet bent down. The water was deliciously cool, running past her fingers as if it were alive.

"You could go in right now," Piers said, watching her. "You look a bit sweaty and hot. Your face is all red. It's probably all that stuffing you have around your waist."

"It's very impolite of you to mention the color of my face," Linnet said, feeling a bit stung. "And I am certainly not going swimming in front of you!"

"Why not? I'm the powder puff, remember? In case you're wondering whether the sight of your undoubtedly delectable body would make me fall in love with you, the answer is no. As a doctor, I see women's bodies all the time, and they never spark any interest."

She straightened up. "I am sorry for that," she said.

"Why? Because I'm not susceptible to your undoubted charms? I can see that would be a bit of a shock."

"Naturally that. But also because men . . ." She trailed off, unsure how to phrase it.

"Because men are lusty creatures, and I'm not? Most women are as well."

113

"I'm not," she said cheerfully.

He cocked an eyebrow. "The prince must have been so disappointed."

"Probably," she said. "Though I was never quite sure why he was flirting with me. We both knew that we had no future together."

"He probably liked to laugh," the earl said. It was the first nice thing he'd said to her.

"I should return to the castle," Linnet said. "I'm going to sprout freckles."

He shrugged. "Pigmentation spots can be quite charming. Though I did once treat a patient who'd bought freckle-water at the chemist. It took quite a bit of skin off her right cheek."

Linnet shuddered and started back up the path.

"Aren't you waiting for me?" he growled behind her. "I was starting to think that you couldn't walk without a prop on one side. At least we had that in common: the basis for a beautiful friendship."

He held out his arm and she took it. "I don't know why I even suggested swimming," he said. "A lady would never put a toe into the ocean here. It's cold."

"I would," Linnet stated. She didn't care how cold it was; she was longing to throw herself into that sapphire sea. "So the household truly obeys you with regard to that sign?"

"They're terrified of me."

"Really?"

"You should be as well."

She gave him a grin. "Maybe you should try harder."

"Maybe you *should* marry me," he said.

She laughed aloud at that one.

EIGHT

Piers walked into the drawing room that evening to find that he was the first to appear, which was precisely what he intended. Sébastien tended to cast a nasty eye at his brandy-drinking, and as Piers didn't care to come to fisticuffs with him, he preferred to drink before his cousin appeared.

Like a drunk, now he thought on it.

He put his glass of brandy on the sideboard. Prufrock opened the door and said, "Miss Thrynne," and closed it behind her.

His fiancée entered, looking, if possible, more radiant than she had that morning.

She was damned beautiful. Really. His father had outdone himself. First he'd produced Prufrock, and now her. Linnet looked like a princess, all curves and sweetness and creamy skin. Definitely more beautiful than the sun and the moon.

And she had a hell of a bosom. Which is nothing more than a functional mammary gland, he reminded himself.

"Fiancée," he said, by way of greeting. "Would you like some brandy?"

"Ladies don't drink brandy," she replied. She was wearing a white evening gown with little pleats on top and transparent floaty bits down below, embroidered with flowers at the edges. Very ingenious, as it gave a man the idea that he could see her legs if he stared hard enough.

"Nice," he said, gesturing toward her gown with his cane. "Though I think you would look better in green."

"My evening gowns are white," she said. "Would you pour me a glass of champagne?"

"No, but Prufrock can. When he comes back. Why white?"

"Unmarried ladies wear white in the evening."

"Ah, virgins!" he said, catching on. "So you're advertising your erotic inexperience on the open market, are you?"

"Precisely," she said, taking hold of the champagne bottle and wrestling with the cork.

"For God's sake," he said. "Let me have that. I didn't know you were desperate." He eased out the cork and poured her a glass. "What's happened to the cushion you were wearing around your waist earlier?"

She was clearly not wearing it. Her body looked like a fine specimen of English womanhood. Slender in all the right bits and plump in all the others.

"I left it off. You were right. It made me hot."

"My father will be horrified. You've barely arrived, and the royal baby lost already. He's completely obsessed by our family history, you know."

"He has to know sometime, so what does it matter? I hadn't realized you were so tenderly concerned about your father's emotions."

"Huh." He took another gulp of brandy.

"Why are you just meeting your father for the first time in years? After all, to have acquired your charming reputation, you must have been living in England for some time."

It was actually rather unnerving being around someone as beautiful as she was. Her eyes were wide-set and blue. The kind of blue he saw in the ocean just before a storm blew in.

"I managed to earn this reputation at Oxford," he said. "I practiced in Edinburgh as well, and news of my winning personality apparently spread. People have nothing better to talk about, obviously. So why aren't your lashes red? I suppose you paint them."

"Of course I do. And I suppose you never met your father because . . ."

He didn't respond, just waited for her to speculate.

"Because you lived in France your whole childhood?"

"After age six. I grew up with my cousin, that blond-headed fool you saw misdiagnosing a fever."

"Is it common for peers to become doctors in France?" she asked. "I must say that it's quite unusual here."

He shrugged. "Sébastien and I shared a childhood passion for cutting things open and seeing how they worked. Neither of us could see any reason to change when we grew up, and besides, the Revolution came along and killed off most of the French aristocrats, if you remember."

He eyed her. "Are you old enough to remember?"

"Of course I am. Were the two of you in any danger?"

"The French medical schools closed in '92, so we came to England and studied at Oxford instead."

"So you missed the worst of the uprisings. That was lucky."

119

She finished her champagne. Piers watched her throat move as she swallowed. The human body was a fascinating thing. "My mother lost her husband in '94, but luckily not her head," he added.

"Why didn't you meet your father when you returned to this country?"

"I didn't want to. I had clear memories of him. He's a weak fool."

"So is my father," she said, rather surprisingly. "But I love him, and he's my father. And your father, by the way, is no fool. I dined with him every night on the way here, and he has twice the brains of my father."

"Why don't you marry *him*, then?" Piers said it mockingly, before he thought. Then his whole body tensed with sudden revulsion. He'd commit patricide before he'd allow that.

She wrinkled her nose. "I'm fairly sure I can find someone to marry who's within twenty years of my age. And given a choice, I'd rather do so."

"But you weren't given a choice when it came to being my wife, were you?"

"Women are rarely given a choice," she said. "We have very little voice in the matter."

"If I asked you to marry me, then you'd have the choice."

She gurgled with laughter. "You don't want to marry me."

"Will you marry me?" he asked.

"No."

"There. Don't you feel empowered? You turned down an earl before supper was even on the table. Surely you can coerce another proposal from one of those poor doctors before bedtime. Bitts has the best background; he's the second son to a viscount, or something like that."

She laughed again. It was alarming how much he liked that laugh. She really was a dangerous woman.

The door opened and Prufrock ushered in the three young doctors currently making a nuisance of themselves trying to learn medicine.

"Penders, Kibbles, and Bitts," Piers said, nodding at each in turn. "Kibbles is the only one with working brains; Bitts is a gentleman, so there weren't any for him to inherit. And Penders is improving, which is good because there was nowhere to go but up. Gentlemen, this is Miss Thrynne, my fiancée."

She gave them the patented smile she'd tried out on him. They melted like butter, and Penders actually swayed a little.

"Show some backbone," Piers said, reaching out and giving him a poke. "You've seen a beautiful woman before, haven't you?"

"Very pleased to meet you," Kibbles said, sweeping into a bow so low that he almost lost his balance.

The door opened once again and Prufrock announced, "The Duke of Windebank. The Marquis LaTour de l'Affitte."

Piers leaned back against the sideboard and waited to see how his ostensible fiancée would handle being the only woman in the room. With one glance, he warned his father to keep his distance, and the man did, wandering over to glance through the windows overlooking the sea.

That left four men to slaver over Linnet. Even Sébastien, whom he'd judged to have more brains than he was exhibiting at the moment.

Linnet gave that throaty little laugh she had, and Sébastien moved closer, his eyes alight in a way that Piers had seen previously only in the operating chamber.

To his utter surprise, he felt a low growl rising in his throat. Jealousy, he diagnosed. Together with a nasty bit of dog-in-the-manger sensibility. *I don't want her myself, but I don't want anyone else to have my shiny new toy either.*

With that thought in mind he pushed

away from the sideboard and hobbled over to see his dear father. It had to be done, after all. He could hardly house the man under his own roof and ignore him entirely.

The duke turned, but then merely stood there, as if he expected Piers to strike him. It was damned annoying.

"I thought we had an agreement," Piers said.

He nodded. "I broke it."

"You're not to come near me. In return I give you tacit leave to place spies in my house —"

His father started to speak, but Piers raised his hand. "Don't think me a fool. Prufrock didn't find his way to the wilds of Wales on his own. I sometimes think I should reduce his wages, given what you are undoubtedly paying him."

Silence.

Piers eyed him, but somehow there wasn't much pleasure in being rude. He'd spent so many years hating the man that it was rather odd to discover — now that they were finally face-to-face — that he was, after all, just a man.

"I take it you're no longer an opium addict," he said. As a doctor, he knew. He'd learned the signs of opium addiction before that, though: at his mother's knee, watching his father.

"It's been twelve years. How is your mother?"

"You probably know that her husband lost his head in the Terror. She was fond of him."

He nodded.

"Of course you do. You likely have spies in her household as well."

"You were right to get her out of France," the duke said, not bothering to deny it. "I don't like the feeling of things over there."

"That was Sébastien," Piers said. "I didn't give it a second thought. He whisked our mothers out of the country a month or so ago and then turned up here himself."

"I'll — I'll stay here until you're married, and then I'll leave you alone again." The duke gave a jerky little bow.

Piers thought about whether to tell him that the marriage was off, and decided not. It was none of his father's business, for all he had produced the bride in question. He glanced over his shoulder to find that Linnet was smiling up at Seb.

"She's exquisite," the duke said, with a trace of pride.

"Even better, she's got a royal babe in tow," Piers said, cutting to the heart of his rhapsody. "Quite a bargain you found for me: wife and heir in one sweet package."

"Prince Augustus would be hard for any woman to resist, let alone one as young and beautiful as Miss Thrynne. But in case you're worried, I asked her, and she's not in love with the prince."

Piers almost grinned at that. No, Linnet was not in love with the prince. She actually reminded him a bit of himself. Chances were good that she would never succumb to such an embarrassing emotion. "What if she's carrying a girl? You're still out an heir."

"Look how many sons the king has," his father said. "The chances are good it will be a boy. And even if she does bear a female, your part of the estate is unentailed, and my solicitor says we could break it on mine as well. The child won't have our title, but she'll have the rest."

"Well," Piers said, knowing he was being abrupt, but unable to stand another second in the company of this old man with longing eyes, "I'd better get back to my fiancée before Sébastien snaps her up and takes her back to France."

His father's brows drew together. "L'Affitte is your cousin. Of course he won't steal your fiancée."

"He is indeed my cousin. But look at the woman you bought for me, *Father*." He gave the label a mocking twist. "There aren't many like her in all of France, nor England either."

"No," his father agreed. "And not just because of her beauty either."

Piers took a leisurely look at Linnet. There was the beauty, sure enough. But it didn't detract from the intelligence in her eyes. And in his opinion the slightly cynical lilt in her voice just made her all the more beautiful, as if Aphrodite had been crossed with Athena.

"Go," his father said, making an abrupt gesture. "You can pretend I'm not in the room. No need to do the pretty with me."

Piers got back across the room and cut in on the conversation between Linnet and his cousin. "*My* fiancée," he growled, giving Sébastien a look.

The Frenchman smiled at Linnet with all that Gallic charm he flaunted so shamelessly. "Are you sure you wouldn't rather marry me? Piers is the very devil to live with. I've had years of him, and I know."

Linnet's eyes danced over Sébastien as if she were seriously considering his proposition, and Piers had the sudden wish to pound his cousin in the face.

What the hell was going on? He'd decided long ago that he was better off alone. He didn't need anyone else to worry about.

"You *should* take him," he made himself say. "He's nicer. I'm richer, though."

Sébastien shrugged. "My lands were confiscated. But I have enough."

"You have enough to dress yourself like a popinjay," Piers said. "Didn't you say that you were going to check on that amputation from this afternoon?"

"I already have."

"So what sorts of things do you cut up?" Linnet asked.

"Legs and arms," Sébastien answered.

"He could be chopping wood, but he took the easier route," Piers said.

"I thought you cut people open from top to bottom," Linnet said. She didn't sound in the least frightened or squeamish, which was unusual in Piers's experience of young ladies.

"There's too much risk of infection," Sébastien told her.

He was opening his mouth, probably planning to regale her with gory details of their dead patients, when Prufrock summoned them to the dining room. At the table, Piers had Linnet at his right hand and Sébastien, thank God, was banished to the other end to talk to the duke.

"Lucky for you the bell rang just then," he told Linnet. "My cousin was about to bore

127

you silly with tales of infection and death."

"It's very kind of you to provide me with a resident marquis to flirt with, insofar as the Continent is likely my next home."

"Do you mean you have to leave the country? Because of that baby that doesn't exist?"

She shrugged. "Marrying you was my aunt's idea of a brilliant recovery from impending catastrophe."

A *gentleman* would probably follow this revelation with a quick proposal of marriage. Piers, however, had no problem maintaining his silence.

"May I offer you some wine?" Prufrock bent over Linnet in such a way that he was probably looking straight down her bodice.

"Go away," Piers growled. "We're having a private conversation. You're going to have to learn to be more butler-like once I marry Linnet, you know. Can't have you barging in on the marital bedchamber, let alone marital confidences."

"As you wish," Prufrock said, gliding away without a backward glance.

"I think you hurt his feelings," Linnet said. "What an odd butler you have."

"Spy for my father," Piers said. "Prufrock can't afford to have hurt feelings, since he's being paid by two households. Listen, I'll take you swimming tomorrow morning."

She opened her mouth, but he spoke first. "If you dive in and drown, people will talk. They'll say I did it just for the pleasure of dissecting you."

Linnet wrinkled her nose.

"And who's to teach you to swim if I don't? Not that I really believe you'll make it in the water. The minute you feel it, you'll be squealing and trotting back up the path."

"It's not proper."

Piers rolled his eyes. "For a young lady who was recently tussling with royalty, you are remarkably prudish. I'm no danger to your chastity. Besides, we can go early in the morning while your chaperone is still snoring. Oh, wait! You don't have a chaperone."

She smiled, not that full-blown dimpled miracle that she used to manipulate the poor sods who fell under her spell, but a small, almost secret, smile. Just a curl of her lips and a smile deep in her eyes.

"Right," he said, pushing back from the table.

"We haven't had our second course yet —"

"Patients dying upstairs, you know." And with that he took himself off.

He was losing his head, sitting there looking at her eyes.

A strategic retreat was called for. After all, he had no intention of marrying. Ever.

NINE

Linnet went to bed thinking about the deep crevice between Piers's brows. Was it there because he was in constant pain, or was it just because he had a wretched temper? Despite her better judgment, there was something about the ferocity in his eyes and the lines of pain around his mouth that made her want to taunt him, to make him laugh, to force him to listen to her.

Which was absurd. He was a man who clearly had made the decision to spend his life alone, and from all indications had never thought twice about it.

Still, she kept thinking about his brow, and fell asleep imagining a Piers whose face had smoothed into laughter, a Piers who wasn't Piers.

She woke to find that particular brow frowning down at her. "You didn't even turn over when I clumped my way into your bed-chamber, cane and all. I've spoken to you

131

twice and you just keep lying there with that odd little smile on your face."

"What hour is it?" she mumbled groggily, pushing her hair off her face.

"Dawn." He sat down on the edge of her bed as if they were the oldest of friends. "My leg hurts like a son of a bitch, so could you please get yourself ready to go swimming? It's the only thing that kicks back the pain."

"Swimming," she said, rolling over on her side, a hand under her cheek. She was still half asleep, and felt as if he had walked straight out of her dream. "You think I'm going swimming with you?"

He dug his fingers into his thigh. "Hurry up. The sun's coming up."

"Does it hurt that much?"

"Massage helps." He sounded as if he were speaking through clenched teeth. "You smell good."

"Honeysuckle," she said, pleased at the compliment. She was starting to wake up. "You know, you really shouldn't be in my bedroom."

"Why not? If we're discovered, the worst that could happen is that we'll have to get married, and we're already supposed to get married. Under the circumstances . . ." He shrugged.

She thought the "circumstances" were probably his lack of manhood. And he was right in that no one could presume her ruined if the man in question was unable to do the ruining. She turned on her back and stretched luxuriously. "Actually, this is sort of fun."

"What? Having a man in your bedchamber? With your reputation, I thought that would be second nature."

"Your reputation led me to think you'd be witty, so we're both surprised." She sat up and swung her feet over the bed so they were sitting side by side.

"Have you had many men in your room?" he said, sounding curious.

"None. Not even the putative father of my alleged child. To be honest, I don't care to find myself alone with a man. Just when you relax enough to feel the least bit friendly, he's sure to leap on you."

"I've never had the experience," he said dryly. "Would you please get yourself dressed? I promise not to leap on you."

"What's the rush?"

"The tide is in. The pool is full and the sun's just up. Trust me, this is the best time to swim."

"I'm not taking all my clothes off."

He shrugged again. "As you like. Though

if you wear full skirts, I'm not diving down to rescue you from the bottom of the pool."

"I'll wear my chemise," Linnet said, suddenly feeling excited. "And you wear — well, you have to wear something too."

"I can wear smalls if you want," he said, sounding completely uninterested in the question.

Linnet darted behind the little screen in the corner of her bedroom, entranced to find out how easy it was to be with Piers. Knowing that he wasn't about to try to kiss her, or throw himself on his knees, or worst of all, lose control and launch into a kind of wrestling match, made it a pleasure to be with him.

"You know," she called over the screen, as she was pulling a morning gown over her head, "I don't want to frighten you, but you're just the sort of man I *would* like to marry."

He grunted.

"I don't feel as if you're salivating all over me," she said, wanting to explain. "I know that you won't start licking your chops and doing a Little Red Riding Hood imitation."

"Wouldn't I be the wolf, not the little girl?"

"You know what I mean." She popped out from behind the screen. "Could you do up the rest of my gown? It's harder to dress without my maid than I would have thought."

She turned her back and he buttoned her up. Again she reveled in an unfamiliar sense of freedom. "No one ever said that being ruined was so much fun," she said happily. "I don't have the slightest fear that you're going to rip off my buttons."

"I have the impression that being ruined is generally a good deal more fun than this. Do you always talk this much?" he growled. "For God's sake, let's go."

They turned the last bend of the path; Piers flipped the red sign to vertical, and there it was.

The sea was a deeper blue today. And the pool looked as placid as a manicured lawn, except that rather than being green, the sea reflected back turquoise blue to the sky. The sun slanted across the water, gilding the tiny waves that sloshed the barrier between the pool and the sea.

"It's so beautiful," Linnet exclaimed.

"Cold as a witch's teat at this hour," Piers said. He was pulling off his coat. Linnet made her eyes slide back to the pool. It wouldn't be right of her to — to ogle him, when he, of course, wouldn't be ogling her.

135

But a moment later she couldn't help looking over again.

He had his shirt off. Shirt. Off. She was in the presence of a nearly naked man. All right, so it wasn't exactly the way that sounded but . . . he *was* beautiful. For the first time in her entire life, on this issue at least, she had to admit that perhaps her mother was right. Those muscles —

He had his back to her, and the way his shoulders moved, and then the way his upper body slimmed down to his waist and —

He was taking off his boots!

Linnet couldn't wrench her eyes away. Stupidly, a high little voice in her mind had started narrating the whole scene. *He's bending down . . . Yes! He is going to pull off his breeches. He's pulling them over his hips. Hmmmmm . . . His — his buttocks are —* the voice seemed to be somewhat strangled. *Different. Different from mine. Muscled, too. It . . .* the voice choked again. *Is he going to turn around?*

"Bollocks, I told you I'd keep my smalls on, didn't I?"

At Piers's growl, Linnet startled as if a gun had gone off. She had to pull herself together. He was incapable, for goodness' sake. And she was ogling him in the most outrageous way . . . as if she were at that brothel her aunt had talked about.

She was a horrible person. Perverted, really.

She kicked off her slippers without untying the bows, wrenching down her stockings. She had to think of it as if she were bathing with — with a sibling. That's all he was. Besides, she was keeping on her chemise and he had put his smalls back on. She stole a glance. They were white and seemed to cover the pertinent area.

"Could you help me with my buttons again?" she called.

He came up behind her and it felt as if her skin went aflame at his touch. If he guessed, she would expire from pure embarrassment.

"So, how does one swim?" she managed. "Do I just jump in and I'll know what to do?"

"I'll show you," he said. "It's going to be cold. You'll have one toe in and then you'll be dashing back up that path."

No, she wouldn't. At this point, anything cold was a good idea. Something had happened to her internal temperature, and she felt as if she were as red as a beet. But she was shivering. "I'll just jump right in, shall I?"

He started to say something, but she

hopped right up onto the flat rock that he had indicated the day before and leaped off. For a second there was a dizzying rush of air. Her chemise flew up and then — oh my God — she'd never felt such cold in her life. It rushed past her as she sank, as if ice were stroking her all over, as if her very bones had frozen.

A moment later a strong arm curved around her waist and the water rushed past her the other way. She broke the surface of the water, stunned, and took a huge gulp of air, hardly believing she was still alive.

"You bloody fool!" Piers was shouting. She was alive. No . . . she was only partly alive, because she'd never been colder in her life. The only thing warm in the whole world was the body next to her.

"I'm fr-freezing," she stammered, winding her arms around his neck and plastering her body against his. It felt good. He was shouting again, but there was water in her ears and she couldn't hear very well. It felt better like this, her arms and legs wrapped around him. And he still had an arm around her as well.

Suddenly she could understand what he was saying. "I don't want to let go of you," she said, shaking the wet hair back from her face because she didn't want to unwrap even one arm from his body. "I'll freeze. Or drown. You're w-warm."

"Swimming, remember?" he said. His teeth were clenched, which seemed to suggest he was as cold as she was. But wasn't he used to it?

"I know we're here to swim," she said. "Tell me how to do it, and I'll — I'll consider it." In fact, she wasn't going to let go of him until they were out of the pool altogether.

But he ruthlessly pried her body away from his. She gasped at the loss of warmth and her teeth instantly started chattering again.

"You need to learn how to float," he snarled. There was something awfully grim about his tone.

She picked up floating instantly. "I'll just die like this, shall I?" she said, her face surrounded by freezing water, her teeth clicking together like castanets.

"I think you'd better get out now," he said, sounding exasperated.

"Wa-warm me up first," she said.

With a muffled curse, he jerked her against him. It was just as wonderful as the first time. With a sigh of relief, she put her head on his shoulder and let the incredible furnace of his body seep into her pores. But

139

a second later, strong arms were around her waist, hoisting her straight in the air and depositing her on the side of the pool. She drew up her toes.

"Towels are over there," he barked.

She looked down at him, so bemused that at first she didn't register what he was saying. Piers was at home in the water, in his element. As she watched, he pivoted and pushed off from the rock wall, surfacing halfway across the pool. First one arm and then the other came out of the water, and then he was shooting away from her, bubbles churning behind him.

There were three towels. Linnet took one and wrapped it around her shivering torso, then she took another and wrapped it around her hair. She returned to the rock and watched Piers slice through the water, length after length. He showed no signs of stopping, so she went back, took the third towel and, once seated at the edge of the pool, wrapped her feet and ankles in it.

After that she sat, entirely swathed in toweling except for her face, and watched the broad planes of Piers's back and shoulders as he tore up and down the pool.

Slowly her body warmed as she sat cocooned and the morning sun poured down on her. Mrs. Hutchins would faint to see her. Faint? She would have an apoplectic fit. Not only was Linnet sitting next to the water, dressed in nothing more than a drenched chemise, but there was a nearly naked man not much farther than an arm's length away.

In this situation, a few freckles didn't seem to matter so much, so she tilted her head back and drank up the sunshine and the clear blue sky. It went so far above her head that she couldn't imagine the top of it. Far, far up a seabird was lazily circling, looking for a fish perhaps.

Piers touched the edge, counted fifty lengths. He didn't stop, just flipped over and swam back the other way. His body was dealing with a feverish kind of energy that didn't require a medical degree to diagnose. Sixty lengths. He was exhausted, but still there was a river of molten lava running under his skin.

Finally he pulled himself out of the water, his eyes going directly to Linnet. Her head was tilted back and her neck was pale cream in the sunshine. The towel had slipped from her hair, which lay in dark red coils all over the white cloth.

As he was trying to gather together the shards of his wits, she straightened up and opened her eyes. "I'm so sorry about nearly drowning you," she said, her eyes giving him that secret smile that he —

Well, that he liked to see.

"I truly didn't mean to," she continued. "You're just so much warmer than I am."

He was when a luscious female body wrapped around him, clinging like seaweed on a rope.

"You look warm enough now," he said, hearing the grating tone in his own voice. Well, it wasn't as if she would guess why he sounded so angry. Thank God for his reputation.

She blinked. "I took all the towels! You must be freezing." She scrambled to her feet, which made all her towels fall to the ground.

It would be sacrilege to refer to those breasts as mammary glands. They were glorious, plump, yielding . . . Her chemise was translucent with water. It clung to her thighs, to a beautiful, dark place between her legs.

"Here, take one of these," she was saying. She threw him a towel and he just managed to catch it and wind it hastily around his waist.

"You know?" She glanced at him, and a little flare of color rose in her cheeks.

142

"What?" he said, rearranging himself discreetly and then rewrapping the towel more tightly.

"You're going to laugh, being a doctor and all, but my mother said something once . . ."

"What?" He had always had control over his body. *Always.* This was an aberration.

"She told me once that men hung."

"Hung?" he repeated. If he looked just at her face, then he wouldn't see the way thin linen clung to her breasts, to her hips. He wouldn't think about the deep hunger flaring in his groins. It was just a biological urge, nothing more.

"Hung," she said, giggling again. "In front. You don't *hang,* do you?" She waved a hand in the general vicinity of his waist. "You don't mind my saying that, do you? I formed this disgusting vision of — of a hanging *thing* and — well, you don't hang at all. You stand straight up."

He burst out laughing.

"I know," she said, laughing too. "I'm a fool."

But he had an uneasy feeling that he was the fool.

TEN

Linnet lingered in a bath for an hour, drinking hot chocolate and finishing Miss Fanny Burney's *Camilla*. But finally there were no more cans of hot water, and she'd finished the book, so she stood up.

"I wonder if this castle has a library," she said to her maid, Eliza. "I only brought five novels, and I read them all in the carriage on the way here."

"Couldn't you just read them again?" Eliza suggested, handing her a towel. "It seems a waste to look at them just the once. Better to buy a ribbon that you can use over and over."

"I might reread that one," Linnet said, nodding toward *Camilla*. "It was quite good. I already read *Miss Butterworth and the Mad Baron* twice. Actually, three times." She sat down at her dressing table.

"It's funny, miss, how you do all that reading," Eliza said, starting to comb through

Linnet's wet hair. "If the gentlemen in London knew you were such a bluestocking!"

"What difference could it possibly make?"

Eliza pursed her lips. "Nobody likes a girl with more wit than hair, but on the other hand, I never heard of a lady who reads the way you do. It would shake them up, all those foolish types who jumped to thinking the prince trifled with you."

"I doubt it," Linnet said. "I expect it's far more interesting to talk about my purported royal baby than my reading habits."

"Well, I do know that there is a library here. Mr. Prufrock mentioned it last night at dinner."

"Have they made you comfortable?" With a fillip of guilt over not accompanying her to Wales himself, her father had sent along not only Eliza, but footmen, grooms, and the boot boy for good measure.

"Oh, yes, miss. We're in the west wing, along with the people who are dying of cankers and such. They told us to never go to the east wing, as that's where they put the ones with infections. That a body could catch, I mean. There's one housekeeper for each wing, and another for the castle. Some patient was groaning just terrible last night so I thought I'd never sleep, but he finally stopped. Mr. Prufrock said that if it happens again, I should complain, and they'll hush him up."

"How on earth can they do that? If the man's in pain, I mean."

"Give him some medicine, I shouldn't wonder," Eliza said. "Why don't you go wait by the fire, miss, until your hair dries?"

Linnet groaned. "Because I haven't anything to read. Could you possibly run down to that library and bring me a book or two, Eliza?"

"I suppose I could ask a footman to help me find it," Eliza said. "There's one who's rather attractive, with the funniest name. He was telling me last night that the doctor threatened to cut off his head and see if he could walk around with it."

Ten minutes later she had returned with a stack of books. "There are oh so many of them," she reported. "I couldn't find anything that looked like the sort of novel you like to read, though."

The books weren't exactly Linnet's general reading fare, but a desperate woman will read anything. "Did you know that eating a melon will cure swelling?" she asked Eliza, some time later.

"Really? Maybe a toe. But I doubt any other kind; my da used to get a terrible swollen nose if he drank too much. Do put that book down now, miss. I have your corset ready."

Rather reluctantly, Linnet put the book to the side. "It also says that onions should be used to freshen the breath."

"Plain foolishness," Eliza stated, lacing her corset and then easing a gown over Linnet's curls, which were now pulled up and fastened all over her head with shining little enameled flowers. When she started buttoning up the back, Linnet caught up the book again.

"My aunt drinks huge quantities of Daffy's Elixir," Linnet said. "She thinks that keeps her slim. This book suggests stewed ox-cheek."

"That's revolting." Eliza paused and then added thoughtfully. "It probably works for that very reason."

"I wonder what Lord Marchant thinks of patent medicines," Linnet said. "Do you know where he might be found?"

"By all accounts he's usually up with the patients. Do stand still, miss. I just need to fix this last button — there. You've an hour before the luncheon bell."

Linnet took a quick look at herself in the glass — front *and* sides.

"No sign of a baby," Eliza said cheerfully.

"I wonder when the duke will notice. By all accounts he's mad on the subject of royalty, just mad. He'll be that disappointed when it turns out you're not the mopsy he wanted for his son."

Linnet sighed. "Does everyone in the household know everything?"

"Not *this* household," Eliza said, shocked. "Though I have to admit that they've started a betting pool below stairs. Mr. Prufrock isn't nearly as stuffy as Mr. Tinkle at home; Mr. Tinkle would never have countenanced such a thing."

"Is the pool over whether I am carrying a child or not?"

"Oh, no! We, that is, all of us from home, know that you had Stubbins drive you about London with nary a stop to pick up that prince. It's on whether Lord Marchant will find himself infatuated with you."

"I sincerely hope you didn't put your life savings into it," Linnet said, heading for the door.

"Every one of us who came along with you, we're betting for you. And the whole household here, well, they're betting for his lordship. He's got them all scared to death. They think he's inhuman."

"For good reason, no doubt," Linnet said. "They work for him after all. You're going to lose your money, Eliza. Lord Marchant and I already agreed that we don't suit."

Eliza grinned. "Why don't you just wander on upstairs and ask him about pickled calf's cheek or whatever it was?" She darted across the room and tugged Linnet's bodice a little lower. "Now you're ready."

Linnet made her way to the infirmary on the third floor, but when she poked her head in the door, there was no sight of Piers, or indeed, of any of the doctors. The patient from yesterday raised his head, though, and said something she couldn't understand, so she walked over to him.

He looked rather like a dog, the kind of shaggy dog who hangs around alleyways looking pathetic and scabrous. "Your skin condition looks quite painful," she said. "We didn't have a chance to meet yesterday, but my name is Miss Thrynne."

"Mither Hammer'ock," the patient managed. His tongue was certainly swollen.

"Is there anything I can do for you?" she asked. "Would you like some water?"

"The doctor said there's nothing to do for him," came a voice from behind her.

She turned about to find a small boy in the next bed. He wasn't much more appealing than Mr. Hammerhock, being all teeth

149

and bones. He too had a kind of dog-in-the-alley scrappiness about him, with brown hair sticking up every which way on his head. He was too pale. She felt a pulse of alarm; surely he wasn't one of the dying patients Eliza mentioned.

"Nothing to do for him doesn't mean he can't drink water," she said. "And what is your name?"

"Gavan," he said, pushing himself up in the bed. "Hammerhock there, see, yesterday they decided he had some sort of a fever. So the nurse comes by once in a while and puts a wet cloth on his face and gives him some medicine."

Hammerhock was nodding.

"Where is the nurse?" Linnet inquired. She was feeling, if the truth be told, rather out of her depth.

"She's taking a break," Gavan said. "It gives her the megrims being cooped up in here with all of us dying folk."

"Dying? Are you dying?"

Gavan smirked. "The doctor says as how we're *all* dying."

Mr. Hammerhock made a strangled noise from his bed, so Linnet turned to him. He pointed to a glass of water, and she helped him take a sip. He lay back and closed his eyes.

Linnet looked down the row of patients, but most of them seemed to be in a stupor, so she sat down on Gavan's bed. "How did you end up here?"

"Me mum brought me," he said, frowning. "And she left me."

"Do you live very far from the castle?"

"Not very far. Well, further than to market."

"And now the doctor is taking care of you," Linnet said. "Soon you'll be able to go home again."

"Can't go home," Gavan said. "I can't go home because I'm sick and here I have this bed, see. So me mum said I should stay here because, well, I have sheets, don't I? And food, all the food I want."

The door behind Linnet's shoulder opened and a flock of men swept in. Before she even turned around she heard Piers's growl. "Well, well, look who's here, trying to burnish her halo."

Linnet was watching Gavan, who was pushing himself even further up in bed, grinning madly.

Then she heard the thumping sound of a cane, and Piers was standing on the other side of the bed. "Slumming with the nearly dead and the newly bred, are you?"

"What's *newly bred*?" And, without paus-

151

ing, "Did you see this lady?" Gavan pointed to Linnet.

Piers's eyebrow went up. "I did see the lady. What do you think of her? I was considering marrying her."

Gavan nodded. "My da says . . ." He hesitated.

"Out with it," Piers said. "She looks like a lady, but she's not."

Linnet glared at him.

"My da says that the best womenfolk have really big peaches," Gavan said. He peered right at Linnet's chest, so naturally, Piers did as well. "You'd better take her," he said to Piers. "That cane means some women won't want you."

Ignoring Linnet's scowl, Piers bent down to take a closer look at the attributes in question. "Are you sure? I always fancied a black-haired girl with a kind of gypsy look about her."

Gavan threw him a disgusted look. "Don't you know anything about womenfolk?"

"Maybe not as much as you do."

"A gal who looks like a gypsy, well, she probably *is* a gypsy. And if you marry her, you'll have to go out and live in the ditches because she won't want to stop in one place, not for long."

"Couldn't I just let her go on her own?"

"Not if you're married," Gavan said. "Then you're chained together, you know. That's what my da says."

"How are you feeling today?" Piers changed the subject. "Been up yet?"

"Nurse let me get up to use the chamber pot. But then I pretended to miss and splash her on the shoe, so she said I was as bad as Old Nick and put me back in bed." He had the clear, happy laughter of children in the park.

"Where is the nurse?" Linnet asked, glancing up at Piers. "Gavan seems to think she's having an attack of the megrims."

"Too much dying around here," Gavan said cheerfully.

"Probably sneaking my brandy," Piers said. "I would if I had to cope with Gavan urinating on my slippers. Gavan, you tell me if Nurse Matilda rolls in here, drunk as a top, won't you?"

Gavan nodded vigorously.

"Do you like the nurse?" Linnet asked him.

"She won't let me get up. She says if I get up, she'll give my bed away."

There was another strangled noise from the next bed. Piers and his little coterie had moved farther down the row, so Linnet leaned toward Mr. Hammerhock. "Yes?"

"For God's sake, woman, move back," came a roar from behind her. "There's a chance he's infectious, you bacon-brained fool."

Linnet ignored him, as Mr. Hammerhock was laboriously managing a few words. "The nurse is a tartar," he said finally, gasping from the effort.

"Are you really going to marry the doctor, then?" Gavan asked. "Because he's not very nice. He's always calling people rude names, and the nurse calls him Old Nick too."

From across the ward, as if on cue, Piers roared at one of his young doctors.

"Me mum would wallop him," Gavan said. "I think if you marry him, you'll have to wallop him now and then."

They both looked down the row at Piers's imposing figure.

"Might not be easy," Gavan added.

"I see what you mean," Linnet agreed. "So would you like to get out of bed?"

"Can't," Gavan stated. "I might lose my spot. There's ever so many sick people who want to be here, you know."

"I won't let them give away your bed," Linnet said, seeing that Mr. Hammerhock was nodding. "You might be a little tired, so perhaps a footman could carry you outside. I know you were probably a very active boy before you came here."

"Couldn't get to the privy yesterday," Gavan said doubtfully, "not without hanging onto the nurse's arm like she was a tree."

"How annoying," Linnet said. "Come on, then." She stood up and rang the bell. By now Piers was all the way down the room, haranguing the doctors, and he paid no attention when a nice footman named Neythen scooped up Gavan and his blanket and headed out the door.

Linnet followed.

"Where would you like to go, miss?" Neythen asked over his shoulder.

"The pool," she said.

"What's a pool?" Gavan asked. His eyes were shining with excitement. "Do you mean a fishpond? 'Cause I've seen one of those. I . . ."

He talked all the way down the stairs and all the way down the path and only stopped when they reached the pool itself — and that was because his mouth fell open.

"It's beautiful, isn't it?" Linnet said, smiling. "Neythen, would you make Gavan comfortable right here on this flat stone?"

"It's so big," Gavan exclaimed, and Linnet realized he was looking straight past the pool at the ocean. "I never knew it was so big. All that water . . . where's it going?"

"It just goes here and there," Linnet said.

They sat, the three of them, and watched the waves for a while.

"How old are you, Gavan?" she asked.

"Six and three quarters," he said. "Do you see the way the sun makes that path over the sea?"

There was a broad golden path stretching to the horizon.

"That's like a road," Gavan said. "Likely the road to heaven that me mum told me about."

Neythen shifted position. "Do you have to return to your post?" Linnet asked him.

"Mr. Prufrock will understand," Neythen said. "He's a decent sort." He reached over and tucked Gavan's blanket more tightly around his shoulders.

"I don't suppose I'll be going to heaven," Gavan said. He didn't sound too worried about it.

"Of course you will," Linnet said. "But not for a good while, I hope."

"I expect they don't let you in the door iffen you don't believe in all the trappings. The clouds and harps, and such."

"You don't have to believe in it," Linnet said stoutly. "When you need it, the door will just open." She looked at Gavan again. Could he be dying from a terrible disease?

156

The very idea was heartbreaking.

Gavan sighed. "Are there any dogs around here?"

Linnet turned to Neythen.

"There's a dog down in the stables. But he's a scruffy old thing who doesn't belong to anyone."

"He could belong to me, then," Gavan suggested. "My brother has a dog, but I don't have one of my very own." Clearly he was no longer interested in further philosophical discussion of the afterlife. "Let's go!" he said.

"Your nurse might be wondering where you are," Linnet said.

But Gavan was of the opinion that the nurse wouldn't even notice that he was missing. And if she did, she'd apparently be ecstatic. "She says I'm a thorn in her side," he confided. "Please, can we just take a peek at the dog?"

So they were in the stable, trying to lure a small grayish mongrel whose only distinguishing features were bright black eyes and a general aura of dirt, when Linnet heard the clumping sound of Piers's cane.

"There you are," he said, not nicely. "For God's sake, the nurse thinks the boy's been stolen."

"She's not giving away my bed, is she?"

157

Gavan cried. He tried to stand up and started to pitch to the side, though Neythen caught him in the nick of time.

"She can't give away your bed, it's got your fleas in it," Piers said.

"I haven't got fleas," Gavan said. "Do you think —"

"Of course I don't think," Piers snapped. "What are you doing with that filthy mongrel?"

"He's going to be mine," Gavan said. "I'm going to tame him and he's going to sleep on my bed."

They had the dog cornered in a manger, but even so, it showed no interest in coming closer, no matter how many times Gavan called "here boy, here boy."

"I expect his name isn't *Boy*," Piers pointed out.

He was scarcely looking at Linnet. And it was the most annoying thing, that way her heart had sped up when he entered the stables. Pretty soon she'd be listening for the sound of his cane like a lovelorn fool.

"What is his name?" Gavan asked eagerly. "Was he yours, once?"

"Of course he wasn't mine. If you want him to come, you'd better offer him some beef." He jerked his head at Neythen. "Prufrock's looking for you. Go tell him where

158

you are, and then come back and carry this varmint upstairs."

"Well, if he's not yours, then he can be mine," Gavan said. "Maybe I'll name him Rufus."

"I suggest Peaches," Piers said, giving Linnet a sly glance. "A name that'll remind you of your father's advice."

"That's not a good name," Gavan said, shaking his head. "That's a girl's name. He's more like a Rufus. Come on, Rufus."

Linnet straightened up, since it seemed that Gavan was occupied trying to coax Rufus to play with a stick.

"And what in the merry hell do you think you're doing?" Piers asked her. "You missed luncheon."

He towered over her in a most annoying fashion. "I merely brought Gavan outside," she said. "Unless I want to sit around your library and read medical tracts, I've got nothing else to do."

"You should do whatever it is ladies do all day long. But stay away from my patients."

"Why?"

"Why? Because I told you to!"

She snorted. "You're afraid of your nurse."

"I am not afraid of Nurse Matilda. She's a fine disciplinarian."

"Then why did you bother stamping all

159

the way out to the stables to find us?"

"Maybe I'm falling in love with you, just the way most of my household thinks."

"They don't think that," she pointed out. "*My* household thinks that."

"My man told me all about the bet. Your household is going to lose a lot of money," he said with some satisfaction. "I hope you pay them well, so they can afford it."

Linnet grimaced at him and then glanced back down. Gavan had crawled forward and Rufus was cautiously sniffing his fingers. "You can't leave that child to die with a tartar of a nurse and no one but sick people around him."

Piers gave a bark of laughter, so she glared at him. "I'm an uncaring bastard, am I?" he inquired.

"Yes."

He leaned more heavily on his cane. "Are we going to stand around and have a meaningful discussion of patient care, or may I go back inside?"

"Why don't you sit on that nice bench over there?" Linnet said.

"Why don't I just go back inside —"

"Because I want to talk about the way you have patients lying in those beds just waiting for the end to come."

"Why the hell would I want to talk to you

160

about it? Your beauty hardly qualifies you as a medical professional."

"One needn't be a medical professional to know that it's not right to leave a dying boy, a child, in there with all those sick people. He's in bed all day. The nurse won't even let him out for a moment."

"I told her not to," Piers said agreeably. "She generally obeys me because I pay her wage."

"That's ridiculous," Linnet said. "You should have seen how happy he was to see the ocean. And now, with —" She glanced down. Rufus had sidled up and seemed to be peeing on Gavan's bare feet.

"Nurse Matilda is not going to like that," Piers said, with a distinct tone of glee. "She's going to blame you."

Linnet shrugged. "Neythen can dip Gavan's feet in the horse trough just outside the door before returning him to the infirmary."

"So just what do you think I ought to do differently with the west wing?"

"Make it more cheerful."

"This is all about dying, isn't it?" Piers leaned a little closer to her. "You're afraid of it yourself."

"This is not about dying," Linnet snapped.

"Good," Piers said. "Well, this has been a

fascinating conversation, but my leg can't take the excitement any longer." He turned to go.

Linnet narrowed her eyes. She could feel her temper rising. "Are you just walking away from me?"

Piers looked over his shoulder. "Am I? Am I what? Walking — *away?*" He snorted. "Yes, I am."

She darted around him and stood in front of the door. "Why won't you listen to me?"

"Because you're asinine."

"You should have seen Gavan's face when he talked about heaven," she said fiercely. "He said the sun on the ocean looked just —"

"He may have looked like a dying cow," Piers said, interrupting. "But I don't see how it's relevant."

"Because he's dying, you fool," Linnet snapped.

"We're all dying."

"Not the way Gavan will. Or, at least not as soon, or as young."

"Who knows when Gavan will die?" He shrugged. "I have to tell you that the chances are pretty good you'll die before him. Even given women's longevity, he's only six, and you have to be twenty-five."

"I'm twenty-three," Linnet said, frowning.

162

"Given what I saw of his mother, I would guess that he'll live to a ripe old age. She's a tough woman, and she was smart enough to bring him here when he fell off the hayrick and sustained a compound fracture."

"Compound —"

"Fracture. A break," Piers said helpfully. "Now would you mind very much if I limp my way back to the house and report that the patient has been discovered, albeit covered with pee and no doubt flea ridden? Nurse Matilda is not going to like that."

"I thought he was dying. He said you made him stay in bed."

"More the fool you," Piers said unkindly. "I did make him stay in bed. We tried a rather innovative method of mending his bone by immobilizing it with a plaster cast, and it worked like a charm, if I say so myself. Now do I need to tell you again that my leg is hurting like a son of a bitch?"

"Is there any need to be so —"

"Rude? You came into my infirmary. You took a boy out of bed who's only been out of a cast for three days. You had him carried down to the water and then to the stables, and now he's crawling on the ground. That boy can't even stand alone. He couldn't walk if you —"

"Look!" Gavan shouted from behind them. "Look at me!"

They turned around.

He had Rufus in his arms and he was standing up. The dog was licking his chin. "He likes me!"

ELEVEN

Linnet dressed for supper in a rather somber mood. So the west wing wasn't entirely full of dying people. She felt like a fool — and she felt belligerent at the same time. Piers was taking care of his patients' bodies, obviously. But he didn't care about how tedious it was to lie in those beds, day after day.

Still, it was hardly her business. They were ill suited, and the idea that he might fall in love with her ever, let alone in two weeks, was laughable. Marriage was out of the question.

So she had written a note to the duke, requesting that they leave the next day. She had to decide what to do with her life, and that meant going back to her father's house, first of all. Then . . . perhaps a trip. Perhaps the Continent.

It sounded rather lonely — but then she'd been lonely ever since her mother died.

Annoyed with herself for whining like a

self-absorbed child, she picked up her book but was incapable of losing herself in descriptions of cures for toothache. She had a feeling that the duke would be unwilling to leave immediately.

She had no idea why Piers and his father hadn't spoken for years, but the look on the duke's face was unmistakable. He was deeply happy to be in his son's presence, even if that son behaved like a complete ass most of the time.

She was sitting at her dressing table reading aloud bits of the medical tract to Eliza, who was nimbly pulling her hair into an elaborate arrangement on top of her head, when a flare of noise rose from the courtyard.

"What on earth is that?" Linnet said.

Eliza put down a jeweled comb and darted over to the window. "It's a carriage," she said. "Just like a pumpkin, all yellow and shiny."

Linnet came over in time to see a dainty ankle wearing an exquisite high-heeled slipper emerge from the carriage. It belonged to a lady wearing a plum-colored traveling costume topped by a jaunty little hat from which curled not one, not two, but three soft plumes.

"Lovely," Eliza sighed. "That hat has to

have come from *La Belle Assemblée.* There's just something about it. You can tell."

Linnet went back and sat down again. "Perhaps a rival for Lord Marchant's hand has arrived."

"More likely, she's sick," Eliza said, picking up her comb again. "The servants say that people come from all over Britain to see him. All over England, and maybe even abroad too. Maybe all the way from Scotland."

Linnet didn't want to think about whether Piers was a good physician, not given the way he laughed at her. His eyes were evil, just evil. He knew perfectly well that she had believed Gavan was dying, and he had let her go on making a fool of herself.

"I hope it's another candidate to be the future duchess," she said. "I shall enjoy watching her consider the prospect of living with that man for an entire lifetime."

"There," Eliza said, tucking the comb into Linnet's curls. "You're all set."

Linnet stood up and drifted toward the door, but she didn't feel like going downstairs. Not after Piers had laughed at her, and made her feel such a big booby. "Perhaps —"

"No," Eliza said firmly. "He may well be the devil's cub, the way they say he is. You'll not be hiding in your bedchamber. Go out there and make him fall in love with you."

Linnet groaned.

"We're all counting on you," Eliza said, pushing her out the door.

Linnet walked slowly down the stairs, morosely counting each step. She thought she'd been humiliated when a whole ballroom turned its back on her. Who would have thought that the humiliation would be even keener when an ass of a doctor laughed in her face?

There was a swell of excited voices coming from the drawing room, and Prufrock was standing just outside the open door, not even pretending to look like a butler.

"Do tell," she said, reaching the bottom of the stairs.

"The duchess has arrived to visit her son," Prufrock said. "That is, the *former* duchess has arrived."

"You mean Lord Marchant's mother? Doesn't she live abroad?" Linnet felt a prickle of interest.

"Apparently she's been in Andalusia for a few months, but got tired of that and decided to travel to Wales and surprise her son."

"Only to find the duke in residence," Linnet said. "Fascinating!"

"The duke has not yet arrived downstairs. So that joy is presumably yet in store for her," Prufrock said. He pushed the door open wide, stepped inside and announced, "Miss Thrynne."

Everyone in the room paused in their conversation and turned toward the door. In a blatant imitation of Zenobia, Linnet posed briefly under the doorframe before entering the room.

There was a small surge toward her: the Marquis Latour de l'Affitte, the three doctors . . . not Piers.

She held her hand out to Piers's cousin Sébastien, who bowed over her fingers like the French nobleman he was. But her eyes slid sideways. There he was. Piers was leaning against the pianoforte, his eyes hooded, as if he was ignoring everything happening in the room.

Of course he looked up. He was about as sleepy as a stalking lion waiting for a gazelle to stumble by. There was mockery in those eyes . . . and something else.

That "something else" stiffened Linnet's backbone. She turned back to the marquis and gave him a melting smile. "Do tell me about your day. Did Lord Marchant tell you that I enraged him by taking one of his patients into the open air?"

Sébastien was truly adorable in a French sort of way. His eyes crinkled with ready laughter. "I enrage Piers so regularly that I can hardly distinguish the state. But come, since he is too ill-mannered to do the task himself, I must introduce you to his *Maman,* my aunt. She arrived a mere hour ago."

A moment later Linnet was curtsying before the petite, utterly elegant lady.

"Lady Bernaise," Sébastien said. "May I present Miss Thrynne? She journeyed to Wales to meet your son, as you've heard."

Piers's mother showed no signs of fatigue from her journey; in fact she was beautiful, with glowing skin and shining hair that belied her age.

"Enchantée," she said with a lazy little smile that reminded Linnet of her son. It said everything — and nothing at the same time. "I understand from darling Sébastien that you are my son's destined wife."

"Not *destined,*" Linnet said. "Possible."

"I have not been in England in so many years," Lady Bernaise said, waving her hand. "You must forgive my errors. Do you wish to marry my son?"

"If you don't, I'd be happy to extend my hand," Sébastien said. He was laughing, of course, but there was a thread of seriousness in his voice.

Linnet gave him a smile from under her lashes. He was everything that Piers wasn't: kind, well-spoken, considerate. And he dressed beautifully. "I'm afraid that your son and I don't suit," she said to Lady Bernaise.

The lady snapped open her fan and regarded Linnet over the top of it. "And how did you reach this conclusion?"

"She was with him for more than five minutes," Sébastien put in.

"Lord Marchant told me so himself," Linnet said. "And I agree with him. I'm afraid that I infuriate the poor man, which would not be a good basis for marriage."

"Since when am I a *poor* man?" said Piers, from behind her shoulder.

"No man can expect to be considered other than poor when he dresses as you do, *mon chèr*," his mother said. "Where did you find that coat, on a dust heap?"

"No, a dust bin," he said. "So, *Maman*, did I remember to mention that my dear, despised father is also in residence?"

Lady Bernaise's eyes narrowed for a fraction of a second. "You must have forgotten it in your excitement at seeing me after all these months."

"Likely that was it," he agreed. "That and my poor memory. Dear me, he should be

171

down any moment."

Lady Bernaise cleared her throat.

"No, he's not taking opium any longer," Piers said helpfully.

Sébastien gave Linnet a rueful smile. "We are treating you like a member of the family already, Miss Thrynne."

Linnet was trying to figure out what precisely was being said. Could the duke have taken opium for some sort of ailment? He seemed quite healthy for a man of his age, in his early fifties, she would think.

"He's an addict," Piers said, apparently guessing her thoughts as quickly as he'd guessed his mother's. "Opium is a painkiller, and therefore addictive, which means he couldn't stop taking it. No doubt he started taking it for a bruised toe or some such. He used to reel around the house giving *Maman* and me no end of entertainment."

Lady Bernaise closed her fan and gave her son a sharp knock on his hand. "You may not be disrespectful of your father in my presence."

"Then when *Maman* finally ran away to France — taking me with her, thank God — he divorced her," Piers added. "Told the whole world that she was unfaithful to him and had run off with a gardener. Which was not the truth, by the way. Our gardener was

172

at least eighty and couldn't have survived the excitement."

"You are washing our *lingerie* in public," Lady Bernaise said, giving him a fierce scowl.

"Linnet is not The Public," Piers said. "She's my fiancée, at least until one of us gets around to sending a cancellation notice to the *Morning Post*."

"My father will address that task the moment I return to London," Linnet said to him. "We'll leave tomorrow."

"Must you leave? You are *ravissante*," Lady Bernaise said to Linnet. "Extremely so. You would do well in France. Though I think you will look even better when you are able to wear colors other than white. Perhaps you should marry Piers for that reason."

"As your husband, I would be happy to go with you to the *modistes*," Sébastien put in. "Whereas Piers would rather expire than accompany you on such an errand."

"Yes, but you are a year younger than my Piers," Lady Bernaise said. "Piers should marry first."

Linnet opened her mouth to make some sort of response, when Lady Bernaise snapped open her fan again and hid behind it.

Everyone in the room turned toward the door, even the gossiping young doctors and the footman standing by the sideboard.

The duke was rather pale, and looked older than he had a few hours ago. But he walked directly across the room toward them, not bothering to acknowledge anyone else.

He was wearing velvet breeches and a remarkably elegant velvet coat, which enhanced the Roman-coin effect of his profile, Linnet had to admit. He didn't look like an opium addict to her. But then, what did she know of such things?

"Handsome, isn't he?" Piers drawled into her ear.

"Yes, he is," she said.

"I won't tell dear *Maman* you said that. Or that he could choose to marry you, if I throw you over. She might still have a grain of affection for the old bastard."

The duke was bowing over his erstwhile wife's hand, kissing it. She had lowered her fan, but her face was absolutely expressionless.

"God, could he look a little less longing?" Piers murmured. "He's a positive disgrace to the male sex. I think you're going to have to reconcile yourself to marrying me. Or someone else, but definitely not him."

"Perhaps he feels he made a mistake," Linnet said back, just as quietly. "Do you suppose your mother might forgive him?"

"For the opium? It's possible. For the fact that he trumpeted her throughout London, not to mention the legal courts, as a cross between a Cyprian and a trollop? Not likely."

Lady Bernaise's back was as straight as a poker, and her glance was anything but flirtatious. "So, Windebank," she said, "Do tell me how you have been in the years since I left England." Her voice had the clear, cold quality of hailstones striking marble.

"Ouch," Piers said.

"Indeed," Linnet agreed. "We shouldn't watch."

"Why not? It's rather satisfying to see that look of anguish on his face. The old fool threw her away in a opium-induced rage, but I gather he regretted it later."

Linnet turned her back and looked up at Piers. "How does an opium addict behave?"

His eyes darkened. "One moment the addict is having a wonderful time, dancing around the house in his smalls and generally acting as if he had sunstroke. The next moment he vomits. It's a very untidy and unattractive condition."

"When you were young, before your

175

mother took you to France, did you have any idea what was wrong with him?"

"Too young to understand it. But I had already learned to look for intoxication. Children of addicts learn quickly to fear slurred speech, signs of confusion, blood-shot eyes."

"You noticed his eyes?"

"Maybe not at the time. But now I would. The pupils contract with chronic opium use."

"It must have been terribly confusing for a child," she said, putting a hand on his arm. "I'm sorry."

Piers looked down at her, his eyes impossible to read. "I'm grateful for it."

"Why? Because your mother took you to France?" His arm was warm under her fingers, and stupidly, she thought about the muscles she'd seen that morning.

"It made me a doctor," he said flatly. "Without his addiction, I'd be sitting around in a London club playing chess and contemplating blowing my brains out from pure boredom."

Lady Bernaise was apparently tired of conversing with her former husband. She appeared at Linnet's side. "Precious ones," she said, "I am feeling the headache."

"The matrimonial headache?" Piers said.

176

"I thought one had to be married to be troubled by such a thing."

"Always, you make the joke," she said, waving her fan at him. "Life is not the joke, always the joke. Your father could give me a headache even when I am a whole continent away from him, I assure you."

"I apologize," the duke said, from behind her. "Please don't retire to your room. I will leave instead."

"No, you stay here with our son," she said, not looking at him. "You have lost too many years with him. Deservedly so, but I suspect that you are now aware of the loss you incurred."

"Yes." The duke wasn't looking at Piers, though. His eyes were fastened on his former wife, on her tiny figure, her perfect curves, the gleam of her hair, the elegance with which she held out her hand, first to Linnet, and then to Piers.

"I think His Grace did well when he chose you for Piers," she said. "Yes, I think he did do something right." Her tone made it perfectly clear that the duke had shocked her by that moment of success.

And then she tripped away.

"Pull yourself together," Piers said to his father. "You look like a dog lusting after a big juicy bone. Hell, you should have found a second wife by now. She married someone else; why didn't you? Then we would have a new duchess standing around trying to condescend to *Maman.* Now *that* would be interesting."

The duke swallowed. "There can never be anyone else for me," he said. "I wounded her so much, because I loved her even more. Though I couldn't understand it at the time, of course. Now, I live with that decision, with the man I was."

"You sound like the lead in a bad melodrama," Piers said flatly.

"Hush," Linnet said to him.

"Miss Thrynne, I received your note asking to leave tomorrow morning," the duke said. There was a desperate look about him.

"Perhaps if we stayed a few days . . . you and Lady Bernaise might be able to converse," Linnet said. "There's no particular hurry."

"I knew it," Piers said, dramatically recoiling. "All along you were just pretending not to want to marry me."

Linnet glanced at him and broke into laughter. "Yes, today made me realize what a paragon you are. Any woman's dream."

"That would be very kind of you," the duke said. "Though I wouldn't want her to become even angrier at me."

178

"Oh, this is marvelous," Piers said. "The unwanted fiancée and the even more unwanted blood relation decide to —"

Linnet gave him a sharp elbow in the stomach, and he bit off his words.

"We'll stay as long as you wish," Linnet told the duke. "After all, I should probably give more thought to my matrimonial prospects. Perhaps there is more to your son than meets the eye." She gave him a sardonic look. "I shouldn't be so hasty to reject him. Perhaps he only *looks* like a childish fool. Or perhaps he only *acts* like one, but there's an adult inside, ready to come out someday."

"I will be a duke whether I leap past my infantile state or not," Piers pointed out. "Unless you marry my father here, you'll likely never get another offer of that magnitude."

"Oh, were you making an offer?" she said sweetly.

"No, my father made it for me," he said. "So, what do you think, Your Grace? Are you going to stay and try to inch back into *Maman*'s good graces? It's impossible, in case you're wondering."

Linnet pinched him. "Of course it's not impossible. Especially since he can depend on good advice from his own son and heir."

179

"I can help if he has hemorrhoids," Piers said. "But I hear marriage is actually the greater of those two evils."

The duke looked at him, shaking his head. "You will never marry, will you?"

Linnet took pity on him. "He'll probably have to make up his own mind to do it," she said. "He will have to find his own wife."

"It's so easy to do around here," Piers put in. "You can't imagine how many young ladies trip their way up the path, complaining of odd swellings, blindness, vomiting . . . all sorts of charming conditions."

"Well, that's the pool you'll have to choose from," Linnet said, shrugging.

"Maybe I *should* keep you," Piers said.

"Don't you get tired of acting like a little boy?" she demanded. "Don't listen to him," she said, turning to the duke. "One of these days a woman will show up with child and he'll marry her because it's the prudent thing to do."

"Not prudent unless I know for sure that she's carrying a boy," Piers said, "and as far as I know, there's no way to ascertain that."

"You could always just substitute one of her other children," Linnet suggested.

Piers howled with laughter.

The duke smiled stiffly. "Primogeniture may be a matter for laughter — for both of you, it seems — but my family has carried this title for hundreds of years."

"Until you trampled your name in the mud by becoming an opium fiend," Piers said, turning away. "It must be time for supper. Prufrock, what the hell are you waiting for? Ring that bell before we start gnawing each other's legs."

Linnet tucked her arm into the duke's. "A difficult day," she said.

He patted her hand. "I chose well with you. But I see what you mean." Piers was striding ahead, already out of the room, paying no attention to the social conventions that demanded he wait — if not for her, then certainly for his father to enter the dining room first.

"You may have noticed that I'm not carrying a child," Linnet ventured. She was feeling more than a tinge of guilt at the falsehoods that had brought her to Wales.

The duke looked profoundly embarrassed and waggled his hand, as if to say that it was unremarkable.

"I do think that your son will marry someday," Linnet said. Though she was fibbing. She couldn't quite imagine the woman who would not only tolerate Piers but also stand up to him.

"Perhaps, perhaps. I had hoped . . . but I

see now that you're very similar."

"Now that, Your Grace, is something of an insult, if you're excuse my bluntness," Linnet said, smiling at him.

"It was certainly not meant as such. What will you do next, my dear?"

"I shall return to London," Linnet said. "I might go abroad. Or I might to go straight to Lady Jersey's house and show her that I am not carrying any child. And then I will force the prince to acknowledge that there was no possibility of that event's occurring. And then I shall marry someone."

"Very good," the duke said. "You can count on my support. I fancy my opinion will prove a significant influence on Lady Jersey."

She smiled at him. "Thank you."

TWELVE

Linnet was dreaming that her mother was sitting on the end of the bed, laughing and throwing cherries. She didn't have very good aim, and one bounced off Linnet's shoulder onto the floor; another fell into the sheets. "Mama!" she protested. "They'll make a mess. They'll stain the bed linens."

Her mother just laughed. "It's all in fun, darling. You have to —"

But whatever her mother would have said was lost when Linnet was roughly shaken awake. She blinked through a curtain of tousled hair to see that it wasn't her mother at the end of the bed. It was Piers, sitting there as easily as if he were the brother she never had.

And yet . . . she took one look at his lean face, shadowed now with beard, and her whole body told her that it wasn't a sibling in the room. He was coatless, and his shoulders strained the sleeves of his white linen shirt. Warmth crept up her cheeks.

"Hello," she said.

This was absurd! He was incapable, and would mock her intolerably if he had even the faintest idea that she liked the look of him so much. That was all it was: a perfectly normal admiration of physical beauty.

"Are you planning to get up one of these hours?" Piers said, his voice as peremptory as ever. "I brought you a cup of hot chocolate. It made me feel just like a lady's maid, though one of those eunuchs who ran around serving emperors would be more accurate."

He didn't look like a eunuch, not that she'd ever seen one. Linnet reached out and took the cup of hot chocolate, curling her hands around it. It was rich and dark to her tongue, almost peppery.

She could see why people liked marriage, at least those who did like marriage. It was fun to have someone else there in the morning to chat with over hot chocolate. What's more, she liked looking at him, and since he wasn't paying any attention to her, she did just that, watching the play of his muscles from under her lashes.

The male body was so different from hers, so enticing in its own way. Silently, she sent up an apology to her mother. *You were right.*

Piers stretched out his arm, and his shirt strained over the muscles of his shoulder.

For the first time, the very first time, she understood what made her mother's eyes so bright when she set off on one of her assignations.

Then, all of a sudden, she realized precisely what she was looking at. Piers had his cane in his hand and he was leaning forward. She glanced along the line of the cane and sat up with a shriek, nearly spilling her chocolate.

"Stop that, this minute!"

He poked again. "It's so hard to wake you up that I thought a little artillery would help."

He had her jewelry box poised on the very edge of her dressing table. Another good poke and it would fall off.

Linnet put her chocolate on her bedside table. "Give me that!" she exclaimed, grabbing the cane and lying back down. "You may not exert your childish sense of humor on my jewelry box. I inherited it from my mother. It's inlaid mother-of-pearl, made in Venice."

Piers leaned toward her, putting a hand on either side of her hips. "That's the second time you've called me childish. Men have been called out for worse."

185

"Not by you," she said, eyeing him. "You're a cripple."

There was a split-second pause. "Now that's just cruel," he said softly, leaning forward.

"It's no worse than the way you talk to people," she said, aware that her tone was distinctly gleeful.

He shifted position, and suddenly his hands were on either side of her waist, so close that she could feel his warmth. She clutched the cane, unable to choke back her smile. Teasing him was intoxicating . . . and dangerous.

Piers confirmed exactly what she was thinking. "Didn't anyone ever tell you that I'm nicknamed the Beast?"

She wrinkled her nose. "As is every two-year-old boy, by his nanny. What are you going to do, call me names? It won't have an effect; all of London already refers to me by the worst names a lady can be called."

"Well, there's something you and my mother have in common," he said. "It should make me feel right at home to cuddle up to a trollop."

A bit awkwardly, she managed to turn the cane around and poke him in the chest. "Would you please move back? This is vastly improper."

He didn't move. His eyes glittered with a kind of emotion that went beyond impropriety. Suddenly Linnet realized that she'd made a mistake about him. She had assumed that an incapable man was — well — incapable of feeling desire.

Piers clearly had no problem with desire.

He knew what she was thinking too. His eyes moved slowly down her face, pausing at her lips, slowly down her neck, pausing . . .

And remained frozen.

She glanced down to find that the fine lawn of her nightgown was caught beneath her, pulling it tightly over her body. Her breasts were barely veiled, rosy nipples clearly visible. She tossed the cane to the side and folded her arms over her chest.

"You shouldn't be ogling me like that," she stated.

"You're my fiancée." His voice was husky and dark, without any of the usual mocking undertones that generally accompanied his every word.

"Not anymore," she said, licking her bottom lip.

"You know," he said, "I think we should explore this whole question of betrothal a bit more thoroughly. We might be tossing out the baby with the bathwater."

He shifted closer once again. His hands were on her pillow now, his face just above hers.

"I've been kissed by a prince," she told him. Her voice didn't come out honey smooth like his; it squeaked.

"Competition," he said, his eyes glittering even more brightly. "I'm fiercely competitive, did you know that?" He dipped his head and licked her bottom lip in one slick, sweet movement.

Linnet blinked at the wave of sensation that rushed through her body. "Prince Augustus wins," she managed.

"But I haven't even got started yet," Piers said. "And do you know? I think we should leave it there for the moment. I should probably brush up on my technique. Read some books. Contemplate my strategy."

Linnet's breath was coming quickly and her eyes were half closed, waiting for his lips to descend to hers, for him to —

"What?" she squeaked. What was it about him that made her lose all her easy charm?

"You taste like chocolate," he growled, his lips still hovering just over hers. Linnet could feel her eyes drifting closed. Yes . . . please . . . her stomach clenched as she caught his breath, chocolate and mint.

"If you were a bonbon, I would nibble

you." He bent his head and — nipped her? Bit her lower lip. Against all rational thought, it sent a jolt of heat down Linnet's body.

Her eyes flew open. "I should think you do need to read a book or two," she said. "Am I the first woman you've ever kissed? If you can call that kissing?"

Piers straightened up and tapped his chin with his finger. "Let me see . . . I seem to remember . . . No! You're not the first woman. Do you find that disappointing?"

"It doesn't matter to me either way."

He stood up. "What in the devil did you do with my cane? Oh, there it is. Now could you please get yourself out of that bed and put on some clothes so that we can go swimming?"

But it was all different now. Piers may have looked precisely the same, as indifferent and sardonic as ever, but Linnet didn't feel the same. She simply could not climb out of her bed and walk across the room in her nightclothes, not after that kiss. Or half kiss.

He looked over and saw what she was thinking. "Number one, I didn't even kiss you. Number two, I couldn't follow up a kiss — *if* I had gone that far — with a deflowering, if you remember. Number three . . . well, there's no number three, but really I think that number two says it all, don't you?"

Linnet cleared her throat. "I'll get up if you sit over there." She nodded toward the chair. "Facing the wall."

"And just how am I supposed to swim? If I face the other way in the pool, you'll drown," he said flatly. "If that's how you feel, I'm leaving. I have to swim every morning or my leg punishes me."

"No!" she said. "I want to go back in the pool and learn how to swim." She'd even taken out a dress, chemise and stockings the night before, in case he came.

"I thought you did. So get yourself bloody well dressed and let's go down there before all the morning light is gone. I have to see my patients soon. They have a pesky habit of dying overnight."

His eyes weren't glittering anymore. In fact, he looked as uninterested as always, so Linnet scrambled out of bed and dashed behind the screen in the corner. "I'm reading one of the books from your library," she told him. "A medical book."

"Oh? Which one?" He sounded completely incurious.

"*Dr. Fothergill's Medical Observations and Inquiries.* It's very interesting."

190

"It's unmitigated rubbish. Don't trust anything it says. In fact, don't trust anything you read in any of those books you find in the library. Most of them were written by jabbering idiots."

She popped her head out from behind the screen. "Do you mean that daffodil juice *won't* cause a man to lose his potency? So disappointing!"

"I can see you're planning ahead," he said, raking a lock of hair from his eyes. "For the next man in your life, the lucky sod."

"Well, would it work?" she asked, ducking back behind the screen.

"Highly unlikely. Do you want the stocking that just fell on the floor?"

"Yes, please," she said.

A silk stocking flew over the screen and settled on her shoulder.

"Why are you bothering with stockings?" he asked. "You're just going to take them off in five minutes anyway."

She was already tying her garter. "I couldn't go outside without stockings on!"

"In a minute you'll be outside with nothing more than a scrap of fabric around your body."

"I can't be seen without my stockings." But she had decided that she could be seen without her corset. It was just too bothersome to lace. "Can you help me again with the buttoning?"

She emerged from behind the screen to find Piers staring out the window. "The sun's up already. I really should go upstairs."

"No. Swimming," she stated. "Button my dress, and let's go."

This time, the rush of freezing water past her body, past her face, was less unexpected, but no less brutal.

Piers hauled her back up and she clung to him, crying, "Oh God, oh God," under her breath. His strong, warm arm wrapped around her body.

"Got your breath back?" he shouted in her ear.

She shook her head. She didn't want to let go, but he ruthlessly pushed her back. "Float."

She floated.

"Good. Now do the same on your stomach." She stared at him, unbelieving, so he reached out and flipped her over.

She instantly sank, but he pulled her back up. "On your stomach," he said in her ear. "I want you to close your eyes and float on your stomach. It's just as easy as floating on your back."

"Warm, warm me up-up first," she said,

192

her teeth chattering madly.

He pulled her over so her back was against his stomach, and wrapped one arm around her again. The arm was just below her breasts, and even in the middle of freezing water Linnet felt . . . something. A rush of hot blood that went down her body and all the way to her toes, that made her skin prickle, made it aware of the muscled body at her back — and the hard part of him that her mother —

But even thinking of her mother in the context of Piers didn't seem right, so she pushed that thought away.

"All right," she said, taking a deep breath. He dropped his arm, she pitched forward and floated, more or less.

"You're almost swimming," he shouted in her ear.

She opened her mouth to answer and took in sea water. "Ugh!" She spat. "Ugh!"

"Time for you to get out. Your lips are turning blue, not to mention your fingers. And important parts of me as well. I have to start moving."

Shaking all over, Linnet stumbled to the pile of towels and swathed herself from head to foot. Then she walked back to the pool and sat down on the flat rock to watch Piers slash his way through the water, up and down.

The sun was even warmer than yesterday, and although she knew that freckles were practically a certainty, she couldn't help raising her face to it and basking in the sunlight. Even, after a while, lying back on the warm rock so the sun could reach her neck and her shoulders.

The rock below her radiated warmth, so she unwound the towel around her head to allow her hair to dry. And then she eased the towel off her legs, so her chemise could warm as well.

By the time Piers pulled himself out of the pool, she was almost asleep, nestled in towels and sunshine. She blinked up at him. "Have you finished?"

"It looks that way. And once again, you have taken all the towels."

She sat up. "I'm sorry. Here — take this one. She pulled the one from under her hair. "I'm afraid it's a little damp."

He took it without comment and started rubbing down his body and his hair, while she lay back and watched. She had no idea — no idea — that men could look like that. So, so intoxicating. So —

Maybe she was more like her mother than she had thought. The idea was distasteful, and she started to sit up.

"No, stay there," he said. "Turn over."

"I will not!"

"I'm going to teach you, on dry land, how to swim. It will be easier than trying to howl instructions in your ear while you shriek about the cold."

"Oh." She rolled over, wiggling to get herself comfortable on the nest of towels and warm rock. Then she looked over her shoulder at him. "All right, what do I do now?"

THIRTEEN

Piers looked down at the utterly delectable body of his fiancée — his supposed fiancée — and knew that he was in deep, dark trouble.

As dark as the crevice running between her utterly —

She was his father's choice. He couldn't have anything to do with her, not if she was the most beautiful woman in all of England.

Which she was, a small voice in his head pointed out. He'd never seen such an exquisite woman. Didn't even imagine that one existed, to be truthful.

He knelt down beside her, savagely suppressing the part of him that wanted to stroke down that lovely plane of smooth back, up the rise of her bottom, down those sleek legs.

"Put your arms out to the side," he said, his voice emerging from his chest sounding as gravelly as that of a man who'd smoked cheroots for years. He leaned over to show her the stroke. "See, on this side, and then on the other. And when you stroke on this side, you turn your head to the other to take a breath."

Dutifully she turned her head and moved her arms. "That's it," he said, his eyes returning to her bottom. "Your legs should be straight and kicking gently."

There was nothing wrong with looking, after all. It was just looking. Though another way of describing it would be to call it torment. He had seen hundreds of women's bodies. Maybe even a thousand. They had bared their breasts, their buttocks, all their most private parts, and he had never blinked an eye.

But now his body was pulsing, literally raging, with passion. Piers pushed himself to his feet and pulled the towel punishingly tight around his waist. He'd be damned if he'd be manipulated by his father, his despicable and despised father, into accepting the bride *he'd* chosen.

He watched Linnet stroke, forcing himself to ignore her sensuality. She seemed to have a fair sense of rhythm.

Of course she has, a voice murmured inside him. He could teach her rhythm, and she would —

He thrust the thought away. "Time to go," he said briskly, turning away. "I have a wing of patients waiting for me, some of them probably cadavers by now. Can't keep those cadavers waiting. It's not polite."

She scrambled to her feet, and he could hear her pulling on her dress. "Wait," she called, as he started toward the path. "I need you to button my gown, remember?"

He turned around. She stood there on the edge of the pool, red hair curling damply all over her shoulders, her cheeks pink from exercise. And she was grinning, properly grinning, not that patented smile that she used to mesmerize his poor students.

"I can't go back to the house like this," she said. "Granted, I have no chaperone. But unless you want my entire household to start believing that we're naked together, you must button my dress."

"Don't be a fool. The servants know exactly what we're doing. There's nothing they can, or wish to, do about it."

"Well, your father would be scandalized."

He grunted, not wanting to get into a discussion of precisely how little he cared for his father's opinion. "Come over here, then. I don't want to struggle across that rock with my cane."

She blinked, and scampered over to him.

"I'm sorry. Watching you swim, you seem so powerful that I forget that your leg is damaged. How did it happen, by the way?" She turned her back and he began buttoning her gown.

A woman's spine is a very delicate thing. Of course he knew it already, but his knowledge came from contemplating spines that had been injured. Linnet's curved in a perfect exhibition of faultless design, one small bump following another, all the bones he'd learned in medical school looking so very different covered with pale skin.

"Where's your chemise?" he asked abruptly.

"Oh, I took it off," she said. "There's nothing colder than wet fabric, you know."

She had pulled her hair away so it didn't get caught in her buttons, and her creamy neck bent before him, like the stem holding up a delicate flower. Her words sank into his mind rather slowly. She had taken off her chemise while he had his back turned. She had stood, naked in the open air, if only for a second.

"Piers?" she asked. "How did you hurt your leg?"

"It's been so long I've forgotten," he said, slipping the last button into its hole.

She made a little chuffing noise, but bent

to scoop up a bundle of wet cloth, her chemise, and then took his arm. He didn't even realize that he'd waited for her until her slender hand slipped beneath his arm.

"So did any new patients appear last night?" she asked chattily. "And can you tell me how you organize the patients' rooms? Eliza told me that there are wards in both wings."

"By what disease I think they have," he said, still thinking about how civility, once bred into a man's bones, stayed there for life.

"How?"

"Infectious fevers with infectious fevers. And they're also segregated by sex. Women in one room, men in another. I can't have the lusty ones leaping on each other in the middle of the night."

"Are there more women than men or vice versa?"

"Women take the prize."

"Why? Do we get sick more often?"

"No, but your sex is much more sensible about going for help. Men tend to keel over in the field, here in Wales. It's a nice, clean way to go and I recommend it."

"And children?"

"Sometimes. Influenzas tend to mow them down, so most of the young ones die before they get here."

He felt her shiver right beside him. "That's awful, Piers."

"That's life."

"You have Gavan at the moment; are there any other children?"

"Two girls." They were at the little house now. She didn't say anything else, but he could practically feel her thinking. "Don't," he said warningly.

"Don't what?"

"Whatever it is you're planning. You're getting a sort of Quakerish glow about you. Whatever it is, I'll just find it annoying."

"I don't have anything to do," she said, in the kind of reasonable tone that rang alarm bells. "I'm almost finished with *Dr. Fothergill's Observations,* and you told me his observations were foolish anyway. I looked at your library, and you have no novels."

"Is that what you generally do? Read novels?"

"There aren't enough of them. I read travel guides too, and plays." She shrugged.

He turned and looked at her, ignoring the creamy skin and curling eyelashes — well, not ignoring them, but trying to look past them. And finding all the signs of high intelligence.

How did his father do it? Where did he find her?

"One of the best physicians I ever met was a woman from Catalonia," he said.

"How did she manage that?" Linnet asked. "Do they allow women into medical schools in Spain?"

"You know where Catalonia is?"

"I told you I read travel books," she said with a trace of irritation.

"Her father is one of the best physicians in that country," he said. "He taught her, and then he forced them to let her into medical school. My guess is that by the time she entered she already knew more than most doctors with a degree, but at least it gained her the credentials."

She was silent as they climbed the steps to the castle door and Prufrock swung it open.

"Waiting for us, were you?" Piers asked.

"Three new patients are," the butler said. "I put two of them upstairs and one of them in the gun room. The marquis and the younger doctors are there now."

"The gun room?" Linnet asked.

"We got rid of the guns and do initial diagnoses there," Piers said, dropping her arm. "If you don't mind, you're going to have to tramp up the stairs by yourself. I've got work to do. For one thing I have to get to the gun room before Sébastien kills my new patient."

"If someone looks particularly ill, I put him there," Prufrock explained. "If he might be infectious, I should say."

"But how . . ."

The doors swung closed on the sound of her voice.

FOURTEEN

Gavan was sitting up in his bed when Linnet put her head in the door of the infirmary some time later. He smiled a big gap-toothed smile and shouted "Hey, miss!"

There was a groan from the bed next to him.

"Mr. Hammerhock, how are you feeling?" Linnet asked.

"His fever broke," Gavan reported. "His face is still all mucky, though, and his tongue isn't too good. The doctor came along and tried to get him to say *yes* a bunch of times 'cause he likes how he says it."

"What?" Linnet asked, confused.

"He says *weth*, don't you, Mr. Hammer-hock?" Gavan said. "And that makes the doctor laugh. Me too."

Mr. Hammerhock grunted.

"Anyway, he's going to live, that's what the doctor said."

"I'm glad to hear it," Linnet said. "See, Gavan, not everybody is —"

"Can you take me out now?" he interrupted. "I've been waiting and waiting for you. Who knows what Rufus is doing? We need to go see him."

"I don't think you're supposed to be out of bed," Linnet said.

"The doctor said that he can start walking today," came a stern voice behind her.

Linnet scrambled to her feet. "Nurse Matilda?"

The woman standing by the bed was wearing a leather apron that went to her knees. She had a black knob of hair on top of her head, a white knob for a nose, and a very long chin. In short, she looked rather terrifying.

"My name is Mrs. Havelock," she replied, witheringly.

"I'm so sorry." Linnet found herself babbling. "Lord Marchant referred to someone as Nurse Matilda, but of course he has more than one nurse, as there are so many patients."

"The doctor refers to me as such because of his impertinent and foolish ways," Mrs. Havelock said. She didn't bother to add *but you may not.* "I am not a dry nurse, but the housekeeper for this wing. Now if you're taking young Gavan out of doors, you may not take him to the stable. I don't want him returned with a single flea on his body. That boy is a magnet, a flea magnet."

Gavan piped up. "We won't go near a flea. Miss will just take me down to the pool again to look at the purty water." His eyes were shining with all the fervor of a missionary before the Pearly Gates.

Mrs. Havelock grunted. Apparently the halo was invisible to her. "I'd say no, but he's driving my other patients mad. I want him out."

"Don't give my bed away," Gavan said, his face falling.

Linnet waved at Neythen, whom she'd stationed at the door. "If you could pick up young Master Gavan, Neythen, we'll get out of Mrs. Havelock's way. I'm sure she has a busy morning ahead of her."

Mrs. Havelock gave her a scathing look that made Linnet suddenly realize just how different a beaten leather apron looked in comparison to a pale yellow morning gown adorned with cherry ribbons.

But she gave the housekeeper a deliberate, defiant smile. It wasn't her fault that she'd been born into a family that thought one could easily spend the morning paying calls, the afternoon sorting ribbons — not to mention buying more ribbons — and the evening galloping around a ballroom.

Any more than Mrs. Havelock had chosen to be born into a family that apparently enabled — or forced — her to hold a position in Piers's hospital. And it was absurd to feel even the slightest twinge of jealousy about that.

"Do you take care of all the patients in this wing by yourself?"

"Certainly not," Mrs. Havelock said. "That would be most improper. I am assisted by maids and male orderlies." Clearly she thought that Linnet was constitutionally worthless; she turned around without a farewell.

Of course they didn't go to the pool. Neythen deposited Gavan in the stable and then returned to his duties in the castle, promising to come back in an hour. Linnet sat on a rough wooden bench while Gavan played with Rufus.

"He looks different," Gavan said. "Don't you think he looks happier now that he has me?"

Linnet looked at the dog. Rufus didn't have much fur, but what he had stuck straight out. One ear poked up, and the other seemed to have been bitten in half at some point in the distant past. His tail bent sharply to the right, so it wagged only on that side of his body. "He is not beautiful."

"He *is* beautiful," Gavan protested. "You're just not looking at him the right way."

"What's the right way?" Linnet asked.

"You have to look at the doggy bits of him."

Rufus sat down and panted. "Well, he has a very long tongue," Linnet observed.

"He has, hasn't he? It's a pink tongue too, that's the best for a dog. I think we should give him a bath. You know Mrs. Havelock doesn't like fleas. And I think he might have them. See how he's scratching?"

He was, indeed, scratching.

"That's because he needs a bath," Gavan said. "We should give him a bath, miss."

She could just imagine that. "I don't think you should get wet at this stage in your recovery. Perhaps we could ask one of the footmen to do it."

"Good morning, Miss Thrynne."

It wasn't Piers. Of course it wasn't Piers, because he had important work to do. It was odd that his father's voice was so similar, though, when they looked entirely different. And it was more than odd — just plain stupid — that Linnet's heart had leaped at the sound of that voice.

She jumped up and curtsied before the duke. "How are you, Your Grace? May I introduce Gavan, and his dog Rufus?"

Gavan looked up. "Yergrace is a funny sort of name."

"He's a duke," Linnet explained. "That's how he's addressed."

Gavan nodded and went back to scratching Rufus's stomach.

"I'm afraid there's nowhere to sit except this bench," Linnet said, sitting back down. She was tired after the swimming lesson. "Did you come to see how your horses are faring?"

The duke sat down on the other end of the bench. "I had to leave the house."

Linnet thought he probably meant that Lady Bernaise was in the drawing room, but she didn't know precisely what to say. And then she realized that the duke had buried his face in his hands, so she reached out and touched his shoulder. "I'm sorry."

"The mistakes were all mine." A tear dropped from between his fingers.

A voice slashed through the air, making Linnet look up with a jolt. "Isn't this cozy?"

How could she have thought that Piers's voice was like the duke's? It was entirely different: darker, stronger, more manly — angrier.

"Gavan is acquiring new fleas," Piers continued, "and dear Dad is acquiring new friends. We're all happy, happy, happy. It must be your influence, Beauty."

"Don't call me that!" she said fiercely.

"It must be your influence," he repeated, thumping his cane.

"Don't be such an ass," she retorted.

The duke took a deep breath and dropped his hands. His eyes were red and glossy. "You told me never to apologize to you again. But —"

"Do you think my mind has changed?" Piers didn't look indifferent now. He looked utterly furious.

Linnet cast a quick look at Gavan, but he had crawled into the corner of a stall, trapped Rufus on his lap, and was whispering into one of the dog's hairy ears. He wasn't paying attention.

"I know nothing has changed," the duke said, his voice cracking. "But I can't help saying I'm sorry. I looked at you and your mother last night and I knew that I once had everything, everything that life could possibly give me that meant anything, and I threw it away. I threw away my marriage. Worse, I injured you —"

"Shut up," Piers said, his voice as cold as the ocean, colder, even. "I told you that I

210

can't give you the pardon you are looking for, and even if I could, it wouldn't magically make your past go away."

The duke swiped away another tear.

"You didn't throw us away. You made a legitimate, if misguided, decision that you preferred the euphoria of drugs to the tedium of family life. Who's to say that you weren't right, after all? I've never been tempted to sleep with the same woman every night myself. Let alone reproduce myself in a leaky, noisy miniature human."

"Stop it," Linnet said, rising to her feet.

Piers's eyes narrowed. "Oh look, now we're going to have an injection of warm female compassion."

"Who's being compassionate? What I see is you making a fool of yourself, and since I grew up with that behavior, it doesn't inspire compassion. Repetition leads to contempt, not compassion."

"If your father was a weeper, all I can say is that I know the feeling."

"You're the fool," Linnet said. "Your father took too much opium. He lost his family. He hurt your feelings." She paused.

"Boo hoo," Piers said.

"That's just what I was going to say." She smiled in a way calculated to irritate. "Was it the medical degree that gave you the idea

211

it was all right to keep acting like an angry six-year-old?"

"No, do tell me. How would that work?"

The duke rose as well, swaying a little. "Please, this is all my fault."

"We agree with you," Piers said. "No need to keep beating that particular dead horse."

"Yes, why bother, when your son can have fun doing it for you?" Linnet said.

"Are you always this sarcastic?" Piers actually looked rather startled.

"No. I'm a very nice young lady," Linnet said. "You bring out the worst in me, however."

"I'll leave," the duke said heavily. "That is, we'll leave. She wouldn't even speak to me this morning. I'm — I'll take you back to London, Miss Thrynne. I don't know why I didn't realize it sooner, but my son could never accept a bride whom I suggested."

"Is that true?" Linnet demanded, putting her hands on her hips.

Piers raised an eyebrow. "What, you'd rather be rejected on your own merits, or should I say demerits?"

"We're not going anywhere," she said, turning to the duke. "We'll stay here until I'm quite sure that I don't feel the urge to marry a nasty, self-absorbed six-year-old tyrant."

"Are you talking about me?" Gavan piped up suddenly.

She looked over. "No, you go back to playing with your dog."

"I'm going to try walking," Gavan announced. "Rufus will help me."

"Good idea," Piers said. "Nurse Matilda won't keep your bed forever, you know."

Gavan stood up, wavering a bit, and walked out of the stall. Rufus stayed at his heels. They all watched as he started down the aisle that ran the length of the stables.

"Once up and down, and then he'd better go back to Matilda's tender ministrations," Piers said.

"If you'll excuse me," the duke said, "I think I'll return to the house." He straightened his shoulders and bowed politely, but his eyes were squinty and small.

Linnet waited until he was gone, and then she said, "You must forgive him."

"Why?" Piers actually sounded half interested.

"It's not good for either of you."

"Do you realize that you sound as if you're hallucinating? We don't talk like that in Wales. *Good for either of you.* Wait! I have heard that sort of language before, from a

213

cracked man who belonged to the Family of Love."

She stared at him, waiting.

"Aren't you going to ask what the Family is, if only so you can run off and join them?"

"I didn't realize you needed a response. When Hamlet is giving a monologue, he just goes on and on by himself."

Piers threw her a disgusted look and turned to go.

She raised her voice. "You must forgive your father because anger is destructive, and it makes you a worse doctor."

"Actually, it makes me a better doctor. I'm more likely to notice when people are lying to me, and believe me, there's no one people lie to more than a doctor."

"Wrong," she said. "Spouses win."

He gave a crack of laughter.

"Your father is sorry that he took all that opium. He's sorry that he drove your mother to France and then divorced her."

His smile was almost feral. "Addicts are often sorry for what happened. I've seen it repeatedly."

"And families forgive each other," she said.

"Oh, they do? What would you know about that?"

"My parents often had occasion to forgive

214

each other."

He limped back toward her, put a hand under her chin. "And you, did *you* forgive them?"

Surprised, she blinked. He dropped his hand. "I didn't think so. It's easier to give advice than to take it."

"Of course I forgive them," she said. Though her voice betrayed uncertainty.

"Shouldn't your father have come along with you?" Piers demanded, going straight for the jugular. "After all, I do have a carefully concocted reputation as a beast. He sent you off to the wilds of Wales without a qualm?"

"Accompanied by *your* father," she said. "A duke."

"We both have irresponsible, not to mention uncaring, relatives." He sounded rather satisfied. "Enough of this charming chitchat. I came to tell you it's time for luncheon."

"Irresponsibility and lack of love don't go together. My father loves me; he simply finds it difficult, if not impossible, to contemplate leaving the comforts of London. Your father obviously loves you, since he puts up with your foul temper and your general unlovableness."

"I gather you're warning me not to get my hopes up based on that small point of

215

harmony between us?"

She hadn't quite noticed how close he was to her. The clean, male smell of him reached out to her like a caress and set her heart racing.

"I think we have a more interesting connection than parental ineptitude," Piers said. He switched his cane from his right to his left. She waited, just waited. A hand brushed by her cheek, curled into her hair. Still, she waited, without saying a word.

It felt as if the whole world waited, the sounds of the stable, the noise of Gavan's unsteady footsteps walking down the corridor, the occasional stamp of a horse's hoof, the creaking wood . . . it all faded before the intent look in his eyes.

"Your eyes —" she said, but he cut off her words.

His lips were like brandy, like an intoxication that swept down her back and stole her breath away. And his tongue —

She had hated it, loathed it, when the prince thrust his tongue into her mouth. Only the good manners drilled into her by the most rigid governess her father could find in the whole of the British Isles had stopped her from slapping Augustus in the face.

But now . . . .

Piers didn't thrust his tongue where it didn't belong, the way Augustus had. Instead he traced the seam of her lips, a touch so sweet that she opened her mouth, asking him in. He didn't take the invitation. His tongue dawdled, savored her, teased her lips.

Her heart was beating faster and she wanted — she wanted . . . Her tongue met his, played for a moment, tasted essence of Piers.

Then, finally, finally, the hand around her head pulled her closer, against the hard lines of his body. He bent his head, just a fraction of an inch, but Linnet, every instinct wildly alert, felt the movement, the change, his intention.

His kiss was no gentle adoration. It was a ravaging, craving kiss, a wildly passionate, tumultuous stand-and-deliver kiss. Her arms went instinctively around his neck. He tasted of the smoky tea he had had for breakfast, and some wilder substance: desire.

It was the sort of kiss that a gentleman never, ever gave a lady.

Linnet loved it.

FIFTEEN

Evening

Linnet was wrong about his father's being a distraction. *She* was a distraction. Piers stared at the patient who had just arrived at the castle, not even seeing her distended abdomen; instead he saw the way Linnet's eyes darkened, from blue irritability to — something else.

It was just sexual desire, of course. Same thing that led a million men to turn themselves into total asses. She was outrageously beautiful and he — well, God knows why she wanted him, but she did. Or at least she seemed to.

Suddenly he heard Sébastien's voice. "You're very large for five months, Mrs. Otter. Have there been any twins in your family?" He tapped her stomach on one side and then the other.

"You look like someone trying to select a ripe melon," Piers said, pushing his cousin

218

to the side. "She's obviously not carrying one baby unless she's been consorting with a bear."

Mrs. Otter gasped. "Well, I never!"

"He doesn't mean it," Sébastien said. "It's his idea of light humor."

"Buttocks here," Piers said, pointing to one little bump. "Another one to that side, though it might be a head. Hard to tell. Have you ever had twins in your family, Mrs. Otter? Yes, well, then you'll want to get yourself a couple of cradles."

"My aunt — and my mother — they both lost their twin babies." Her voice trembled. "That's why I came here, because their babies were born dead."

"Born dead, or died thereafter?" Piers demanded.

"Died after," she said. "I think. They were too small. I remember my mother saying that her babes had hands just like a walnut, a shelled walnut."

"Well, yours are both alive at the moment," Piers said. "Go home and go to bed. For the next four months."

"What?"

"Go to bed," he said, spacing out the words. "Get up only to take a wee, and probably not even then."

"I couldn't possibly do that! Why, my

husband needs me. And my father-in-law lives with us; he's old and I have —"

"Go on out and tell Mrs. Havelock that you need a bed in the west wing. For a few months at least. We have to try and get your babies' hands past that dangerous walnut stage."

"A bed?" she said, almost shrieking. "You want me to stay here?"

"Oh, you'll love being here," Piers told her. "All my patients adore it. I have a housekeeper who's saint-like in her loving care. In fact, she's due for canonization any moment."

"I can't just go to bed for months! My husband couldn't do without me, and I'm the leader of the sewing circle, and I run the benefit for —" Her voice died at the expression on Piers's face.

"I can see that you are entirely worthy and likely a comfort to the entire county. But you have a better chance to bringing these children of yours into the world actually breathing if you lie down for four months. Of course, twins *are* a great deal of trouble, so if you'd prefer to trot along home, we would all understand. I daresay your mother slept better with only you, rather than two of the same."

She shook her head.

"Are you sure? Your mother obviously had better luck the second time. Go on upstairs, then," he said when she remained silent, glaring at him. He turned toward the door, dismissing her from his mind. "Is that it for the day? I didn't go to all the trouble of changing for supper just so I could make rounds again."

"I don't like the fever case that came in this morning," Sébastien said, following him.

"Petechial, most likely," Piers said. "There's a rash of it going around." He was thinking about swimming. Tomorrow morning.

"It doesn't look like it to me. It looks worse."

"How can it be worse? Half my patients with petechial fever die, and I'm not even bleeding them. Besides, you're no good at diagnosis, may I point out?"

Sébastien shook his head. "That man is really sick. I told the housekeeper to put him in a room by himself."

"Fine," Piers said, pausing for a second to ease the pain before they headed down the stairs.

"How's the leg?" Sébastien asked.

He glared at him. "How's the twig of a dick you carry around in your breeches?"

221

"Feeling no pain," Sébastien said cheerfully. "Unlike your leg, given the fact you're tilting to the side like a drunken man at a Yule feast."

"Bollocks," Piers said, thumping his way down the stairs. And then, "Have you seen my mother?"

"She's flitting about, trying to find your father so she can torment him by not speaking to him. And she's dressed up like she's going to meet the queen."

Piers stopped for a moment, leaned against the banister.

"You're overdoing it with the swimming," Sébastien said. "Cut back. Every other day."

Not a chance of that. Not now that he had a playmate in the pool.

"I'll think about it," he said, starting down again. "Do you suppose my mother wants to take him back, then?"

Sébastien thought about it. "She's got on one of those corsets that's pushed her bosom out where you can't miss it."

"You're a pervert to take notice of such a thing in your aunt."

"I didn't take notice in a desiring sort of way," Sébastien protested. "Your father did, though."

"She's just tormenting him," Piers said. But his voice sounded uncertain even to

222

himself.

"Likely she does want him. It'd be a good thing too. She would go back to being a duchess, and stay safe here in England, and I would send my mother to London as well."

"Why —" But there was really no point in asking Sébastien. He was prancing down the stairs in front of Piers, looking like a cockerel at dawn. Clearly he understood women better than Piers did. He was practically a woman himself, given the embroidery on his waistcoat.

"She won't take your father back unless you mend fences with him, though," Sébastien tossed over his shoulder. "At the moment, she has to be angry for you as well as for herself."

"Bollocks," Piers said again.

Sébastien reached the bottom of the stairs and turned into the drawing room. Piers heard his voice emerging. "Ah, *ma tante,* you look as ravishing as if you were a mere eighteen."

"Bollocks!" Piers told Prufrock, who was standing about looking as if he was enjoying himself.

Sure enough, his mother had crammed herself into a gown that had to have been made for a woman with half her bosom. *"Maman,"* he said, bowing and then kissing her fingertips. But when he looked about, the target of all this feminine extravagance was nowhere to be seen. "Where's the duke?"

"Who?" his mother said disdainfully.

"You know: hawk nose, cheekbones, sober look? We used to live in his vicinity."

She took a sip of wine. "I suppose he doesn't care for a preprandial drink. And I hear that he's leaving at dawn tomorrow. We'll have the castle to ourselves."

She smiled gaily enough, but Piers could see the shadow in her eyes. Damn it, Linnet was right. Sébastien too, probably. "Where's my fiancée?" he asked, looking around. The doctors were clustered around the sherry. Sébastien was kicking the fire, endangering the high polish he maintained on his boots.

"I don't know," his mother said. "Perhaps she's directing her maids to pack her trunks."

"She's not leaving," he said, accepting a glass of brandy from Prufrock. "She's trying to drive me into fits of violence by flirting with the idea of accepting my hand. Not that I ever really offered it."

His mother looked at him with pity in her eyes. "She'll never marry you, darling. Linnet will cause an uproar in Napoleon's court, just by walking in the door. All this fuss about her reputation . . . no one will care about that."

"You're saying she's too good for me?"

"*Good* I know nothing about," his mother said, waving her fan. "But too beautiful: of a certainty. You should have married her the moment she got here, before she had a chance to get to know you."

Prufrock actually broke into a trot crossing the room, and Piers turned, knowing exactly who was about to enter.

Linnet's evening dress was cut in a vaguely classical style. Piers had heard the rumor that Roman matrons wore no undergarments beneath their tunics, and apparently Linnet took that historical aspect of her costume very seriously.

The muslin of her gown was so sheer that he could see the bump of her knee as she posed in the doorway, waiting for Prufrock to announce her. And as for the muslin around her bosom — well, there wasn't much. Bits of lace here and there, and a string of pearls that did a subtle job of calling attention to the swell of her breasts.

He could feel an unfamiliar grin on his lips. His mother didn't know everything; that dress was intended for him.

He started limping across the room, but Sébastien flitted ahead, cutting directly before him with a muttered "Excuse me, I'm in a hurry."

So Piers slowed down. There was no use competing with Sébastien's Continental flummery; his cousin took a glass of champagne from Prufrock so he could ceremoniously give it to Linnet. Watching him kiss her hand was enough to make him a bit nauseated, so he turned around and stumped back to the sideboard to retrieve his glass of brandy.

She would come to him. Not that it mattered, because they were both merely toying with each other. It wasn't the flirtation, but the similarity to himself that intoxicated him.

In her own way she was a female version of him: dislikable. Too beautiful, too intelligent, too sharp-tongued.

Not that he was beautiful.

She didn't come to him. Instead, maddeningly, she seemed to find Sébastien's chatter delightful. Five minutes later, his father walked into the room, looking drawn and tired and like a man who'd given up. Which Piers found he resented even more than he had loathed His Grace's longing glances.

In the end, Sébastien brought Linnet over. "I thought perhaps you didn't notice that your fiancée had entered the room."

226

"Good evening, fiancée."

"Beelzebub," she said, inclining her head. There was a secret smile in her eyes.

"I've been demoted," he said lazily, leaning back against the sideboard. "I'm sure people have called me Lucifer in the past. Wasn't Beelzebub just a lesser devil?"

"In fact, I think you are confusing your demons. Beelzebub is another name for the Evil One himself."

"Oh good," Piers said. "I'm ferociously competitive. I think I told you that before."

"Enough of this charming conversation," Sébastien interjected. "If I want to watch dogs snarling at each other, I can go to the fights."

"Now, now," Piers said. "You mustn't call Linnet a snarling dog. As soon as she decides to throw my father's proposal back in my face, you'll be free to snatch her up. But not if you've insulted her."

Of course Sébastien took the opportunity to bow again, and kiss Linnet's hand, and protest that she was the most charming, agreeable, and exquisite member of the fair sex whom he'd ever, et cetera, et cetera. Piers watched him, marveling that Sébastien didn't seem to realize how much Linnet loathed that sort of fawning attention.

Oh, she was smiling at him, and holding

out her hand. But her eyes were completely unmoved, even as she gave him that lavish smile she seemed to use as ammunition.

It certainly worked on Sébastien. Piers had known him all his life, and he'd never seen quite that expression on his face.

"Enough," he said to Linnet. "If this were a dog-fight, you'd be a mastiff and he a mere spaniel. Save your artillery for stronger opponents."

Sébastien frowned at him. "What are you talking about, Piers? You're making less sense than usual."

Linnet tucked her arm through Sébastien's and laughed. "He's jealous," she said, though her eyes showed perfectly well that she knew he wasn't. "You're such a dashing figure, my lord. It's hard to believe the two of you grew up together."

"I'm a glass of fashion," Piers stated.

Sébastien and Linnet stared for a moment at his costume. He was wearing the same sort of thing he always wore: a plain-cut coat with plain buttons, plain breeches, a neckcloth tied in under five seconds. The skirts of Sébastien's coat, in contrast, were greater in circumference than Linnet's gown. Not to mention the fact that said coat was a garish mustard color.

"You're deluded," Sébastien said.

"A *glass* of fashion," Piers repeated patiently. "Without me, you would hardly shine with the glory that you do currently, would you?"

"A particularly strained metaphor," Linnet observed. "But I take your meaning. A mongrel always makes a greyhound look more regal, does it not?"

"Or a poodle more absurd," Piers retorted.

"Insult me all you wish," Sébastien said. He was looking down at Linnet with an utterly fatuous expression on his face. She had apparently seen that look on men's faces so often that it hardly registered; there wasn't a trace of triumph about her.

"You two couldn't be more different in your dress," she said.

"You should have seen us as boys," Piers said. "I could hardly walk, of course, so Sébastien used to run twice as fast. And then as we grew older, he started dressing twice as elegantly, to compensate for my slovenly ways."

"But you were both interested in medicine," Linnet said. "How on earth were you able to pursue your interests? Not a single gentleman I know in London has any skills of that sort."

"Or of any sort?" he asked, eyebrow raised.

"They can dance," she offered.

"Perhaps that's why: I couldn't dance, so I turned to cutting people up."

"And he couldn't cut people up all that well, so I had to do it for him," Sébastien chimed in.

Linnet laughed. Her laugh . . . it was far more enticing than that practiced smile of hers. It was both husky and sweet, like warm brandy with honey.

"He's not joking," Piers said, taking another gulp to fortify himself against that laugh.

"I thought *you* were the famous doctor," she said.

"I'm good at figuring out what's wrong with people. The trouble is that I do that best when they're already dead. Sébastien, on the other hand, is good at the tidy sort of surgery, the kind where the patient is living and would prefer to stay that way."

Linnet gave Sébastien another smile, and Piers fancied he could actually see the poor man buckle at the knees. "It's very reassuring to think that you'd be here if I were to need surgery," she cooed.

"Yes, if you want a leg lopped off, he's the man to do it," Piers said.

"That would be a crime," Sébastien said, his voice as soft as a dove's.

Damn it, Piers was starting to feel a bit guilty. Sébastien had no idea what sort of temptress he had hanging onto his arm and his every word. He'd end up getting his heart properly broken if this kept up.

"Stop it," he said to Linnet.

She gave him the smile.

"And don't ever smile at me like that again," he ordered. "It makes me want to vomit, and given that your slippers appear to be sewn with pearls — an inordinate waste of money — gastric acid would not be good for them."

Sébastien frowned at him. "Is this your idea of proper conversation, cousin? If so, you're worse than I thought. Miss Thrynne is a delicate flower, who should be treated with the utmost respect. Instead you're talking about lopping her legs and vomiting on her toes."

Piers raised an eyebrow at Linnet. She sighed and patted Sébastien's arm. "I'm sorry," she said. "His lordship has quite correctly noticed that I am as adept at flirtation as he is at its opposite."

"Nice," Piers said, with genuine appreciation. "Damned if you aren't one of the nastiest conversationalists I know. Especially given the extra ammunition you carry."

"You mean the smile?" she asked. "I find

it very useful. You should try it sometime."

Sébastien was scowling now. Likely it was starting to dawn on him that Linnet was not merely a delicate flower.

"You're not up to her weight," Piers told him. "She's a master. No wonder all of London thinks she had a prince under her thumb."

"It runs in the family," Linnet said. She looked almost bashful for a moment. "I would really like to hear more about your surgical practice," she told Sébastien. "You said that you can't avoid infection. What sorts of things have you tried?"

Piers often thought his cousin was a bit of a dolt, but he never underestimated him when it came to surgery. Sébastien was the finest surgeon he'd ever seen, his concentration unyielding, his fingers quick and impossibly deft.

"If we didn't have a problem with infection," Sébastien was saying, "I think it would be possible to intervene in ways that we can't even imagine now. For example, up in the west wing we have a woman with a swelling in her stomach. It's almost certainly some sort of cancer causing a tumor, a kind of growth. It's probably around the size of an apple, or even larger."

"I'm certain of the tumor," Piers put in.

"I won't know the size for sure until a few months from now, of course."

Linnet blinked, but to her credit, she didn't flinch or squeal, the way most ladies did once faced with the exigencies of medical practice, and his own fascination with dissection.

"If we had something that could control infection, I could open up her stomach and cut out the tumor," Sébastien said. "She could go back home and live out her life."

Piers had to concede that his cousin was particularly appealing when he was talking about surgery. A lock of hair had fallen over his forehead, and his eyes were bright.

Maybe he should steer the subject somewhere else. Linnet was obviously enthralled.

"Doesn't alcohol work?" she asked. "I've read that soldiers in the field pour brandy over their wounds, and it limits the risk of infection."

"Not good enough," Piers said. "When we were younger and less morbid, we tried everything we could. But our patients died with distressing frequency."

"Almost all of them," Sébastien said. Now his face took on the sort of sweet distress that women found so appealing. Piers couldn't make an expression like that if his own life depended on it. Of course, Sébastien really meant it. He was genuinely distraught when his patients died.

"So we stopped," Piers said. "Sébastien couldn't take the body count."

"Limbs are one thing," Sébastien said. "But the interior of the body is just too much of a risk."

"That poor woman," Linnet said.

Piers had forgotten whom they were talking about. "Ah. Well, at least she came here. We put her on so much opium that she feels no pain."

"Is she awake?"

"Almost never. Which, for her, is by far the best situation. Stomach cancer — if that's what she has — seems to be particularly painful."

"What about her family?"

He shrugged. "I wouldn't know about that. Perhaps she hasn't got any."

"Don't any of the patients have families? No one seems to have any visitors."

"That's Nurse Matilda's domain. I really wouldn't know."

Linnet's eyes narrowed. "Mrs. Havelock seems to have very decided opinions. It's possible that she's told your patients that they aren't allowed to have visitors."

"Oh, she wouldn't do that," Sébastien said. "She's rather brusque, but she has a good heart."

That was Sébastien. He always saw the best in people.

"Actually, she doesn't have a very good heart, if by that you mean a capacity for human sympathy," Piers said. "That's one reason I keep her around, given her utter lack of charm. She can hold down a screaming child without a flicker of an eyelash."

"A screaming child?" Linnet shuddered.

So she did have a soft spot.

"Gavan screamed like the dickens when we had to set his broken leg," Piers said. "But look at him now. He stopped screaming, and he's walking again. The boy will be going home soon."

"Yes, but how long as he been here without being allowed to see his mother?"

Sébastien frowned. "I'll look into it, Miss Thrynne." He threw her a hopelessly addled look. "What a kind spirit you have. Piers and I have been in and out of that room for months without considering the question."

"Well, you have the patients, not to mention all those Ducklings, to look after," she said, gesturing across the room. "I can ask Mrs. Havelock about visitors."

"The Ducklings?" Sébastien inquired.

But Piers was already chuckling. "Those foolish boys," he said, nodding at Penders,

Kibbles, and Bitts. They were hovering around Lady Bernaise, likely absorbed by his mother's exuberant display of bosom.

"Oh, I see," Sébastien said. "I suppose they follow Piers as if he were a mother duck. A sweet, lovable mother duck."

"It does strain the imagination," Linnet agreed.

"I like *that* smile better," Piers told her.

It vanished.

"That was a mean, sarcastic little smile," he continued. "It showed the real you."

Her eyes narrowed, and for a moment he thought he was going to get a glass of champagne in the face. But Prufrock rang the gong for supper, and she simply turned her shoulder to him and sauntered off with Sébastien, making a point of clinging to his arm.

After the meal, Piers's mother rose and with a twinkling, sweeping smile that encompassed everyone at the table, including her former husband, said, "Why don't we retire to the drawing room together? Prufrock has been kind enough to arrange for some small entertainment."

One look at her face and he knew that his *Maman* had some devilish plan in mind.

"Dancing!" he said moments later, seeing

the floor cleared and Prufrock at the piano, accompanied by a weedy-looking footman with a violin. "How very kind of you, *Maman.* That's just what I was hoping for."

His mother swanned over to him in a cloud of jasmine. "Darling, the world does not revolve around you, and I'm sorry if I ever gave you the impression that it did. Now sit down there and rest your leg. Sébastien will dance with me, of course."

"Of course," Piers echoed, sitting down, because when one's mother decides to stage a comedy, why not enjoy it?

His father sat down on a straight-backed chair at the other end of the sofa and watched. He didn't even make a pretense not to, just sat, his eyes fixed on his former wife as she circled the floor in a waltz, laughing up at her nephew.

"She's as light on her feet as she ever was," Piers said, after a time. He would rather have a conversation than watch the dancing. It was making him irritable to watch Bitts grinning down at Linnet, for one thing. He liked to think of Bitts as a doctor, however incompetent, not a young gallant.

"Your mother?" His father nodded. "You should have seen her when she was seventeen. She was as slender as a willow, with a sparkle in her eyes that made all the men in the room fall in love with her."

"Are you going to ask her to dance?"

His father glanced over at him, a little twist on his lips that Piers realized, with a shock, he'd felt on his own face, time and again. "Oh, I shall ask. She's arranged the entertainment, and it would be unchivalrous for me not to allow her to refuse me. We didn't waltz back then, of course."

"Back then?" Piers repeated, rather dim-wittedly.

"I broke all the rules of society," his father said. "I didn't wait to be introduced, to request her hand in the dance. I simply pulled her onto the floor."

"Well, go then," Piers said. "Pull her onto the floor."

"She doesn't want to be pulled. She wants the chance to turn me down."

Yes, Piers definitely recognized that sardonic smile. It was his own.

"And my transgressions mean that she deserves that pleasure," the duke added.

His mother might well refuse to dance with his father, but Sébastien wasn't going to turn down the chance to dance with Linnet, and he'd be damned if he'd sit watching from a sofa as Sébastien whispered into *his* fiancée's ear.

238

He got up to leave, and then hesitated. "Good luck," he told his father.

"Too late for that," the duke said. "Good night."

Sixteen

"You're a pig," Linnet informed Piers. He had woken her by dangling a ribbon over her face so it tickled her nose.

"I brought you hot chocolate."

"That goes some way toward ameliorating your piggishness," she said, pushing herself up against the backboard so she could drink her chocolate. And watch Piers surreptitiously, though why she was beguiled by such a boorish character she could hardly say.

But a woman who's dreamed all night that a certain doctor was kissing her — and not stopping with mere kisses — can hardly pretend to herself that she isn't fascinated.

"Don't make such a dead set at Sébastien," he said. He still hadn't met her eyes. Instead he was playing with the ribbon the way a small child might, tying it in knots and testing its strength.

"You're ruining that ribbon and it's one

of my favorites."

"Made of silk?" He tied another knot.

"Of course. Why?"

"We need something better with which to tie patients to the table during surgical procedures. We're using ropes, and they complain of burns later. Maybe silk would work." He tested it again by running it against the edge of the footboard. It promptly snapped in half.

"Oh for goodness' sake," Linnet said. "Did you have to break that? Wind silk around the ropes."

"Good idea. Did you hear what I said about Sébastien?"

"Yes. Are you worried about losing your playmate?"

Piers snorted. "I wish I was the boy you keep calling me."

"Why?"

"In thirty, forty years at the most, we'll have something to control infection. Surgery will be revolutionized."

"You're what, thirty years old? You could be operating at seventy-five, propped up against the table."

"Taking my patient's nose off with my shaking hands," he put in.

"I call you a boy because you act like a child whose parents have disappointed him,

241

and he's determined to pay them back."

"I love my mother." He seemed to be truly listening to her. But then Linnet realized that it wasn't in Piers's nature *not* to listen.

"Of course you love your mother. But you love your father, too. And he loves you."

"All this tender emotion so early in the morning is curdling my stomach."

"You seem to have problems with your stomach," she said pointedly. "Maybe Sébastien will be operating on *you* in thirty years."

"Damn, I hope not. He's as good as they come, but it's not a pretty affair. Let's go, shall we? I can't take this much intimacy, and definitely not with a woman I haven't slept with."

Linnet drank up her chocolate and then swung her feet out of bed. She felt a pang of real sadness at the idea that Piers could never make love. "How *did* you injure your leg and — and the rest of you?" she asked, going over to the screen. She'd put her clothes out the night before.

When he didn't answer, she turned around to find him gazing at her back. "What? Did I spill the hot chocolate?"

"That nightgown is practically transparent," he said, his voice low and growly. "I can see your buttocks."

242

She whisked herself behind the screen, feeling a rush of heat in her stomach — and a corresponding twinge of sadness. She, who never really wanted to sleep with a man (if she admitted the truth to herself) — well, she could envision herself in bed with one.

Piers.

Piers, who was incapable. It was the cruelest of ironies.

"I don't like that word *buttocks*," she said, controlling her voice so that not even a hint of desire emerged. "That's a doctor's word."

"What would you prefer? Bottom? Arse? Ass?"

"Bottom, I suppose."

"I think I like *ass*. It has such a round sound. Round and luscious."

Linnet pulled her gown over her head and let it settle around her. Then she reached behind her and felt her bottom. It certainly felt round. Hopefully it was luscious, too.

She walked out and over to her dressing table. "I just have to brush my hair. I decided I would braid it today and see if that keeps it from getting too tangled. It's giving Eliza no end of trouble."

He walked up behind her and started doing up her buttons without being asked. Linnet drew the brush through her hair, and then caught his eyes in the glass, and paused.

"Just as if we'd been married ten years already," he said with a lopsided smile.

"You don't mean to ever marry, do you?"

"I don't see any point."

"Why not?" Then she realized why. "Oh, because you can't have children?"

"The institution is designed for precisely that," he said. "No point in it otherwise."

She opened her mouth, but realized that she didn't feel like defending love, or even companionship, to a misanthrope. Besides, she agreed with Piers that love and marriage often had little in common. She tied the half ribbon around the bottom of her braid and rose. "Shall we?"

He looked her up and down. "You look about fourteen with that braid. And you've left off your stockings."

"I've come to agree that there's no point. We never see anyone on the way out of the house anyway."

"Prufrock is not one of those butlers who believe the staff has to be up and about at the crack of dawn."

"He is a very unusual butler," Linnet said, falling into step as she tucked her hand under Piers's arm.

"I told you. He's not a butler; he's a spy

for my father."

"But why does your father have a spy in your house?"

Piers shrugged.

"Stop shrugging; you do that entirely too often when you want to avoid a question. Why does your father have a spy in your house?"

"I suppose he wants to know what goes on here."

"And you said he has one in your mother's house as well."

"Yes."

"He's still in love with her, you know. And the feeling is mutual."

"Sébastien said as much to me. They'll have to make up their own minds about whether they want to act on it."

Linnet glanced at him, but could see from his jaw that he didn't want to discuss it further. Besides, it really was no business of hers. "So you told me that the rooms in the castle are all organized by various diseases."

"As well as by sex," he said, using his cane to knock a rock off the path before he stepped forward. "Patients are so pesky about decency and propriety."

"Why is Gavan next to Mr. Hammerhock, then? You told me that Mr. Hammerhock could be infectious."

"It's unlikely. Petechial fever seems to stop being infectious after the skin lesions break open. I was just trying to stop you from falling in love with him. His charming rash makes him a danger to any woman. Not to mention that adorable lisp he developed. Although sadly, it seems to be going away as of last night."

"I think the air is warmer today," Linnet said as they turned the last bend, passed the guardhouse, and could see the pool.

"I don't like the sky," Piers said, squinting up.

"What's the matter with it? There aren't any clouds." She dropped his arm and turned her back to be unbuttoned.

"That brooding color means a storm. Maybe."

"Maybe? You're a diagnostician of diseases, not weather." She pulled off her dress. "Just get undressed, would you? I practiced swimming last night —"

"You did?"

"On the floor. Eliza came in, which confirmed all her suspicions that I've completely lost my mind." She ran over to the rock overlooking the pool.

"Slow down. You'll make me feel like a cripple."

"By wounding your non-existent feelings?" she taunted. She moved to the very edge of the rock. There was a light wind blowing from the sea, bringing a kind of salty fever to the air.

Piers was pulling off his boots. He had taken one look at her, and then gone back to undressing. Obstinately, she wanted him to look again. She could tell that the wind had molded her chemise to her body, revealing every curve. She wanted . . .

With a start of guilt, she realized how cruel she was being. It was truly unkind to flaunt before him what he could never enjoy.

She sat down, pulling her knees to her chest. Piers was taking off his shirt, and she watched him while pretending to stare at the water. His chest was beautiful, with a sprinkling of hair that darkened just as it arrowed into his breeches. Her fingers trembled to touch him, to run her fingers over his chest, around to his back, down to his —

Buttocks. Or perhaps the right word for a man's behind was arse, she thought, watching as he turned to put his breeches and shirt to the side.

A moment later they were both plunging down into the water. Rather than feeling mortally cold, she loved the thrill of the drop, the way the water shocked her, as if

247

she had been sleeping until the instant she hit water.

And then she loved the way Piers hauled her up and against his body. But he didn't let her cling there long.

"One hand on the side," he barked. "Now, try swimming."

She took a deep breath and pushed away from the side of the pool. And promptly sank.

He pulled her back up and shoved her toward the side again. "Float for a moment and then start moving your arms," he ordered. "And don't forget to kick."

She was shivering so violently that she didn't think she could move . . . . but she did. A moment later she was moving through the water: slowly, but she was moving, not sinking. Piers stayed beside her, shouting instructions, most of which she couldn't hear. But finally she got the idea, the way the arms moved separately, up and around, the way her head turned to the side, the way her legs —

He grabbed her legs with those clever hands, surgeon's hands, and held them straight to show her how to kick.

Being a weak fool, she instantly stopped thinking about swimming and thought, slide your hands up, *up.*

He didn't.

Five minutes later she had made it all the way across the pool. Her heart was racing, and she couldn't stop grinning.

"Are you all right to go back the same way?" he shouted.

Without answering, she pushed off from the side and began to fight her way back through the water. Halfway across, her eyes stung, her mouth was full of saltwater, and her arms were exhausted.

A wave slopped over her head, and she hesitated, just long enough so she began to sink.

Piers's arm curled around her waist. "Good enough," he said into her ear. "Come on." He pulled her to the side and then against his body. She curled against him naturally now, like a baby clinging to its mother. Except the way his hard body felt against hers had nothing maternal about it.

"Your heart is racing," he said. "Too much exertion for someone who does little more than dance."

She wasn't going to explain why her heart was racing, so she let him hoist her out of the pool, and didn't even watch as he thrashed away, back through the water, beating the waves to the side as if they were no more than ripples in the bathtub.

Linnet's legs felt like soggy bread pudding. Perhaps he was right. She found the stack of towels that Prufrock had sent down and took all of them again.

Really, she should tell Prufrock that they needed an extra towel, one just for Piers. But lying back on the rock, she had to admit that she liked taking one off her body to give to him. Or two off her body.

It made him look. It made her feel fiercely alive, as if the blood sang in her veins.

Of course, that was why her mother set out so cheerfully on her assignations. They made her feel alive, one had to suppose. Poor Mama.

Linnet turned on one side in her nest of towels, remembering her mother's laughter. She must have been addicted to the kind of pleasure Linnet felt around Piers. As easy to explain as Piers's father's being addicted to opium.

As simple as that.

And Piers was right: she hadn't ever really forgiven her mother for wanting to be with strange men more than she wanted to be with her daughter. Enough so that she set out one rainy night to meet a man — they never knew who — and died when her carriage crashed into a piling.

I would never do it, Linnet thought. I

would never . . . but that doesn't mean I can't understand it. Not when Piers's very touch set fire raging through her blood.

Somewhere around her heart, some sort of emptiness, as icy as the water, eased and fell away. "Love you," Linnet whispered, telling the wind, the warm rock beneath her shoulders, the smell of fish and the sea, the memory of her mother.

Piers came up, dripping, and flicked cold water over her face. "Are you planning to share one of those towels? Never mind the fact that my body is so much larger than yours."

She pulled the towel off her head and gave it to him.

"I need another," he said, rubbing his hair.

She gave him the one wrapped around her feet.

"Do you know how many people have diseases that cause their toes to drop off? I'd like a different towel."

Linnet blinked. "My toes are firmly attached."

There was something wicked in his eyes, something primitive that made her whole body respond. Instantly. She felt like a slave girl lying at the feet of a raja, boneless and without will.

"Another towel," he demanded.

She took her time, pulling the edge of the towel from under her shoulders, rolling a little to the side, unwrapping herself as if she were a present. She didn't have to glance down to know that her nipples stood out under the wet chemise. She didn't have to glance up to know that he was devouring the sight.

She tossed the towel in his direction and settled back, her arms above her head.

He rubbed his body, looking down at her the whole time, without a shred of remorse or propriety. *"You,"* he said finally, wrapping the towel around his waist, "are —"

His head jerked up. "Bloody hell!"

Seventeen

Linnet sat up and followed Piers's fixed gaze toward the horizon. Coming toward them was a kind of dark mass, as if the night sky had appeared out of nowhere, come down to the sea and was —

Piers yanked her to her feet, reaching with his other hand for his cane. Then he dropped her hand. "*Run!* Run as fast as you can back to the castle."

She looked back over her shoulder. The dark, roiling cloud was coming, so close that she could see it moving. But the uncanny thing was that the sky opposite was still blue, the sun still shining.

He had started up the path. "Linnet!" he bellowed, not looking back. "Run, you blithering idiot!"

She dashed after him. He was going quite quickly in a sort of three-pronged run, watching the ground intently to manage where his cane landed on the rocks. Once

253

she caught up, she turned around again.

The cloud wasn't black. It was a kind of dark green-blue, and it bulged as if it were alive. Fear replaced fascination. She ran after Piers again. "What is it?" she asked. "What is that?"

"Weather," he said tersely. "Bloody Welsh weather, that's what it is. Would you please start running?"

"I'm not going without you," she said. A wind running ahead of the cloud reached them, and the words were ripped from her mouth.

One glance over her shoulder and Linnet knew they wouldn't make it to the castle. Whatever was in that cloud was eating up the blue part of the ocean, racing toward the coast like a ferocious animal. And yet, oddly, the sun still shone in the sky directly above them.

Piers was going even faster now, the power of his left leg clear as he thrust himself forward. "The guardhouse," he shouted, his words barely intelligible in the howl of the wind. They were almost at the curve of the path, and just beyond that stood the little building.

The wind was shoving them from behind, and all of a sudden Linnet felt needle points of icy rain strike her shoulders and back.

Piers, impossibly, put on such a burst of speed that he drew ahead. Then he was at the door, yanking it open, reaching back for her as she came up panting, grabbing her hand and pulling her so strongly that her feet left the ground.

Slamming the door behind them.

One second, in which they looked at each other in the dim twilight of the house. Then as if gunfire had erupted, the wooden door shook from blows so strong that the frame visibly trembled.

"Oh, my God," Linnet whispered. "What is that?"

"Hail," Piers said, turning and limping into the room. "That's why we leave the shutters closed on this house at all times." He paused and cocked his head. "The size of tennis balls, from the sound of them."

"I've never heard of anything like this," Linnet exclaimed. She stared, transfixed, at the door. It was shaking as if hundreds of fists were pounding from the outside, as if a wild mob were trying to gain entrance.

"But surely you've heard of Welsh weather? It'll be over in two or three hours, I should think. Does your maid have any idea you came swimming?"

Linnet nodded.

"Prufrock will tell her not to worry; this

255

happens frequently enough that I've instructed him not to send out a search party. My patients will have to get by with the tender ministrations of Sébastien."

"Your Ducklings will help him," Linnet said, over the noise of a renewed hammering, as the wind flung more hail against the house. She became aware she was shivering, in reaction and cold. "Do you suppose there might be some clothes here, or a blanket?" she asked, her teeth chattering.

Piers turned around and leered in an appreciative kind of way. "Forgot your towels?"

"I'm freezing," Linnet said, wrapping her arms around herself. "Blankets?"

He pointed with his cane to a door to the left of the fireplace.

"Make a fire," she implored. "Please."

"As you command," he retorted. But he put his cane to the side and took a flint from the mantel-piece. Thankfully, it was already laid with shreds of kindling and a few logs.

Linnet pushed open the door to find a small bedchamber. It had nothing other than a big bed, with a window that looked inland so the shutters weren't being buffeted by hail.

She found a cupboard next to the door, and pulled open the doors. The shelves were empty, but for a heap of cloth bundled into

256

one corner. She pulled it out, her fingers shaking with cold, and saw that it was a man's shirt. It wasn't a shirt of the kind Piers wore, made of fine linen. It was homespun, thick freize.

She sniffed it cautiously and discovered to her relief that it was clean, if rumpled. Her freezing, wet chemise was off in a second. But she was still damp, so she poked her head out the door. "Piers, may I use —"

Only to see what she unaccountably had overlooked. Piers Yelverton, Earl of Marchant, was stark naked.

He was squatting in front of the fireplace, banging the flint against a firestone.

"Your towel?" she asked.

"The wind took it."

"It took your smalls too?"

"I must have forgotten to leave them on. I'm used to swimming naked." He looked up at her, his eyes as warm as French cognac. Just as if she'd drunk that cognac, warmth slid down her throat, to her breasts, her stomach, lower. She couldn't help looking. His body was all heavy muscle, his legs, back, shoulders . . .

"Want me to stand up so you don't miss anything?" His voice was amused, but there was a strain of something feral in it, deep and male and dangerous.

Linnet's whole body responded to it. The gentle glow, the brandy-like cheer, turned into a kind of desperate heat, pooling in her legs. "No!" she gasped. "If you don't have a towel — never mind." She saw him start to move, and pure instinct whipped her back inside the bedchamber, door closed.

The door's wood was rough against her back and bottom. I'm naked, she thought. I'm naked, and I'm in a house with a naked man, and I need —

Linnet had the shirt over her head in two seconds. It fell to her knees, which was scandalous enough. The thick fabric concealed her figure fairly well, though her breasts strained the buttons a trifle. It seemed to have been made for a man with a slender chest, which solved the dilemma of whether she should allow Piers to have their only garment. His chest was most decidedly not slender.

She turned back to the bed. It was covered by a rough blanket; she pulled it back to find a coarse sheet. It would cover that huge expanse of naked man out in the front room, and that was all that mattered.

She pulled the sheet from the bed, opened the door and pushed it through without looking.

Piers's voice came around the wooden

door perfectly clearly, even over the wind. "What's this?"

"Put it on," she shouted.

"No need."

"Yes, there is a need." The door moved under her hand. "And don't come in here without that sheet around your body!"

The door opened, pushing her backward. "I found a tablecloth." Sure enough, he had a blue cloth tied around his waist.

"The sheet would be better," Linnet said, her eyes instinctively sliding over Piers's broad chest. She looked lower and gasped. "That's indecent!"

The tablecloth was knotted in a jaunty sort of way over Piers's right hip, but even so it barely covered the — that — "You can't wear that!"

"Well, I can't wear the sheet, unless you want to sit on that blanket," he said, an odd grin playing around his lips. "It looks as if it might harbor as many fleas as Rufus, which is really saying something."

Linnet glanced with horror at the bed. "I'm not sitting there."

"There's nowhere else to sit," Piers said. "There's an unaccountable lack of furniture in the house. My guess is that it was borrowed by neighbors. Very thrifty, these Welshmen. I suppose they didn't think the house needed a table or chairs, since no one is living in it. We're lucky the bed is still here."

Sure enough, Linnet peeped around his shoulder and realized that the front room was empty but for a heavy sideboard. She looked back at the bed.

"My understanding is that fleas can't live without a blood meal of some sort for more than a few weeks," Piers said, tossing the sheet back on the bed. "Could you put the damned thing back on? My leg didn't take to that jaunt we had up the hill, and I am going to either sit down or fall down. At the moment my cane is the only thing holding me upright."

Linnet scrambled back to the bed and started trying to tuck the sheet in on all sides. "This is harder than it looks," she said, vainly making idle conversation so that she didn't look at Piers again.

"Should I give the maids an extra truppence per bed?" He sounded bored.

Linnet gave up on the foot of the bed. She must have put too much sheet under the top, because it wouldn't stay tucked. "Sit down," she said, waving at the bed.

He sat down with a groan.

"Better?" Linnet asked. After a moment, she perched on the end of the bed, giving

260

him plenty of space. She could hardly remain standing for the duration of the storm, improper though this was.

Piers was digging his fingers into his right leg, giving it a rough massage. "Anything's better than standing on it after that run," he said, not looking up.

"Have you had the injury a long time?" Linnet asked.

"Almost my whole life."

"Why doesn't it heal?"

He shook his head. "I won't know until I autopsy myself." She blinked. "Stupid joke. I think the muscle died, inside. I've found patients who seem to have experienced muscle death following a traumatic injury. In some cases the pain goes away. In others . . . it doesn't."

"Is there no chance?" She watched his fingers for a moment. "You don't even have a scar, that I can see."

He turned his leg slightly to the outside, and she gasped, seeing a wicked, jagged scar, extending from his upper thigh down past his knee on the inside. "How did you survive?"

"I probably shouldn't have," he said coolly. "Huge risk of infection, for one thing. But I'm a tough bastard." He looked up, at last, and grinned at her.

261

Linnet couldn't smile back. She was too shaken by the terrible pain implied by that huge scar. Without thinking, she reached out and ran her fingers down the rippled skin. "Does the scar itself hurt, or only the muscles inside your leg?"

"I think you're the first woman who's touched me there," he said slowly. His face was unreadable. "An odd thought."

Of course no woman had touched him, given his incapability. Her fingers looked pale, creamy against his darker skin. Still, she suddenly realized that she had her hand on a man's inner thigh.

She jerked her hand away.

"I liked it," Piers said. His voice came from deep in his chest.

Linnet felt so embarrassed that her cheeks were probably peony red. She risked a glance at his face. She knew that look by now. Desire. She took a deep breath. "I just wanted to . . ." She foundered to a halt.

He seemed to be having trouble controlling his laughter, the wretch. "I don't see what's so funny," she fired at him. "I'm trying to be sympathetic to your plight."

Piers leaned back against the headboard and crossed his arms behind his head. Which did something to the tablecloth, she couldn't help but notice. It didn't seem to contain him very well.

"I haven't allowed any women to stroke that part of my leg," he said.

Linnet nodded. "Of course. I completely understand." Her own hands were clenched in her lap, but her fingertips still tingled from the feel of his skin.

"I quite liked it, though. Perhaps I should get myself a ladybird. What do you think? We could house her in the west wing with Gavan and the patients who are dying but not infectious."

The wind was howling around the little house, making it feel as if they were the only two people in the whole world. "Why?" she asked, with genuine curiosity. "Just so the lady could rub your scar now and then?"

"She wouldn't be a lady," Piers objected. "That's the whole point." His eyes were full of laughter. Laughter and . . . something else.

Just desire, Linnet told herself. Garden-variety desire. She pulled her legs up and tucked them to the side. His eyes followed her movements. "What would a ladybird do for you that a lady couldn't?"

"Ladies come with too many strings," he said, shifting so that his outstretched leg brushed her feet. It felt like an electric shock.

"Strings as in marriage?" she managed, priding herself on not showing any reaction to his touch.

"As in," he agreed. "As in living with the same woman for far too many years. Don't tell me you haven't thought about the drawbacks of that."

She had. No one could flirt with a prince for two months and not contemplate what it would be like to see his face over the breakfast table for the rest of her days. And if the prince was Augustus, it was hard to avoid the sinking feeling that accompanied that particular vision.

"You have!" he said, laughing. "You're as much a lone wolf as I am."

Linnet shook her head. "I'm not. I do want to marry. I also want to fall in love, though I realize the two are not necessarily compatible."

He snorted. "You're a romantic, even if you do seem to be contemplating adultery without turning a hair."

"I read too many novels not to be."

"Novels have nothing to do with real life."

"They are better than real life," Linnet stated. "There's a great deal of pleasure in seeing bad people receive their just desserts."

"Why don't you come sit beside me? That

bedpost looks very uncomfortable, whereas the headboard makes a decent chairback."

It was uncomfortable, actually. But . . . she eyed him.

"The storm isn't letting up," he pointed out. "We're stuck here for at least a couple more hours. Besides, there are some interesting gaps in your knowledge of real life that we could discuss. I've always wanted to chat with an adulterous woman. By the time they get to me, they're generally riddled with syphilis and don't feel like gossiping about their trollopy pasts."

"I'm not adulterous, given that I'm not even married. Though I might as well point out that in real life, I would be compromised by this storm, and we would have to marry," Linnet said, scrambling to the head of the bed and sitting down next to him.

"Don't give up hope," he said amiably. "A dukedom is still within your reach. Just not my dukedom, since there's no one in Wales who gives a damn what we get up to. My father is probably back in the castle praying for a miracle. Yours is back in London, thinking you're a countess, well on your way to duchess."

"What sort of miracle does your father want?" Linnet inquired.

"Oh, that the past never happened. That

my mother would forgive him. That my injury will disappear."

She nodded. "He's desperately sad."

"No grandchild," Piers said. "Very disappointing."

Linnet elbowed him. "Don't be so tiresome. You know as well as I do that your father is no monster. It's stupid of you to keep pretending he is."

"Aren't you going to say childish?"

"You don't mind being childish," she observed. "But I would guess that you dislike being told that you're not using your brains. You're too observant not to see his pain."

"Well, if you put it like that . . ."

"I do put it like that. He's in pain because he loves you and your mother."

"Now you're beating the dead horse," Piers said, mildly enough. "I'll give the old bastard a kiss, will that do?"

She turned to smile at him.

"No!" he said, shuddering and throwing his arm over his face. "Don't try to poison my will with that grimace of yours. Aristotle believed in free will and so do I!"

Linnet broke out laughing and pulled down his arm. "Here." She let the smile spread over her entire face. "Are you mine to command, now?"

266

"Oh dear," he said mockingly, "it didn't work that time. Maybe you're losing your touch." With one swift movement he swung over her.

Linnet's mouth fell open. Suddenly she was flat on her back, her hands caught in his above her head.

"Give me another smile; let's see if the magic is slow to take, or whether I'm impervious," he said. His words were mocking, but there was a caress in them, a rough, insolent caress.

She gave him a smile. But it wasn't the family smile. It came from a different place altogether: a hungry place, a longing, fierce, desiring place.

He said nothing.

She could feel every inch of his muscled body on hers. "Mine to command?"

"Not quite," he said, staring down at her. "But damn . . . you're good."

Linnet opened her mouth and ran her tongue delicately over her bottom lip. "I like to kiss you."

She could feel his deep, shuddering breath.

"And I would rather like to kiss your leg," she said, wondering in some part of her mind whether she'd gone mad.

"You —" he said.

"Yes?"

"You will do anything to win, won't you?"

She grinned at that. "I'm very competitive. Did you think you were the only one?"

"Not anymore," he muttered and then finally, finally, bent his head to hers.

A trace of brine lingered on his lips. And his kiss was pure Piers: rough and demanding, without a trace of civility. Linnet felt as if she were the slave girl again, lying at the feet of her master. No, not at his feet, since her whole body was thrilling to the weight of him.

Lying under her master, submitting to his —

"Bloody hell," Piers said, lifting his mouth and glaring at her. "Why do I feel as if I'm making love to a rag doll here? You seemed to know how to kiss yesterday."

She pulled her hands free and wrapped her arms around his neck. "We're not making love."

"Right. Let's go back to my initial comment, stripped of the love part. Why am I bothering to kiss a limp —"

She stifled a groan. "Shut up, Piers."

Their eyes met for a single, electric moment. Then his eyes darkened, and his mouth took hers again.

She tossed the slave girl idea, and just

268

concentrated on the way he tasted: hot and male. The feeling of hard body lying on top of her. The way he was devouring her, the way she was kissing him back.

Kissing him made her body melt under his, and her hands move down his back, tracing his muscles, the way his back curved to his waist, stopping short at the tablecloth.

He was nudging his leg forward, between her legs, and the shirt — what happened to her shirt? It must have . . .

Piers broke free of her mouth and trailed his lips in a burning caress across the line of her jaw.

Linnet looked blindly at the ceiling, her senses flooded by the touch and smell of him. He was pushing the shirt even higher, which meant that she could feel more of him, more hot skin against hers.

His head dipped lower, and a groan tore from his chest. "Damn, Linnet, you have the sweetest breasts I've ever —"

She didn't hear what he said because he had her breast in his hand, and his mouth on her nipple. It felt lovely, intoxicating and — he suckled. She gasped. Or perhaps screamed. Or that was too hoarse for a scream. She shouldn't be making noises like that, she should —

"Stop it," he said, raising his head, rearing

269

over her and looking down into her eyes.

"Don't stop," she begged.

"You started thinking again. You went all rigid."

"No." She drew her fingers over his chest, just as she'd imagined, over the broad muscles, and the flat bronze nipples. "You're beautiful."

"And you're cracked if you think so," he said flatly. Her fingers brushed over one of his nipples, and a ragged sound came from his throat. She did it again, more firmly. His neck dropped back, which gave her room to slide down and put her mouth where her fingers had been.

She could feel him shaking, so she tried this and that . . . licking, even a little bite. Anything that got him to throb against her. Half her mind was on him, and half was on the way she felt every time he bucked against her.

"Enough," he said, rolling off her onto his back and bringing her with him.

"Your leg!" she gasped. "I'm sorry, I —"

He thrust a knee between her legs. The words died in her mouth. Every sensation in her body focused on the sweet spot between her legs. "Oh," she moaned. "Please . . ."

Dimly she heard him chuckle, but his lips

were on her nipple again, feasting, licking, tasting. Moving to the other nipple, suckling there until she was pulsing against his leg, crying out.

She braced herself against his shoulders, eyes closed.

"Want to come?" he said, his voice raspy and low.

His thumb rubbed across her nipple again, and she moaned.

"I think I could make you come just from this," he said.

Linnet caught his voice, the detached, physician tone, and knew what he was doing. She leaned over and bit his lip. "You're being an idiot again."

"Why?" He played with her breasts, making her shake.

"Observing," she gasped. "You do it when you're uncomfortable. Oh!"

"I'm not uncomfortable. Neither are you." A hand slid down her stomach to between her legs. He nudged her backward. "Though I think I could make you a good deal more comfortable."

Linnet's mouth fell open, but nothing came out. She quivered all over. "More comfortable on your back," he said, flipping her over as easily as if she were a pancake. "More comfortable, if I kiss you here —"

271

He put his mouth to her breast "— while I touch you *here.*" His fingers dipped back between her legs, coaxing, caressing.

Linnet didn't know whether he was observing her. She hardly noticed when his mouth left her breast and trailed down her stomach. What he was doing with his hand was making her twist, her hips bucking against his fingers, hoarse moans flying from her lips.

But then he pushed her legs wider.

She raised her head, dazed, to see his dark head between her legs. "What are you doing?" she cried, trying to push herself away. "That's — what — stop it!"

Too late. His lips turned to the sweet curve of her inner thigh. A tongue trailed delicately, closer and closer.

"You smell so good," he said dreamily. "Essence of Linnet along with a touch of the ocean. And you taste . . . ."

She gasped.

"You taste like the sweetest honey." He turned back to what he was doing. He shoved her knees up, and his tongue claimed her, took her, threw her into the fire. Her head turned from side to side, and she strained against him, crying out, over and over, with each soft stroke.

A finger thrust inside her, and she broke,

screaming so loud that she heard only the sound of her own pleasure, rather than the wind.

Then she heard the wind again, but also the whisper of Piers's voice as he kissed her, very gently. "Oh so delicate," he said, crooning. "Such good working order."

"You're diagnosing me!" she said, managing to pry her head off the pillow so she could look down at him.

He looked up at her, the devil in his eyes. "I'm diagnosing the pinkest —" he dropped another kiss, and she quivered again — "sweetest" — another kiss — "most delectable part of Linnet."

EIGHTEEN

Linnet scooted backward, pushing herself up against the headboard. Piers let his hands fall away from her legs, and she pulled her knees together, against her chest, reflexively thinking to cover her most intimate parts.

She could hardly believe that she had allowed such a thing to happen. Her stomach was curdling with embarrassment. "That was very improper," she stated, apportioning some of the blame to him. "I'm sure that people don't — where did you learn to do such a thing?"

"How would you know what people do or don't do?" Piers rolled over on his side and propped his head up on one hand. "As a doctor, I can tell you that they get up to all sorts of things that you and I haven't tried yet. Has anyone ever instructed you as regards the proprieties and improprieties of the bedchamber?"

She shook her head.

"I thought not," he said with satisfaction. "Given that there are some obvious holes in your education."

"What do you mean?" Against all common sense, her body was still quivering.

"Do you know what just happened to you?"

Laughter escaped from her mouth before she could stop it.

"I'll take that as a yes," he said. "Well, the first rule is that nothing is improper between lovers."

"You sound as if you're instructing the Ducklings," she objected. "I've heard you haranguing them with questions that were meant to trap them into foolish answers."

"Trust me, I'd never consider lecturing them on intimate matters. For one thing, they have far more chest hair than I like in my partners."

Linnet wrapped her arms around her knees. "You're absurd."

"Not as absurd as the fact that you are a young woman who knows nothing of the reproductive system."

She couldn't argue with that.

"I suppose your mother died before she could get around to explaining the basics."

"I know the basics," she protested.

"Oh? Then why did you think that men hang down in the front? Just how would that work? Like stuffing a sausage?"

"A minor error," she said, her eyes sliding to that part of him. The tablecloth had long ago given up the fight. "My mother was obviously speaking metaphorically."

"This" — he said, running his hand down himself — "is an erection. And I, by the way, am not incapable, as you should have known the moment you saw me standing up rather than flopping around."

Linnet's throat tightened. She would rather like to touch him that way herself.

"A man gets an erection only when he would like to bed a woman. If not, he hangs."

"Oh. My mother was correct, then. Can you make yours hang, so I see what it looks like?"

He ran a slow hand over himself again. "No. Impossible."

"It's not within your control?"

"Not at the moment, and rarely around you, to my surprise."

Linnet felt a little better hearing that.

"In case you're wondering, I'm no virgin," he said, conversationally. "Not that I would say I've made love to a woman. I've been with one, or two, or more. But obviously, you *are* a virgin, and a remarkably unin-formed one. Why don't you tell what you think the basics are," he said, his eyes provocative, "and I'll correct your inaccura-cies."

"So you can shout at me the way you shout at the Ducklings when they guess something wrong?" She shook her head. "No."

"Do you want to skip the lecture and go straight to the demonstration? I'm touching myself." Instinctively her eyes returned to his hand and what it was doing. "I could use some help."

"I truly believed that you were incapable," she whispered. "I thought you couldn't do this."

"Think about it," he said. "I suspect you have enough knowledge to know exactly what I would like to do with the tool at my disposal. It's in functioning order."

She took a deep breath, still watching his hand. "You might not fit," she pointed out. "I would say not, myself."

"I would say yes, myself," he retorted.

"But I thought you, that is, your father told me . . . Is it just that you can't sire children?"

"You've asked me one or twice how I injured my leg," he said, watching her. His eyes were as dark as the blackest velvet.

"I've asked three times," she corrected him. "Maybe four."

"One day my father was in a euphoric state due to opium intoxication. I entered the room — I was six years old — and he thought that I was a fiend come to do whatever it is devils do. Steal his soul by various nefarious means."

"He thought *you* were a devil? At age six?"

"Bizarre, isn't it? Any number of people might agree with him now, but I assure you that I was quite pretty at that age, without a hint of sulfur about me. Though apparently I was the right size for a smallish devil, to my everlasting regret. At any rate, he hurled me into the fireplace, thereby protecting his soul. I suppose I should be glad that he's such a devout Christian."

Linnet gasped, her hand flying to her mouth.

"Happily, it was unlit, but there was a pair of forged andirons, one of which gave me this lovely memento of the occasion."

She scrambled to his side. "That's horrifying. You must have been so terrified and hurt. How awful for you. For both of you, actually."

"I don't remember much," Piers said. "Flying through the air, some pain. But the aftermath . . . I remember that. Because the pain just wouldn't go away."

"So your mother took you to France."

"Followed by Bavaria. Better doctors there. Still, no one could understand why the leg didn't heal. It didn't. And it won't. While we were gone, my father instituted divorce proceedings. It cost him a good quarter of my inheritance to have his wife — my mother — legally declared a degenerate."

"He wasn't himself," Linnet said, stroking his leg with her fingers again. Her fingers slipped over the ravaged skin. "As a doctor, you know that."

"As a son —" He shook his head.

"And so you told him that you were incapable! Because he's so proud of his family history. You knew precisely what would hurt him the most, the idea that he himself was the cause of his line dying out."

"It doesn't sound like a very intelligent thing to have done, now you say it." His hand was on her leg too, tracing fiery little circles on her thigh. "I might have to consider reconciliation."

"I think you should."

"This was all just to say that I'm not really incapable. I hope you'll forgive me if I don't break into snuffling tears and dash off to

279

comfort Papa this very moment."

Linnet concentrated on his leg, her fingers moving from the scar to skin that was roughened with hair and stretched taut over muscle. She didn't look at his face. "We agreed to end our betrothal, such as it was."

He nodded. "That means that you should make up your mind about what we do here. I have nothing to lose, whereas your virginity hangs in the balance."

That was so characteristic of Piers. Another man might lie to her, or finesse the fact that he wanted to sleep with her, yet not to marry her. Not Piers.

"What would you say if I refused?" Her fingers spread over the roped muscle of his thigh, and she knew already that she wouldn't refuse. This might be her only chance to make love to someone she truly desired.

He shrugged. "You're an intelligent woman. You have a commodity that is extremely valuable on the open market, doubly so because of your beauty. Why on earth *would* you give it to me, for free?"

"You make it sound as if I'm for sale to the highest bidder."

He was silent.

"Well, I may have been for sale to the highest bidder," she said, "but the bidding dropped because everyone believes that I no longer own this oh-so-valuable commodity of mine."

Still, Piers said nothing.

"If I choose to give it to you, can you guarantee that no child will result?"

"No," he said. "This house doesn't have all the amenities one might desire."

There was a thread of amusement in his voice that woke a smile in her eyes. "What if there is a child?"

"We'll marry," he stated.

She nodded, feeling terribly shy.

Piers pulled her down onto his chest. "I think we should investigate exactly what we're proposing to do." His lips settled on hers, aggressive and delicious. "After all," she heard him say a few moments later, his voice muffled by the way his lips were skating over her skin, "where there is a chance of marriage, one must proceed with care. Deliberation. Make absolutely sure that neither of us has the slightest qualm."

She arched against him, not interested in careful thought. She couldn't even concentrate on touching all that skin she had been furtively ogling. She felt inebriated, drunk, as if brandy were pouring through her veins and pooling between her thighs.

She wanted *more.*

In fact, the only thing she was really interested in was pressed against her thigh. Piers was still talking, in that sardonic kind of way that she found irritating. So she slipped her hand down by her leg and grabbed.

He went abruptly silent. He felt hot and smooth in her palm, pulsing with life, and far too large.

He eased back. "You're holding me like a prize cucumber that you're planning to pick." But something in his voice indicated that he wasn't as blasé as he sounded.

She let her fingers ease, slide up and down, the way he had been doing. A broken moan came from his lips. It was fascinating the way his skin moved . . . her fingers tightened again. Piers's head fell back.

He was soft and hard at the same time, an odd combination that her body understood better than she did. She curled her fingers more tightly and stroked him again. The feeling of it made her shudder, and the breath caught in his throat, emerging in a strangled moan.

Desire lanced through her again, making her breathless, exhilarated. "I think this will suffice," she whispered, letting him go and pulling his body toward her. "I have no doubts."

"Suffice?" He was laughing again, but she was too busy tasting his neck, running her tongue up that strong column, and incidentally, bumping her hips against his.

"Come on," she said, trying to pull him on top of her.

"We should be slow," he whispered, his tongue sliding across her lips while his fingers did the same thing below. "You're a virgin. You may well have an impediment inside. You must have heard about the pain caused by losing one's virginity."

Linnet hardly heard him, so entranced was she by how he was stroking her. Still, what she wanted wasn't strokes or caresses or even sweet kisses. So she pulled hard at his shoulders. *"Now,"* she said fiercely.

She felt him *there,* and arched toward him instinctively.

"Slow," he whispered.

She didn't want slow. She felt a deep hunger for heat, and rush, and possession. The feeling was so intense that she couldn't find words, just sobbed once, against his shoulders.

He knew . . . somehow he knew what she was thinking. A strong hand lifted her hip higher, fingers biting into her curves, and then he said into her curls, "You're sure?"

Linnet didn't bother answering, just

283

growled in his ear as if she'd lost the ability to speak.

Apparently he knew how to interpret that because he came to her, in a smooth ferocious rush, with a twist of his hips and a lunge.

"Pain?" he said a second later, his lips on her cheeks.

It wasn't pain. She felt stretched, occupied, possessed . . . delirious.

Linnet arched her hips, took him deeper. "Could you —" She lost her breath as he shifted, sending cascades of fiery sensation down her legs.

"I can stop," Piers gasped. "Wait for you to adjust. Your body will accommodate me, if you give it a moment." His voice was deeper than she'd ever heard it.

Linnet hardly heard him. She was arching again, trying to get back the sensation, the fire. It felt good but . . . She clutched his shoulders. "Is that it?" Then she realized how her comment sounded. "It's very nice. Really. Very —" Her voice cut off when his hips shifted.

He was laughing again, a kind of deep, breathless laughter. His elbows were just by her ear so she could feel his body shaking . . . She opened her eyes and stared at him, annoyed.

"I don't think laughing is appropriate."

"Mmmmm," he said, reaching down and nipping her lip. The motion of his body made another ripple of sensation spread from her middle to the very ends of her toes. Her eyes started to close again.

"Are you feeling comfortable?" he asked her.

Really, was this all there was? She was comfortable. This couldn't be all there was.

"Quite comfortable," she said, tilting her neck to kiss his chin.

"In that case, do you suppose I could start to move?"

"Move? Move where?" Instinctively she clutched his shoulders. She might be slightly disappointed by the act, but she definitely didn't want him to go anywhere. "Is it over already?"

He dropped his head into the curve of her shoulder, but she could hear the snort of laughter.

"Stop laughing at me!" she ordered, thinking that maybe she would just shove him off, before he had a chance to leave. That would show him. She pulled up her knees, bracing her feet on the bed, and the breath caught in her throat. Pleasure spread out like slow liquid ripples, right down her legs.

Piers's breath sounded harsh in her ears.

Without another word, he reached back and pushed her left knee up.

"Oh," she breathed, understanding his silent command and winding her legs around his hips. It brought the two of them closer, shifted him somehow so he was even deeper inside her. She liked it. Even more after she wiggled a little, adjusting so that they were a perfect fit.

"This is very nice," she said, kissing his chin. "I like it."

"I'm going to have to move now," he said, between clenched teeth. "The pause for virgin accommodation is over."

"All right," she said, disappointed, letting her legs uncurl. It felt so good. She was throbbing all over.

He pulled back. The sense of loss was dizzying. Her flesh instinctively clung to him, mourning. And then he thrust forward again.

A sob flew from her lips, and her legs flew back around his hips. Her body arched to meet his. "What —" she managed.

He didn't answer. Instead he pulled back to thrust, and thrust again.

Linnet clung to him as if she were a limpet and he a rock, letting the wild pleasure of his ride echo through every bone in her body.

She could hear herself whimper, hear the harsh sound of Piers's breath in her ear. Slowly, slowly, a sort of incandescent heat was building in her body, making her toes curl and her fingernails dig into his shoulders.

"Linnet," Piers growled, pausing. His voice sounded so unlike himself, his controlled, observant self, that she pulled him even closer, dropping kisses on his shoulder, his neck, his chin.

"We need to —"

"What?" she asked, startled out of her daze. "Am I doing it right? Should I be doing something else? Shall I —"

"Shut up," he said in her ear.

That wasn't very nice. Linnet would have felt annoyed, but at that moment he slid a hand between them, right to the part where they were joined, and touched her there. One slow rub of his thumb, and her body reacted like a bonfire doused in brandy.

A strangled cry burst from her lips. The feeling of him, thick and hot and possessive, felt like a fever in her blood.

A satisfied rumble burst from his lips and he thrust again. She saw stars, literal stars. Whatever he was doing with his hand, combined with the delicious friction, made the fever burst through her body.

"Piers!" she cried. "Piers!"

He let go of any semblance of control, pounding into her with such force that the sound of the bed thumping the wall rivaled the beating hail.

Heat exploded in her body, and she fell into a pleasure so vivid and fierce that she could never have imagined such a thing. She couldn't see, nor hear, only feel as her body went liquid, relaxing into a delirious kind of spasming heat that burned through her blood.

Vaguely she heard a strangled groan, an animal hoarseness, and opened her eyes blurrily to see Piers's head arch backward as he pulsed into her one last time.

The look on his face, the total abandonment, total pleasure, set off another cascade of red-hot sparks through her body, making her clench at the very moment he shouted, literally shouted.

And collapsed on top of her.

NINETEEN

Later in the afternoon

"Lady Bernaise retired with a headache; the duke is playing chess with the marquis," Prufrock said, walking up the stairs backward before Piers. "I put a new patient in a room by himself; the Ducklings are with him."

Piers raised an eyebrow. *"Ducklings?* She's contaminated you."

Prufrock had a trick of appearing perfectly innocent when he wished to.

"Where's Nurse Matilda?" Piers demanded.

"In the morning room, with Miss Thrynne," Prufrock said. "As you requested, the young lady is reviewing Mrs. Havelock's responsibilities regarding the patients. When I saw them last, it didn't seem to be going smoothly."

Piers hesitated for a moment and then mentally shrugged. What did it really mat-

289

ter? As soon as Linnet left, he could let his housekeeper go back to her obstinate ways. Patients had their families with them, or they didn't. They still died, unless he and Sébastien could figure out some way to keep them going for a while.

He entered the small room they used to isolate new patients until he determined their illness. *If* he determined their illness.

The Ducklings — damn it, he was taking on Linnet's name for them — were clustered around the bed, arguing.

He whacked his cane against the bedpost and they fell silent. "Bitts, who is the patient?"

Bitts pulled himself upright. "Mr. Juggs is a sixty-eight-year-old publican from London."

"Sixty-eight?" Piers demanded, pushing Kibbles out of the way so he could consider the man himself. "You've had a good run at the pub; leave a few beers for the rest of us. Why don't you close down your taps and go peacefully?"

The patient was tubby and bald, but for an extraordinary pair of eyebrows, so untamed that they looked ready to jump from his face. "Bunkum!" he said with a splendid cockney accent. "My father lived to ninety-two, and I've got no plans to be put to bed

290

with a shovel any earlier than me da. If you're as good as they say, that is."

"Well, I'm not," Piers said. "Symptoms, Bitts?"

"He can't hear."

"Nonsense," Piers said. "He just treated me to *bunkum.* I'm hoping for *burn my breeches* next. Did you spend time in the navy, Juggs?"

"Twelve years as a corporal in the Fourteenth Light Dragoons. I can't hear all the time. I hear fine, and then it goes away, like it fades."

"Old age," Piers said. "Tip him out of that bed and give it to someone else."

"And sometimes it happens with my sight too. It just fades out," Juggs added. "Comes back, though."

"Not old age. So, Bitts, what do you have to say for yourself?"

"His lungs sound clear. I used the acoustic method we've been practicing. His limbs are strong, and his reflexes are normal."

"Anything to add, you two?" Piers asked Penders and Kibbles.

"He's lost his vision three times," Kibbles said. "While watching the entry of the King of Norway into London, during his wife's sixtieth birthday party, and at a military review. Those occasions seem indicative."

"Tsk, tsk," Piers said. "You married a younger woman. Cradle robber."

"Only by eight years," Juggs said defensively.

"What's your diagnosis?" Piers asked Kibbles.

"Based on the three occasions in question, overexcitement leading to a rapid heartbeat."

"Since when does a rapid heartbeat cause loss of vision?" Penders put in. "I think he experienced heart stoppage."

"A heart attack doesn't cause loss of vision," Bitts objected.

"It does if he suffered a temporary loss of blood to the head," Penders retorted. "Were you dizzy during those episodes, Mr. Juggs?"

He shook his head. "Awful hot, though."

The door opened behind Piers. He knew it was Linnet before she entered because he smelled her, a light flowery scent with a hint of lemon. He started wondering whether the olfactory nerves are heightened by sexual arousal.

Nurse Matilda's charming tones snapped him back to the present. "Doctor, I am deeply offended by what has occurred today, apparently with your permission, if not encouragement. Deeply offended. And while I'm sorry to interrupt you, this cannot wait."

"The patient experienced a possible fever during the episodes in which he lost his vision. What does that tell us?" Piers asked the Ducklings. Then he turned, reluctantly.

The truth was that Linnet was terrifyingly beautiful. Perfect lips, perfect cheeks, perfect . . .

A perfect secret smile in her perfect eyes.

It was irritating.

He bit back an answering smile. "What the hell are you up to?" he asked her.

The smile faded. "I am questioning the housekeeper of the west wing — that would be this wing — about her procedures for patient care, including diet and family visits."

"Right," he said. He nodded at Nurse Matilda. "That's what she's doing. Your role is to answer, insofar as you're the housekeeper in question."

Nurse Matilda's chest swelled in an impressive way, rather like that of a toad on a sturdy lily pad, preparing to sing. "I am grossly insulted by the tone of these impertinent inquiries. If you have concerns about my housekeeping and care of the patients, you should consult me directly."

Piers turned back to the Ducklings. "Temporary vision loss, ditto hearing, possible fever. What other questions have you asked?"

The Ducklings were silent.

"I gather, none," he said. "You, in the bed. You weren't dizzy. Did anyone mention whether you turned red in the face?"

Juggs shook his head.

"Did you feel weak in the knees? Hot and then cold?"

"Just hot. Well, and I spewed some of those times."

"You didn't think to mention that? Anything else you're not telling us?"

"My wife says that I was on the toodle. But I wasn't." Juggs frowned so that his eyebrows joined in the middle, an interesting look, though unlikely to be taken up by dandies, in Piers's opinion. "I've owned the Mermaid's Ankle for twenty years and I know when a man is three sheets to the wind. I wasn't."

"Drunkards are usually the last to realize," Piers told him. "In fact, most of them only admit inebriation the morning after. You of all people should know that." He turned back to Nurse Matilda. "Just what has you so excited, in fewer than five words? I take it Miss Thrynne's questions don't please you."

Her chest swelled again. "This young lady

has no idea of nursing care whatsoever. She implied that I was cruel —"

"*Inhumane* was the word I used," Linnet put in. She had that smile going again, and all the Ducklings were melting on the spot. Even Juggs was hanging over the side of the bed, the better to see her.

"Because I tell the patients once they're here, there'll be no visitors," Nurse Matilda said firmly. "You know as well as I do, Lord Marchant, that there's many of our patients that never leave. I can't be dealing with weeping and such like. The family can make their good-byes just as easy when they leave the patient here. There's no reason to prolong the pain of it."

"So it's really in their best interests." Linnet frowned, but Piers ignored her. "Did you give this speech to Mrs. Juggs?"

Nurse Matilda nodded. "I did indeed." She flashed Linnet a look of profound dislike. "Unfortunately, this young lady countermanded my orders and sent the woman down to the kitchens, where she is just causing extra work and bother, no doubt."

"Which means we can request that she come upstairs and explain exactly how Mr. Juggs looked on the pertinent occasions," Linnet put in. "Mrs. Havelock, why don't you fetch her?"

Interestingly, though Linnet weighed at least three stone less than the housekeeper, there just must be something about her, because Nurse Matilda stamped from the room.

"By Jaysus, I wouldn't want to be on the wrong side of your housekeeper," Juggs observed. He cast Linnet a worshipful glance. "It's right kind, what you've done. My missus would feel terrible, driving off and leaving me here. She'd worry herself half to death."

"It's the smile, isn't it?" Piers said to Linnet.

"My smile had no effect whatsoever on Mrs. Havelock," she said. "How long have you been married, Mr. Juggs?"

"Going on twenty-four years," Juggs said. "First time I had this happen to me was our twentieth wedding anniversary."

"You didn't mention that before," Bitts pointed out, scribbling it down. "That's four occasions, now."

"Maybe there were a few more," Juggs admitted. "It took me a while to get up the steam to see a doctor in the first place. It's really the missus that did the worrying."

The door opened again, and an infuriated Nurse Matilda swept back in, followed by a round, anxious-looking woman wearing a bonnet covered with cherries that appeared to have been fabricated from knobbly wool.

"What did your husband look like during these attacks?" Piers asked, not bothering with greetings.

She blinked at him. "He looked the same as usual, I reckon."

"Red in the face?"

"Not more than usual when he's drunk."

"I'm never drunk," Juggs shouted from the bed.

"You was." She nodded her head so vigorously that a whole bunch of cherries rose lightly in the air and then subsided. "As you will get when it's a special occasion, and don't deny it, Mr. Juggs."

"That time in York, I hadn't had more than a pint," the patient said triumphantly.

"You was slurring your words," his wife said, moving over to pat his foot. "There's nothing wrong with a pint or two, but it takes more than that to jumble your tongue. This last time in York was the straw that broke the camel's back," she told Piers, but somehow talking to Linnet at the same time. "He had promised me before as how he'd see a doctor iffen it happened again."

"Blow my dickey," Juggs said with frustration. "I wasn't drinking near as much as I could have!"

"What sort of occasion was it?" Linnet asked. "Were you wearing that utterly captivating bonnet, Mrs. Juggs?"

Mrs. Juggs beamed. "I was, that I was. Well, it was the military parade, wasn't it? And there was Mr. Juggs dressed in his uniform, though it is a bit small these days. But he always likes to wear it of a special occasion. I made this hat just for the day, even though it were already summer and hot for it."

"I expect Juggs here was sweating to beat the band," Piers said.

"Oh, no, he never sweats, Mr. Juggs doesn't," his wife said proudly. "I hardly ever have to wash his uniform a-cause of sweat, which is a blessing. His mates in the parade, they were all mopping themselves dry."

"And then I went blind and couldn't see a thing until the next morning," Juggs said mournfully.

"Our preacher suggested it's the wages of sin," Mrs. Juggs offered.

"That's when I said I'd go to the doctor. 'Cause I ain't been sinning more than is strictly normal."

"Well, Bitts? Kibbles? Penders? I think it's quite clear what has happened to Juggs, don't you think?" Piers waved his hand at

298

their blank faces. "Confer amongst your-selves, you blithering idiots."

He turned back to Nurse Matilda. Linnet was examining the fruits of Mrs. Juggs's crochet hook. "You just lost the battle," he told her. "Mrs. Juggs solved the problem of her husband's blindness. I'm an idiot not to have insisted on seeing family in cases like this."

Mrs. Juggs's mouth fell open. "I did? It's the drink, isn't it?"

"No," he said to her.

Nurse Matilda was hissing like a teakettle on the boil.

"What symptom was the most impor-tant?" Linnet asked curiously.

"They all are." He caught the Ducklings' eyes. "Juggs has lately gained weight, his uniform is uncomfortably tight, he suffers episodes only on celebratory occasions dur-ing which he feels hot and drinks ale — likely to cool himself, though he ends up vomiting. Add to that the fact that the dress uniform of the Light Brigade is heavy wool, with triple braiding at the shoulder, not to mention the truly crucial detail that Juggs cannot sweat."

"Heatstroke!" Kibbles exclaimed, while Penders and Bitts were still thinking it through.

"Right. The good news, Juggs, is that you can hop out of this bed and go back to the Mermaid's Ankle. The bad news is that an inability to sweat, a woolen uniform, and a hot day are a dangerous combination. You're likely to die one of these times, and you're damned lucky you're not already planted."

"But what happened?" Mrs. Juggs asked, bewildered. "It wasn't all *that* hot."

"He needs to drink more water," Kibbles explained.

"And no ale if it's sweltering out," Piers ordered. "Not even one pint."

"That was it, that was all it was? Just not drinking enough water?" Mrs. Juggs still looked confused, but Juggs swung his legs out of bed.

"I knew I wasn't sick, not really." He stood up. "I stay away from water if we're going in the parade, being as there's no place to piss without breaking ranks."

"Adding to the problem," Bitts said, scribbling madly.

Piers let Juggs and the missus leave with the Ducklings. "Mrs. Havelock, you can decide whether you want to go along with Miss Thrynne's plans for my hospital, or you can find another position."

She looked at him, her mouth so tightly

shut that it looked like Sébastien's suture work.

"Scratch that," he said. "You're sacked." He took Linnet's arm and led her out of the room, but she stopped in the corridor, holding him back until the nurse stamped into the corridor.

"His lordship was only jesting," she told Nurse Matilda, giving her the smile that supposedly didn't work on outraged house-keepers.

Piers opened his mouth, but she pinched him so sharply that he shut it again.

"We can discuss how to manage family visits tomorrow," Linnet said. "Of course, we'll have to figure out a way to disrupt your schedule as little as possible. I know how smoothly you run the wing, Mrs. Havelock."

The smile clearly didn't work on Matilda. Still, she froze there for a moment, obviously calculating whether to give in or not.

"I know the doctor's humorous ways," she finally said, heavily.

"Good day, Mrs. Havelock," Linnet said, pulling Piers down the corridor.

Twenty

"You're an interfering little witch," Piers said. "Wait a moment. My leg is aching." He pushed open a door. "Look at this! An empty bed just waiting for a patient." He limped in. "Perfect place to sit down and rest our weary limbs."

Linnet leaned against the door frame, laughing.

"Big enough for two," Piers said, making sure his tone wasn't overly hopeful. "Or are you too sore?"

She scowled at him. "That's none of your business."

"Of course it's my business. Here, come in and close the door. We don't want to give poor Nurse Matilda any more shocks than she's already been dealt in one day."

Linnet walked in and closed the door. But she made no move to climb on the bed with him. "Come on, then," he said, patting the bed. "Time for a private consult with your favorite doctor. Come tell me all about that nasty raw feeling caused by that seducing devil who took advantage of you."

She laughed. "And I have to get on the bed to tell you about it?"

"How am I going to ascertain the injury until I do an examination?" he asked reasonably. "A close examination."

"It doesn't hurt that much. Besides, we can't do that again."

"Why not?" He held out his cane toward her. "Will you take that for me?"

She stepped forward and took the end of it, whereupon he jerked backward, reeling her in like a fish on a line. Linnet fell on top of him in a fluttering soft bundle of sweet-scented womanhood.

Piers's arms tightened. "Damn, you smell good."

"You smell like soap," she said, sniffing. "Unpleasant soap."

"Castor soap. We're trying to cut down on hospital fever."

"What on earth is that?"

"Fevers go around hospitals, and kill patients who weren't even in line for a coffin," he said, nuzzling her hair until he found a delicately shaped little ear. "This castle's perfect because it's got so damn many rooms that we can just stow most of the patients by themselves until their fever breaks."

"I'd like to hire some village women to come in and read to the patients who are awake and not infectious," Linnet said.

"Village women and reading. I see a problem there."

"A village woman who knows how to read," she said, not all that patiently. "I'm sure there are some. And another woman or two to entertain the children and perhaps work on teaching them to read."

"Entertain? This is a hospital, or next thing to it. We're not playing host to a traveling show."

"The patients will get better sooner if they have something to think about. Why, look at Gavan."

She shut her mouth, but Piers caught a tone in her voice that made him give her ear a little nip. "What are you up to?"

"Nothing. Gavan walked up and down the stables five times after luncheon. His leg is much stronger."

Piers thought about her voice while he ran a hand over her truly magnificent bosom. "Are you sore?"

"Yes," she said, a bit shyly, pink climbing in her cheeks.

"Want me to take a look and make sure

it's all in working order? It would be my pleasure." And he meant it. Just in case she said yes, he kissed his way down her neck and onto the curve of her breast. Closer to the site of the problem, as it were.

"No," she said, her voice sounding pretty definite.

But her hands were on his chest too, gliding over his shirt. He reached down and wrenched his shirt from his breeches to give her better access.

She pulled up his shirt with a charmingly greedy look. Then her fingers were running over his chest, leaving little trails of fire in their wake. Piers rolled to the side to let her explore as she would.

Linnet bent her head delicately, politely, as if she were a long-necked heron considering something in the water.

"Please," he said, watching her, and was almost ashamed at the husky, needy tone in his voice. But not quite.

And particularly not after a small pink tongue curled over his nipple. A hoarse grunt escaped his lips. "Why do you have your eyes shut?" he made himself ask, forcing himself to think sensibly.

"You taste wonderful," she said dreamily. "And you smell so good, just a little salty still, but like soap — not that awful soap,

305

nice soap." Small white teeth closed, nipped him, and his body instinctively arched toward hers, begging for what it could not have.

She was kissing lower now, on his belly, on the soft parts of his skin that no one had ever paid attention to before. Piers closed his eyes only to have them fly open when she said, "Hadn't you better take off your breeches?"

He raised his head. "Take them off? We can't do anything serious, Linnet. Your poor little twat cannot take another intrusion from —"

"This?" she said, stroking along it. "I'd just like to see it. Properly, I mean. If you have time."

"Time?" he repeated, hardly believing his own ears. "I think, yes, I have time. Though perhaps we should put the latch on the door."

So she got up and put the latch on the door, which meant that he noticed that her cheeks had gone a lovely rose color, and her eyes were sultry and a little wild. Her lust was like tinder to his, and he could hardly manage to shove down his breeches and smalls . . . but he did.

And lay back on the bed to see what she would do.

What she did . . .

She knelt and then relaxed onto her side, her lovely curves just before him, the straight line of her backbone going down to the curve of her hips, her arse.

"Globes," he said, his hand running down to her hips and then behind. "Another word for buttocks. A more poetic one, perhaps." His fingers were trembling.

Linnet had just been looking, but now she reached out and curled her fingers around him.

The sound that came from his lips was undignified to say the least. It was a carnal sound, and he thought Linnet's face turned a little pinker. Fighting not to simply lie back and let her do her will, he ran his hand more firmly into the curve of her bottom, around the most delicious curve of all, between her legs.

She flinched.

"Very sore," he said, withdrawing his hand. "I do apologize."

Linnet's eyes glinted with amusement. "But you wouldn't take it back?"

Take back the most ecstatic sexual experience of his life, not to put too fine a point on it? "Never."

She seemed to like that answer, since she shifted down in the bed, her head dipped, and her tongue touched him.

His head fell back at the sweep of it, the liquid, hot touch of her. Still . . . "Linnet," he managed.

"Yes?" She was looking at him consideringly. He wrenched his mind away from the possibilities she might be considering.

Cleared his throat. "I feel bound to mention . . ."

She bent forward, licked him again, and then her lips slipped around him like wet silk.

A hoarse cry tore from his throat.

"Yes?" she asked, looking up at him. Her eyes were bright with mischief, and dark with desire . . . She was the very picture of trouble.

"Most ladies, that is, women who aren't paid for their time, don't pleasure men in that particular way," he said hoarsely.

A little frown crinkled her brow. "They don't? Why not? You did so to me, and you told me that it was quite proper." She reached out and ran her fingers swiftly up his length, as if a feather brushed there. "I like this part of you. Such an interesting shape, as if it were made for a kiss. See?"

And before Piers could do anything, not that he would have stopped her, she bent over again. Her mouth was tight on him, like delirium, like a fever in his blood, like . . .

"You don't sound as though you dislike it," she said, stopping again.

"Wretch," he said, raising his head. "Don't —"

"Don't continue?" she said, full of mock sadness. "I was just starting to imagine what you might like. For example . . ."

She did it again, deeper, at the same moment that her hand curled tightly around the lower part of him. His hips jerked forward, and Piers realized that he had exactly five seconds to make sure that Linnet, delicious Linnet, knew exactly what she was doing.

"If you keep doing that," he said, his voice strangled. "I'm going to come. And that means my sperm will rush out and directly into your mouth."

"Are they injurious?" She sounded curious, unafraid. Something in his body relaxed, some deep powerful caution in him.

"No," he whispered. She was playing with her right hand too, touching his balls, rubbing him. Her hair glinted in the sun slanting through the window as she bent to him again — the silky hair of a princess. But no princess ever gave her lord such pleasure.

He could withdraw. He told himself to

withdraw. He had never allowed a woman to perform such an intimate service, never.

But he couldn't hold in the sounds erupting from his throat. His balls tightened, he arched toward her one final time. Her tongue gave a playful little twist, a caress that burned all the way to his balls and down his legs . . .

Piers lost himself as he never had before. His mind shut down like a box with a lid, leaving him no more than a man in the hands and mouth of a woman who was enjoying herself. There is no greater aphrodisiac, he thought dimly.

And stopped thinking altogether, because her hands . . . her mouth . . .

He forgot to withdraw. He forgot his name. He forgot he was a doctor. He forgot . . .

He forgot everything except for Linnet and the curve of her neck, and the wet warmth of her mouth, and that little hum that told him she was happy.

In fact, his mind was still completely blank when she crawled back up to him and said in a husky, lustful voice: "Now you owe me."

Indeed.

TWENTY-ONE

That night after supper they all retired to the drawing room for a postprandial brandy (for the gentlemen) and tea (for the ladies).

Linnet was having a hard time keeping herself within the bounds of ladylike behavior. She wanted to touch Piers, to speak only to him, to smile at him in unmistakable invitation. She was in the grip of ravening hunger, as if lust were the only emotion in her body.

Every once in a while a thought of the future — even, it had to be said, a pulse of anxiety — would float across her mind. After all, she had thrown away her virtue, her most precious possession. Her father would be horrified, even more so if he knew that Piers had promised to marry her only if she were carrying a child.

But one glimpse of Piers's lean body, and her heart started beating high in her throat, and heat crept up her legs. She couldn't hide the truth from herself: given the chance, she would throw her virtue to the wind again. And again.

It was like madness. It was like being drunk, as if she were drinking brandy with her tea.

After a few minutes in the drawing room, Linnet found herself wondering if perhaps Lady Bernaise had slipped brandy in *her* tea. Her ladyship insisted on dancing, taking the marquis as her partner and consigning Linnet to Mr. Bitts. Even when the waltz was over, she was remarkably gay, her eyes sparkling, her fan in constant motion.

Linnet looked down at her white gown and sighed. Lady Bernaise was wearing an exquisite gown, of lilac tissue caught up just under the bodice with ribbons the color of mulberries. Though it might be a misnomer to talk of a bodice, since her décolletage was so much in evidence that her breasts appeared to be decorated rather than concealed.

Piers was leaning against the wall, watching with a sardonic expression as his mother grew more and more outrageous, flirting with the young doctors, tapping them with her fan, laughing her throaty little French laugh.

Linnet caught his eye, and put her hand

on the sofa beside her.

"You summoned?" he asked, a moment later.

Her whole body shivered as he sat down, his broad shoulder brushing hers. "Did your mother have too much champagne?" she said in a low voice, trying not to look too delighted that he had responded to her summons.

"I doubt it. I think she's discovered a new pastime, which could be summed up as *Torment the Duke.*"

"*Torment* as in make him jealous?" Linnet asked, her eyes sliding to the duke. "I believe it's working." Piers's father was sitting bolt upright, his eyes fixed on his former wife.

"It might be a bit more complicated than that," Piers said. "You see, my father divorced her on the grounds that she was a —"

"Oh, I see," Linnet breathed. "Do keep your voice down, Piers. Your father will hear you."

"And?"

"If I understand you, she is flaunting her independence: as a trollop she may take pleasure from whomever she wishes, including young men. Though of course she's not really a trollop."

"It looks to me as if the Honorable Bitts has become the leading contender," Piers said. "Who would have thought the man had such a courtier turn in him? Though I suppose he comes by it honestly, being the son of a viscount or some such."

"But would she —" Linnet whispered.

"Never," Piers said calmly. "My father knows that too. My mother loves to flirt — she is French, after all — but she was a devoted wife, to my father as well as to her second husband."

"What was he like?" Linnet watched, fascinated, as the former duchess delighted Mr. Bitts by sitting down at the piano. The other two doctors clustered around as well.

"They can probably see straight to her navel," Piers remarked. "And to answer your question, *Maman*'s second husband was an excellent spouse. An antidote to my father, certainly: solid, not too bright, thoroughly civilized. Unfortunately, also headless, after the Revolution caught fire and he refused to leave his estate, insisting that *his* peasants weren't as angry as everyone else's."

The duchess was singing now, her eyes sparkling and her fingers flying over the keyboard.

"What a charming tune," Linnet said. "And she's singing in English!"

"There would be no point otherwise," Piers said dryly. "My father's French isn't good enough to catch the words in her own language."

Linnet listened more closely. "A lascivious wench was she," caroled the duchess merrily.

"Marvelous!" Linnet exclaimed, giggling. That was a song worthy of her aunt or mother, though she could hardly say so to Piers.

"My father isn't quite so amused," Piers said, nodding.

"I feel as if I'm watching a play." Sure enough, the duke was scowling so fiercely that the resemblance to his son was unmistakable.

"I had the same sensation last night. If we were in a box in the theater," Piers said, "it would be rather dark."

"And?"

The duke's lower lip was jutting out, and he was tapping his fingers on his knee.

"I would put my arm around you," Piers said, "risking public censure." He did just that, pulling her back into the depths of the sofa.

Linnet looked up at him. "I suppose if I were very, very tired after some unexpected activity during the day, I might rest my head

315

on your shoulder." And she did.

Piers's fingers traced little circles on her bare arm, making it hard to think about the drama unfolding before them. Lady Bernaise finished her song and got up from the pianoforte with a flutter of skirts. The Ducklings clustered around her.

They were all laughing — indeed, they were convulsed with laughter.

"Dear me," Piers said, "those actors shouldn't forget that they have an audience — to wit, us."

But just then, his mother obliged, her light voice coming through the laughter perfectly clearly. She had her fan open, and her eyes glittered dangerously over the edge. "I have always thought, Mr. Bitts, that a hard man is good to find."

Linnet choked back a laugh, but Piers was looking to his father. "She's brought the old lion out of his cave with that witticism," he said into her hair.

Sure enough, the duke was on his feet. The doctors scattered like chaff in front of him; he slipped his hand under the lady's arm and towed her out of the room before Linnet could do more than blink.

"What a shame," Piers said, not moving.

Linnet tried to sit up. "We should —"

Piers caught Kibbles's eye and jerked his

head. In a second the Ducklings were gone.

"The entertainment is over," Piers said mournfully. "Only you and I left in the darkened theater."

"Where is your cousin?" Linnet asked, suddenly realizing the marquis was nowhere to be seen.

"Prufrock pulled him out of the room a few minutes ago. A patient must have shown up with a broken limb, since that's Sébastien's speciality."

Linnet relaxed against Piers's shoulder, letting him pull her closer, and then tilted her head up to examine the ceiling. There was nothing much up there to examine, but it did give Piers the chance to dust kisses over her neck.

"Mmmm," Linnet hummed, deep in her throat.

"I love it when you do that," Piers said, raising his head to drop a kiss on the corner of her mouth.

"Do what?"

"Make that little sound in your throat that means you're willing and able."

"Are you implying that I'm easy?" Linnet asked, nettled.

"Are you implying that I wouldn't respect you if you were? After all, you're not the one who just extolled the virtues of hard

317

men," he pointed out. "That was my mother, the woman whom I have the most reason to honor."

"I'm not easy," Linnet said stubbornly.

"I, of all men, know that." He nuzzled her ear. "But do you think that perhaps you could do an imitation of an easy hussy later this evening?"

Linnet found herself trembling. Piers was holding her tightly, and licking — he was licking! — the edge of her ear. "*That* is a very strange thing to do," she said, avoiding his question.

In answer, he nipped her ear lobe, and a little pulse of fire went straight to Linnet's thighs. "Very strange!" she managed.

"All this hair of yours is in the way."

"As for tonight," Linnet began — but the door opened.

It was Prufrock. "I apologize for interrupting, but his lordship the marquis has requested your assistance."

"Tricky operation?" Piers asked, still nuzzling Linnet's ear.

Linnet tried to sit up straight, but he didn't let her.

"So I understand," Prufrock said. And then, obedient to some unseen signal, or unwritten code, he backed straight through the doorway and closed the door behind him.

"Damnation," Piers sighed.

"How tricky can it be to lop off a limb?" Linnet said. "I would think it would be rather straightforward, like sawing a log, only messier."

"Where's your maidenly squeamishness?" Piers demanded. "You sound as if you wouldn't mind holding one end of the saw."

"I wouldn't," Linnet said, thinking about it. "I expect it would be interesting. You really must let me sit up. I'm sure Prufrock was horrified."

"Prufrock? Nothing horrifies that man. Besides, you *are* my fiancée. We're allowed to nuzzle each other."

"Not without a chaperone somewhere in the vicinity," Linnet said firmly.

"Pooh. I expect you never went anywhere without a chaperone during the season, did you?"

"Never."

"And look where it got you . . . pregnant by a prince, and betrothed to a maniac."

Since Linnet had often thought the same thing, she could hardly protest. So she turned her head, just a fraction of an inch, and caught his lips as they slid across her jaw.

His lips were unruly, demanding, not gentlemanly. She opened her mouth to him, allowing — nay, welcoming — him in all his lavish greed. In his kiss was an inquiry that she meant to refuse. They couldn't do *that* again.

She tore away, her chest heaving. Only to find the beast laughing at her, his hands, both hands, clasping her breasts. Her bodice may not have had the claim to lasciviousness that Lady Bernaise's had, but on the other hand, it was held in place by nothing more than a gathered ribbon. And Piers, deft, clever Piers, twitched the little bow on her right shoulder, causing her bare breasts to tumble straight into his hands.

"You're beautiful," he whispered. His thumbs rubbed over her nipples. She actually squeaked aloud, it felt so delicious.

He had full possession of her breasts now, squeezing them almost roughly, bending his head . . .

Linnet's back arched instinctively, and a kind of little scream flew from her lips. It woke her up.

"Prufrock, he's just outside," she stuttered, pushing at Piers's shoulders.

He let go of her breasts only after her second shove. Linnet's whole body thrilled again at the look in his eyes, the wild, uncontrolled desire vibrating from his face.

"We can't do this," she said, taking a deep breath. Which made her breasts rise in the air, and Piers's eyes return to them like a drowning man sighting a rope.

"God, you're perfect," he muttered.

"You don't think I'm too large there?" she asked, feeling stupid even as the words left her mouth. "My father said that I — that is, my governess once said I looked like a cow."

"If cows looked like this . . ." Piers said, but he didn't seem to be able to think of a second half of the sentence. Instead he reached out again, reverently this time. "Your breasts are perfect, Linnet. Every man's dream."

"Your dream?" she asked.

"I never dared to dream of someone like you," he said, finally meeting her eyes.

She knew the smile in her heart had spread deliriously onto her face.

Instantly something changed in his. He reached out and pulled up her bodice, gently tugging on the ribbon and then tying it. She didn't move, just sat watching his lowered eyes and wondering.

"Just because I never dreamed of you, doesn't mean that I'm going to marry you," he said finally.

"I know," Linnet said, scrambling to put

her wits together. "We aren't suited. We agree on that."

"Look, I brought you something," he said, reaching into his pocket and pulling out a little muslin bag neatly tied with string.

"What's in it?"

"Mineral salts. Take a long bath this evening, and you'll be set for swimming tomorrow."

She took the bag. "A second bath! The footmen will complain of hauling all that hot water to my bedchamber."

He shrugged. "As you wish."

Then he stood, grasping his cane with one hand and holding out the other to help her to her feet. "I must go."

He seemed suddenly irritated, as if he were blaming her for something. She caught his arm. "What's the matter?"

"Nothing."

"We were having a perfectly good time a moment ago, and now you're stiff and un-friendly."

He turned around with a little snarl. "A man never likes it when he almost loses his head over a woman."

Linnet frowned at him. "I see no sign of your losing your head."

"I made up my mind long ago that I wouldn't marry," he said, scowling back at her. "I can hardly take care of myself, let alone someone else."

Linnet nodded. "That seems a foolish reason to abjure matrimony, but you did say so. I haven't asked you to change your mind, have I?"

"No."

"Then why are you blaming *me* for any errant thoughts that might have flown through your thick head?" she retorted. "*I* was not thinking of matrimony when you kissed me."

A rough bark of laughter escaped his throat. "Neither was I."

"Then why the fit of sullens?" She let go of his arm.

"Because I'm an ass?" he offered, relenting. "But I really must go assist with Sébastien's patient, or he will be furious at me." There was a smile in his eyes, so she took his arm and let him escort her from the room.

Just before he opened the door, he stopped and dropped a kiss on her nose. "If I were to marry anyone, Linnet, it would be you."

"I always knew these breasts would come in handy," she said with satisfaction.

He laughed at that. "If I were a different man, this would be a different story."

"Imagine that," she said. "I could be dallying with a fiancé who doesn't turn on me like a viper when he has a fit of megrims."

"Megrims! You make me sound like a sour maiden aunt."

"Megrims," she repeated, giving him a saucy smile. And then, more reasonably: "You really do have to control your anxiety, Piers. I promise that I haven't suddenly decided that you're the spouse I always wanted, no matter how much I enjoy your kisses."

He blinked, glanced down at his cane. "I'm a fool. A vain fool, in this case."

"It's not your leg," Linnet said quickly.

But he was grinning, pushing open the door to the entryway. "My vile tongue, I assume?"

"A woman would have to take that into account," she pointed out. "She might not welcome that vile tongue of yours making havoc at the breakfast table." She hesitated and decided to just say it: "We're playing. And I — I *deserve* to play, after all that has happened to me recently."

He was nodding. "You do. And I'm a fool, just as you said." And then, in front of the footmen and Prufrock and anyone else who might be in the entryway, he bent his head and kissed her, one of his lustful kisses that took no prisoners.

A demand.

And she gave, she gave instinctively, her hand clutching his coat lapel, her body swaying toward his, her lips clinging to his when he raised his head.

He leaned forward and said in her ear, so quietly that no one could hear. "You're one hell of a playmate."

Then he was gone, clumping up the stairs.

Linnet forced herself to meet Prufrock's eyes. "I'd like a bath, if you please."

He nodded to one of the footmen. "Of course, Miss Thrynne. I believe your maid is in your chamber, waiting for you." He cleared his throat. "The mongrel who now goes by the name of Rufus has been washed and trimmed, though I can't say it has improved his looks to any measurable amount."

She'd forgotten all about that. "He can come to my room," she said, with a sigh.

Prufrock did not approve. "The dog will be perfectly comfortable in the stables, or even in the boot room, if you insist."

She shook her head. "I promised Gavan. He's terrified that Rufus will run away during the night."

"The boot room will prevent that."

"I promised," Linnet repeated. "If someone could deliver him after my bath, I would be most grateful."

Of course, the butler was all business, as if he hadn't witnessed their kiss.

But as she walked up the stairs, she could feel eyes prickling her shoulder blades. We're in Wales, she said to herself. Wales. No one cares what happens in Wales. It's not as if the servants can gossip with their counterparts next door.

What happens in Wales, stays in Wales.

TWENTY-TWO

Robert Yelverton, Duke of Windebank, sometimes thought with some despair that he had bequeathed only one characteristic to Piers, his son and heir: the capacity for addiction. Piers's fierce, single-minded devotion to his work reminded him of nothing so much as his own benighted fall into opium use. Though whether it was possible to talk about work — even such laudable work as being a surgeon — as an addiction was unclear to him.

It perhaps would not have pleased Robert very much to realize that in fact he *had* given Piers more than a predisposition toward obsession; the scowl on his face as he pulled his erstwhile wife Marguerite out of the room was the duplicate of one often seen on his son.

"Alors!" Marguerite cried, trying in vain to twist her wrist from his grip. "Robert, you have no right to handle me in this rough

fashion, you — you —" Apparently she couldn't think of the right words in English, because what followed was a torrent of French.

Robert ducked into the library, towing her behind him. The minute they were inside he released her hand. She whirled in front of him, a vision of luscious breasts and fluttering skirts, and he felt such a pulse of longing that he almost fell to his knees. It wasn't only her physical beauty that made his hands tremble: it was the dearness of her, the memory of the way she would smile at him over a cup of tea or a silk sheet, the lost joy of having Marguerite as his wife.

"You — you — *cretin!*" she cried, so furious her voice broke. "How dare you handle my person in such a manner! How dare you even touch me?"

"I don't know," Robert said. He was determined to be completely honest with her. "But I thought your performance in the drawing room had gone far enough, and that it was time for me to play a part."

"There is no call for *you* to play any part at all in my life. I will select a man from the street — yes, from the gutter — before I would ask you to be near me again."

"I know."

She blinked, and a bit of the fire left her

eyes. "Then why did you bring me here? We have nothing to say to each other."

"I've changed, Marguerite. I am not the same man you married."

"You were not the same man I married within five years of the ceremony," she stated, turning toward the door.

"If there were any way — any way at all — that I could take back the hurt that I caused you and Piers during the years of my opium use, I would do it," he said desperately. "I would cut off my arm. I would give my life to undo it."

She paused, her hand on the door. Her narrow shoulders were rigid. A few, just a very few, strands of white gleamed among her bronze locks.

"I am not the man you married. Nor am I the fool who divorced you. I am older and far wiser," he continued, praying that she would stay for a moment longer. "I did not understand then how much you were to be treasured."

Marguerite turned around slowly, and then leaned back against the door. "There were so many times that you told me you would stop taking that drug. You promised so many times."

"I know. I couldn't keep my word."

"But I gather you finally did stop. Piers

says that you have not taken opium in years."

"Seven years. Almost eight."

"So you could not stop for me, but you stopped for — for what? What did you find that you loved more than that opium dream of yours?"

"Life. I was near death, I think. And I found, to my surprise, that I wanted to live." He was revealing his saddest truth to her. He walked a little closer, just enough so that a hint of her French perfume reached him. They stood there for a moment looking at each other, two middle-aged people with years of anger and regret between them.

"You're as beautiful as ever," he said, clearing his throat.

"You were always one to talk about beauty, and see only what is superficial in a person." But the fury had drained from her voice.

"Was I?" He couldn't remember. "I loved you for more than your beauty. I admired your strength, Marguerite, and your intelligence. The way you stepped into the role of a duchess and did so gracefully, and the way you dealt with my mother. The way you raised our son."

"So you say now."

"I do say now. And I'm sorry that I never told you then how greatly I admired you.

There has been only one woman in the world whom I admire as I admire you, love as I love you."

"Who?"

"You."

"Oh. My English is a bit rusty. I did not follow."

He chose his words carefully. "I know that you would never consider being my wife again after the pain I caused you and Piers. But if you could ever forgive me for what I did to you —" He stopped, swallowed, kept going. "I expect it is unforgivable, but I think of little else."

She gave a little shrug, an entirely Gallic gesture. "*Alors,* Robert. I am long past the point where I wish to kill you for ruining my reputation, or even for loving that drug more than me. But what happened to my baby, our son . . . That I cannot forgive."

Robert took a step closer to her. "I would not expect you to."

"Yet I think *he* needs to forgive you," she said, her eyes troubled, not seeming to notice that he now stood just before her. "Piers is more harsh with you than he ought to be."

"I know. Perhaps . . . someday." But he didn't really want to talk of Piers, and he couldn't stop himself. His hands came up of their own volition and cupped her face. And swiftly, before she could refuse him, he bent his head and kissed her. He put everything into that kiss: his regret, his love, his longing. The long, cold years of sobriety, when she was married to another, and he had nothing to contemplate but his own stupidity.

For a moment — one blessed, exquisite moment — she kissed him back. She tasted like apricots: at once sweet and tart, and heartbreakingly familiar.

But then she put her hand to his chest and pushed him away. Without a word, she turned, pulled open the door, and walked out, leaving nothing behind but an elusive thread of perfume in the air.

Still . . . there had been something in her eyes, in the way her lips yielded to his . . .

To hope was to put himself at risk. In all likelihood, his hopes would turn to dust, to rejection and pain. He hadn't dared such a foolish emotion in years. But hope billowed from some secret place in his heart all the same.

TWENTY-THREE

Linnet was rather hoping that an irascible doctor with a cane might burst into her bed-chamber at some point during the night, but no. He was there in the morning, though, dripping warm chocolate on her face.

"What are you doing?" Linnet gasped. She licked at the chocolate.

"Giving you the look of someone with pox," Piers said. "One more drop on your left cheek. Yes, you're a proper horror now. Did you know that Queen Elizabeth was badly scarred by pox?"

"Ugh," Linnet said, grabbing a handker-chief and rubbing her face vigorously. "How beastly of you!"

"Why?" Piers said, leaning back against the bedpost at the foot of her bed. "Would it be so terrible to have scarred skin after the pox?"

"Of course it would," Linnet said crossly.

"Is my face clean again?"

"Blooming. Why would it be so terrible?"

"Because," she replied, nonplussed. "It just would."

"But many women aren't as beautiful as you, and they live perfectly happy lives," he pointed out. "Even the scarred ones."

"Yes, but —"

"Queen Elizabeth had a fine time of it, by all accounts," he added.

"She never married, did she?" Linnet took her hot chocolate away from Piers and took a sip.

"There's no rule that says women with bad skin can't marry."

"Yes, but there are all sorts of unwritten rules about what makes a woman desirable. Beautiful skin being paramount."

"And you have every single criterion, haven't you?" He narrowed his eyes, looking as if he were examining her minutely for faults.

She didn't answer. Anything she said would leave her open to mockery.

"I wonder if it's worse for an ugly woman to get the pox or a beautiful one," Piers said.

"A beautiful one," Linnet said without hesitation. "She has more to lose."

"I can't go swimming this morning," he said, changing the subject. "Sébastien has to operate on that patient who appeared last night, and I need to stand by and harangue him."

Linnet felt her mouth droop. "Oh, of course."

"I thought we might go in the afternoon instead."

"That would be acceptable," she said demurely. He wasn't looking at her, but was concentrating on poking the pile of novels on the far bedside table.

"What's the pleasure in knocking them over?" she asked.

"I'm not knocking them over. I'm seeing what percentage of the top book has to overhang the rest before they all fall."

They fell.

"Around forty percent. I told Prufrock that I want the guardhouse refurbished," he said, getting up from the bed.

She blinked at him. He stepped forward, and then swooped down for a kiss. "Mmm," he said, "essence of Linnet with a dash of chocolate."

Linnet sat looking at the closed door, her cooling chocolate in hand. He told Prufrock that — and why?

But she knew why. Her burning cheeks knew why. The little tremble that went through her thighs knew why.

One more time, she promised herself. That wasn't too trollopy. *She* wouldn't be too trollopy.

But when they actually got to the guard-house? Trollopy.

There was no other way to describe her behavior. Nor the day after, nor the day after that.

Certainly not the day when Piers caught her in the corridor after she had read *Camilla* to a group of patients, pulled her into an alcove and with a quick hand between her legs, reduced her to . . .

Well, trollop-hood.

It's just playing, she told herself every night before sleep. Though the phrase began to sound a bit anxious.

We're just playing, giving the duke time to . . . to reacquaint himself with his wife. Or vice versa. No one could miss the fact that the formerly married couple seemed to be spending more and more time talking to each other in a reasonably civil manner.

Then came a week in which Linnet had absolute proof that no baby had been cre-ated in their first encounter. Even so, Piers argued that he was not yet ready to send a retraction of their betrothal to the *Morning Post.* "One never knows," he said, and then explained exactly how French letters might fail in their duty.

"In that case, perhaps we should stop now," Linnet said, knowing full well that neither one of them wished to do so.

"We're just playing," Piers stated.

And trolloping, as Linnet pointed out.

"I don't think *trollop* can be used as a verb like that," Piers retorted. He never came to her bedchamber to make love to her, never slept with her. But that night he had come upstairs around midnight, pulled her straight out of bed and brought her down to the library to show her a very important text, specially written (he said) to mark the end of her courses.

It turned out to be written on little scraps of paper that he had strewn over the sofa before the fire. And on each little scrap was a suggestion.

"Nor as an adjective," he continued, thoughtfully. He was sitting on the sofa stark naked, firelight gleaming on his chest, his muscled legs stretched out before him. "I couldn't say, for example, that my *Maman* is acting in a trollopy fashion, parading around as she does, dressed in a handkerchief for the most part."

"But you couldn't say she was a trollop either," Linnet said, "because she's not. So the word is more useful in degrees, as an adverb or an adjective."

"You are not a trollop, because such a woman moves from man to man," he said, tacitly giving in to her grammatical point, but, characteristically, countering it with a different argument.

"In fact, any woman who goes to a man's bed without the benefit of matrimony deserves the label," Linnet said. "She needn't visit more than one such bed. I have become everything that most of London believes me to be."

"Does that bother you?"

She was nestled on the opposite end of the couch from Piers, sitting on her chemise rather than wearing it. "Just look at me."

He did, and she liked the gleam in his eyes.

"That's not what I meant," she said. "Here I am in a gentleman's library, without a stitch of clothing on my body. I begin to think that I am truly my mother's daughter. Though I still hope that I won't earn a reputation akin to hers."

Inside, she wasn't afraid of losing her reputation . . . she was afraid of losing her heart. But there was no reason to share that lurking fear.

They had found they both liked to sit by the side of the pool, or in the guardhouse, or in the library, and dissect things. Words. Bodies, though only through Piers's descriptions. People, at least metaphorically. Patients, as regarding their behavior.

Because Linnet was regularly visiting the rooms of the non-infectious patients, she had funny stories about Mrs. Havelock, sometimes known as Nurse Matilda, and her skirmishes with those few who, rather surprisingly, dared to rebel.

One night, Linnet had reduced Piers to helpless laughter by mimicking the antics of a certain Mr. Cuddy, who had taken advantage of his wife's visits to have her smuggle in a flask of gin, whereupon he promptly became inebriated, to Nurse Matilda's disgust. "I don't know that hearing this kind of thing is good for me," Piers said.

"Why not?"

"Patients," he said, waving his hand. "One shouldn't know too much about them. They're just illnesses, after all. That's all I can treat."

Linnet was sitting on the floor between his outstretched legs, wrapped in a blanket. "You're a hopeless fool," she told him.

He bent forward, scooping up her hair in his hands. "We should sell this."

"There's no market."

"It gleams in the firelight like guineas, if

guineas had more red in them."

She leaned back against him and let him play, piling all her ringlets up and then letting them flutter back down.

After all, they were only playing.

TWENTY-FOUR

One fine morning a few weeks after Linnet first met Gavan, he was carried downstairs by Neythen and plunked in the sun at the front door of the castle to wait for someone to fetch him.

Linnet found him there and sat down beside him. "Will your father be along?"

He shrugged. "Probably Mum, in the wagon. That's how she got me here. My dad, he's in the field, or with the sheep."

"So you're a farmer's son," Linnet said. "Do you want to be a farmer as well?"

"My dad's not a farmer; he manages a big estate for somebody who's never there. I'm going to be a doctor," Gavan said, with easy confidence. "I'm going to be better than those two." He jerked his head back at the castle.

"They did a good job with you," she said, hiding her grin. "What do your parents think of your plan?"

"They don't know yet, do they? On account of how old Havelock told my mum she had to leave me here. We only live over there in Tydfil." He gestured, rather vaguely, toward the east. "My mum told me she'd visit, and then Havelock said she couldn't come, ever."

"So Tydfil is quite close?" Linnet asked, but Gavan was suddenly struggling to stand. Linnet jumped up and hauled him to his feet.

"There's the cart!" he bawled, beside himself with excitement. "It *is* my mum!"

When the cart drew up in front of the castle, a woman jumped down, ran over and swooped Gavan up her arms. "There you are!" she cried. "Bright as a ha'penny and good as gold!"

He had his arms tightly wreathed around her neck. "I never cried," he said. But he was crying now. "Not even when they held me down, and —" but whatever he was saying was lost in sobs.

Linnet patted the bench she and Gavan had been sitting on, and Gavan's mother walked over, her son clinging to her front. She wasn't much older than Linnet, all told, her hair black and gleaming under her bonnet.

She sat down, stroking Gavan's hair.

"There's nothing wrong with crying," she told him. "Nothing at all." After that, they just sat there in the sunshine, his head buried in her shoulder as she rocked him back and forth.

The door opened behind them, and Linnet heard the sound of Piers's cane. She turned around to give him a warning glance. This was no time for incivility. But he was well-mannered, for him. "Mrs. Wing," he said, "the boy is healing like a charm. He should be on his feet for an hour a day at the most for the next week, and then go gradually from there. He has a cane; he must use it."

Mrs. Wing nodded. "Thank you, my lord. We can't thank you enough." She squeezed Gavan a little tighter. There was a gloss of tears in her eyes, but she was clearly an energetic soul with little time for weakness.

Piers turned on his heel to leave.

"Wait!" Mrs. Wing called.

He paused and half turned. "Madam?"

"I want to say something to you, my lord," Mrs. Wing said. She uncurled her son from around her neck and dropped him, quite naturally, into Linnet's outstretched arms. Gavan had stopped sobbing, and was just hiccupping.

"These weeks without Gavan, and without

343

knowing what's happened to him, have been terrible for his father and me. Terrible. And there's no call for that. We live just over the hill. We could have visited easy, without disturbing anyone. That, that housekeeper of yours, she said —"

"We're changing our ways," Piers said, cutting her off. "Talk to Miss Thrynne. She's the frivolous-looking one next to you." Then he clumped through the door.

"Well, I *never*," Mrs. Wing said, plumping down on the bench. "I told Mr. Wing that I would have my word with him, and I knew the doctor wouldn't like it." She pulled off her bonnet and started fanning her face with it. "But the way he looked at me! As if I was some sort of rodent he found in the grain bin!"

"He's not *that* bad," Linnet protested.

Gavan suddenly scrambled off her lap. "Mum, I didn't show you my dog, my dog Rufus!"

Mrs. Wing blinked. "A dog?"

"The miss here, she found me a dog in the stables," Gavan said, hauling Rufus out from under the bench where he was lying in the shade. "Isn't he the bestest dog you ever saw, Mum?"

Rufus sat up, his tongue hanging out, and his remaining ear cocked.

344

"Well, he looks like a good ratter," his mother said, eyeing Rufus. Then she turned to Linnet. "You found my son that dog?"

"Yes, she took me to the stables before I could even walk, and we found him there," Gavan said, sitting down on the grass, and then lying down so that Rufus could lick his face. "She kept him in her bedroom at night so he wouldn't run away. And she took me to see the sea too."

Mrs. Wing's lip trembled, and she reached out and gave Linnet a rather blind pat on the knee. "I can't tell you what that means to me," she said, her voice wavering. "I've been lying awake night after night, thinking about Gavan all alone in this castle, and maybe something going wrong, and us never seeing him again." She stopped and took out a handkerchief.

"I wasn't here during Gavan's entire convalescence," Linnet said, "but I think he was rather happy. He has a cheerful soul."

"He does, doesn't he?" Mrs. Wing dried her eyes. "All I can tell you is that I made four quilts while he was gone. *Four.* Pieced, sewn, and finished off."

Linnet had no idea what it took to make a quilt, but one had to imagine it involved a great deal of work.

"Of course, I had help," Mrs. Wing said.

345

"We all of us women over in Tydfil" — she jerked her head — "quilt together. And if something's happened, as happened to Gavan, then we quilt more often. It's a distraction."

Linnet had a sudden idea. "Quilting doesn't take anything like a loom, does it?"

Mrs. Wing shook her head. "It's all piecing squares together at that stage. We sit around in a circle and sew together. And talk, back and forth. Later I put it on a quilting frame and finish up."

"I wonder if you could ever come here, to the castle," Linnet said. "Because you see, Mrs. Wing, there's a room full of women in the west wing who are terribly bored. There's a woman who's carrying two babies, for instance, and so she can't get up for a few months yet. And Mrs. Trusty had a terrible thing happen to her foot, though she's starting to hobble about now."

"Would the housekeeper allow such a thing?"

"We could arrange it," Linnet said firmly. "A quilting circle, here at the castle. Would you please come, once a week, Mrs. Wing? Could you spare the time?"

"Of course. The doctor may be prickly in his manners, but he saved my Gavan's life." She nodded. "It helps, you know, with

346

people in pain too. Distracts them. Not labor, though. It doesn't help for that. I've never seen a woman in labor who could sew a straight seam."

"Mrs. Wing, I see you're going to be marvelous at this," Linnet said with a happy smile.

"I like to get things done," Mrs. Wing said. "I see what needs to be done, and I do it. Luckily, my husband is never bothered by anything. If both of us went haring off every time we see something wrong, we couldn't get on!" She broke into laughter.

"I will speak to Mrs. Havelock, the housekeeper for the west wing," Linnet said. "Perhaps you might pay a visit in a week or two, after Gavan is stronger on his feet?"

Mrs. Wing nodded. "That I will." She looked at Gavan. "I suppose he shouldn't be rolling around down there in case it hurts his leg?"

"He doesn't seem to be in any pain," Linnet said. "He's a dear boy."

"And *you* are a dear lady," Mrs. Wing said, turning toward her, and taking her hand. "I can't tell you how this has soothed me. You being there, miss, and giving him Rufus, and making it so I can pay the doctor back with some quilting."

"Linnet," she said impulsively, squeezing

347

Mrs. Wing's hand back. "My name is Linnet."

Mrs. Wing chuckled. "Diana," she said. "It's a strange name, something to do with a goddess who was likely no better than she should be. I reckon you'll be learning to quilt as well, won't you?"

Linnet's smile dimmed. "I'm afraid I'm just visiting, and I'm not likely to be here in two weeks, so I'll miss the quilting."

"Now that's a shame," Diana said. "A real shame. Well, if you fix it with Mrs. Havelock and warn the doctor, I'll manage all right."

"Don't let him frighten you," Linnet said. "He's more bark than bite."

"No one will stop me helping those women," Diana said. She laughed again. "Gavan, you hopeless boy, get up."

"I need my cane," Gavan said. He managed to get to his feet with its help. "See, miss? See? I'm just like the doctor now, aren't I?"

He stood there leaning on his cane, grinning in the sun with his hair over his eyes. Linnet couldn't help laughing. "You look like a doctor already, Gavan."

"That's 'cause I'm going to be one," he said with satisfaction. "The best one ever."

TWENTY-FIVE

Evening, the next day

"Two more patients admitted to the east wing with that fever," Sébastien said.

"Which fever?" Piers asked.

"The one that you think is petechial and I don't. I couldn't find you this morning when I wanted you to take a look."

Piers had pulled Linnet into an empty bedchamber after breakfast, and when she'd fallen asleep, he lay with her on the bed for an hour, boneless and satisfied, slowly stroking her shoulders. He had heard his name called, and had ignored it.

He was thinking about his father. Linnet, his father, Prufrock, his mother, Sébastien. His father again. Linnet.

"I'll look at them after the meal," he promised. They walked into the drawing room. Kibbles and Penders were at the sideboard, hovering over the wine decanter. Linnet was sitting next to his mother, while

349

his father sat opposite with that hungry look in his eyes again.

"Where's Bitts?"

"He was rather peaked and admitted to not feeling well. I sent him upstairs."

Piers met Sébastien's eyes. "Ill?"

"Headache, no fever." He shrugged. "Probably not hospital fever, but it's best not to have him in the west wing until we're sure. Let alone around your family."

His *family*. A cold shiver went down his spine.

"I've seen that look before," Sébastien said in a mocking voice. "Yes, I will have a glass, thank you, Prufrock."

"What do you mean, you've seen that look before?" Piers asked.

"The face that launched a thousand . . . *scowls*," Sébastien said, obviously enjoying himself. "I mean that you're thinking about doing something that will hurt yourself in the long run. Seen it before, and I see it now."

"You think you've suddenly developed the ability to diagnose me, of all people? You can't even manage a simple fever."

"I know that you have an affinity for unhappiness," Sébastien said, tipping his glass to his lips. "In fact, paradoxically, you don't feel truly happy unless you *are* unhappy. The way to do that is to push away the people who give a damn about your nasty hide. Me, for one — except that I'm impossible to dislodge, so you seem to have given up on me. Your parents." He turned and raised his glass in the direction of Linnet. "Your utterly beautiful fiancée."

"Beauty is not everything," Piers said.

"Linnet has everything else a man could desire as well," Sébastien said. He put his glass down on the sideboard. "You and I, we've always been together."

"Just break it to me gently, will you? You're running off with a dairymaid."

"No. No."

Piers followed his gaze. "You're running off with Linnet." Every muscle in his body went rigid. She was *his.* His, and no one else's. *His.*

"If she'd have me, I'd run anywhere with her. Or after her." Sébastien turned back to Piers. "I've always run faster than you, Piers. And I'm a better surgeon. And a better lover, though it's crass to point it out."

"I've never bothered to love anyone," Piers said. Linnet was laughing. Diamonds shone in her ears, twinkled at her throat. She looked like a fairy princess, someone created by a magic wand.

"That's true enough. You never bothered.

351

And you're not bothering now, are you? Even though your father wrapped her up like a present and dropped her in your lap."

Piers flinched, and Sébastien let out a crack of laughter. "So that's why. You can't contemplate Linnet because your father chose her. And you're too busy hating your father for his past sins to admit that he found the right woman for you."

Piers reached out and grabbed Sébastien by his pale pink neckcloth and twisted him closer. "My leg hurts like a son of a bitch," he said, between clenched teeth.

His cousin didn't move, just stared into his eyes. "You and your leg can keep each other company at night, then. No room for a woman, given the terrible injury you suffered."

Piers let go of his cousin's neckcloth. Sébastien was right, even though he meant it sarcastically.

He had to stop making love to Linnet. Now. There wasn't any place in his life for her. Not when he knew well that there would be days, even weeks, when the only thing he could feel or think about would be the agony in his leg.

Those were the days when he lost his temper at the drop of a pin, when he shouted at Prufrock and all the rest of them if they so much as twitched. When the pain in his leg spread to his head and he ended up in a darkened room, shivering.

"You're right," he said. "Of course, you're right."

Sébastien, still angry, looked at him narrowly. "It's not like you to concede. So, if you recognize how stupid you're being to reject Linnet, why don't you go over there and woo her?"

"I thought you wanted her."

Sébastien grunted. "I do."

"Well, then, go do the pretty," Piers said tiredly. Perhaps tonight was the night to have two glasses of brandy, rather than one.

"There's no point."

"Merely because my father carted her here from England for me? Nonsense. She needs a husband, and you'll make a pretty one." Something twisted, agonizingly, in his stomach at the idea of Linnet with a husband. Another man. Sébastien? Inconceivable. "You can't live here, though."

His cousin leaned back against the arm of the sofa, holding his glass of brandy up to the light. "Why not? I'm comfortable here. The castle is big enough, Lord knows. And, like it or not, you need my surgical skills."

Piers threw him a look. "I won't have her," he said, making it clear and simple, so even

353

his romantically minded cousin could understand. "I'm not having her." *Anymore,* he added silently.

"And before you start bleating about my father," he continued, "it's not that. I see — Linnet made me see — that I'm just making an ass of myself on that front. Prufrock is the king of butlers, and Linnet . . ."

"The queen of women," Sébastien said quietly.

"But I'm too injured for someone like her. For anyone. I'm too much of a beast, Sébastien. You know that as well as I do."

His cousin shrugged. "I rather like you, even when you are in a temper."

"You grew up with me. You had no choice but to get along with me. I can't pretend to myself that I'm not the utter bastard that I am. Maybe if I were different, if my temper weren't so fierce, if —"

"If you didn't indulge yourself by letting it fly," Sébastian said, dryly.

"You don't understand." As if to prompt him, his muscle spasmed, sending a flash of agony up his leg.

"No man in his right mind with a functional tool," Sébastien said, "would understand. If I had a chance at Linnet, I wouldn't give a damn how much pain I was in. I'd grab her and get a ring on her finger, and trust that we could work it out later."

"That's why you're no good at diagnosis," Piers said, trying to ease the muscle by straightening his leg.

"Why?"

"You can't put symptoms and observations together. One pain-ridden bastard with a wicked tongue —"

He raised his hand when Sébastien opened his mouth. "That's a good description of me, and you know it. At any rate, someone like me, together with a woman like Linnet, adds up to one thing."

"What?"

"Unhappiness," he said flatly, bringing his boot back to the floor.

"Not necessarily —"

"Unhappiness for *her.*"

Piers let the golden, fiery brandy slide down his throat.

Beside him, Sébastien was silent. Then: "Couldn't you control it?"

"I am who I am." He swallowed. "I don't want to watch her wilt when I'm out of my mind from pain. Or grow afraid, the way my mother did with my father, if I turn to laudanum to relieve it."

"You never do."

"I might. It's always there, the possibility, the temptation, at the back of my mind.

Like father, like son, perhaps. I will not put Linnet through that."

"Damn, you're in love with her," Sébastien stated, staring at him.

Across the room, Linnet was chuckling and rapping Penders on the shoulder with her fan. The man was practically groveling at her feet.

"Who wouldn't be?" Piers said, acknowledging the truth aloud. "Who wouldn't be?"

Prufrock entered the room, walking swiftly up to the two of them. "The orderly in the east wing feels that the fever patient admitted yesterday has taken a turn for the worse."

"I'll go," Piers said, putting down his glass with a clink. "I've no business here anyway."

"Don't —" Sébastien said, but Piers lost the end of his sentence in the thump of his cane, the door shutting behind him.

He looked at the stairs before him with some exhaustion. Behind him was a world of fragrant women and golden brandy. But up those stairs was his real world, that of dying patients with their strained faces and terrified eyes.

He started climbing.

The orderly met him at the top of the stairs. "The patient broke out in a rash three days ago, a couple of days after he had the

356

first symptoms."

"And those were?" The orderly held open the door to the east wing so Piers could limp along beside him.

"It began with a stiff neck and shoulders, but since he's a miller, he thought he'd simply strained himself moving sacks of flour. Chills came on that night, alternating with fever. He turned, as he described it, red as a boiled lobster within a few days."

"And now?"

"He hasn't eaten since admittance yesterday, and vomited after drinking some broth. He's feverish, complains he can't breathe. The reason I asked Mr. Prufrock to fetch you is that his skin is blistering terribly. And his lips seem to be blackening."

"Hell and damnation," Piers said, with feeling.

Sure enough, when he examined the patient, the inside of his throat was covered with small brown colored specks, and there were swellings behind his ears. "Double damnation. Who's seen him? Who's been in the room?"

"Well, Dr. Bitts admitted him yesterday," the orderly said. "I have, of course." He looked a bit nervous, but steady enough. "His lordship came by after Dr. Bitts, and said that the man should be kept in a room by himself; Dr. Bitts had directed me to put him in with the patients with petechial fever."

"It's not petechial," Piers said, closing the door as they left. "It's scarlatina anginosa. Scarlet fever. Or more probably, scarlatina maligna. This means real trouble, unless he's unique. Where are the two other patients admitted earlier today?"

"Down the hall," the orderly said. "They're in a room together, because they're cobblers who own a shop together, and they became sick at the same time."

"Where did they come from?"

"Little Millow."

"Around two miles from here."

"The first patient is from Aferbeeg."

"Only about one mile. Did the cobblers say whether anyone else they knew was ill?"

"I asked all three. The miller was delivering grain for the two days before he finally collapsed. He thought he just had a cough and would get over it."

"Delivering grain . . . likely in a wide circumference around Aferbeeg." They turned into the room with the cobblers. They both had the rash, the peeling, ulcers in their throats. The miller had stopped by five days ago to have his boots repaired.

"Bad to worse. There's a good possibility

358

of an epidemic," Piers said grimly. "The first thing we have to do is protect everyone in this castle who's not already on death's door." He ran the bell for Prufrock, and then went to the top of the stairs, holding up his hand to stop the butler midway.

"Do you remember the plans we made last year in case of epidemic?"

Prufrock nodded.

"Time to put them in force. Get everyone out of the castle who is not essential to patient care. Every patient who's not actively dying goes back home — unless they have a sore throat, any stiffness, or signs of fever. Send footmen to borrow all the carriages within a few miles to take them off. All the rest go home — get the duke and my mother out of here, Miss Thrynne with them, of course."

Prufrock's eyes widened and he trotted back down the stairs without a word.

Piers felt a pang somewhere in the area of his heart for the fact he would never see Linnet again.

But then he turned back to the east wing. Scarlet fever was a killer, and it looked as if the miller had time and opportunity to infect quite a number of people. But Piers was famous for not losing fever patients, even those with scarlet fever, and he meant

359

to battle the disease with every tool he had at hand. He had argued in front of the Royal Society that anginosa did not have to turn into its deadlier cousin, maligna, and it was time to prove it.

Within an hour, he began to hear carriages rolling up the drive and then trundling away again, as each patient who could be moved was sent away. Meanwhile, he and Sébastien began a careful inventory of the east wing, finding to their dismay that the disease had already spread among their own patients, seriously complicating matters.

"It's the cough," Piers said. "But I think it may be spread by touch as well. I want buckets of water mixed with alcohol and liquid soap outside every room," he told the orderly. "Wash your hands constantly."

Some of his patients, weakened already, might die, but not as fast as patients would die in the outlying towns, if fools tried to bleed them or give them emetics. "Weak tea and broth," he told the orderly. "We'll treat the fever by cooling patients as much as possible. Open all the windows, and keep pouring fluids down their throats. I want a notice going out to every church within five miles of Aferbeeg that anyone showing signs of a fever or sore throat should be quarantined immediately.

"We should make sure Penders and Kibbles didn't miss any incipient cases in the west wing," Piers said, some time later. "We've got six here so far, but I'm hopeful it hasn't spread to that wing."

Dismayingly, he was wrong. "How did this happen?" he demanded a few hours later, in frustration. They had five cases in the west wing, all in the early stages of scarlatina anginosa.

Sébastien shook his head. "We're the only ones who go back and forth. How are you feeling?"

"It's Bitts!" Piers exclaimed. "God Almighty, it's Bitts. I wonder if anyone's checked on him."

Two minutes later they were on the second floor, in one of the guest bedchambers. Bitts was burning up. "I'm all pins and needles," he gasped. His man was hovering nearby.

"The important thing is to keep him cool and give him water," Piers said. "Bitts."

The young doctor opened his eyes.

"You're going to make it. You have white spots on your tonsils, not brown. Keep drinking. God knows I've lectured you on the need for patients to take liquids, so put all my barking to good use."

A ghost of a smile touched Bitts's lips.

"He'll do," Sébastien said, striding ahead

361

of Piers. "Why don't you get some sleep, and then wake me in a few hours?"

Prufrock was waiting for them, halfway up the stair. "His Grace and Lady Bernaise refuse to leave," he said.

"You're wringing your hands, Prufrock," Piers said. "I'll speak to them."

"I can hardly force them into a carriage. And Miss Thrynne is with them."

Piers sighed. "I'll take care of this," he said to Sébastien. "Do you remember the lecture we heard that recommended applying the froth from fermenting malt to the throats of scarlatina patients?"

Sébastien shook his head. "Details like that leave me on the way out of the hall."

"Get Nurse Matilda on it," Piers said. "We might as well try." As he outlined the treatment details, there was a pounding on the front door, and they both paused. A footman opened the door, whereupon four — five — no, eight patients entered, two on their feet, the others dragged or carried.

"I'll take these," Sébastien said. "You deal with your parents and then get some sleep. We'll have to take turns."

Piers nodded. "Try to put anginosa in the east wing and maligna in the west." He thumped down the stairs, and detoured around the patients, heading for the drawing room.

His mother, his father, and Linnet formed a charming family group. Piers felt a sense of profound exhaustion even looking at them. They were talking of the sculptor Michelangelo, the table before them littered with cakes and cups of tea. They seemed to be in another world, of porcelain and Italian artists, of French perfume and gentlewomen's voices.

His mother jumped to her feet as soon as she saw him. "I will not leave here, Piers. Not without you."

"Are you mad?" he demanded, not moving from the door. "We're in the midst of a serious scarlet fever epidemic, *Maman*. If you stay here, you're quite likely to catch it."

She tossed her head with fine French disdain. "I snap my fingers at scarlet fever. Who will nurse you, if you fall ill? That shall be I."

"Are you condemning your maid to die for you? Younger people are more likely to develop a severe form of the fever."

"We sent our personal servants away immediately," his father intervened. "They're waiting for us at an inn some distance from here."

"You cannot stay here," Piers said stubbornly. "I cannot have you to worry about."

"I won't leave without you," his mother snapped back. He knew where he got the fierce strain in his nature, and it was looking back at him from her eyes.

"The guardhouse," Linnet said.

He turned to her, barely understanding what she was saying. "What are you talking about?"

"Lady Bernaise could go to the guardhouse, and the servants could leave food for her outside the door. It's just down the path on the way to the sea," she told his mother. "You'd be safe there, but close enough so that if Piers did become ill, you could nurse him."

"I'll be damned if I'll allow it," Piers stated.

But his mother was already rising. "I shall be in the guardhouse."

"Don't come near me," Piers said, giving up. He had other battles to fight, and they were far more important. "And don't go out the front door. The corridor is full of patients, all of them coughing, no doubt. You'll have to go out a window."

He turned to Linnet. She was as delectable, and as remote from him, as the fairy queen herself. Stupidly, foolishly, he tried to memorize her: the sweet little nose, stubborn chin, curling eyelashes, flawless skin. Which just made him think about the effects of scarlet fever. "You must leave," he said. "Now, quickly."

"I will." She had her hands clasped before her. "Oh, Piers —" She took a step toward him.

"No." He said it fiercely. "I need you to be gone. I can't think about you, or worry about you."

She nodded.

"Forever," he continued. "Go back to London, or to France, or wherever you want."

"No!" she gasped.

"It's over between us," Piers said, feeling a strange sense of remoteness. Upstairs, his patients were dying, and even so, his heart was twisting; even so, the gleam of tears in her eyes felt mortal. "You always knew it would be the case," he added, more gently. "We have no future."

Her jaw set, and suddenly she looked remarkably like his mother.

Piers looked to his father. "Pry open a window, if you would. Take my mother to the guardhouse, down the ocean path. Linnet will be ready to leave with you in two minutes."

He and Linnet stood like marble statues

while the duke pushed a window out of its frame.

"Be well, Piers, my love," his mother said as the duke held out his hand next to the window. "Be careful."

"I never catch anything, *Maman,*" he said, with perfect truth. He always thought it was nature's compensation for his injury.

At last, they were gone.

"You don't know that you won't be infected," Linnet said. Tears gleamed in her eyes.

He shrugged. "If I do, I shall care for myself properly. I lose very few patients to this particular disease, as long as they reach me in time. I myself have no plans to succumb."

"I don't want to leave you."

"I don't want to marry you."

There, the truth was out, clearly spoken.

"You'll have to wait outside for my father," he said. "Stay away from anyone you see out there, including Prufrock. Do you hear me? In fact, wait by the side of the house. I think it's spread by coughing."

Linnet took a deep breath. Piers was leaning heavily on his cane, exhaustion in every line of his body. "I don't want to leave you."

"You've got no choice," he said. "God almighty, Linnet, how many ways can I put this? I don't want to marry you."

"I haven't decided whether I wish to marry you," she said, trying for a small jest in the face of nightmare. "I think I might."

"The possibility is not in question. It never was, not really."

Linnet looked at him, the shadow of his beard, the shadows under his eyes, and knew she loved him. That she would never love another man. Piers's fierce wit had tempted her, but it was his passionate heart that had won her.

"Go on," he said impatiently. "I don't want to marry you. I won't marry you. Is that clear enough?"

"No." She saw the pain in his eyes and could recognize it for what it is. "We belong together," she said with a feeling of perfect truth. "You will never love anyone but me."

"You are blinded by your own claims to beauty," Piers said, avoiding what she had just said. "Will you please leave now, before I say something I regret?"

But Linnet's heart was flying on a wave of passion and love. "I love you!" she said again. "And you love me."

"I don't give a damn," Piers said.

For a moment she didn't hear him. Then she didn't understand him. "What do you mean?"

"Just what I said. I don't care what you feel for me, or believe you feel for me."

"Why are you being so cruel?"

"I'm not. Indiscriminate niceness is not indicated in this situation. Honesty is."

She ran to him and grabbed his lapels. He recoiled violently. "I might be infectious. Stay back!"

"You are not ill. You never get ill. I believe you."

"Then why don't you believe me when I say this: Linnet, I don't want to marry you. I don't want to marry you!" He was shouting it.

"Yes, you do," she said, and reached out, clasping his face, bringing it down to hers. Her lips sought his, hungry, welcoming, even adoring.

"I won't marry for sex," he said, pushing her away.

She couldn't understand him, and her hand reached out to catch his sleeve as he turned away.

"For God's sake, have you no dignity? I tupped you, and we were good together. But you're not the first, and you won't be the last."

Linnet felt her throat tighten. "Why are you speaking to me like this?"

"Because you damn well won't listen to

me any other way," he said with obvious frustration. "You know what kind of man I am, Linnet. We had fun dallying together, rutting, shaking the sheets, whatever you want to call it. But I never pretended to you that it would result in marriage."

"No, you didn't," Linnet whispered, a chill creeping over her. "You were very clear about that."

"I suppose I should have turned you down," he said. "But you were there, you were eager."

Linnet swallowed. "Because I was — eager?" It seemed she *was* like her mother, at least in Piers's eyes. "Is that why?"

"You're also damned beautiful," he said, raking his hair back. "But yes, you were eager. You might want to practice more discretion if you find yourself in that situation again."

Her heart fell like a stone.

"Look, you have to go. I need some sleep. Sébastien and I have a castleful of patients, and Bitts is already down, which means the other two might go down as well."

"I could —" she said, and the words died in her throat.

"Go," he said wearily. "You can't help. We don't need you here."

"And you don't want me," she said, needing to say it aloud.

"If you mean, do I want you in a sexual way, then the answer is yes. Reference your beauty and general enthusiasm. Every man wants that in his bed. But do I want you in a marital kind of way, a death-do-us-part kind of way? No. And I never will."

His eyes were faintly kind. That kindness, Linnet felt, was rather horrid. "You don't want to admit to loving me because that would mean you have to take responsibility for being miserable — or in this case, not being miserable," she said, raising her chin and staring back at him.

"What?"

"Just what I said," Linnet retorted. "If you married me, if you admitted to your feelings, it would mean that misery is not a given, but a choice."

"Bollocks!"

"Well, I love you," she said. "I'm not afraid to say it aloud. And I want you too."

"I don't —"

"I see you don't," she cut in, moving away from him, toward the window. "I hope all goes well in the castle."

"It will," he said. Now that she had her back to him, it seemed that his voice had pain in it. But when she turned, his jaw was set, his face unyielding.

370

She stopped, just one more time, because she was a stubborn woman. "I'll wait for you in London," she said. "For a time. In case you change your mind."

"Has no one any dignity around here?" he said, half shouting it. "You're as embarrassing as my father."

"I don't mind being a fool for you," she said. "I love you."

There was no response behind her, and she rather thought there never would be one. So she clambered over the windowsill.

"Get in that carriage," Piers said from behind her, nodding to a large one standing to the side, the horses blowing and stamping. "It's the duke's, given the crest."

"Good-bye," she said. "God bless."

She left before he could say anything, because it wouldn't be what she wanted to hear, and she was blinded with tears anyway.

TWENTY-SIX

Robert leaped down from the window after handing out Marguerite, but she refused to move. She was standing, frozen, listening to Piers's voice emerging from the drawing room.

"We must go," the duke said quietly, catching Marguerite's hand to pull her away, just as their son said flatly, "I don't want to marry you."

"He is a fool," Marguerite whispered, "Such a fool. Linnet is the *one* for him. There will never be another, not like her."

But Robert drew her away, down the path toward the guardhouse, listening silently as she told him what he already knew: that Piers seemed to be determined to bring himself more unhappiness. That their son was unable to accept the woman whom he obviously loved, and who loved him.

She stopped talking only when they walked into the guardhouse's sitting room.

The interior of the little house didn't look like a servant's dwelling, but like the country home of a gentleman, albeit in miniature. The walls were hung with paintings and the room glowed with color, punctuated by a scarlet throw tossed over a settee before the fireplace.

"How odd," Marguerite said, looking around. "From the outside, it looks quite rough, but in truth, it is charming. Look at that little sofa: surely that was in the small drawing room only last week?"

Robert had his own theories about why the house resembled a snug little nest, but he didn't think Piers's mother would appreciate the insight.

"You may leave now, Robert," Marguerite said, pushing open the door to the bed-chamber and poking her head inside. "I shall be perfectly comfortable here. The servants will tend to me, and if Piers becomes ill, you may depend on me to care for him."

"I always knew you would," he said, coming up behind her.

She looked over her shoulder, smiling. He had not kissed her again after the first time, unwilling to risk the chance that she might repudiate him for good. But they had talked and talked about the last few years, about how he had slowly emerged from an opium haze, only to realize that his family was lost to him. During the lonely years that followed, his only happiness was the certain knowledge that Marguerite was taking the very best possible care of their son.

"I know," she said now, accepting it.

"If you become ill, Marguerite, what then?" He wrapped his arms around her, from behind, and dropped a kiss on her cheek. "What then?"

To his enormous pleasure, she didn't pull away, but stayed in the circle of his arms. "Oh, I shan't," she said, with a perfect confidence that echoed Piers's. "I am never ill."

"I remember differently."

"Never!"

"When you were carrying our son. Don't you remember how ill he made you?"

She laughed at that, and actually leaned back into the circle of his arms, remembering. "How I came to detest that wretched green basin we kept in our bedchamber! I threw it away after he was born."

"So I *have* seen you ill," Robert said, holding her even tighter and daring to kiss her ear. "I cared for you then, remember? When you were ill in the middle of the night. And I shall be there to care for you again, if worse comes to worst. If Piers falls ill, we shall both be at his side."

"Nonsense," she said, pulling free and turning about. "What are you saying, Robert?"

Even the way she said his name, with her enchanting accent, made his heart thump. "I am saying that I shall not leave you," he said steadily.

Her brows drew together. "That is foolish."

"No."

"Foolish," she persisted.

For a moment he just stood looking down at her, and then he stated with absolute truth, "I shall never leave you again."

"What on earth do you mean?"

"If you throw me out of this house, I shall sleep on the path outside. If you return to the Continent without me, I shall follow you. I will build a willow hut at your gate; I will sleep under your window; I will be waiting for you at your own front door."

Her hand went to her mouth, laughter escaping from behind her fingers. "You have lost your mind, Robert!"

He shook his head. "On the contrary: I have found it. I'm in love with you. I was always in love with you, always. Even when I couldn't think straight, there was one thing

I knew, even in an opium dream: that I loved you."

"It is a tragedy that you could not remember your beloved ones the day Piers entered your study unexpectedly." But her voice was not harsh.

"I will always, to my dying day, beg Piers to forgive me. But Marguerite . . . At this moment I don't want to talk about Piers. He is now a grown man, a wonderful man, which is entirely to your credit. But you are not only Piers's mother. You are my wife, the only woman I ever wanted to marry, and the wife of my heart, even though I behaved like a fool after you took Piers to France. You were perfectly right to leave."

"You were *un idiot*," she observed. Her eyes encouraged him, though.

"No one will ever love you as I do," he said, catching her hands and bringing them to his lips. "No one ever *has* loved you the way I do. You are my heart and my life, Marguerite."

A little smile played at the corner of her mouth, an enticing, utterly feminine smile.

"Take me back."

His words seemed to hang in the air, to echo in the small house.

"I am sure what you did is unforgivable,"

Marguerite said, finally. "All my friends say so."

"They're right. Don't forgive me. Just — just take me back." His fingers tightened on hers.

"And if I say no?"

"Then I shall leave this house."

"And?"

"I will not allow you to be at risk for scarlet fever. I will be outside, should you need me. I will take the food from the servants so they cannot infect you."

"You may get the fever yourself," she said softly.

"I would die for you in a heartbeat."

Hope had exploded from his heart and was pouring through his veins: a torrent of joy and fear and desire.

Marguerite took a step closer, pulled her hands free and wound her arms around his neck. She fit there as sweetly as she always had. "You may stay."

He pulled her to him, put his cheek against her hair, closed his eyes. *"Mon amour."*

"But I am not sure that I will marry you again," she observed.

"I don't care. We can live in sin for the rest of our lives."

He heard a gurgle of laughter. "I am

French. We are very prudent."

"Prudent and delectable," he whispered, his hands moving slowly down her narrow back.

"What if this opium did some permanent injury to you?"

He pulled back, looked down at her. "I don't —"

Her smile was impish, and her eyes slid to the bedchamber door. "A Frenchwoman never, ever takes important things for granted."

With a rush of joy, Robert took his former wife — no, his *wife* — up in his arms and stepped across the threshold to the bedroom, placing her gently on the bed. "It would be my very great pleasure to assuage your alarm."

He straightened with the sound of her laughter in his ears. "I must make sure that Linnet is safely away in a carriage. Then I shall tear back here with such speed the servants will think me mad."

"You *are* mad," Marguerite said, giggling like a young girl.

"No," he said, bending over to kiss her once more. "I am sane. For the first time in years."

Twenty-Seven

"I'm so sorry," the Duke of Windebank said to Linnet, after he climbed into the carriage and discovered she was sobbing. "I apologize for bringing you here, Miss Thrynne."

"Linnet," she managed. "After all, we were almost related by marriage. Do you have a handkerchief by any chance? Mine is wet."

"My son is a difficult man," the duke said, handing her a huge linen handkerchief embroidered with his crest.

"He's a — a fool," she said, her voice breaking.

"That too."

"He loves me, I know he does, and he still says he won't marry me. That he doesn't wish to marry."

The duke was silent.

Linnet blew her nose. "Perhaps he will change his mind."

She could see the answer to that in the duke's eyes. "He won't, will he?" Tears started rolling down her cheeks again.

"My dear, my dear, I wish I could give you a different answer."

"It's quite all right," Linnet managed. "Could we leave now?"

The duke hesitated.

She understood immediately. "You plan to stay with the duchess, I mean, with Lady Bernaise."

"I cannot leave her," he said quietly. There was a firm resolve in his eyes that was the mirror of his son's. "And I can't leave Piers either. For all my transgressions, they are my family, and they will always be my family."

Linnet sniffed ungracefully. "I would do the same. Don't worry about me. I shall be just fine."

"I'm sorry about all this," the duke said. "Deeply, deeply sorry. My carriage will take you to a village where the servants and your maid are waiting. We mustn't delay any longer, since I told them to continue without us if we didn't arrive before this evening. I want the household and you well away from this epidemic."

"I am ready to leave," Linnet said, hiccupping.

"I'm afraid it will be a lonely journey back to London."

380

She managed a smile. "I'm used to being lonely."

"Oh." The duke looked even more distressed, if possible.

"Ignore me," she said, venturing a watery smile. "I'm merely feeling sorry for myself. I fell in love with your impossible son. Rather hopelessly so. And now I need to craft a life without him. Which I *shall* do." Though she couldn't imagine it. The pain of even thinking about it tore at her heart.

"It will not be easy," the duke said, leaning forward and patting her knee. "But you can do it. I did."

"Perhaps when I'm sixty," she said, laughing a little, "I shall come to Wales and force Piers to live with me in the guardhouse for a week or so."

"Yes, do that," the duke said. "I would feel better about him if I imagined you pulling him from the castle someday."

"If you tell him so, I'll have nothing to look forward to at age sixty," she said frankly.

"I realize that. I won't say a word about you. If I had understood how profound his dislike of me runs, you wouldn't be in such pain now. I deeply regret that."

"In that case, I would not have met Piers." She dried her eyes again. "I will take the broken heart."

He reached out again, and squeezed her knee. "You're a rather wonderful woman, you know."

Her smile was shy, this time. Not a bit of the family talent in it. "Thank you. I wish you the very best of luck."

The duke's eyebrow shot up in precisely the way his son's did. "Thank you." He started for the door. "I shall call on you as soon as I return to London."

"I think you will not be alone," Linnet said.

He paused for a moment on the carriage steps, and she hardly heard his response as he stepped to the ground. "I hope not."

The door closed behind him. There was a rumble of men's voices outside the carriage, and it started rolling down the road. Away from the castle, away from the ocean and the pool, away from Kibbles and Bitts, Prufrock and the patients. Away from Piers.

She let the duke's handkerchief fall to the floor. Crying had given her a terrible, blinding headache. In fact, it seemed inconceivable that the day wasn't over yet. That she was in a carriage rather than a bed. It was impossible to imagine going all the way back to London, day after day in this carriage.

After a bit she lay back on the padded

seat, staring at the swaying ceiling of the coach. It was hard to get comfortable. She must have strained her neck and her shoulders while swimming.

Finally, she closed her eyes and let the gentle rocking of the carriage carry her away from Piers's harsh words, though they echoed through her dreams.

TWENTY-EIGHT

Six days later

"He's dying," Piers said, with the frustrated pang he always got at moments like this. He looked down at the patient, a stout man in his sixties.

"Every time I give him water, it just rolls out of his mouth," the orderly said.

"Make him as comfortable as you can," Piers said, heading for the corridor. "It could be that red eyes are a sign of impending mortality."

"He looks like a ferret," Sébastien said. He was leaning against the wall in the hallway.

"Go to bed," Piers said. "You were up all last night. You'll be no good if you keep on like this. Besides, there haven't been any new patients for at least two hours."

As if in answer, there was a banging on the front door.

Sébastien's laugh had a hollow sound to

it. "How is Bitts doing?"

"Quick pulse, but the fever broke. I told his man to start with chicken broth sometime today. He's out of the woods."

Sébastien pushed himself away from the wall. "I think it's slowing down."

"That would make sense," Piers said. "We have the orders out about isolating patients. Thank God it was limited to the miller's route."

"I'm off to bed," his cousin said, and then paused. "Did you know that your father is still here?"

Piers jerked his head up. "What?"

"Living in the guardhouse with your mother. I went out for a breath of fresh air yesterday. They were sitting in the gardens. I waved, from a distance, of course."

"They were?" Piers was so tired that he felt as if his brain had been pickled. "Together, in the guardhouse?" Even thinking of the guardhouse brought a pain to his heart that felt as if it would break him in two.

"I suspect there will be a newish duchess soon," Sébastien said, rather cheerfully. "He had his arm around her. Very cozy."

"Wait! That means he sent Linnet home without an escort," Piers said, fury surging through his veins. "He sent her all the way to London without an escort."

Sébastien frowned at him. "Other than a crew of footmen, maids and grooms. Three carriages' worth in all. For God's sake, Piers, you threw her out. Put her out of your mind. She'll be perfectly safe. Remember, your mother traveled here all the way from Andalusia."

Linnet was fifty times more at risk than his mother. But Piers bit back the words before he could voice them.

Kibbles appeared, halfway up the stairs. "One of the new patients is in a bad way. The village doctor treated him with leeches."

"Get a grip on yourself," Sébastien said, his voice growling with fatigue. "Linnet is *gone.* Put her behind you."

"Go to bed," Piers snarled back, waving his cousin off. Then he turned to Kibbles. "I thought we got the news out about proper care."

"His wife says they heard about isolating the sick, but nothing about treatment."

"What village was it?"

"Llanddowll."

"We've already taken three patients from there. Send Neythen over on horseback. He seems to be good at this sort of thing and he's a local boy. Tell him to talk some sense

386

into the doctor. And if that doesn't work, knock the man on the head and bring him over here. We'll put him downstairs in the dungeon."

Kibbles shook his head. "Neythen is down. A mild case, I think. He's in the west wing. My guess is that Prufrock would be hard-pressed to spare someone."

"They'll have to get along on their own, then," Piers said tiredly. "Take me to the patient."

"Mr. Connah is very hot, with a feeble pulse," Kibbles said, standing by the patient's bed a moment later.

"Throat?"

"Dark-colored ulcers. And," Kibbles turned the patient's arm over, "the peeling is so violent that he has lost his fingernails."

Piers looked down at the patient. His eyes were closed, and his breath rattled in his chest. "How many days has he been ill?" he asked his wife.

"This is the sixth day," she said. She was standing by the bed, twisting her hands. "It came on sudden-like, so we put him in a room by himself, just as the minister said, and I sent the children away."

"You probably saved their lives," Piers said.

"And my husband? My Barris, what of him?"

He had found that it was best to be direct. "I don't think he will survive. There's a chance, of course. Your husband looks like a strong man, and we will fight for him. Tomorrow will tell."

Her hand clenched on the bedpost. "If I'd brought him here right when he got the fever, would he have lived? Tell me that."

"No," Piers said flatly, meeting her eyes. "The course of the disease is the course of the disease. We can't say who will live and who will die."

"It weren't because of those leeches? I didn't want the leeches, but the doctor insisted. He's come all the way from the next village, so it seemed as if we were wasting his time if I didn't let him. He put them right on the throat, the part that hurt, to get the poisoned blood out, he said."

"There's nothing you could have done that might have made a difference. Only God knows when it's a man's time to die."

"*God,*" she repeated with a little gasp. "That's right. Barris went to church every Sunday he did, and always something for them poorer off as well. Iffen he dies . . ."

Piers waited until she collected herself.

"Iffen he dies, he had a good life. He loved

the children. Me. He said it to me, as soon as we knew he was sick. We had twelve years together."

"A great deal of happiness in those twelve years?" Piers asked.

"Hardship too, but yes, yes," she said, tears falling onto her hands. "He is a good man, Barris is a good man."

"Then you have much to be proud of," Piers said. "And so do your children."

In the corridor he said wearily, "Tell the orderly to keep giving him water, as much as possible. Enlist his wife's help. We need to cool him down; try wet cloths. I don't think the malt foam is doing a damn thing but stinking up the rooms, so drop that."

"Why did you say that to her?" Kibbles asked. "About whether she could have done it differently? We haven't lost a single patient who got here early enough. We should tell people, so they know that scarlatina can be beaten back." For all his exhaustion, there was pride in his voice.

"She has to live with herself," Piers said, turning to go. "And she has to live with his memory. That's enough for one woman."

"And why did you say that about God?" Kibbles said, trotting after him. "I've never heard you say anything like that."

"*Observe,* you idiot," Piers snapped. "I'm

389

always telling you that. She was wearing a cross at her neck."

"The other two new patients aren't so badly off. I think you should go to bed as well."

"I just sent the marquis to bed."

"Penders and I had a good five hours' sleep," Kibbles said. "And we know what we're seeing now. We can manage. Go to bed."

"You're the best of the lot," Piers said, eyeing him. "You listen."

"So, trust me. Go to bed."

"I'll just look in on Neythen," Piers said. "Anyone else in the household down?"

"Not since the two maids a few days ago," Kibbles said. "I think the hand washing is having an effect."

Neythen was sleeping, so Piers didn't enter the room. He could see from the door that the footman had a mild case; his face and arms looked uniformly red, which suggested a fairly quick recovery.

Then he made his way to bed, swaying a little from pure exhaustion as he went down the corridor, leaning on his cane as if it were a third leg.

His man had been there at some point; his sheets were turned down and a cold supper waiting. He stopped only to pull off his boots before he fell between the sheets.

The dream was waiting for him, as it had been every night since she left.

Linnet was laughing as she pulled her chemise off, just as she had that last morning together. She stood on the rock overlooking the pool, her eyes shining, her beautiful, curvy figure lit by the sunshine so that she looked positively angelic.

He waved at her as he came down the path, planning to throw off his clothes and join her . . .

And then he saw, down in the pool, the glint of teeth.

There was danger in the water.

Something had got into his pool, and it was waiting for her, hungry and destructive.

He tried to shout, but she didn't hear him, and then he started running down the path toward her, except he couldn't run. Pain flared in his leg, but he kept running, violently throwing his cane forward and thrusting himself off the ground, desperately trying to reach her.

Linnet waved back at him — and then leaped into the water with that kind of ferocious joy she had, the fearlessness that propelled her into icy water the very first day, before she even knew how to float.

He woke shaking, heart pounding, face

sweaty. For five minutes he couldn't even think, just lay there staring at the ceiling, telling himself over and over that Linnet was on her way to London. She was safe. She was perfectly safe. His father's servants were inestimable, trustworthy in every way. He should know how good the duke was at hiring staff. He would trust Prufrock with his life.

The dream is merely the result of the epidemic, he told himself. Imagination running amok because of the condition in the castle. Because of the scarlatina. Because he was an ass.

And yet even as his heart calmed, something was nagging at him . . . something he couldn't quite remember, something about Linnet. It couldn't have been said to him. No one had mentioned Linnet's name since she left. It was as if she had never existed.

Even Sébastien had forgotten her, it seemed.

Only he thought of her, every five minutes or so. He'd be bending over a patient and instead of sloughing skin, he'd see her delicate hand. One morning Nurse Matilda called his name, and he whipped about, thinking it was she.

Mistaking Nurse Matilda's voice for Linnet's was just short of a sign of impending insanity.

What was it? What should he remember? Whatever it was, it stayed just out of reach, tormentingly elusive. Something about dancing . . . which was madness. He had never danced in his life.

Finally he turned over and went back to sleep.

TWENTY-NINE

It was agony to rest on her back, so Linnet
rolled to her side, but that was just as bad.
She rolled back, and found herself tangled
in blankets. They had put blankets on her,
so many blankets.

"Water," she muttered, hearing a voice.

She peered up, seeing a stout figure wavering far above her. He bent down and picked
up her wrist. She watched her elevated arm
with a kind of fascinated horror. Her
skin . . . what was happening to her skin
was alarming. Disgusting.

"Of course we could take her to the
castle," came a voice from somewhere . . .
somewhere by her feet. "But I have to admit
that Mr. Sordido didn't think the expense
and time was justified. After all, we've no
idea who she is. I'm caring for her at my
own expense, doctor. My own expense."

"The castle," she tried to croak. But they
didn't seem to hear her. Her throat hurt so,

and her tongue didn't fit in her mouth any longer. "Water," she tried again.

The man holding her wrist put it down again and straightened up. "She wouldn't survive the journey, Mrs. Sordido," he said. "I'm afraid this disease is too strong. Her eyes are open, but she's clearly not *compos mentis.* Looking into the other world already, I shouldn't wonder."

"She seems a little less hot, though."

"I've found that the fever comes and goes. I might write a treatise on it when this is all done. I'm thinking of it."

"Oh, yes, you should, doctor. It would be a great help to others, I'm sure."

"A Treatise on Febrile Diseases," he said. "Perhaps with a subtitle that ran something like *Including the Intermitting, Remitting and Continued Fevers and the Profluvia.* I shall report that we've had modest success with application of leeches to the poisoned areas, as well as use of rhubarb as a laxative."

Mrs. Sordido gave a little gasp that seemed to indicate approval.

"Have we heard anything from the duke?" the doctor inquired. "It was a duke who owned that carriage, wasn't it?"

"That's what we think from the blazon on the carriage. It will take some time for our man to reach London and bring back news.

395

It's a plumb shame about the coachman."

"Buried, is he?"

"Never woke up, not after that first night. Just raving, thinking he was in London. We buried him straight off. Mr. Sordido didn't see any point in waiting."

"This woman can't be a lady," the doctor said thoughtfully. "She's traveling without a maid, or luggage of any sort, and just look at that chemise she's wearing. I expect she's a maid in the duke's household, or a servant of some sort. You're very kind to look after her so, Mrs. Sordido. There's many an innkeeper who wouldn't bother."

"She's in no one's way. This old chicken coop was just sitting about," Mrs. Sordido said modestly. "I send the scullery maid morning and evening to offer water, just as you said."

"It's not as if she could complain of the smell from the chickens," the doctor said. "It's a rank disease."

"Terrible swollen, isn't she?" Mrs. Sordido said. "And what's that running from her ear, doctor?"

The doctor's face loomed closer to Linnet. "Fetid liquid," he said, straightening up. "There's nothing that can be done here, Mrs. Sordido. You can assure yourself that you've done your Christian duty by these poor travelers."

"Do come out into the fresh air, doctor," Mrs. Sordido said, her footsteps echoing on the wooden floor as she walked toward the door. She stirred up little swirls of dirt that floated before Linnet's eyes like fairy dust.

The doctor straightened and turned to leave as well. "I've no doubt but that the duke will reward you for your care."

"Yes, but Mr. Sordido isn't happy with having her here. Nor with me coming in the coop with you, I have to tell you, doctor. But I told him that I would have you visit her one more time, because I don't want her death on my conscience."

"You did right, you certainly did," the doctor said heartily. "Phew, it is rank in here, isn't it?"

"No," Linnet said, struggling so that she almost sat up. "No, please!"

She saw dimly that Mrs. Sordido had paused at the door. "What's happening to her now, doctor?"

"Seizure, I expect," he said, glancing over his shoulder. "Come along, madam. We've tried all that's humanly possible, and now we should just consign her soul to God. In fact, you might want to alert the minister."

"Oh, I couldn't bring the minister out just for a . . ." Her voice died away.

397

Trembling, Linnet brought her hand to her face. It wavered before her eyes. How long had she been here? It felt like weeks . . . months.

Slowly, slowly, she moved her hand to the glass next to her pallet, and managed to bring it to her lips. It flowed into her mouth, cool and lovely. But a moment later she realized that she had forgotten to swallow, and now her neck was wet.

She tried again, and the water sloshed against her nose. A tear trickled down her cheek.

She could feel heat lurking, coming back. Water, she thought. This time she managed to swallow. But when she put the glass back on the floor, next to her pallet, it rolled on its side, and the rest of the water poured onto the dirt floor.

No more water. No more water. It beat in her head to the pace of her heartbeat.

The terrible heat was coming now, drawing her back into that feverish whirlpool where she couldn't hear or see anything. But still, water . . .

The pool glimmered in front of her, exquisite blue, cool and refreshing. And there was Piers, his lean, sardonic, lovable face grinning at her.

For that moment, before the fever called

for her again, she concentrated on loving him, the way he made his fierce way through life, in agony but never stopping. The way he smiled. The intelligence in his eyes.

He never gives up, she thought. Little speckles, black speckles, were gathering before her eyes so that she could hardly see the weather-beaten boards at the bottom of her pallet.

Then the fever claimed her, and her eyes closed again.

THIRTY

The next day

By mid morning there was no question but that the epidemic was contained. Only three new patients arrived at the castle, and they weren't in extremis.

For the first time since the epidemic began, Sébastien and Piers actually paused for luncheon, falling into chairs in the small parlor, where Prufrock served them braised chicken and glasses of wine.

"This is civilized," Piers said with a sigh. "Have you brought some of this to my parents, Prufrock?"

"Yes, my lord," Prufrock said. "His Grace came out to bring it inside, once I had moved back a safe distance, of course." He cleared his throat. "He seemed quite happy."

"Lucky bastard," Piers said. "She's forgiven him." And somehow, he had too. Life was what it was. It was time to put away his rage at his father and simply get on with it, defective leg and all.

"Happily ever after," Sébastien said, taking a deep draught of wine. "Christ, it feels good to be clean again. I didn't want to get out of that bath."

Prufrock offered Piers a plate of tender, young asparagus. "Dr. Bitts is out of bed. He's still quite weak, but his man reports that he is asking questions about the patients."

"Bitts," Piers said moodily. "He's not a bad doctor, especially for a gentleman. Better than Penders. That fool came up with an infusion of roses yesterday for cleansing patients' tongues. I couldn't see any harm to it, but no benefit either."

"I think gentlemen make the best doctors," Sébastien said. "Look at the two of us." He grinned, exhaustion shadowing his eyes, but still triumphant. "We did a hell of a job with the scarlatina outbreak, Piers. And it didn't even involve cutting off people's limbs, which is what we're best at. Or I am, at any rate."

"We're an anomaly," Piers said, swirling his wine and trying not to think about Linnet. Which was futile, because the only time he didn't think about her was when he was actively working on a patient. "Most men, like Bitts, at home in the ballroom, aren't —"

He stopped.

Bitts . . . dancing with Linnet, laughing down at her. Bending his neck toward her. *Breathing* on her. Every night, almost every night. He shoved back from the table so hard that his chair fell over. "Linnet!"

Sébastien opened his mouth.

"She danced with Bitts. I'm a bloody, bloody fool. She danced with Bitts the night before he fell ill, and then she left in that carriage by herself." The blood was gone from his head; he felt dizzy. "Where's my cane, where's my perishing cane?"

It had fallen to the floor. Prufrock rushed to pick it up. Sébastien was standing now too, frowning.

"Bitts's symptoms appeared the next day," Piers said hoarsely. "The next day, Seb! She could be anywhere, sick. She could be —"

He turned, pushed Prufrock out of his way so roughly that the butler fell back against the sideboard. "I'm going after her."

"Wait!" Sébastien shouted. "We have to think this through."

"There's nothing to think through," Piers said. Panic was pouring through him like quicksilver, burning in his veins. "I'm going after her. Get my coat, you fool," he snapped at a footman. "Prufrock, a carriage. The fastest we've got. The curricle."

"You don't know where she is," Sébastien protested. "What route she took to London. You can't take a curricle all the way to London."

"I'll ask my father for the route. And if she dies because he allowed her to travel alone, I'll come back here and kill him."

"Piers!"

He ignored Sébastien's shout, running down the castle steps, watching his cane carefully to make sure that he didn't misstep.

The duke came out of the guardhouse and turned white when he heard Piers's explanation. "The road to the Swansea," he said. "I told the servants to wait for her in Llanddowll."

"Llanddowll or Llanddowrr?" Piers demanded.

The duke grew even paler. "I think I said Llanddowll. I'm not sure."

"Llanddowrr makes more sense; it's on the road north to Carmarthen." Piers pivoted on his heel and thrust himself back up the path to the castle. It was his nightmare, all over again. Trying to get down the path, up the path, it was all the same, and too slow because of his bloody leg, unable to save her.

The carriage was ready and waiting in front of the castle, four fresh horses attached.

"That's not a curricle," Piers snarled at Prufrock, who was standing at the coach's door.

Sébastien ran down the castle steps. "You don't know where she is. *If* she's caught scarlet fever from Bitts — and there's a good chance she hasn't, as your mother seems perfectly well — still, if she has contracted it, she'd have had the first symptoms within a day's journey. Two days at the most. But you're not going to find her so close, Piers."

"Why not?" he snapped.

"Because she's not ill. If she were, the duke's servants would have brought her back directly. They would have sent someone here on horseback, if she were too ill to be moved. It's been six days. Even if she hadn't fallen ill until the second day, someone would have brought us news by now. They're not all sick. None of them danced with Bitts."

Piers stopped, one foot on the carriage's step. "Seven days since she left, not six. They could have gone a long way before she felt symptoms. Some patients are — Oh. I see. No curricle as I might have to go all

404

the way to London. I understand."

Sébastien put a hand on his shoulder. "She's not ill, Piers. They continued on to London, and she's there, safe and sound, waiting for you."

"You can't know for sure." Piers swung up into the carriage.

"You will never know for sure if she's dead or alive unless you keep her near you all the time," Sébastien said with perfect, if maddening, accuracy.

Piers threw himself into a seat. His cousin handed a satchel through the coach door. "Take this. Just in case . . . all the salves the orderlies have been using, though I've no idea if they work. A bit of frothing mash, even a jar of Penders's acidulated rose water. Do you want footmen?"

"You can't spare them," Piers said. "Neythen is still in bed. I'll be fine with Buller." He put the satchel on the seat beside him.

"I'm convinced she's fine, and you won't need that, but do go fetch her." Sébastien was grinning. "We'll be all right here."

"I'm not going for that reason," Piers snapped. "She might be ill, you fool."

"You're going for her, no matter how much you protest you aren't," his cousin asserted. "I knew you would. You can't catch

405

her on the way; she's had too much of a head start. You'll have to do your groveling in London."

"I'm not . . ." Piers said.

Sébastien reached in, and gave him a slug to the shoulder, the kind of friendly blow they exchanged as boys. "I like her too. We all want her in the family. And . . . she's yours. There's just something about her. She's yours."

"She's mine," Piers said, tasting the words on his tongue. They fit, they fit in his heart. "She's mine." It wasn't really a question.

"So, go and fetch her back," Sébastien said, laughing.

Piers reached up and whacked the carriage's ceiling. "Out of the way, Seb. I have —" The door swung shut before he finished the sentence.

"A wife to find," he said into the empty carriage. "I have Linnet to find, to bring home, to marry."

THIRTY-ONE

Llanddowrr was a small village, dreaming in the afternoon sun. Piers stamped through the door of the inn that sat squarely on its high street, wielding his cane like a maniac. He saw no signs of sick travelers . . . in fact, no signs of scarlatina at all. No warning crimson cloths draped from windows, no apparent distress.

"We heard about it, of course," the innkeeper said, his eyes fearful at the thought. "A great crew of people came through here, a duke's household. They stayed for a meal and then rushed on, getting away."

"The Duke of Windebank's servants," Piers said. "They were here for some time?"

"Until early evening."

"Were they joined by a young lady in another of the duke's carriages?"

The innkeeper blinked. "Well, I couldn't really say as to that. There were three carriages, and the wife and I were getting a meal for all of them. Fourteen it were, all at once, piling into the common rooms, see?"

"All at once," Piers repeated. "But the young lady? She would have arrived in the late afternoon."

"That I don't know about, unless she didn't want a meal."

Piers thought of Linnet as he last saw her, of the bruised look in her eyes. "She might not have wished for a meal."

"We'll ask the hostler," the innkeeper said, coming out from behind the counter. "He's the one to know if a fourth carriage came along after the others. They were terribly nervous, that I do know. Kept saying that the duke told them to keep going if he didn't come by twilight."

"But surely they did wait for the duke," Piers said, controlling his voice.

He must not have done a good job, because the innkeeper glanced nervously over his shoulder before bustling out the door shouting. "Daw! Daw, where in the blazes are you?"

Daw was inspecting Piers's horses, wiping them down and having a good gossip with Buller. He jerked upright at the innkeeper's roar.

"Did a young lady come along in another carriage and join them three carriages as

408

belonged to the duke?" the innkeeper demanded.

Daw shook his head. "They waited, 'til 'round about eight. Which was a mad time to take off down the north road, but they were all tetchy-like and afraid of getting sick. They meant to drive through the night, I think."

"She never came," Piers said, his heart sinking. She had left the castle around three that afternoon. She should have arrived with time to spare before the caravan departed.

"They talked about the duke coming," Daw put in. "But nobody came, so they left."

She must have gone to the wrong village. Piers tossed a guinea to the innkeeper and turned to shout at Buller. "We've got to turn around. Go to Llanddowll."

"Llanddowll," Daw said. "That's not better than a privy, it's that small."

"It's smaller now," Piers said. "The village was badly hit by the fever."

The hostler moved back, and the horses were off. Piers sat in the carriage, his fingers drumming against the windowsill. She never came to Llanddowrr. That meant . . . that meant what? She must have driven to Llanddowll.

Why hadn't she returned to the castle,

once she couldn't find the duke's servants? She couldn't have proceeded to London by herself.

Impossible. She had no belongings, no maid. It was all in trunks, gone with the duke's servants. She couldn't even unbutton her gown by herself.

What he said to her wasn't *that* terrible, that she should run away without a stitch of clothing.

Forest, acres of forest, spun by the window. Llanddowll was in the opposite direction from the castle as Llanddowrr. Finally, he saw the turrets of his castle in the near distance. The horses slowed, then stopped.

"We can't stop, damn it!" Piers said, swinging open the door and shouting up at his coachman.

"The horses are blown," the man said apologetically. "If we don't change them, I'll have to slow down, and I reckon it will take less time if we just put on a new team."

What Piers said to this was unprintable, unsayable. It didn't help. The tired horses ambled home. The sun was drawing in now. Time, time was running through his fingers, and he was still running down that ocean path. He was going to be too late.

Prufrock emerged. "My lord?"

"She never made it to Llanddowrr," Piers

410

said. "We're off to Llanddowll."

"Damn," the butler said succinctly.

Piers swallowed. "She might have set off for London herself, when the servants weren't there to be met."

Prufrock nodded. "That's probably it. Miss Thrynne wouldn't have wanted to —" He stopped.

"She wouldn't have wanted to return here," Piers said, his heart beating in his rib cage like a trapped bird.

"Then that's what she did," the butler said, though he clearly didn't believe it.

"Any new patients?"

"No," Prufrock said. "And one of the ones that looked dead for sure, Barris Connah, seems to be pulling through."

Fresh horses were ready, and Piers climbed back into the carriage, stumbling, almost falling through the door. They were off again.

If Llanddowrr was small, Llanddowll was a speck, hardly carved out of the forest. A weather-beaten inn, a cobbler, a cluster of houses. No mill, which put it squarely on the original patient's flour delivery route. Fifty souls in all, if that.

It was getting toward dark as they pulled up to the inn. The innkeeper emerged as the carriage drew to a halt. He had a thin

411

nose and hollow cheeks, with a grubby beard and an even grubbier red handkerchief around his neck. He was rubbing his hands, looking guarded but welcoming.

"Good evening to you, sir," he called, as soon as Piers had his feet on the ground. "And welcome to the Gambling Fool. I'm Mr. Sordido, your host, but I should mabbe tell you now that we've had a spot of bother in the village —"

"Scarlatina," Piers cut him short. "I'm the Earl of Marchant, and we admitted four patients from this village."

"We've done our best," the innkeeper said, sensing criticism. "Isolated them just as soon —"

"Did a young lady arrive here in a carriage bearing the crest of the Duke of Windebank?"

Piers saw it in Sordido's eyes before he spoke, the way they avoided his own, the way his weight shifted from foot to foot. In an instant Piers had him by the grimy neck cloth. "Where is she? Is she dead?"

"We done nothing!" the innkeeper squealed, his face turning persimmon red. "We're taking care of her, good care. And we done so for the coachman too, afore he died."

She was still alive. Piers let go of the red

412

cloth, stepped back. "Where is she?"

Sordido's eyes shifted again. "We isolated her, same as the minister said we should. If you'll just step into the common room, me lord, I'll get my wife to check on the young woman and make sure that she's able to take visitors."

"Young woman?"

The innkeeper actually fell back a step. "We thought — the doctor said — we thought she must be a maid in service to his dukeship."

"A maid? You thought a future countess was a *maid?*"

Where there had been persimmon red, now there was just sallow yellow. "We had no call to think she was a lady, me lord. No maid, and no trunks."

"The coachman would have told you, before he died." Piers took one precise step forward.

Sordido's eyes flickered to Piers's cane and back to his face. "He didn't say nothing. The man was sick, mortal sick. He raved some, but none of it made sense that we heard. Then he died quick."

Piers closed his eyes for a second. What was he doing, bickering with the innkeeper when Linnet . . . "Take me to her." It was not a request; it was a demand.

413

The man looked behind him desperately. Then he bawled, "Moll!"

His wife was a trifle cleaner than her husband, but her eyes were small and close-set, like a ferret's. There was a rising panic in Piers's throat. His coachman had been attending silently from his seat; now he stepped down, tossed the horses' lead rein over a hitching post, and moved to Piers's shoulder.

"His lordship has come here a-looking for that woman" — the innkeeper corrected himself — "the lady who's been lying sick. At our own expense, we've been caring for her," he said, jutting his chin. "On account of how she had no money with her."

Piers frowned. It was entirely possible that Linnet had not carried a reticule with her, or had left it in the drawing room when she escaped through the window. The duke's coachman would have been equipped by his master for ready expenses, but if, when they'd arrived, he succumbed immediately as the innkeeper claimed . . .

The innkeeper's wife dropped a curtsy. "She's been terrible sick, I'm sorry to say. I had the doctor to her just yesterday, and he said that we'd done all a mortal body could do."

Piers jaw was clenched so hard that he

could barely say the words. "Take me to her."

"Like I said, if you just wait in my common room for a moment, the wife here, Mrs. Sordido, she'll make sure the young lady is acceptable for visitors."

"Take me to her."

Mrs. Sordido dropped another curtsy. "Begging your pardon, me lord, but I couldn't do that of a right conscience. The young lady is of a tender age, and not married. I'll just go and make sure that she's —"

Piers's voice cracked like a whip in the quiet inn-yard. "Take me to her *now*." He was walking toward the door, his cane thwacking the rough cobble stones, when his coachman said, "My lord."

The innkeeper's wife was trotting around the corner of the inn, her husband standing rather helplessly where he was.

Piers altered his path. Of course they hadn't put her in the inn. He had ensured that himself, when he sent out the orders for quarantine. They rounded the corner, Mrs. Sordido hastening ahead. Piers looked over his shoulder.

His coachman, Buller, had her elbow in a moment. "We'll all walk together, shall we?" he said. Buller was a large man, and his

415

voice, though soft, seemed to frighten her.

"It isn't proper!" she squeaked. "She's not properly attired."

Piers just concentrated on picking his way across the stones in the falling dark. He was aware of the innkeeper trailing behind, of the gathering shadows fingering out from the woods surrounding them. But fear filled his mind. Fear pounded in his head and his heart.

It took two or three minutes to walk there; it felt like an hour. Mrs. Sordido protested the whole way, but Buller kept a firm grip on her elbow. "There," she said finally, spitting it out defiantly.

Piers looked, but Buller spoke first. "That's for chickens. That's a chicken coop."

"It's a good coop," she said. "Tall enough to walk in. And there haven't been any chickens in there for months, six months probably. We put her in there, and I had my girl visiting her morning and night of my own good Christian will, let me tell you. And I had the doctor to her two times, and had him try everything in his power, the leeches and all, though there was no one to pay him."

Piers was frozen to the spot. The chicken coop had no windows, and the door was

416

hanging from one leather hinge. It was made of rough boards that had apparently started falling apart at some point, as random pieces of wood had been nailed this way and that.

"What is that *smell?*" Buller said, his voice dropping an octave. His hand on Mrs. Sordido's arm must have tightened, because she squeaked in protest.

"It's the chickens," she said. "That is, chickens do smell, and we didn't have time to clean it."

Piers had shaken free of his paralysis and was going as fast as he could through the little clearing before the coop. One part of his mind was screaming silently in panic, the other was grimly aware that he was reliving his nightmare, trying to reach Linnet . . . too late.

Behind him he could hear Mrs. Sordido's protests and Buller growling back at her. He reached the door, flung it open. The hinge snapped, and the door fell with a crash onto the ground.

Once inside, Piers couldn't see anything in the gloom, and his eyes immediately started watering from the foul air. Carefully he inched his cane forward, pulling himself a step, waiting for his eyes to adjust.

"Linnet," he said, quietly. Quietly, because

417

in his heart he knew the truth. She was dead, and it was his fault.

No answer. He walked forward another step and finally his eyes began to adjust. There was no bed. He looked down to find he was about to step on her.

The woman at his feet had no resemblance to his laughing, beautiful Linnet. But the doctor in him came to the fore, pushing aside his grief, dropping his cane so he could kneel beside her and take up her wrist.

For a moment he despaired of finding a pulse, and then he felt it: thready and weak, but there. "Linnet," he said, hand on her cheek, seeing not her ravaged skin or tangled hair, but the shape of her dear face, the way she curled slightly to the side as she always did in sleep. He loved her; he loved her so much that his heart was breaking.

There was no answer. A cloud of chicken effluvia rose around his knees as he shifted. She was burning up, of course. Numbly he catalogued such symptoms as he could see in the half-light — and couldn't bring himself to add them up to the obvious conclusion.

Instead he reached for his cane, got himself to his feet, and then bent to get out the entrance.

"It weren't our fault," Mrs. Sordido

yelped, the moment he exited. Buller still gripped her arm.

"I assume you have no guests in the inn," Piers stated.

"No," she said, half panting. "Not at the moment, but —"

"I'm taking over your inn. You and your husband will have to get out."

"Where's the duke's carriage?" Buller said suddenly. "I don't see where you stabled his horses, either."

There was a second of silence, then Sordido said, "We sent them on to the duke, of course. In London."

Buller grabbed Mrs. Sordido's arm again. But there must have been something in Piers's eyes that was more frightening than the threat of force. She quailed and said, "Behind the inn, in the shed."

"No, they're not," Sordido said, blustering. "We —"

"You stole the carriage," Piers stated. "You stole the horses. You likely stole my wife's clothing."

"You never said as how she was your wife!" Sordido put in.

"She's *mine*. You stole her clothing, and the money they had with them, and I'm fairly sure that you killed the Duke of Windemere's coachman."

"We didn't," Sordido said, panting. "We'd nothing to do with it."

"He died from what ailed him," his wife said, the words tumbling out now. "They came late at night, and he went to bed above the stables, but the next morning, he was in a high fever, all hot, mumbling and coughing. He never really came out of it."

Piers looked at her.

"He didn't!" she repeated shrilly. "He raved of this and that, but we couldn't stand by his bedside every minute of the day. Besides, she was sick, and the smith was down with it too, and his wife. We had our hands full, trying to get the doctor from the next village over to visit. And then the minister came through, and said as how the sick ones had to be isolated." She lost steam.

"He died," Sordido added. "He died quick-like. But she didn't. So we had to put her somewhere."

"You and your husband, get out," Piers said. "If you're on the premises in an hour, I'll have you put in the dungeons in my castle. They are marginally worse than where you put my wife."

Her mouth gaped open. "You're — no, you're not!" With a fierce wrench, she freed her arm from Buller's hand. "You can't come in here and just do as you wish with a

420

person's property! That's my inn, my and Sordido's. We bought it free and clear for fifty pounds, and we're not going — Sordido!"

"If you leave the inn now, I won't haul you up before the magistrate."

"You can't do that!" she said shrilly. "Sordido, say something! We did no more than our duty with that woman. Out of the goodness of our hearts."

"You have no heart," Piers stated. "What you do have is one hour to gather your possessions and get out. I don't want you within ten miles of my castle. I don't want you in Wales at all. If you're not out of here in an hour, I'll have you deported to the colonies."

Mrs. Sordido was obviously the power behind the throne, as it were. She had her fists on her hips now. "You can't!" she screamed. "It's our property, free and clear. We paid for it."

"If you're out of the inn in one hour, I won't prosecute. If you're not, I'll have you before the magistrate by morning light."

"We can't," Sordido said, starting to whine. "It's coming on night, and what would we do for money? I put everything into this inn, every tuppence I had."

But Piers was done with the conversation.

421

"Buller, I need you to carry my — to carry Linnet into the inn. One hour," he snapped at Mrs. Sordido. "In case you're wondering whether my word carries weight with the magistrate, I just saved his daughter from dying of scarlatina."

"I did what I could out of pure Christian mercy," Mrs. Sordido cried.

Piers held up his hand. "She is at the point of death. I am telling you to leave out of pure Christian mercy. Because if she dies . . ."

Mrs. Sordido backed up, scrabbling her apron in her hands. "Sordido!" she cried, turning to run. "Hurry, man, hurry!"

"Carry Linnet into the inn," Piers said, turning to Buller. "I'll go ahead and find an acceptable bed. Then give those fools a few guineas and a chit for fifty pounds, and take the carriage straight back to the castle. You can get a few hours of sleep and return in the morning. We need help."

Buller nodded, and went to the chicken coop, stooping to enter. Piers turned and made off across the yard toward the inn.

He could hear Mrs. Sordido shouting at her husband as she racketed around upstairs.

He made his way directly to the best bed-chamber. "Them's my sheets," Mrs. Sordido said, appearing in the doorway. "You said as how we could keep our things."

The guinea spun through the air, and she caught it neatly. "And what of the kitchen?" she demanded. "I expect you'd need a pot or two, and I've a full larder already set in for the winter."

He doubted that, but he threw her a couple more. Then: "Get out."

She ran.

At least the bed linens were clean, and reasonably soft. He pulled back the covers, opened the curtains, and threw open the windows as he heard the sound of Buller coming slowly up the stairs.

Together they laid her on the bed.

"God almighty," Buller whispered. "What did they do to her? I've never smelt anything like it. And her face . . ."

Piers glanced at her ravaged face and skin. "That's the scarlatina, not the chicken coop. I need water, Buller, lots of it. A pail right away, and several pots on the stove set to boil. And the satchel from the carriage. Once you see those louts off the premises, you need to go back to the castle and fetch help. We'll be all right without you in the meantime."

"You'll be all right?" Buller whispered. His eyes were fixed on Linnet. "I wouldn't know it was her. I never seen anything like it. She was the prettiest little thing . . ."

"Go," Piers said, jerking his head. He waited until he heard the man's footsteps start down the stairs, and then he ripped off the shameful excuse for a nightgown Linnet was wearing. It was ragged and torn; clearly the Sordidos had taken all her clothes when they consigned her to the coop. He threw it in the corner.

Still she didn't move, her neck and head utterly limp as Piers pulled her filthy hair away from her face, piling it on top of the pillow. So he began talking to her, a slow, steady conversation, telling her exactly what he was doing as he checked her ears, checked her throat, her blackened tongue, her skin. He found signs of leeches at her throat and let fall a curse word that interrupted his soothing monologue.

Buller's heavy feet sounded on the stairs again, so Piers went to the door. "I need you to bring clean mattresses from the castle, at least two. I'm going to ruin this one, getting her cooled off and clean, and I think there's a fair chance of vermin in any bed on the premises."

Buller nodded. "Pots of water are on the stove. The Sordidos are gone. They whipped out when I had my back turned." He hesitated.

"What?"

"They stole the duke's carriage, I'm pretty sure of that. And his horseflesh. I didn't see them go, but that wasn't the sound of a cart leaving. And they said something about a scullery maid, but there's no one to be seen around here. The girl must have seen the way things were going and run off."

Piers shrugged. "They have Linnet's clothing too, so you'll need to bring her something to wear. Go back to the castle and get some rest, Buller. I'll expect you first thing in the morning."

The coachman nodded, but then waited, his eyes fearful.

"She'll live," Piers stated, making it fierce, a statement, not an opinion.

He closed the door to the bedroom, threw off his coat and began the fight of his life.

For her life.

THIRTY-TWO

"We have to get you clean, sweetheart," he said to Linnet. She didn't move. "You're in a coma, so hopefully you don't know how filthy you are." He devoutly hoped so. "I'm going to wash you down the way Nurse Matilda washed Gavan once a week, and if you feel like squirming or shouting the way he did, please do not hesitate."

Silence.

"Until I have some boiled water, I can't wash the parts of your skin that are raw, as they might get infected." Unfortunately, that was most of her body.

God, she'd lost so much weight. How could this happen so fast, in a week? She went from a curved, delicious woman to a near skeleton, her hair like straw, her skin . . .

From head to foot she was covered in a layer of grime, all her sores and raw skin layered in chicken excrement. He started with her feet, because they weren't peeling, and washed every toe carefully.

"Whatever all this dirt is," he told her, washing her toes for the second time, and realizing that the water in which he was wringing the rag was already turning brown, "I'll write an article about it after you recover. The miraculous properties of chicken manure. It can't be worse than the fermented mash, though the smell is certainly more penetrating."

He kept talking, and talking, though not even Linnet's fingertip quivered in response. He told her when he was going down to fetch more water, and greeted her when he returned to her room.

"An ungainly progress," he told her. "I had to hoist the pail up each stair first, and then hoist myself after. Now we're starting the hard part, darling. It's going to hurt. You're covered in dirt, and I have to clean your skin. With soap, which will make the open blisters hurt all the more."

Mercifully, she didn't seem to feel it, although the pain would have been torment to a conscious patient, as they often screamed at a mere touch. He kept checking her eyes to see if her lids twitched, indicating discomfort. And he listened to her chest again and again, finding the deep rattle that reassured him she was breathing.

At some point he simply poured the now-tepid water over her, desperate to get her clean, but terrified to rub skin that was open and raw from the scarlatina rash. It didn't work. The dirt clung to her body, giving way only to soap and water.

Darkness fell. He lit the one lamp he could find, without closing the windows. She'd been locked in that coop for days; fresh air could only help.

"You're cooler now," he told her. "The fever's come down, though whether that was because of all that water or just the course of the disease, I don't know. The fever does come and go, we've found."

He had slowly worked his way up her body, past her breasts, her arms, her neck.

"I've reached your face, Linnet. This is going to be torture. Gavan would scream bloody murder."

Her hair, thick and rank, had fallen back around her face, so he pushed it away again. It was matted with sweat and water and dung. "I have to cut it off," he said. "Speak now, or never."

She lay unmoving, and Piers found himself swallowing a cry, a sob, some involuntary response that he hadn't allowed himself since the early days of his injury, when he learned that crying over pain made it worse.

Who would have thought that there was worse pain in the world?

He made his way back down the stairs to the kitchen, and returned, hauling another pail of water and a knife. "It has to go," he told her. "It will grow back. But right now it's likely harboring God knows what sort of vermin."

It wasn't easy, cutting hair with a none-too-sharp knife. He hacked it off as close to her scalp as he could, and attacked what was left with soapy water, treating her face as gently as he could. By the time he was finished, water was running off the bed, rivulets streaming across the floor in all directions. "I think we'll have to double Nurse Matilda's wages," he told her. "This is harder than what I do with patients."

He turned her over, carefully, supporting her neck as if she were a day-old infant. Her back was cleaner, but the rash was more violent, blisters breaking at his touch.

"There's nothing I can do about the pain," he said, his voice ragged. "Damnation, Linnet, I need another bucket of water. I'll be back."

Walking back through door with fresh water he found her so still, so corpse-like that his heart stuttered. He stumbled to her bed, grabbed her wrist . . . the pulse was still there.

By the time he finished washing her entire body, the rivulets of water on the floor had merged into a sudsy pool. "It's running through the floorboards to the room below," Piers told her. "Likely the first time this floor has been so clean. Now what am I going to do?"

She was clean, but he couldn't dry her, not in a sodden bed. He turned her over again, carefully arranging her arms by her sides. "Dead of midnight," he told her. "I'm going to have to take the lamp, dearest. Can't see a bloody thing without it. I'll look for another lamp, but I have a nasty suspicion that the Sordidos took anything moveable. There's not a candle to be found in the kitchen."

He picked up the lamp and his cane, and hobbled from room to room. There were no more lamps, and in fact, only one room still had linens. "Bloody hell," he said aloud. He went back to Linnet. "You weigh less than those mattresses."

Not even an eyelid flickered.

He looked down at himself. His clothes were filthy and covered in chicken excrement. He couldn't touch her like this. "I'm taking my clothes off," he said, conversation-

430

ally. "I know you always liked to watch me. Did you think I didn't notice that you were peeking at me?"

She didn't answer, but in his head he heard her laughter.

"There's some clean bedding next door that Mrs. Sordido unaccountably missed," he explained. "I have to carry you there, and unfortunately you're more ungainly than a bucket of water."

When he was naked, he leaned the cane against the bed, took a deep breath, and slid an arm under Linnet's neck and the other under her knees. For a moment he just held her while he gathered his strength, her cheek pressed against his chest as that sob fought to escape again.

"No," he said out loud, straightening up. He turned on his strong leg, and pitched forward on the bad one. "I won't fall," he reassured Linnet. Her arm fell free and swung before them. Step, lurch, step, lurch. Another step and he was through the door into the corridor.

"This gives new meaning to the need for wall lamps," he said to her. Step, lurch, step, lurch. "Damn, I'm going to have to sit down." His voice was a ragged gasp. But if he sat down on the floor, he would never be able to get up, not without his cane and with her in his arms. So he leaned against the corridor wall, head back, took deep breaths, and tried to ignore the pain exploding past his leg into his hip.

"A few more steps . . . perhaps three, only three, and then the door will be there. I'll turn in. Three more to get you to a dry bed."

Pain lanced through him as if in answer.

He shoved himself away from the wall and took a step. Another lurch, a step. "That swimming is coming in handy," he said to her, getting the words out between grunts of pain. "You're a feather in my arms."

Not precisely true, but good enough. Finally, he made it to the doorway, the bedchamber lit only by moonlight streaming in the window. He hobbled across the floor, managed to place her on the bed, and pulled the sheet up.

"If you'll excuse me, my lady," he said, the words coming in short bursts. And without further ado, he crumpled to the floor.

Some time later, he raised his head. "Have to retrieve that cane of mine," he told her. Walking was out of the question. So he crawled, stark naked, out of the room, down the corridor, onto the wet floor of the bedchamber. Found the cane and got himself upright.

Profanity didn't help. The pain in his leg was excruciating, so much so that even the drenched bed looked inviting. "I have to get back to her," he said aloud. The moon was traveling across the sky. "Water. Linnet has to drink water."

He'd saved one precious bucket, so he slung his satchel over his shoulder, put the wire handle of the lamp over his forearm, and picked up the bucket. It was too much to carry; he knew it immediately.

But it had to be done, even if a man found himself grunting every time his weak leg moved forward. If not crying out.

She lay under the sheet, as still as death. "That corridor," he said from the door, panting. "I'll never forget it, Linnet. It's the inferno, hell itself. I'm afraid that I can't make any more trips downstairs. I'm done for the night."

Since she showed no sign of disagreeing with him, he got the lamp onto the table somehow, the satchel over to the bed. Only half the precious water remained in the bucket. "Lurching is not recommended for water carriers," he told her, pulling her chin down slightly and dribbling some into her mouth.

"That will do for now. Ointment next," he said, opening the satchel. "Frankly, I doubt that any of these work. But they don't hurt, as far as I can tell. Back first." He rolled her over and carefully applied ointment all over her rash. "Poor bottom," he said, dabbing carefully. "Or do you prefer *buttocks?* I can't remember. Now your front."

Some time later, he scrabbled around in the satchel again and pulled out a jar. "Penders's rose water. I'm going to clean off your throat and tongue," he told her. His voice was rasping now. It was a messy business, not helped by the fact his patient was in a coma.

"But if you weren't in a coma, I would be hurting you," he told her. "I couldn't bear that, Linnet. Not after the way I already hurt you."

She was clean and sweet-smelling now. But she looked like a fragile baby chick. What hair she had left was standing straight up, and for some reason that made her head look large, and her neck too frail and slender to carry such a weight. Her closed eyelids were blue.

His doctor's instinct told him what he couldn't put into words. The patient was close to death.

He turned down the lamp, looked at her again, and finally extinguished it. Moonlight was enough . . . moonlight and the thread of her pulse.

Carefully, carefully, Piers hoisted himself onto the bed, lying on top of the sheet so he didn't touch any open wounds. But he had to hold her, so he tucked the sheet around her neck and then wrapped an arm around her waist.

And if the sobs escaped then, if the sheet grew salty and wet, there was no one to see but the moon.

THIRTY-THREE

Linnet heard Piers's voice first as a faraway trickle, like running water in a brook somewhere off in the distance. She herself was far away in a safe place, the pool near the sea. It wasn't cold as it always had been, those mornings, but pleasantly warm, sometimes even too hot.

Still, she wanted to say good-bye to him, she really wanted to say good-bye to him.

He was her lodestone, after all. Her beating heart. And although he'd pushed her away, he would be broken when he learned of her death. She knew that.

In the last days, as she lay in that place, drifting into and out of the fever, she'd come to the certainty, the sure knowledge that he loved her. For all he said cruel things, he loved her.

And she had let him scold her out of the room and out of his life. It was just as she thought when she saw Piers for the very first time. If they were to be married, she'd have to stop him from bullying her.

If she lived, she would go back to him and make him stop. She would tell him . . . something.

She drifted off again, but when she woke his voice was closer and less melodic. Piers, melodic? That was an amusing thought. What could she be thinking? He was never melodic.

As if on cue he burst into a string of curse words that would have made her smile except she was too strangely enervated to twitch a muscle.

In truth, she didn't seem to have the energy to open her eyes. But she'd stopped opening them lately, anyway. She was too exhausted to drink, and her eyes were sticky with dirt.

So she sank back into the water, the blue crystalline water of the pool. She was drifting down and away, her hair rippling through the water, when she heard him swearing again.

Really, she should speak to him about his profanity. It —

Then she remembered that she was dying. In a chicken coop, and Piers was nowhere close, since he'd thrown her out of the castle.

Dying . . .

He would care, dreadfully.

Then she clearly heard Piers say something about her buttocks. *Bottom,* she thought. But she was still trapped under the water. Though was *trapped* the right word? It was pleasant there. The pool was fearsomely hot sometimes, but now it was cool, and the water brushed her face like the hand of someone who loved her.

Her mother's hand. A sudden memory came into her head of a fever, some fever she'd had as a child. Her mother's voice, her nurse's voice . . . her mother irritably saying, "Of course I'm not going anywhere tonight! Linnet is ill . . ."

But it wasn't a hand touching her, it was an arm. An arm around her waist, heavy and male.

It must be Piers. She'd never been to bed with anyone else.

For a moment her mind reeled wildly between the pool, with its watery silken sheets and its drifting peace — and a bed with Piers. His arm around her, tight. The smell of him, male and a bit sweaty.

Sweaty? Piers was never sweaty.

Just like that, her face broke the surface of the pool as if she were thrust from the water

438

by a pair of arms that threw her, threw
her —

Where?

She opened her eyes. It was terribly dark,
so it must be the chicken coop. But the
coop . . . She sniffed again, but carefully,
without moving. She had learned not to stir
a muscle because of the sores on her skin.

It didn't smell like the chicken coop.

And then, as her eyesight slowly returned,
she realized that moonlight was coming in a
window. She was in a bed. And the arm . . .
there was an arm around her.

She turned to her side, wincing. Piers *was*
there. He'd come for her. For a moment
Linnet just feasted on the look of him: his
lean, fierce face, darkened with beard. His
eyes, closed now in sleep, but so powerfully
intelligent when he was awake. His lips were
surprisingly full for a man, his bottom lip
rounded.

Piers, she whispered, before she remembered that she couldn't talk, that she hadn't
been able even to whisper for a long time.

He didn't stir. Her eyes began to close
again; the pool beckoned . . . but he was
here, next to her. Didn't she want to say
good-bye? Hadn't she something to tell him,
something important?

Yes. She had to stay awake, not fall into

the pool until he woke, until she could tell him the important thing.

She forgot what it was, feasting on his cheekbones, long eyelashes, the tumble of hair over his brow, the frown that he wore even in sleep. He had never slept with her before, though she had secretly longed for it.

And here he was, naked on the sheet. Sleeping *with* her, in the same bed, at night.

The moonlight faded, replaced by the very first rays of morning light.

"Piers," she whispered. Her lips moved, but no sound came out.

Still, he must have heard her that time, because his eyes opened.

For a moment he just smiled at her, sleepy and possessive. "Linnet," he said, and her whole soul rejoiced.

Then his eyes snapped open. "You're awake!" His hand came down on her forehead. "How do you feel?"

"Hurts," she said, knowing no sound was coming from her lips.

"It must hurt like hell," Piers said. That was all he said, but for Piers, that was sympathy. "You need to drink, Linnet. That's the most important thing. You're not out of the woods."

It was as if he were talking to himself. So

she drank some water, though most of it trickled down her neck.

Still, she felt . . . different.

"Clean," she said. He read her lips.

"Do you remember me washing you, Linnet? Do you?"

She almost shook her head, and then remembered not to. "No," she breathed. Her eyes were drifting shut. His hand was huge on her forehead, touching her gently, and she could hear him talking.

"The fever's back," he was saying. "But that's to be expected, Linnet. I'm putting a wet cloth on your forehead."

It made her flinch.

"I know those sores hurt." His voice was grim. "But I have to bring your temperature back down."

Suddenly she remembered the important thing she had to tell him, and opened her eyes. "Love you," she breathed, eyes meeting his.

"Then live for me," he said, bending over her, his voice fierce as a hawk's cry. "Live."

She fell asleep with a little smile on her face. The pool was farther away now, dim and receding. She found herself dreaming of the chicken coop instead, and woke with a gasp.

Piers was still there, dressed now, with a

snowy white neck cloth. He was standing at the door to the bedchamber, talking to someone in the hallway. "More water, if you please. Boiled, of course."

She went back to sleep. Time seemed to stretch out, elongate itself and then suddenly disappear. She'd sleep, and wake up to find it was the middle of the night. Sleep again, wake to find it still nighttime, but Piers was wearing a different neck cloth.

Finally, after three days, she tried to say something, and a squawk came out.

"You sound like a barnyard rooster with a cold," Piers said, coming to her side. His face was exhausted, his eyes bruised.

"Tired," Linnet said, going back to a soundless whisper.

He misunderstood. "Fatigue is a side effect of a brush with death," he said, a triumphant grin spreading across his face. "Damn it, Linnet, I'm going to write you up. I'm the only doctor in Wales who could have pulled you through."

"You peacock," she mouthed. Her body felt boundlessly weary, but mercifully, the prickling pain was fading. Remembering, she raised her arm, and gasped. It was dark red and scaly.

Piers sat down on the edge of the bed. "It isn't a pretty disease, Linnet."

She tried to make sense of that.

"This is not your finest hour. I had to cut your hair off."

She blinked in horror, her mouth falling open.

"You're covered in scabs, head to toe. Well, actually for some reason your feet are fine. But you even have them behind your ears."

Linnet raised her arm again and stared at it in disbelief.

"You could have gone blind," Piers said with his usual directness. "Or died. You should have died, by all rights. It's a miracle you didn't get an infection, lying on the floor of that chicken coop."

Linnet shuddered at the word *chicken* and let her arm fall. But she had to ask. "Scars?" she asked, propelling the word out with such force that it was easy to comprehend.

White lies were not in Piers's repertoire. "Most likely," he said, looking at her analytically, like the doctor he was. "Sometimes yes, sometimes no. You won't look quite as much like a boiled lobster in a week or two."

Linnet closed her eyes and tried to understand what he was saying. She looked like a boiled lobster, perhaps permanently. *Not* a beauty any longer. Not by any measure.

More like a monster, she thought. A scaly beast.

She could hear Piers rising, probably thinking she had gone to sleep. Her body was rigid, the arm under her sheet feeling her leg and then her waist carefully. Everywhere she touched, her skin felt uneven, scaly and hard under her fingertips.

Piers was there again. "Broth," he said. There was no point in refusing; she'd learned that over the last three days. Piers would not accept no. So she opened her eyes and took the broth, spoon after spoon. Her left fingers twitched at her side, but she didn't move.

Then the bowl was empty, and Piers walked away with it. For a moment she was frozen, unable to make herself move — and then she did. She put her hand squarely on her breast.

There was no mistaking the skin under her fingers. Her breasts were in the same condition as her arm, as her stomach, as her leg.

She lay there, hand on her breast, and felt one hot tear go down her cheek, and then another.

Piers was still at the door, having given someone the empty bowl. "I'll just go next door and take a nap," he was saying.

444

She knew he would come back, lean over her, say good-bye. In the last three days, he had never left the room without telling her where he was going, and how long he'd be gone.

"Maid," she breathed, as soon as he was close enough. "You go back to the castle. I'll be fine with my maid."

For a split second, his eyes changed, turning desolate. But then he said readily, "Of course. She can be here by supper time."

Eliza was no better at hiding the truth than Piers. She fell back upon entering the door, hand on her heart. "Lord Almighty!" she gasped.

Linnet waited.

"Your hair, your poor hair," Eliza breathed, but her eyes returned with a kind of fascinated horror to Linnet's face and neck. "That's not . . . you don't have that all over, do you?"

Another tear ran down Linnet's cheek. She nodded.

"Well, you were like to die," Eliza said, coming over but looking as if she was thinking twice about touching Linnet. "You easily could have died. By all accounts, his lordship thought you would, at first."

Linnet wished she had, rather than face

life with this skin.

And Eliza guessed what she was thinking. "It'll get better," she said, rattling out the words. "I'm sure of that. We'll — we'll bathe you in mineral salts, every day. Twice a day. I've never seen anyone who looks like you, which means that it has to get better. Of course —" She stopped.

"What?" Linnet croaked.

"Oh, your poor throat," Eliza cried. "Your voice is just gone."

"What?" Linnet repeated.

"His lordship said as how you're almost the only one to get this sick and survive," Eliza said. "Maybe that's why I've never seen skin like that before."

Linnet closed her eyes, feeling utter despair. She had lived, but she was left with this face. This skin.

"Would it hurt if I touched you?" Eliza was saying.

She shook her head again, wearily.

Eliza's fingers were soft and cool. "It's like scabs," her maid said. "All-over ones. Well, this is a perishing state of affairs."

"Home," Linnet croaked, catching her eye.

"You want to go home? It's going to break your father's heart, that it will."

At the moment Linnet didn't give a damn about what her father thought. She just

446

wanted to be back in her own room, away from anyone who —

Away from Piers.

Away from the man who had loved her body and thought her hair was like burnished gold.

"I'll ask," Eliza promised. "But his lordship, I'm not sure he'll let you go. He tended you all by himself, you know. Kept you alive when no one else could, spooning water into you every hour, covering you with wet cloths, and then warming you up again."

Linnet felt a pang. Piers had always warmed her with his body when they swam together. She had no doubt he had done everything possible to make her live. Piers couldn't bear to lose, especially to Death.

"From what I hear," Eliza continued, "you were a proper sight when they found you in that chicken coop."

Linnet remembered bits and pieces, and what she remembered wasn't pretty. The smell . . . the smell was foremost in her memory. She shuddered.

"We'll have to get you back to the castle first," Eliza was saying. "You should see the duke and the duchess now. Like a pair of lovebirds, they are. The duke wanted to get a special license, but Lady Bernaise made him post the banns right in the little church in the village. Second week now, so they'll be tying the knot again next week. Did you ever hear anything so romantic?"

Linnet shook her head.

"I'm not sure that you'll want to go to the ceremony, though," Eliza said. She ran her fingers over Linnet's hand again.

"Never," Linnet managed, meaning that she would never, ever leave the house again. Not like this. Not . . . *ever.*

"Well, as to never," Eliza said, "it'll get better. There are salves that we can put on, and salt baths, and in a week, maybe a month, you'll be as good as gold. There's all those creams they advertise in the papers," she added. "For clearing up red skin. I know I've seen those. We'll buy some back in London. Your father will buy all of them. The earl sent him a message, by the way, in case he was worried at not hearing from you for so long."

Linnet closed her eyes and tried to imagine her father worrying about her long silence.

"And even if your skin isn't *quite* what it was before," Eliza went on, "it doesn't matter, because you're going to be a countess, and a duchess someday."

Linnet snapped her eyes open.

"Anyone can tell the man loves you to distraction," her maid said, smiling. "Besides, he told his father *and* the marquis that he was marrying you. They came over here the second day to see how you were doing. He wouldn't let them in to see you, but he told them that you were going to live long enough to marry him. Three footmen heard it, so I know it's true."

"No," Linnet stated. She would never marry Piers. In fact, she would never marry any man, but in particular not the Earl of Marchant.

Eliza didn't hear her. "I'm just going to pop out and see what I should be doing for you. There must be *something* we can put on that skin."

Linnet could hear her, through the door. "I don't care if he is asleep, there must be something we can put on her skin." More murmuring. "All right then." She was back in the room, brandishing a jar. "I'm going to put this stuff all over you." Eliza took a sniff. "It smells like beer. Well, beer and pine needles. Who cares as long as it works?"

Linnet let her spread the oily, smelly stuff all over, front and back.

"Lord Almighty, it's worse here," Eliza exclaimed, gently rubbing it into Linnet's rear. "Though I wouldn't have thought that possible."

More tears trickled into the pillow.

By the time Piers walked into the room —
without a knock, as if he were master of the
bedchamber — Linnet had made up her
mind. She couldn't go home to London yet,
obviously. She had to gather strength. She
drank more broth than she wished, because
the sooner her strength returned, the sooner
she could leave.

He bent over her, almost as if he were going to kiss her. "Go away," she said, turning
her face to the side. The words came out
like squawks, but they were perfectly under-
standable.

He straightened and scowled down at her.
"You smell like a brewery. What's all over
you?"

"I put on this salve," Eliza said, bustling
forward with the now-empty jar.

"I told Neythen to send that along for the
scullery girl's chapped hands," Piers said.
"Though it can't have hurt."

"I had to do *something*," Eliza said defensively. "The poor dear can't stay like this.
Why, she couldn't be seen on the street
without causing a riot."

She would never look in a glass again.

"Go away," she croaked at Piers.

"It stands to reason you'd be one of those

450

cranky patients," he said.

So Linnet looked at Eliza. And Eliza, bless her heart, stepped forward to fight the beast. "My mistress would like you to leave the room, Lord Marchant. Since she can't make herself understood, I'll speak for her."

"Fine," Piers snapped. He walked to the door, turned around. "I'll come back later with your supper. I think it's time to try something more sustaining than broth."

Linnet threw Eliza a desperate look. Her maid moved forward again, as if she were guarding the bed. "If you'll bring me the supper, my lord, I'll make sure that my mistress eats every drop. She's not fit for company at the moment."

"I'm not company!" Piers roared.

Eliza folded her arms.

"Oh, for God's sake," he said suddenly, and got himself through the door. Linnet could hear his cane thwacking down the steps, and then receding into the distance.

Eliza came back. "I won't be able to hold him off for long," she said, peering down at Linnet. "He is a doctor. He's seen the worst of it. He was here all alone with you the first night."

A tear trickled down Linnet's cheek. Eliza sat down and put a hand on her arm, not even flinching at the feel. "There, there," she said. "If a body ever deserved a good cry, you're the one."

It went on like that for a week. Piers would push his way into the room, and Eliza would manage to thrust him back out. Sometimes she thought they were actually enjoying it, the two of them. Eliza took to shouting at the earl with relish. And Piers had never hesitated to shout back. They were a pair.

But once or twice, she caught Piers's face when he looked at her, and she understood that she was hurting him. She did understand that.

"But it doesn't matter, it can't matter," she whispered to herself in the depth of the night, thinking of it. "I can't — I cannot be a duchess. Never. It's inconceivable."

Finally, Piers declared her ready to travel, back to the castle at least. Eliza wanted to put her in a gown, but Linnet said no. She could talk now, albeit in a low voice. "The sheet," she said hoarsely. "It's bigger."

Eliza immediately caught what she was saying. "Your hair's curling all over," she said. "So that's good. It looks like that short haircut some ladies get. It's *à la mode,* which means French ladies probably did it first."

Her hair didn't matter; she knew it would

grow back. Yet even thinking about leaving this room and people staring at her face made Linnet want to vomit. Or faint.

But leave the room she did, wrapped up like a mummy and carried by Mr. Buller, Piers's coachman.

It wasn't so terrible leaving the inn . . . but when they got to the castle, Prufrock was there, and the footmen. The duke came down the stairs to greet them, and Linnet actually prayed for a quick death after she saw the kindness in his eyes.

But as death didn't seem to be offered, she closed her eyes, and pretended, as fervently as she could, that none of this was happening. That she was in London, dancing with Prince Augustus. The prince was smiling down at her with that besotted expression he tended to have around her.

"Of course she's fine," Piers's rough voice said, interrupting her daydream. "She looks like a lobster, and she's twice as irritable."

The dance . . . Prince Augustus turned her in a circle and she caught a glimpse of a row of faces ogling them, frankly envious. Her skirts were swirling —

"No, she's just having a fit of the megrims," Piers barked. And then, offhandedly, "Someone show Buller the way to her bedchamber."

With Linnet's eyes closed, she could hear Eliza tapping up the stairs before them, and the sound of Buller's heavy breathing.

"I'm sorry if I'm too heavy," she said. Her voice was no longer rasping.

"Not at all, miss," Buller said. His voice was kind. All the kindness was mortifying, worse than the moment when the whole ballroom gave her the cut direct. Honestly, she preferred Piers's irritatability.

A moment later she was in bed. "His lordship said as you should get up today," Eliza said. "Perhaps Lady Bernaise might join you for tea."

"No," Linnet said, firmly. When evening came, she closed her eyes but she couldn't sleep. Instead she lay in bed, listening to the sounds of the castle, distant clinkings, floors squeaking, the sound of the front door opening and closing.

Over the next few days she ate everything Eliza brought to her, and she obediently walked in circles around the bed to gather strength, but she refused to leave the chamber. Piers had stopped trying to visit her; she had taken to rolling over with a pillow on top of her head the moment he entered, and no matter how he ranted, she didn't listen.

"I am strong enough to return to London," she told Eliza one evening. "Will you please inform the duke?"

"I'll tell him," Eliza said uneasily. "But what of —"

"I am grateful for the earl's care of me," she said steadily. "But I have made up my mind not to marry him. Which is no more than he said to me, before I became ill. I'm not marrying anyone who pities me, Eliza. Never."

Eliza sighed and left the room.

THIRTY-FOUR

"She wants to leave," the duke said to Piers.

"Bollocks," Piers said angrily. "She can't leave."

"Her maid says that she is quite strong and sat up for the entire day yesterday."

"Her skin is still scabbed over, which may well lead to infections. She should be under medical care."

"Are such infections common?"

Piers hated the fact his father's eyes were so sympathetic. It was bad enough that he and his mother were gazing at each other like feverish adolescents. He turned away, raking his hand through his hair so the ribbon fell away. "No," he admitted. "No."

"Perhaps if you let her go, she will come back to you," the duke said. "When she is well."

"She won't." Piers took off across the garden in front of the castle, his cane digging savagely into the grass.

His father kept pace with him. "She loves you. Why wouldn't she come back to you? I came back to you."

"Oh God, is that the cue for a tender reunion?" Piers said, stopping at the edge of a flower bed.

"Not unless you wish it."

He stood still, a tacit yes.

The duke took a deep breath. "I know you hate to hear this, but I'm sorry for injuring you, for ruining your life, Piers. I would cut off my own leg, if I could. I would —"

"Killing yourself wouldn't achieve much," Piers said. His father's eyes, oddly enough, were just like his. In his imagination, he always saw them with pupils contracted and the wild gleam of opium intoxication.

But those were childhood memories. What was in front of him was a grieving man, but a strong man. A loving man.

"I forgive you," Piers said flatly. He wasn't good at this sort of thing, so he thought for a moment if there was something else Linnet would think he should say. Too bad she was locked in a bedchamber playing Sleeping Beauty.

His father's eyes glistened with tears. "I will never forgive myself. Never."

Then he knew what Linnet would do. He opened his arms and his father came to him,

457

just as he had when Piers was small and his father was large.

All this emotion was making him feel even more irritable, so he pulled back and snapped, "By the way, my life isn't ruined."

"You suffer intolerable pain," his father said, dropping his arms.

Piers whacked off the head of a nodding daisy with his cane. "That hasn't ruined me. I'm a hell of a doctor. I wouldn't even *be* a doctor if you hadn't developed a liking for opium." He scowled at his father. "I'd rather be dead than not be a doctor."

A smile tugged at the corner of the duke's mouth. But: "You have no family and no friends."

"Bollocks. I have Sébastien. You sent Prufrock to me. And I have Linnet, if I can manage to keep her."

"You'd better keep her," his father said. "If your life isn't ruined, that is."

"She wants to go." Piers decapitated another flower. "She won't talk to me. I wrote her a letter, and her maid reported that she ripped it up without reading it."

"When I decided that I couldn't bear not knowing you any longer, I took a carriage to Wales knowing you'd be furious. Linnet was just an excuse."

"Every time I go to her chamber, she rolls

458

over and hides." Two more flowers lost their heads.

His father gave a little shrug, and that came back to Piers too. That little shrug of amused acceptance. He had always thought that the only memories he carried of his father were of intoxication. But apparently, not so. "I suppose I could go to her room in the night."

"You could. At least that way it would be dark. She wouldn't have to worry that you were looking at her."

"That's absurd. I was the one who rescued her from that chicken coop. I know exactly what she looks like!"

"Your mother thinks that her skin is at the root of the problem, however."

"Why?" Piers ran his hand through his hair again.

"Linnet is mortified by the loss of her beauty."

"She hasn't lost her beauty! Her skin is not the same, but the rest of her is just as good as it ever was."

"To Linnet, she has lost her beauty, and for a woman that exquisite, it must be a tremendous shock."

"No doubt." Moodily he took out three more flowers. "She's vain enough to drop me for that reason, so it must be important.

You know, she pleaded with me in the draw-ing room that day, after you and *Maman* climbed out the window. She begged me to marry her. She said she didn't mind playing the fool for me."

His father nodded.

"But apparently all that love was contin-gent on being beautiful enough to control me," Piers said, thrusting his cane back into the ground. "Or something."

"Or believing that she was good enough for you," his father suggested. "I didn't see any signs that Linnet had hope of control-ling you."

Piers gave a bark of laughter. "*Good enough* for me? For a cripple with a fero-cious temper and a vile tongue?"

"You're the one she wants. I have the distinct impression that you are the only man she has ever wanted, though she has been courted by princes, as well as every eligible man in the *ton*. Likely very few vile tempers in the group."

"Fools, all of them," Piers muttered.

"You'll join that crew if you let her go."

"I never dared to imagine someone like her. Or a life with someone like that."

"That's no reason not to dare now she's standing before you. There's something about the two of you together —"

"She's like my other half," Piers said savagely, keeping his head down. "My other bloody half, like some sort of joke that Plato made up. Like nothing I ever wanted, and then, there she was."

His father put a hand on his shoulder. "Go tell her that."

Piers swallowed. The idea was horrific. Blurting it out to his father was one thing; telling a woman who wouldn't even look at him was another. His feet were surrounded by flower petals. "Is that what you said to *Maman?*"

"No. She wouldn't listen to me."

There was something amused in his voice. Piers raised a hand. "I do *not* want to know."

His father grinned, shrugged. "Do whatever you have to."

THIRTY-FIVE

It took until the next afternoon to think of a plan. His instincts told him that visiting Linnet at night would just make things worse. He couldn't say why, exactly, but he trusted his instincts as a doctor, so he might as well trust them when it came to Linnet.

Humiliatingly, he had to ask for help. It was like the bloody labors of Hercules, courting Linnet. And he wasn't exactly hero material. Remembering the way he had crawled along that corridor, arse-naked (albeit in the dark) made him shudder.

But he swallowed his pride and asked for help, and never mind the fact that Hercules never needed help.

"What do you mean, you want me to go to Linnet's bedchamber?" Sébastien said, looking horrified. "I certainly will not!"

"I'll be with you, you cretin," Piers said. "You're going to pick her up and carry her out of the castle and down to the pool."

Sébastien's mouth fell open. "I certainly will not!" he squealed again. "Are you mad?"

"Have I ever been wrong when it comes to a diagnosis?"

"Of course you have!"

Piers waved his hand. "Ninety percent of the time I'm not, am I?"

"What does that have to do with anything?"

"I've diagnosed her, and now I must cure her."

His cousin eyed him. "She'll likely scream bloody murder."

"No, she won't," Piers said. "I've already told Prufrock to get everyone out of the way. And she's too embarrassed by her appearance to want to draw attention to herself."

"Is it still quite terrible?" Sébastien asked.

Piers shrugged. "Who cares?"

"*She* does, you lout."

"Just come with me to fetch her and spare me the sermonizing."

"What if she never speaks to me again?" Sébastien moaned.

"Once she marries me, you'll both be living in the castle. She'll have to break down and greet you at breakfast."

But Sébastien still protested all the way up the stairs. At the door of Linnet's bedchamber he caught Piers's arm. "She'll hate me for this. I don't want her to hate me."

"Don't be a fool," Piers snarled. He was having enough trouble suppressing his own doubts without having to contend with Sébastien's. He turned the handle.

In the end, it was quite easy. At the first sight of him Linnet dove under the sheet. Which meant it was the work of a moment to roll her up in that sheet.

She made muffled noises and tried to struggle, but her arms and legs were pinned.

"Are you sure she's still breathing?" Sébastien asked, as he made his way with some difficulty down the path.

Piers prodded at Sébastien's cargo, provoking a new struggle. Furious sounds were coming from the bundle. "It appears she is."

"What now?" Sebastian said when they reached the pool.

"Put her over there," Piers said. "On that flat rock. I couldn't have done it without you, but feel free to leave immediately. No need to come back; my fiancée is going to walk back under her own steam."

The words emanating from the bundle took on a tone that suggested profanation.

Sébastien left, shaking his arms. Piers waited until his cousin rounded the curve leading to the guardhouse, and then said, "All right, you can take the sheet off. He's gone."

Instantly the sheet exploded in thrashing movement. Piers stood, arms folded, until Linnet popped out. She was wearing nothing but a light chemise, and he took a moment to enjoy the sight.

"Don't you dare look at me like that!" she shouted. And then she realized where she was.

It was a lovely day. The sky was hot and blue, with just wisps of clouds, like ragged lace high above the wheeling seabirds.

"Oh," she breathed. "You brought me to the pool."

"Why don't you take off your chemise before we swim?" he asked.

She seemed not to hear him, her eyes dreamy as she stared down at the blue water.

"Your chemise," he repeated, pulling off his boots. "Take it off."

She finally turned and frowned at him. "I will not."

"Your choice," he said. He tossed his shirt to the side.

Her eyes flicked away from his chest with indifference. He pushed down his breeches.

"You needn't bother undressing," she said. "I will not swim, and I am not interested in anything more intimate." In fact, she seemed to be shuddering a little at the very thought.

That was annoying. In wordless reply, Piers reached out and gave her a shove between her shoulder blades.

She hit the water with a shriek, and came up spluttering. "You pull me out this second," she shouted, hanging on to the side of the pool. "My skin prickles, and it's freezing!"

"Better start swimming," he said, pulling down his smalls. He had an erection again. It wasn't his favorite thing in the world, jumping into an ocean pool with an erection, but there it was.

He saw Linnet look at that part of him, then he dove off the rock over her, and swam back to the edge where she was clinging. Of course her teeth were chattering now.

"The water's not that cold today," he said. "The sun's been out for three days. You should get moving." But he scooped her against his body, as he always had. He hadn't held her close for days — and it was so . . . so . . . His heart clenched, like the beginning of a cardiac attack.

"We need to swim," he said, pushing her off. "Go!"

"I've been ill." But her voice lacked conviction.

"You're well now. You're just malingering." He grinned at her furious expression, and then reached out and pinched her bottom.

She narrowed her eyes. "Don't you dare touch me. Ever."

"I shall whenever I want to," he said. "You're *mine*. You might want to start swimming or you'll freeze." Without another word he turned and started swimming slowly down the pool. It took a second, but she began swimming after him.

When he had his worst days, during which the pain in his leg was all he could think about, coming here to the pool set him free. It cleared his head, stopped him from thinking about laudanum and brandy. Stopped him from contemplating suicide.

So, he swam just in front of Linnet in case she needed help, hoping that the water would have the same soothing effect on her. At the other end, she caught hold of a rock and panted for a moment. He tried to pull her against him, but she said, "I'm fine," pushed away, and started swimming.

This time he swam behind. She was doing fine without his help, and besides, it gave him a fine glimpse of her legs kicking up and down.

When she reached the flat rock, she was blown, puffing and wheezing; he popped her up on the side, and climbed out after her.

"Is that all the swimming you're doing?" she said, running like a rabbit over to the towels.

"I have to make sure you're not going to steal away."

She kept her back to him. "Where would I go? I have no clothing."

"That's right, I forgot," he said. "You're too much of a coward to be seen in red." Then he dove back in and started swimming, checking every so often to make sure she was still there. She had lain down on the rock, so bundled up in the sheet as well as towels that he could see nothing more than the tip of her ruddy nose.

By two lengths later, it seemed the peace and the sunshine had worn down her resistance. She had unwound the towels and sheet and even taken off her chemise. She was lying like a mermaid on the rock, soaking up the sun.

Five more lengths, and he decided her skin had probably had enough.

He hoisted himself out of the pool and walked over to her, shaking his head so that cold drops flew all over her and made her squawk with annoyance.

Just like that, he got his erection back. One glimpse at her, draped across the rock, and his body forgot about being cold and rather tired.

"Take a towel," she said crossly. But her gaze wasn't quite as dismissive as it had been. "How can you?" she burst out.

"How can I what? Do you suppose you could dry my legs? You know I can't do it, with this cane."

He tried to look pathetic, but her eyes narrowed. "The sun will dry you."

He gave himself a slow caress, his eyes fixed on her. "You heat me faster than the sun."

"How can you desire me when I look like this?" She swallowed hard, but Piers had already decided that the last thing she needed was pity. Besides, any inclination in that direction died when she added, "And that's one of the most ill-phrased compliments I've ever heard."

"Unlike you, I fell in love with more than beauty. Your sharp tongue, for example. I adore that."

"I don't love you for your looks," she said crossly. "If I were that way inclined, I'd choose Sébastien."

"Well, if I were that way inclined, I'd

469

choose Nurse Matilda."

She snorted.

"These days, she's better looking than you are."

Sure enough, she sat up, eyes blazing. "You are a hoggish lout to say such a thing to me!"

"Her creamy skin," he said dreamily. "Like orchid petals."

A puff of air escaped from her lips in a fashion that could never be described as lady-like. "Was that another snort?" he asked. "Dear me, what an annoying habit. I hope that darling Matilda doesn't develop the habit before I ask for her hand. Oh wait, I think I already have a fiancée."

She pulled the sheet over herself and flopped back down, eyes closed. "You're ridiculous."

He lay down too, next to her. For a time they merely lay there, silent. As if they were the only two people in the world, and no other creature in it but a curlew, singing rather tunelessly on a rock nearby.

When he finally sat up, Linnet's eyes were open, and so full of pain that his throat tightened. She didn't look away, didn't say anything.

Before she could intuit what he had in mind, Piers grabbed the sheet and tossed it to the side.

He expected her to screech and try to cover herself, but instead she lay still, her face turned away from his, though not before he saw tears.

"I'm looking at you all over," he said conversationally, doing just that.

"Look your fill," she snapped. "You're going to, no matter what I say."

"You're still red, but now you're peeling too. God, you're a mess."

She snapped upright like a jointed wooden doll, looked down, and shrieked so loudly that the curlew flew away.

"Saltwater is healing," he said, picking up the sheet and rubbing her skin very, very gently. "Look at that. You're not quite boiled underneath. And no scars, on your stomach at least."

She watched him, a stunned expression on her face. "It's coming off?"

"Of course it's coming off," he said. "These are scabs that covered the scarlatina blisters, protecting them while they healed. I expect" — he rubbed a little bit more — "that your whole body is ready to molt, except perhaps your back. The salt helped, and the sun."

"I didn't think it would ever come off," she said, so quietly that he could hardly hear her over the waves splashing up on the rocks behind them.

"If you'd asked me, I could have told you. But because you wouldn't speak to me, I didn't know you were frightened of something so foolish."

She had the most rebellious lower lip that he'd ever seen.

"But what's worse," he persisted, not looking at her, "you lost faith in me. You said you loved me enough to play the fool. But when it came to it, you hadn't the courage for the slightest bit of humiliation. You wouldn't see me in private in case I mocked you, and you wouldn't see me in public, because you felt humiliated at being seen by Prufrock."

This time he was the one who lay down and flung an arm over his eyes.

"I do love you," Linnet said, feeling as though Piers were stealing her capacity for rational thought by looking so hurt. "But I can't be a duchess looking like this. I don't want anyone to marry me out of pity. And I can't marry you if I'm a horrible —"

"Beast?" he interjected. "Is that the word you're looking for?"

"No," she said.

He sat up again, and his eyes burned into hers. "You only loved me when you were beautiful. So that you could control me, the way you think you can control other men with your smile."

"No!" she cried. "That wasn't it."

"Then what was it?" he demanded. "One minute you were begging me to marry you, telling me that you would wait for me, and the next you wouldn't even look at me." Anger and hurt vibrated in his voice.

She looked down and took stock of her body. It was still red, still peeling, but somehow, sitting next to Piers in the sunshine, it didn't seem monstrous. "I thought you would be horrified," she said, choking a little. "I didn't want you to marry me out of pity. I couldn't do that to you, give you an ugly wife."

"Pity is not exactly an emotion I'm known for. What's more, I haven't the faintest hesitation about giving you a beast for a husband."

"That's not really true," she said slowly. "You told me that you wanted me, but that you'd never marry me. You said that I was beautiful and eager, but that you'd rut other women, so I should just forget you."

The ugly words hung in the air between them.

"You're right," Piers said. "That was a contemptible thing to say." All the outrage disappeared from his voice; it was so bleak that she couldn't think what to say next. "I pushed you away because I'm afraid I might become a drug addict, someday. I was — and am still — afraid that I'll lose my temper and make your life miserable."

Suddenly her whole heart was bursting with the fear that he would leave her, even though a mere hour ago she had wanted nothing more than to never see him again.

"You broke my heart when you threw me out," she said, hugging her knees. "*That* made me miserable. But when I fell ill, in the chicken coop, I realized that you loved me."

There was a pause. The curlew was singing again, a bit farther off.

"I said, that you love me," she repeated.

"I do." He said it almost irritably.

"I made up my mind that if I lived, I would never let you bully me again, the way you did when you refused to marry me." She reached out to touch him, just to touch him, running her fingers over his thigh. "But afterwards, I was so ugly. I don't see how I could possibly be a duchess."

"I suppose all duchesses are beautiful," he said. "It's likely a requirement of the position."

"At the very least they shouldn't terrify

people in the streets."

"And for this reason you thought that, since you were circus material, you'd throw me over. What was supposed to come thereafter? Suppers in your room for fifty years?"

"I thought I'd hide," she said, her voice trembling a little. "Just hide, that's all."

Silence. Then: "You weren't supposed to want to hide from *me,* Linnet."

"I'm sorry," she whispered.

"You broke my damn heart by nearly dying, and then you broke it again when you threw me out of your room."

She couldn't bear the pain in his voice, the fact she had hurt him, so she pushed him back onto the rock. His body was warm and large under her leg. Familiar and dear.

"Are you going to kiss me and make it all better?" he asked, at once sardonic and tender.

"Shut up," Linnet said. She brushed her lips across his. Her tongue stole out and tasted his lips.

"I suppose now you're trying to seduce me the old-fashioned way, having lost your looks."

But she knew when he was angry and trying to hurt, and when he wasn't. This time, he wasn't. Her heart rejoiced and she hummed, deep in her throat. "Something like that." She nipped his bottom lip, the way he'd taught her.

Piers opened his lips to her plea and raw passion caught them both for a moment. But then he pulled away. "I can't."

Linnet leaned after him. There was something in his voice that made her excitement build, rather than diminish. "Why?" It came out a husky murmur, perhaps because she was kissing the line of his jaw.

"You're too ugly. I never make love to ugly women. I could never love an ugly woman."

For a split second Linnet's heart stammered, and then she realized what he was really saying. "And I, my lord, can only love a man who can carry me over the threshold. Who can promise me that he will never, ever touch laudanum and will certainly never raise his voice. Can you do that?"

His eyes met hers: deep, lustrous, intelligent — loving. "In the inn I carried you down the hallway and over the threshold," he said, and his voice was as husky as hers. "Does that count?"

"I might be beautiful again someday," she offered. "Or not."

He rolled to face her, and their eyes met in a way that had everything to do with love, the kind strong enough to snatch someone back from the grave, the kind that never fades and never fails.

The kind that has nothing to do with beauty, temper, or damaged legs.

"I can't promise you that I won't lose my temper," he said. "Though I have a feeling that you may have changed me for good. I might not be such a beast anymore."

"I can't promise that I won't die and leave you alone. I think I forgot to say thank you for saving my life."

"I love you," he said, his voice catching. "When I thought you were going to die, I wanted to die. And as soon as you climbed out that damned window, I wanted you back."

She ran a hand softly up his cheek. "I'm back."

"I would have gone to fetch you, even given that I had no idea that you might be ill. I just couldn't leave my patients yet. Well, actually, I contemplated leaving my patients more than a few times, mostly in the middle of the night."

"That wouldn't have been right," she said firmly. "It would have put a damper on our wedding."

"Is there going to be a wedding?" His eyes searched hers. "It wouldn't be easy to take our vows in your bedchamber, but we could manage it."

She took a deep breath. "Do you mind marrying a peeling lobster?"

His eyes showed that he didn't mind at all. "You're not a lobster," he said, brushing his lips over hers. "Where the new skin shows you're more like a strawberry. A ripe, delicious strawberry."

"Berry is my middle name," Linnet said, a giggle escaping.

"*My* Berry." But he was done with talking, so he rolled over onto her, big and strong and — yes — domineering. "If I don't mind making love to you while you molt, would you mind making love to a man whose temper gets the best of him sometimes?"

"No," she gasped, because his hand . . . well, there were parts of her that were seemed to be exactly as soft as they used to be.

He had to rub her breasts with the sheet until they were a beautiful strawberry pink, but they both enjoyed that. And they were both happy when it turned out that for some mysterious reason the scarlatina hadn't touched her inner thighs.

There were other things to be happy about as well.

Afterward, they lay on the rock while Piers concentrated on polishing his beloved into a uniform rosy pink.

"Is my face scarred?" Linnet inquired anxiously, after a time. "Tell me the truth."

"Not at all. You're no Queen Elizabeth. In fact — though I hate to tell you this — a little rice powder and the Ducklings will be slavering over you again." He had apparently decided her breasts needed even more attention.

Linnet began tentatively feeling her face, her fingers sliding over her cheekbones, chin, lips. All smooth again. "I don't know that I'll ever be able to forget it," she said with a shudder. "The chicken coop, the rash, and I was so hot and thirsty."

Piers cupped her face in his hands. "I will never forgive myself for not being there with you."

"You mean, the way your father won't forgive himself?"

"We talked," he said gruffly. "I tried to think what you would want me to say."

She brightened. "So you said that he was a dedicated —"

"No."

"You don't even know what I was going to say!"

"Nothing along those lines."

"What did you say then?" she asked, somewhat disappointed.

"That I loved him. Not in so many words,

but he knew."

"When I was very ill, I dreamed my mother was with me in the pool."

"In the water?"

"Under the water. I kept floating away, because there wasn't any pain there, and it was cool and wet. But she would push me back."

Piers clutched Linnet against his chest. "Good for her."

"I forgave her too," she said softly. "She loved me."

"Well," he said, "you're very lovable. And not because you're beautiful, either. And not even because you're a delectable pink that I've never seen on a woman before."

Tears spilled over in Linnet's eyes. "I didn't think anyone would ever —"

"Hush," he said, brushing his lips over hers. "I didn't think I would ever care for another person."

"We were both wrong," Linnet said, her hand sliding around his head to pull his lips to hers.

"Sweet Berry," Piers whispered, some time later.

"Yes?" She surfaced from his kiss dazed, her lips swollen, her heart pounding.

"I can't make love on this rock again. I hate to sound conventional, but my knees

480

are scraped. Shall we go home? I have a wonderfully soft bed. It's in the master bed-chamber, which you have not yet seen, but which you might as well lay claim to."

"Home," she repeated, pulling herself together.

"Our home."

So they got up and fashioned a Grecian gown from the sheet, and made their way home, hand in hand.

When they arrived, Linnet beamed at everyone from Prufrock to the duke. No one really noticed that her skin was strawberry pink.

Because the joy on her face and in her eyes was dazzling.

EPILOGUE

Some years later

"I don't see why you call Mama 'Berry,' " a small boy said to his father, one summer day. He was lolling on a rock, watching his sister paddle around the sea pool with their mother.

"It's a private name," his father said. He was watching Mama with a peculiar smile on his face that the boy couldn't quite interpret.

"It's not logical," John Yelverton, future Earl of Marchant and Duke of Windebank, pointed out. "Mama doesn't look like a berry. Evie does, because she's round and fat and she has that red hair."

He regarded his younger sister with some disfavor. Even at age seven, he was aware that his sister seemed to have some powerful charm over strangers. If she smiled at them, they simply melted. They gave her whatever she wanted.

Not that his mother and father did, of course. They were more likely to poke her until she laughed. He preferred to pinch her, himself.

"Once upon a time, your mother had quite rosy skin," his father said. "So she was like a particularly delectable berry, a strawberry."

John had seen that look on his parents' faces before, and he didn't think much of it. It wasn't rational. He was fond of categorizing the world; things were either rational or irrational. That sloppy look? Irrational.

"Could we go back to the castle now and dissect another frog?" he asked.

"No. One frog a week. Frogs are not created simply for your amusement, you know."

"But you do remember that I had trouble finding the gallbladder, don't you? I need another try."

"Next week," his father said. "I'm sure there will be many gallbladders in your future."

That was just the sort of nonsensical thing that parents said all the time, and which John didn't appreciate. "I want to dissect a frog *now!*"

His father stopped looking at the pool and glanced down at him. He raised a finger.

"Remember what we discussed this morning?"

"I have to learn to control my temper," John said obediently. "An' if I feel it coming up in my stomach, I have to count to ten."

"Do you need to count at the moment?"

"No," he said, somewhat darkly.

Evie was at the side of the pool, and his father got up to pull her out. He had his cane in one hand, but he bent down. Evie grasped his arm with both hands and he swung her out in a big circle while she shrieked and shrieked.

Then he put down his cane and reached down with both hands to help Mama out of the pool. There they were, smiling at each other in that way again.

Papa had a towel slung over his shoulder, which he used to dry her off.

John rolled his eyes and went to look around the little tide pools. Maybe if he found his own frog, Papa would let him dissect it.

There didn't seem to be any frogs.

"They don't like saltwater," Evie said, lisping a little. She cocked her head on the side and gave him that smile he hated so much. "Don't you know *anything?*"

He pulled her hair.

Then she cried, so he counted to ten.

484

"I didn't *yank* her hair," he explained to his papa a second later. "Or *wrench* it. That would have been mean. It was just a little tug."

"You are a chip off the old block," his father said, taking him by the hand as they all started up the path back to the castle. "Next time, count to ten before you tug."

John grinned. His greatest ambition was to be just like his papa in every way. Well, and a little like his grandfather the duke too, because he loved the way His Grace told stories.

But mostly he wanted to be like his papa. "Maybe I'll operate on the next frog before I dissect it," he offered. "Give it a cast on its leg. We could pretend it jumped too high."

"Hmm," his father said, and John realized he was looking over at Mama again.

She was holding hands with Evie, who was still heaving with sobs, though John knew perfectly well that he hadn't really hurt his sister.

"You love Mama a lot, don't you?" John said, pulling on his father's hand to get his attention.

"Yes, I do," his papa said. "I certainly do."

"And she loves you," John stated. He liked

to have things organized and clear in his mind.

His mother laughed. "I do love your father, Johnakins."

He frowned. "That's my baby name. I'm not a baby any longer."

"My apologies," she said, dropping a finger on his nose.

"Then if you love him," he said to his father, "and she loves you, and you love *us,* why do you have to have another one?" He had been told that there was another baby in Mama's tummy, but it didn't seem logical, even if her tummy was rounder than it used to be.

His mother smiled down at him and then took his free hand in hers. "Loving each other is what this family does best."

That was illogical to John's mind. Dissecting people was what his papa did best. But there was no point in fussing over it, and besides . . .

He guessed the four of them could probably spare a little love for a baby.

As long as it wasn't another girl.

HISTORICAL NOTE

"Beauty and the Beast" is a very old tale; Madame Gabrielle de Villeneuve wrote *La Belle et la Bête* in 1740. I shan't cite any particular adaptation, because I discarded most of the details, including the magically transfigured hero. Piers was transformed by a far less wondrous, but no less life-changing, event: infarction — tissue death — in his right quadriceps muscle.

My greater debt, as you may have recognized, is to a far more modern tale, the Fox television show *House, M.D.;* I tip my hat to *House*'s brilliant, quirky, and thoroughly entertaining scriptwriters. Piers, my version of their Dr. Gregory House, differs from his prototype as much as Linnet does from Beauty. But his personality, not to mention his damaged leg and his life's work, was inspired by the irascible diagnostician from Princeton-Plainsboro Teaching Hospital.

If the gifted Dr. House deserves mention,

so do the eighteenth-century doctors and surgeons who struggled to combat diseases without the benefit of the tests, technologies, and treatments on which Dr. House relies so heavily. Many of the details regarding scarlet fever you read here came from a book first published in 1799. *A Treatise on Febrile Diseases,* written by Dr. A. Philips Wilson, offered detailed information about the progress of scarlet fever, along with commonsense treatments. In his hands, or so he said, an attack of scarlet fever never became fatal. Wilson's *Treatise* fought against the ineffectual and too often harmful practices of doctors such as a certain Dr. Sims, who in 1796 recommended treatment of scarlet fever with laxatives and emetics. In his own way, Wilson was a similarly arrogant, and truly heroic, version of House.

I also pay homage to Enid Blyton's series of books about a girls' boarding school in Cornwall, named Malory Towers, which boasted a pool cut from the cliffs and filled by the tide. Reading her novels aloud to my daughter sparked my imagination, and by the time I finished this novel, Piers's sea pool had taken on a character all of its own.

And finally, T. S. Eliot's "The Love Song of J. Alfred Prufock" sang through my mind while writing, though Eliot would surely have palpitations to think so (you'll find the text on my website, www.eloisajames. com). His poem raises questions about time and courage — whether there is "time for you and time for me," whether there is time to prepare "a face to meet the faces that you meet," and time to wonder, "Do I dare?" So I leave you with Eliot's love song, in which the mermaids sing, and humans risk lingering too long in chambers of the sea.

ABOUT THE AUTHOR

Eloisa James is the author of nineteen award-winning romances. She's also a professor of English literature, teaching in New York City, where she lives with her family. With two jobs, two cats, two children, and only one husband, she spends most of her time making lists of things to do — letters from readers are a great escape! Connect with Eloisa on her Facebook page (*www.facebook.com/EloisaJamesFans*), through her website (*www.eloisajames.com*), or through e-mail at *eloisa@eloisajames .com*.